CAIN AT GETTYSBURG

FORGE BOOKS BY RALPH PETERS

The War After Armageddon
The Officers' Club
Cain at Gettysburg

CAIN AT GETTYSBURG

RALPH PETERS

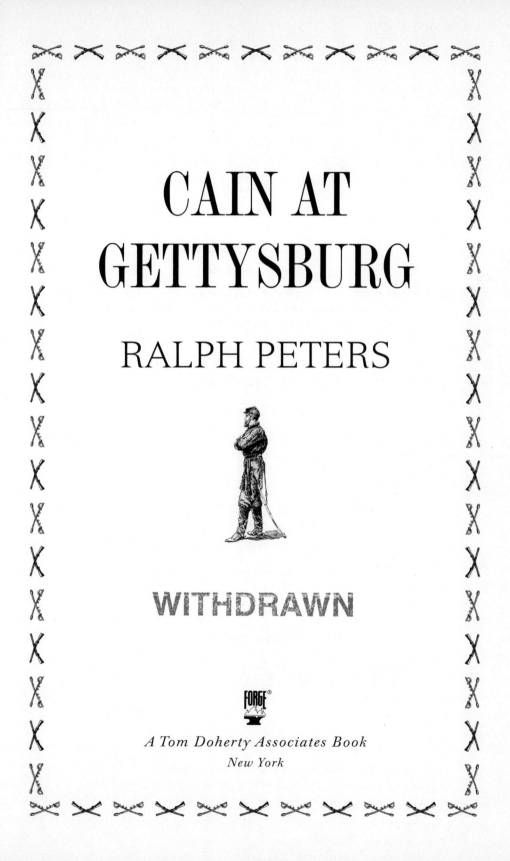

WITHDRAWN

FORGE®

A Tom Doherty Associates Book
New York

This is a work of fiction. All of the characters, organizations, and events portrayed
in this novel are either products of the author's imagination
or are used fictitiously.

CAIN AT GETTYSBURG

Copyright © 2012 by Ralph Peters

A Forge Book
Published by Tom Doherty Associates, LLC
175 Fifth Avenue
New York, NY 10010

www.tor-forge.com

Forge® is a registered trademark of Tom Doherty Associates, LLC.

Library of Congress Cataloging-in-Publication Data

Peters, Ralph, 1952–
Cain at Gettysburg / Ralph Peters. — 1st ed.
 p. cm.
"A Tom Doherty Associates book."
ISBN 978-0-7653-3047-5
1. Gettysburg, Battle of, Gettysburg, Pa., 1863—Fiction. I. Title.
PS3566.E7559C35 2012
813'.54—dc23

2011024970

First Edition: February 2012

Printed in the United States of America

0 9 8 7 6 5 4 3 2 1

To my mother and father,
who drove us down to Gettysburg each year,
where my brother and I would clamber
over the cannon at the Angle;
restrain ourselves through a picnic lunch
(white-meat-of-chicken sandwiches)
eaten where gray waves slapped a wall of blue;
and always, always, always
visit the "Electric Map" with awed delight

And he said, What hast thou done?
the voice of thy brother's blood
crieth unto me from the ground.

—GENESIS 4:10

PART
I

THE IGNORANT ARMIES

JUNE 28, 1863
LEE INVADES PENNSYLVANIA

ONE

June 28, 1863

Annoyed by flies, Meade fell asleep at last, only to wake with a hand upon his shoulder. The intruder's lantern cast fantastic shadows. Hardie wore civilian clothes and crouched under the tent's slant. It took Meade a moment to recognize him.

"What the devil?"

"I'm here to give you trouble," the colonel said.

Blades of alarm pierced weariness. Meade sat up sharply.

"My conscience is clear," he declared.

Margaret had warned him to check his temper. Now Hooker had charged him with insubordination, with Halleck's acquiescence and bespectacled Hardie as henchman. He was being relieved of his command, arrested in the middle of a campaign. There would be a court-martial. Reputation's assassin sneaking into camp, this colonel from the adjutant general's office had come in the dark, in disguise. And he had always thought Hardie a decent fellow.

"I've done . . . nothing dishonorable," Meade protested. "Nothing." He yearned for coffee just off the fire, for the light of day, for a friend. "My differences with General Hooker . . . have been matters of professional judgment, nothing more."

The colonel raised a hand to quiet him. The gesture struck Meade as insolent. Hardie grinned.

Black and devilish, flies looped around the lantern the colonel held. Settling the light on the camp desk, Hardie drew a pair of envelopes from a pocket.

"General Meade, you are ordered to assume command of the Army of the Potomac. Effective immediately, sir. I'm to accompany you to General Hooker's headquarters, to witness the transfer of authority."

Dumbfounded, Meade took the documents. He didn't open them, but held the papers atop one knee. He wondered if arrest would not have been preferable. He began to wake fully and bitterly.

Outside, the camp clattered, despite the wretched hour. A sergeant barked and soldiers answered. Chains chimed and horses whinnied. Hardie's arrival had yanked them all from sleep. His staff officers would be gathering by his tent, waiting to hear the news that had come from Washington.

How much had they guessed? Meade needed coffee. Coffee and John Reynolds. Reynolds was the man for this. Men followed him and loved him. Handsome John. He was the man to take command of the army. How foolish he himself had been to resent Reynolds' advancement. He rued his pettiness now.

Meade sighed. He meant to rise and put on his uniform coat, to wrap his old bones in a guise of authority. But the flesh hesitated.

"I'm not qualified," he told Hardie. "I'm the devil's choice for this. I mustn't command this army."

"It's the president's decision."

"What about Reynolds? Is it true he turned it down?"

Hardie shrugged. "I don't believe there was a formal offer. Anyway, the president chose you, sir. General Halleck and Mr. Stanton concurred. They sent me to Frederick by special train. There's no time to lose."

Meade snapped, "Don't you think I understand that?"

Halleck. The man was devoured by jealousy. Of Reynolds, that much was evident. Of Reynolds and so many others. Apparently, though, he wasn't jealous of everyone. What does that say of me? Meade asked himself.

He did his best to button up his temper. His wife had warned him, more than once, that his tongue cut worse than his sword.

"I haven't the seniority on the Army rolls," Meade insisted. Then he added, "I thought things had been patched up with General Hooker?"

"Mr. Lincoln lost faith in him."

So has the rest of this blasted army, Meade thought. Yet, removing Hooker now was madness. With battle looming. On a field yet unknown.

"Hardie, I don't want this," he said in a tamed voice. "I'm not the man for this."

His visitor gestured toward the envelopes, which remained unopened. Meade unfolded the fateful order, bending to make out the words. Hardie took up the lantern again and brought it closer.

It was true. He had been selected as the latest general half-expected to fail and be damned forever.

Expected to fail? Was that the nub of it?

Meade tested each word of the order, then studied the accompanying correspondence from the general-in-chief. "Considering the circumstances," Meade read, "no one has ever received a more important command."

A sharp-fanged creature slithered through his bowels.

Had it come to this? With the Confederates already marching on Philadelphia, for all he knew? For all anyone knew? The evening before, he had worn himself out riding through the Maryland countryside trying to find Hooker, the man who held the string and hid both ends. The raw, hot roads had been burdened with batteries and commissary wagons, with regiments coming late to their camps and with stragglers, some of them drunk. No one knew where the army's commander could be found.

"I don't want this," Meade said. "It's impossible. I shall send a message to Halleck."

Fixing his spectacles higher on his nose, Hardie said, "It won't do any good, sir. The president's mind is made up." He set the lantern back down on the desk.

Meade arched his back. The camp bed creaked. "Does General Hooker know?"

"He sent in a letter of resignation." A quarter-smile cut into Hardie's cheek. "I'm not sure he meant it to be accepted. But it was." The smile turned cruel enough to tell Meade that Hooker had earned Hardie's enmity. "I suspect he'll know by the time we reach army headquarters."

Meade snorted. "I don't even know where that is."

"I'll guide you there, if you'll loan me a horse. I came in a rented buggy."

Irritated anew that he had failed to find Hooker's camp the

evening before, Meade asked, "Since you're so well-informed, Hardie, would you happen to know where General Lee and his army are strolling just now? No one else seems to have any blasted idea. Certainly not this army's corps commanders."

The colonel shook his head. "General Hooker's communications with Washington have been . . . limited." Posture deformed by the slope of the canvas, he shed another layer of formality. "To tell you the truth, sir, he hasn't told us much of anything. He wouldn't even share his plan of campaign with Mr. Lincoln. All we heard from old Fighting Joe were calls for reinforcements and wails that the army's outnumbered. He sounded more and more like Little Mac. It set the president out of temper. And that's putting it soft."

"Hardie, do you know where the corps of *this* army are right now?"

"Not all of them. It took some work to find you."

The situation reminded Meade of a game he had seen blindfolded children play in Tampico. Spun round, they lashed out with a stick, trying to shatter a dangling plaster animal filled with treats. Except that there would be no treats this time. Only the blind lashing out.

Meade reached for his watch. Instead of metal, his hand met the sweat-heavy cloth of an undergarment. *Wake up,* he commanded himself. *Take hold of yourself.* "What time is it, Hardie?"

The colonel drew out his watch and clicked open the cover. "Half past three, sir."

"Well, we'll have a ride before us. If we must go through with this." He cleared his throat, tasting bile. "I'd like a few moments alone. And you'll want your breakfast."

"Yes, sir." The colonel turned to go.

"Hardie?"

Hand on the tent's flap, the visitor turned again. Reflections of the lantern's flame flickered on his spectacles.

"I've been tried and condemned without a hearing, and I suppose I shall have to go to execution," Meade said. He attempted a smile and failed. "Send Captain Meade to me. And tell my staff I'll join them shortly."

"Shall I let them know, sir? About the order?"

Meade brushed a fly from his beard. "Do as you see fit."

Left alone, Meade clutched the paper that damned him. His bowels winced again. The flesh always reminded a man of the constraints on human dignity.

In those last private moments, he thought about young George. It had wounded Meade when the boy was cast from West Point for his follies. Now he himself had been pointed toward failure, toward a far greater failure, a failure that would resound for generations. Was it a curse on the family? His father, too, had failed, in a different way, in a different world.

Still waking to the charge that had been given him, Meade felt a wave of shame, as if one of those Barnegat rip currents had changed the direction of an inner sea. He needed to control himself, if he hoped to control the army. To put up a manly show. How could he have indulged in such fretting in front of Hardie? How could he have shown such weakness? Weariness was no excuse, nor was confusion.

He imagined the colonel telling tales at the bar in Willard's Hotel. He could hear the laughter of clerks and politicians.

Well, the thing was done.

In the sour air of his tent, Meade viewed himself with an engineer's cold eye: too dark of thought, too dour, a man alert to the smell of sulfur, but not to Heaven's scent. He could hear Margaret teasing, "George, I know you can smile!" His wife was a proud, loyal woman, of good family. She had got him a brigadier's rank at the start of the war, when his merits had not sufficed. He would have to do his best for her. And for the Union, of course.

Major General George Gordon Meade had been happiest building lighthouses.

At the cue of hoofbeats, General Hooker emerged theatrically from his tent. Stepping into the humid dawn in his full dress uniform, he looked a perfect military specimen. Only his gold-trimmed hat was missing, left behind to exhibit his fine shock of hair. Flanked by his staff, the dismissed commanding general posed for a martial portrait. Meade stilled his horse and dismounted, slopped with sweat and more than a little mud.

Accompanied only by his son and Hardie, Meade hardly felt apt to complete Hooker's tableau. An officer once had remarked within

his hearing that "Old Meade resembles a bishop who's sucked a lemon." He had mastered a steely dignity, but knew he would never be a favorite of crowds.

Hooker extended his hand. Meade wiped his own on a trouser leg, then took it.

"You've got the bag of wildcats now," Hooker told him. "And I wish you luck." He released Meade's hand. Anxious to catch each word, Hooker's coterie edged closer.

"General Hooker," Hardie interposed, "we need to—"

"A moment, Hardie, a moment. You needn't be so impatient for my head." Piercing eyes unclouded by drink this day, Hooker returned his attention to his successor. "I've already published my farewell order, so we can abridge the formalities." He smiled wryly. "We wouldn't want to inconvenience Colonel Hardie by delaying his return to Washington. Butterfield has a copy of it for you. You won't find it objectionable." He patted Meade on the upper arm, in a show of amity neither man could feel. There had been too much bad blood before this day. "Shall we go to the headquarters tent?"

Meade knew he would have to clear out the worst of Hooker's men, but it couldn't be done all at once, not in midcampaign. He would have to live with the ill will and the spies alert for missteps. He would have liked, at the least, to remove Butterfield, who was Hooker's given creature through and through. But Warren had refused the chief of staff's position, preferring to remain chief engineer and telling Meade he'd be mad to get rid of the only man who might know what Hooker had been up to with the army. Meade took the point, but suspected Warren of avoiding the prospect of failure at his side.

Who would stand by him? John Reynolds, of course. Despite some petty bickering in the past, he knew he could count Reynolds as a friend. But he needed Reynolds in the field, in command, not at headquarters. Gallant John. Their spats aside, he and Reynolds understood each other. Lancaster and Philadelphia, two Pennsylvania men. Perhaps it was as simple as that. He had sent off a courier even before riding out of the Fifth Corps camp, asking Reynolds to come to army headquarters.

The labor of transferring command began. With a map of Maryland spread over a borrowed farmhouse table, Butterfield reeled off

the approximate—very approximate—locations of the various corps of the Army of the Potomac. Fiddling with his mustaches as he spoke, the chief of staff kept glancing from Meade to Hooker.

Meade was appalled that the army remained so dispersed, an invitation to defeat in detail and a gift to Robert E. Lee. But he said nothing. He would give his orders soon enough. First, he needed to listen. Nor did he wish to humiliate Hooker further in front of his acolytes. Bad blood enough already, bad blood enough.

Hooker, too, remained silent.

Colonel Sharpe of the Bureau of Military Information took his turn. He had not prepared a map.

"It's been confirmed that General Ewell . . . in command of Jackson's old corps, somewhat reduced . . . has passed a division through York. One brigade reached Wrightsville on the Susquehanna, but the militia burned the bridge before the enemy could cross."

The colonel paused to look at Meade, as if expecting a question.

"Go on, Sharpe," Meade said. "Where's Ewell now?"

"Carlisle, we believe. Threatening Harrisburg, according to General Crouch and Governor Curtin's people."

Hooker leaned forward. He was a man who loved to speak and could resist no longer. "Bobby Lee isn't interested in Harrisburg. He's attempting to lure this army into a trap. I've done my best to stay out of it."

"Where's Lee now?" Meade asked.

Sharpe lifted his eyebrows and whisked the air with a hand. "It's unclear, sir. Somewhere north of Hagerstown and still west of the mountains. No doubt, he intends to reunite with Ewell."

"Longstreet?"

"He'll be with Lee, sir. Now that Jackson's gone."

"And Hill?"

"We don't know, sir. Probably west of the mountains."

"Is that your answer to everything, Sharpe? 'West of the mountains'?" Meade turned to Hooker. "What were your orders to the cavalry?"

Butterfield answered for his former superior. "They're conducting a screen on a broad front, covering our flanks and the passes on our left, up to the Pennsylvania line. To prevent surprise."

Chancellorsville leapt to every mind. No one dared say the name in front of Hooker.

"And General Stuart?"

"We've lost contact with him. Since the affair at Upperville."

"I want to see Pleasanton," Meade said. "Today."

A staff man in a cavalry jacket exited the tent. Meade cautioned himself again. Occasional flashes of anger enlivened subordinates, but constant anger demoralized them. Still, he couldn't but feel outraged at finding the army spread halfway to China. And Lee on a romp through Pennsylvania, awaiting his chance to strike.

When he reached for his watch this time, Meade found it. "Gentlemen," he said, "I'm obliged to send a message to General Halleck." He turned to the man he had replaced. "General Hooker, I beg your indulgence." Addressing the little group again, Meade continued, "I have twenty-five minutes past six. Let us reconvene in one hour. General Butterfield, is there a place where I can write without interruption?"

And write Meade did. He knew Halleck's temperament and the backbiting in the War Department well enough to make himself two pledges. First, he would see that each message from his headquarters would be as clear as the English language could make it, even if he had to write every last one himself. Second, he would keep Halleck so well-informed that he'd have no excuse for meddling. He was not going to make Hooker's mistake. At least, not that one.

Left alone in Butterfield's personal tent, he paused and held the pen suspended an inch above the paper. The army's dispersion haunted him. The first order of business would be to concentrate his force so every corps could rush to support another. He was not going to let Lee eat him one bite at a time. The first of them to concentrate might well emerge the victor.

Nor did Meade intend to let his adversary surprise him. He remembered the follies of past commanders too well. If George Meade had any say in it, the next time Robert E. Lee fought the Army of the Potomac, he was going to have to fight all of it.

It was all a matter of time. And how could there be enough time now? He began to write:

The order placing me in command of this army is received. As a soldier, I obey it, and to the utmost of my ability will execute it. Totally unexpected as it has been, and in ignorance of the exact condition of the troops and position of the enemy, I can only now say that it appears to me I must move toward the Susquehanna, keeping Washington and Baltimore well covered, and if the enemy is checked in his attempt to cross the Susquehanna, or if he turns toward Baltimore, to give him battle.

On the edge of his consciousness, horses galloped off. But there was more to write. He wished to complain, but did not. He remembered Hardie's remarks about Hooker sounding too much like McClellan. Lincoln read the telegrams received by the War Department.

When he finished, he blotted the paper, wiped the ink from his fingers, and stepped out of the tent. The morning was bright, hot, fierce. Terrible marching weather. But the men would have to march, and more than one of the marches would be long. He handed the message to the waiting courier, who leapt to the saddle and spurred his mount toward Frederick. The man's alacrity drew a faint smile from Meade, who saw that his reputation as "Old Snapping Turtle" was already having its effect on the headquarters.

Enjoying a new pulse of confidence, he returned to the tent where the staff awaited him. The canvas sides had been rolled up to let the air pass through.

Hooker wasn't there. And several officers were missing. Meade turned a quizzical look on Butterfield, but the chief of staff remained mute.

Meade's son, face pale, spoke up. "General Hooker's gone, sir. He just rode off. Colonel Hardie left with him."

Suppressing a burst of fury at the snub, Meade told himself that it was better so. Now he could get down to the business of organizing the army, without unnecessary niceties. If Hooker had funked it, good riddance.

He allowed himself a single sigh as he strode to the table that still bore the map of Maryland. "Butterfield? Have one of your officers fetch a map of Pennsylvania. There's work to be done, man. We need to designate points of concentration for this army."

Butterfield passed on the order to a major, who stood close enough to have heard each word the new commanding general had spoken.

Meade glanced around the reduced group of officers. "Would you gentlemen excuse us? General Butterfield and I have a few affairs to discuss."

Obedience wasn't a problem. The big tent emptied rapidly.

Meade stepped closer to the man on whom he would have to rely. The chief of staff smelled of cologne water. "Well, Dan, we'll have to make the best of things, you and I."

Butterfield's face was a mask without emotion.

"I know I haven't been in the good graces of this headquarters of late," Meade went on.

"Nor I in yours, General Meade."

"But I think we shall manage. We must."

Butterfield remained impassive. It exasperated Meade, who had reached the limit of his affability. He didn't like Butterfield, never had. He only hoped he could trust him to do the right thing for the army, if not for its new commander.

The major sent for the Pennsylvania map returned, hesitating at the entrance to the tent. Meade beckoned him inside.

"Spread it on top of the Maryland map," Meade told him. "General Butterfield and I will need them both. Then tell the rest of the staff to come back in."

The major did as ordered, then eased away. Meade stepped to the table.

"Major!" he called after the man. *"Major!"*

"What is it?" Butterfield asked calmly.

Meade turned on his chief of staff. "Damn me to bloody blue blazes, I asked for a map of southern Pennsylvania."

Butterfield considered the map. "That's southern Pennsylvania," he told Meade.

"I need a topographical map, man. This is nothing but a sketch of towns and roads. I need to see the terrain, the relief, the watercourses. That major should know as much."

"That's the only Pennsylvania map we have," Butterfield said.

Meade looked at the man in astonishment.

The chief of staff shrugged. "We never expected to give battle

in Pennsylvania, there seemed no need. Proper maps have been ordered, of course. They just haven't arrived."

Once again, Meade managed to rein in his temper. "All right, Butterfield. I'll speak to Warren, he'll see to the business. Just start at the beginning and explain General Hooker's plan of campaign to me. I need every detail, no matter how small."

"I can't do that," Butterfield said.

"What do you mean, you can't?"

The staff officers had gathered outside of the tent, but waited to be bidden to come back in.

"He kept it all in his head," Butterfield told him.

You seen it, too. Ain't I right?" Cobb asked. "All through the preaching, Colonel Burgwyn had the look of death on him. He's a marked man, Quaker. I know you seen it. I seen you looking. Things don't get past you." Cobb widened his grotesque smile.

Sergeant Blake buttoned up his trousers and kept his breathing shallow. After one night, the green glade close to the regiment's camp smelled foul. Cobb reeked, too, but that was his normal condition. This grove, where the morning coolness had drawn up its weakened lines for one last stand, deserved better.

"Shut your mouth," Blake said. "You're talking craziness."

"Hell I am," Cobb said, still spraying the ferns. "Hell, if you don't know it, either. I seen you looking right at him. Plain as day, Quaker, that man ain't long for this world." He shook his head in mock sorrow. "Pretty fellow, too. And so young. Going to be a shame to see him go, a crying shame."

In the distance, the regimental band started up, instantly recognizable by the music's precision. Moravians from Salem, the musicians were the pride not only of the 26th North Carolina, but of the entire brigade. General Pettigrew was fond of calling them up to the head of the column whenever his men were about to march through a town. Even Yankees came out to listen, some of them.

"Guess the praying's over," Cobb said as the band leapt through a polka. "They're meaning to cheer us up, I expect. But you and me . . . we know better. Don't we now? You and me, Quaker, we know what's coming. Old Marse Robert didn't march us all the way up just to let us live off the fat of the land and scare Dutch

girls. No, sir, he didn't. They just give us these pretty new uniforms to be buried in."

Blake looked at the little man. At God's hideous excuse for a man. A nose eaten by sores topped a mouth whose last teeth ran black. Cobb's new gray tunic was already stained by tobacco juice or worse. A leathery creature of unknown age, his only pleasing feature was thick black hair, but that crawled with lice. Now and then, the men tossed him into a creek, which Cobb accepted as part of his fate on earth. He was the only man in the company with whom no other soldier would share a blanket.

"I didn't know you had gypsy blood, Cobb," Blake remarked.

Finishing up his business, Cobb smiled again. "My ma was a McCaslin, she had the sight. Guess it passed on down to me, after all." His smile widened, revealing a grim chasm. "Though it don't take no second sight to see as how the colonel's marked for death." He laughed, a mean sound. "Anyhow, you know the McCaslins and what's said about them. From your shopkeeping days."

Yes, he knew of the McCaslins. They were the only clan in the hills to whom no one would give credit, not even when they sent the children to town to beg. Other, worse things were said about them, too. But even the bony, sliver-faced McCaslins compared favorably with little Cobb.

"I should charge you for a court-martial. For talking about Colonel Burgwyn that way."

Cobb cackled in delight. "You won't, though, Quaker. No, sir, you won't. 'Cause we understand each other, you and me, and you know that's right. Goes all the way back to New Bern, when you and me were the only ones didn't turn tail. You know you'll need old Billy Cobb, sooner or later, when things get doing proper." He laughed yet again. "Always wondered why you didn't run off with the rest yourself. I mean, we all know why you joined up, Quaker. But I never could figure why you stood and fought like a man, when you didn't need to. Now I know, though. Figured that out back at Culpeper Court House. And I expect I'm not the only one."

Blake didn't want to hear any more. He marched from the glade, toward the busy encampment, passing a boy squatting at the edge of the bushes. The soldier looked up, embarrassed and quivering.

"For pity's sake," Blake told him, "go farther into the trees."

"I meant to, Sergeant," the boy said in a pleading voice. He didn't rise from his squat. Shivering all the while like a sick man. Although he had probably just eaten too many green plums.

"Better hide that pretty white bottom you got there," Cobb told the lad. "Might some of the boys take a fancy to it."

Cobb was the most repellent man Blake had ever met.

The morning sun had already turned mean. It looked to be another day of baking heat interrupted by sudden downpours. Blake was glad they weren't marching, that this Sunday, at least, would be a day of rest. The men needed it. As he did himself. They had never marched longer and harder in his recollection. He needed to see about the hole in his right shoe, too. How thoughtlessly he once had arranged good, strong shoes on the bottom shelves of the store. Blake curled a rueful smile. Holes notwithstanding, at least he *had* shoes. Cobb and plenty of other soldiers didn't. The 26th had the fine new uniforms the governor had sent as a gift to his former regiment, and the outfits made them the best-turned-out regiment in the Army of Northern Virginia. Until you looked down at their feet and saw that they were no better off than the rest.

If only Governor Vance had sent them shoes, Blake thought for the hundredth time. The winter-weight uniforms were only a torment in the summer heat. Even with their tunics rolled up and carried, men collapsed by the roadside on each day's march.

Striding past the cook-fires of a sister company, Blake believed he had rid himself of Cobb, who was careful to be insubordinate only when there were no witnesses about. But Cobb was more agitated than usual and had stayed on his heels like a hound.

They passed two bearded men slaughtering a steer amid happy laughter. In the background, the Moravians played "Bonnie Blue Flag."

"I know, don't I, Quaker? Why you didn't run off? Back then, when you and me kept the Yankees off, and they made you a sergeant and left me sucking a straw?" Eager and bright as a child he was, with his sordid nose and filth. "I've known why ever since that evening at Culpeper Court House."

Blake stopped. "I should knock you down."

The words only intensified Cobb's glee. "But you won't. You

and me, we both know that. 'Cause you want them to take you for a gentleman, ain't that right? Still hoping to be made up a lieutenant, a fine, high officer. But you won't be. Not after Culpeper Court House. Everybody knows what you're all about now, Quaker. And it ain't just 'Lost Lenore.' They know. They just don't say. Out of politeness."

Blake turned. Fists balled.

Cobb cackled again and danced off. He always knew how far he could go, and that was how far he went.

Blake watched the narrow shoulders recede, the soiled black hair clotted below the brim of a worn straw hat. Most of the men already claimed to have lost the governor's new kepis, favoring their worn slouch hats or straw that shielded them from the sun.

Disdainful of the Sabbath, a nearby game of cards spurred cries of victory and disgust. The band struck up "Wait for the Wagon."

"I'm not a Quaker anymore," Blake said.

His words were a breath, and only God could hear them.

Blake sat apart with a tin cup of coffee, concealed by a shade tree and trying to let things be. Cobb had unsettled him.

The coffee was fine, though, and that was something. The drink was the last of a "gift" pressed from a Dutch family in Fayetteville. The local men were timid, when they were in evidence at all, but the big Dutch housewives were bold and forthright. The man of the house, with a beard like a bib, had produced the measure of coffee only after his wife turned them down with an earful.

Blake admired the Pennsylvania countryside. All the men did. The great barns and the houses of stone or brick, as strong as fortresses, and the gardens dense with vegetables, the abundant fields of corn, astonished the men with whom he served, who knew only sag-walled cabins and rock-toothed fields that broke the men who chewed them with a plow. As terrible as war might be, for many a man from the hills it was a lark that spared his back, if not his feet. For a time, at least, the Bunyan twins and Hugh Gordon, Pike Gray and Tam McMinn, had entered a world in which they no longer needed to worry about feeding a pack of children or replacing an old mule that had died in harness. The Cause absolved them of all

other obligations. All a man needed to do was to stand up and kill or be killed when the time came.

Pennsylvania was a foreign country to those men, so exotic it was unthinkable that it ever could have been governed by the same hand that ruled their knobs, narrow fields, and hollows. But it was not a strange land to Blake. He had not come to their mountain world until his fourteenth year. Before that, he had been housed by his mother's family in Waterford, Virginia, where Quakers and other industrious sorts had drawn their own wealth from hard work and better soil. For Blake, the orderly towns of Pennsylvania, with their redbrick fronts and scrubbed stoops, brought a sense of homecoming he would have preferred to avoid.

The last of the coffee went cold. Blake drank the dregs. Although there were orders to give, Sabbath or not, he was not yet ready to move. He sat on in the shade a while longer.

The damnable thing was that Cobb was mostly right. It was uncanny. Blake, too, had noticed a queerness in Colonel Burgwyn, who had looked almost feverish during the psalms and sermon. Blake would not have put his impression into the words Cobb had spit out, but it chilled him to feel their rightness.

Yes, there would be a fight. Only God knew where. Probably beyond the high ridges to the east. As always, rumors thrived and grew extravagant. They were marching to Harrisburg. No, to Philadelphia. Or all the way to New York City. They would circle back to Baltimore, or descend upon Washington from the north and hang Lincoln from a sour apple tree.

No one knew what General Lee had in mind.

But there was this quiet day for which to be grateful. Blake wished he could find comfort in its Sunday-ness, but he could not. His upbringing had been left too far behind him, to the sorrow of so many. He had still read the Bible for a time after leaving his mother's faith, but that came largely from habit, partly from guilt. Then the Good Book had drowned in the blood of Malvern Hill.

The regiment had gone in late and done little. But the carnage had stunned Blake. The regiment's skirmishes in North Carolina had not amounted to war. Malvern Hill was war. What killed the last

prayers left in him wasn't a sense of revulsion at the suffering and death, but how much he loved it.

Old George, ever cheerful . . . ," Reynolds kidded. "You sound as if you've been sentenced to hang at daybreak."

"Haven't I been?" Meade asked. They walked along a farm road beyond the headquarters picket line. A cavalry unit had followed the track some hours before, leaving its visiting cards. The two generals stepped carefully.

"I suppose you'll have the Sixth Pennsylvania for your headquarters guard now?" Reynolds said. His grin was friendly, but devilish.

Embarrassed to be caught out so readily, Meade tried to smile.

"Oh, come on, George," Reynolds told him. "It wasn't a brilliant deduction. Philadelphia society would never forgive you, if you didn't. And Margaret would pin back your ears. Social standing has its obligations." He chuckled. "At least your Rittenhouse bucks got rid of those sticks of theirs. 'Rush's Lancers' indeed. They read too much Walter Scott in Philadelphia."

"They took young George in," Meade said, defending himself. "When he left West Point."

"And they would've been damned fools, if they didn't. He's a fine young man. Just a bit too energetic for the old jail on the Hudson, I suspect. Come on, cheer up."

Meade stopped to stare out across a field of wheat. Staring at nothing. The world smelled burnt.

"I'll need your help, John," he said. Unable to look the man who was now his subordinate in the face.

"Don't underestimate yourself."

The heat pressed down. Sweat bloomed. "I don't. I never have. I'm a proud man, John. You know it. That's part of my dilemma, I suppose. I don't want to fail. The shame of it."

"Then don't fail."

Meade turned to his friend. Reynolds was the shorter man, but more pleasing to the eye. The white hairs threaded into his beard graced him, while graying whiskers just made Meade look older.

"You should have had the command, John."

Reynolds shrugged, smiled. "Well, I don't. Now what the devil

was so important that I had to ride over immediately?" He wasn't bothered, though. His good smile held.

"I can't do this by myself," Meade told him, reversing their direction and strolling back toward the picket line. "I'm keeping you in command of the army's left wing. Doubleday can handle your household duties at First Corps, while you apply the switch to Sickles—he's back, you know—and to our sainted and reverent General Howard." He grimaced. "The Eleventh Corps's in a bad way, and we both know it. His Germans hate Howard, and he despises them. And, frankly, I'm not sure I blame the Dutchmen." Meade's expression tightened. "It wasn't just Jackson at Chancellorsville. Or bad luck. Howard hasn't a jot of imagination when it comes to the things of this earth. He can't envision anything he can't see right in front of him—unless it has to do with abolition—and he won't listen to anyone who doesn't rank him. The man can only lead if he's properly led."

"Well, you stumped me," Reynolds said. "I thought you'd be more worried about the Third Corps. Sickles is the joker in the deck, George."

Meade almost smiled, but his mouth was etched with bitterness. "That's why you're keeping him, too. His corps is able, if he's not. Good division commanders. And I can't very well relieve Abe's favorite War Democrat and Mrs. Lincoln's slinking Tammany pet, can I? Sickles is the burden I can't be rid of, and there's folly and damnation in the creature." Meade grunted at his image of the man. "He'll have his marching orders this afternoon, to close in your direction. You'll move north to Emmitsburg with the First Corps, keeping the Eleventh on your flank." Slowing, he turned toward his golden companion. "You wouldn't have a spare map of Pennsylvania, would you? To call Hooker negligent would be merciful."

A cloud of green flies rose from a pile of horse droppings. The soldiers called the flies "Berdan's Sharpshooters."

"I expected more of Butterfield," Reynolds reflected. "He hasn't just been Hooker's boon companion. Dan always kept one duty officer sober."

"He can't even keep up with the orders I pass along. John, I just

can't trust the man. He's Hooker's creature. You should've heard
him this morning, claiming Hooker told him nothing of his plans.
I asked Warren to take his place, and Seth Williams, but nobody
wants it."

"You can't replace him as chief of staff now. With Lee out there."

"That's what Warren said."

"And he was right. Anyway, Warren's where he needs to be. He's
a splendid engineer."

"But I can't depend on Butterfield to be loyal to me. And he
and Sickles are thick as thieves." Meade swept off a veil of flies.
"I've never hated the army, but I've hated army politics since West
Point. Even you and I have had our differences. To my regret, John.
But now, with these volunteer officers . . . the whole business stinks
like an Irishman's drawers. I'm not certain whether they've given
me command of an army, or of a political convention. But I know I
can't trust Butterfield."

A lone cow looked up from its grazing, as if about to join the
conversation. Instead, it just flicked its tail.

"No, you can't," Reynolds said. "Not personally. But he'll be
loyal to the army. Butterfield's a good Union man, if nothing else.
As is Sickles, for that matter. I don't think Butterfield will let you
down, as long as we're on campaign. Not intentionally, anyway.
And I'd say the same for Sickles, if no more."

Meade roused. "Sickles is a murderer and a thief. The man's a
whoremonger."

"He'll fight."

Meade snorted. "But will the man *think*? He's leading a corps, not
a regiment."

Reynolds dosed his voice with warmth again. "Well, I'll watch
Dan Sickles for you. And I'll see that Howard doesn't pray too ex-
travagantly for his darkies on army time." He laughed. "Then we'll
see if you can manage Hancock. Old Win's the wildest savage Phila-
delphia ever nursed."

"Win's not really a Philadelphia man," Meade said. "Not in the
true sense. Humphreys is more the thing."

Amused, Reynolds shook his head and dropped the matter.

"And perhaps this army should take General Lee into account,"
Meade said abruptly, resentment back in full gallop. "Sharpe waves

his hands and tells me the Army of Northern Virginia is 'somewhere west of the mountains.' He has no blasted idea."

"Come now, George. You're being harsh. I'd have Sharpe any day. If he hasn't yet found the current address of Robert E. Lee's chamberpot, who do you think would? Without Sharpe, this army might still be in Virginia. You're damned lucky to have him."

Meade never liked being chastened. He kicked a clod of dirt before realizing that it wasn't dirt. "I'm trying to drag this army together so we won't have another disaster on our hands. And I can't help believing that Lee knows more about us than we do about him. Damn it, we can't even find Stuart, who's always ranging about across Lee's front. It's as if a curtain's been drawn." He shook his head. "I'm *not* going to let Lee set the rules this time. I swear it. I'm going to fight him on ground *I* choose, not where he wants to fight. And that means I need to find him before he pounces."

"Buford's out in front of me. He's an old Indian-fighter. If Lee closes on our left, John won't let him slip by."

"We're not fighting Indians this time."

"No. But I trust Buford. And finding Lee should be a tad simpler than trailing a Comanche war party."

"Well, keep pushing Buford north. Ignore any sobbing from Pleasanton."

As the two generals neared the picket line, a young sentry weighed the wisdom of challenging them. He chose to keep his mouth shut and present arms.

Rejoining the commotion of the camp, Meade said, "Thank you for riding over, John. In this heat. I needed to see you, I had to let some of this out. I really must depend on you, you know."

Reynolds kept silent, but his eyes were good.

"It's all an odd business," Meade continued. "I thought I'd be remembered for my method of reading longitude. That, and the better of my lighthouses. Now look where we are. . . ."

Before they parted, Meade to see that his orders had been dispatched and Reynolds to rejoin his soldiers, the new commanding general of the Army of the Potomac seized the hand of his friend and sometime rival, gripping it hard. As if to draw strength from it.

"I fear," Meade said in a voice only Reynolds could hear, "that, if we lose the next battle, we've lost the war, John."

"Then we mustn't lose it." Reynolds laughed.

Abruptly, inexplicably, wonderfully, Meade found himself able to laugh along. And he did. So vigorously it startled those within hearing distance. Reynolds was right: He had to climb out of himself. He couldn't do worse than Hooker, after all. Perhaps the army just needed an engineer's discipline.

Before Meade could gather more confident words, his son dashed madly toward them, bareheaded and struggling to keep his scabbard from tripping him.

Both generals stiffened.

"Father!" young George cried, drawing up before them. Immediately, he corrected himself, "I mean, General Meade, sir." Eyes young and wild, he turned to Reynolds and touched fingers to an eyebrow in a salute. "General Reynolds, your indulgence, sir."

"What's got you all lathered up, George?" Reynolds asked.

Captain Meade turned back to his father. "A message from General Halleck, sir. Fitzhugh Lee's cavalry captured a wagon train at Rockville. Smack in our rear, between us and Washington. They made off with a hundred and fifty wagons."

In the sliver of quiet that followed, summer's hum swamped the noises of the camp.

"Well, George," Reynolds said at last, "it seems you've found General Stuart."

TWO

June 29

G eneral Stuart will not let us down," the old man said. "I expect to hear from him at any hour."

Longstreet grunted. "It wouldn't hurt him to worry less about getting into the Richmond papers and more about his duty to this army."

"General Stuart will not let me down," Lee repeated.

The two men sat on camp stools under an elm tree, a few steps from Lee's tent. The air was hot and thick, with dark clouds rolling. Out on the road, an artillery battery passed between lines of infantry, all of them bound for the high hills to the east. The men on foot heckled the mounted gunners, their words unclear in the distance, but their tone unmistakable to anyone who wore a uniform.

Longstreet was sour. He liked Stuart well enough, was even fond of him, but the man had grown too confident. Perhaps they all had. Even the ideal gentleman before him, with his immaculate uniform—worn despite the heat—and his well-groomed beard.

Reading his mind, Lee added, "Stuart's young. High-spirited. We don't want to break those spirits." The old man thought about his own words, then half-sighed. "They're all so young."

Yes, the army's officers were young. And getting younger. Not least after Chancellorsville, that magnificent victory, Jackson's crimson sepulchre. Jackson had been the noted loss, but there had been so many others, all of their deaths eclipsed by his alone. The army could not afford many more such triumphs. The Union could replace men, the South could not. They had to fashion their battles after Fredericksburg, not Chancellorsville. Make the Federals charge a wall of fire. Bleed them. Raise the cost intolerably.

"Well, while we're waiting for General Stuart to grace us with his presence," Longstreet said, "perhaps Imboden's unwashed slave-catchers could spare some time from chasing niggers to go on a scout?" He made as if to spit, but did not. Spitting was a habit Lee deplored. "The irregulars are worthless, all of them. Worthless and useless. They disgrace this army, sir."

Longstreet's outburst left the old man aggrieved. In silence, the two men looked past the cluster of tents and the soldiers at their labors. The road in the middle distance, a tunnel of dust, belonged solely to the infantry now. Men plodded forward.

The commanding general and his favored subordinate had pitched their headquarters near to one another, the way it always went now. Lee's quartermaster had chosen a picnic spot for the encampment. "Shatter's Woods," the locals called it, a name the soldiers soon altered by one vowel.

"There are matters," the old man said at last, "that trouble us both, I think. But Mr. Davis has his political flanks to guard, as we have our military flanks. The runaway-slave issue excites certain factions in Richmond."

"Factions conspicuous by their absence on any battlefield."

Both men chose to let the subject go. But Longstreet had been bitten by a scene he'd witnessed while riding to the artillery trains. Judging his importance by his retinue, a captive darkey, the tiniest man in a rope chain of a dozen, had called to him, "I'm no runaway, Gen'rul, I'm a freeborn man, I'm freeborn!" A cavalryman in a ragged pretense of a uniform had smashed the man across the face with his pistol, knocking him down. To Longstreet's surprise, the other captives had laughed, one singing out, "You ain't freeborn no more, boy, no you ain't."

Longstreet had ridden on, only to regret it. He would have whipped the man who treated a dog like that. Instead, he had cantered away from the bloody-faced nigger. War hardened the heart.

He had no right to spend his anger on Lee, though. The old man had troubles enough.

Longstreet went to work to improve the mood he had worsened. "Porter Alexander told me a howler this morning, sir. And young Porter's the man to tell a joke. Happened in Chambersburg. Brigade of Hood's boys come marching along, the whole wild pack

of 'em, and the good citizens are watching this fine parade from their porches and windows, some of them waving Yankee flags, defiant as all get-out, and all of them sour as pickles. . . . Well, the boys come marching up past this big yellow dog in a front yard, and it's leaping and barking to beat the band, just growling and snapping away. And this little, bitty girl runs back to her porch, crying, 'Pappy, Pappy, don't let Beave bite the army!'"

Lee laughed. It was a soft sound. "Have your men been comporting themselves well, General? We will not behave as those people have done in our own country."

"They've followed your orders. Better than I expected, to tell the truth. Plenty of temptation around here."

"Hood's men? The Texans?"

Longstreet grinned through his beard. "I told Hood to keep his men out of the Pennsylvania whiskey. And he told me that wasn't a problem at all, that the trick was keeping the whiskey out of his men." With Lee's spirits revived, Longstreet decided to raise another subject. "Sir, I'd be obliged if someone could take that high-toned Englishman off my hands. The one who turned up yesterday."

"I thought he and your people were getting on," Lee said.

"Oh, the boys get a laugh or two out of him. Moxley stands him well enough. But he won't give me any peace. The man has more questions than a drunken newspaperman at a fire. And he looks at my men like he's gawking at native troops somewhere in India."

"I'll make time for him tomorrow," Lee said. "Perhaps that will satisfy the man."

Longstreet waved away a fly. "No, sir. He intends to see a battle." He laughed. "He's a proud fellow, the way they are. Tries to be affable, but it feels like a counterfeit bill." Lofting his beard and remembering, he went on, "Got more than a little put out last night, after he made sure to let us know he's a lieutenant colonel in their Coldstream Guards at the ripe old age of twenty-seven years. Well, Tom Goree's all Texas and won't put up with much, so he mentioned to Fremantle that we have a passel of full colonels younger than that, including that boy-colonel over in Pettigrew's dancing school. Our English friend was crushed like the belle nobody asked to dance at the cotillion."

"Bear with him a while longer," the old man said. "Tolerate him a little yet. If we win the coming battle and do so on Federal soil . . . England may come in for us at last."

Longstreet didn't believe that, but kept his opinion to himself. He judged that, had Britain meant to back the Confederacy, it would have done it the year before. But a great defeat, a Fredericksburg writ large, might be enough to bring the Union to ask for a peace without English interference.

Longstreet did not trust his own hope. But there it was. All men hoped for something.

Above the line of high hills, thunder boomed.

The old man's thoughts had moved along to the battlefield that would be. "I'll beat General Hooker again," he confided. His tone expressed uncharacteristic disdain. "And if God is with us, this time it may be less costly." The ghost of Jackson passed between them. "I have a sense of Hooker now. He'll worry about having his flank turned again. And he has to cover Washington, Baltimore, and Philadelphia. So he'll spread out his corps and weaken himself. He'll weaken his center to brace his flanks." Lee punched a fist into his open palm, entranced by what he foresaw. "And then we'll have him. We'll pick his apples one at a time, instead of shaking the entire tree at once."

"We didn't know Hooker had his army in Maryland until Harrison showed up. We need Stuart."

At the mention of the spy, Lee had lifted his nose, but Longstreet drove on. "You heard what he had to say about the rumors that Reynolds may replace Hooker. John Reynolds is a different proposition."

Lee shook his head. "Those people won't do that. The campaign's too far along." He gave Longstreet a sideward look. "I trust General Halleck to make a bounteous share of poor decisions, but nothing so madcap as that. No, we'll fight Hooker again. And whip him again." Lee reached out and patted Longstreet's forearm. "My old warhorse," he said, voice as warm as ever it could grow. "It'll be Hooker. And our victory again. And then we'll see if their president chooses peace."

Longstreet almost brought up Vicksburg, which was likely to fall by summer's end, if not sooner. But he chose not to spoil the

old man's better mood. The thought of Vicksburg brought Grant to mind, though. Longstreet loved Grant. As deeply as he could love any man. And he feared the degree to which Virginia's cavaliers underestimated him. Sam had needed only a war to bloom.

Overhead, dark clouds thickened. Thunder neared. But the heat refused to weaken.

Longstreet recalled the last time he and Grant had been together. In St. Louis, before the war, at the Planters' Hotel. Out of the army, Grant had fallen low, reduced to selling firewood in the streets. But people kept in touch with him, and mutual friends called him in as a fourth at cards. The evening had gone well enough, but with no time for private talk or displays of sentiment. Grant was threadbare, but unashamed, and pleased as could be to see Longstreet. When Grant returned to the hotel the next morning and thrust a five-dollar gold piece into his hand, Longstreet had tried to decline it. "No," his ragged friend had told him, "you take it, Pete. I've owed you that for years, and it's gnawed me."

Now Grant was far away, on the Mississippi, a conqueror making a fool of Joe Johnston, a fine general, and cornering Pemberton like a cat backs up a mouse. Even a victory on Pennsylvania's soil might not end the war so soon as the old man hoped.

And whether they faced Hooker or Reynolds, it was bound to be a tougher fight than the old man would admit. Jackson was gone, along with so many other capable men. Now a third of the army fell under Dick Ewell, with his peg leg and thinned bravado, and another third had gone to Hill, who was meant to command a division, not a corps. Hill was a fighter, that was true enough. But only when he wasn't laid up by the aftereffects of a loathsome disease no gentleman would mention. And the last third of the army fell to him, Pete Longstreet, Old Dutch. Before the reorganization in the wake of Chancellorsville, he had commanded half of the Army of Northern Virginia. Now his command was reduced to three divisions. But the old man still clung to him.

"I believe we will have three days yet," Lee said out of the blue. "Perhaps a fourth. That will be enough. Ewell starts south, and Hill will be there to greet him. You, General, will have time to lead your corps across the mountains. Then we shall pay a call on General Hooker." The old man's brows tightened. "How far back is Pickett?"

"Two days. I've sent a man to hurry him on."

"Two days will do well enough."

"If we have three."

"Hooker will not take the aggressive," Lee said. "We'll have the time. Hooker will be cautious."

Longstreet almost raised Stuart's absence again, but saw it was pointless. The old man would hear nothing against his beloved fellow Virginian. Stuart was almost a son to him. And perhaps he was right, Stuart might ride into camp that afternoon.

"Then we should have time to pick our ground," Longstreet said. "To choose good ground and make Hooker attack us. Outflank him, move between him and Washington. Force his hand."

Lee did not answer immediately, but said at last, "When the army is gathered in, we'll take the aggressive. We should find those people still dispersed in Maryland. Should we meet any closer to hand, we'll defeat them piecemeal. Otherwise, I intend to turn toward Harrisburg again, to make Hooker follow, to give him the chance to worry himself into errors."

"And we'll force him to attack on ground we choose," Longstreet repeated. He wanted to hear the old man say it aloud. "A strategic offensive that ends in a tactical defense."

Again, Lee weighed his words before responding. Then he spoke as if he had not heard a word Longstreet had offered. "I will not bring on an engagement until this army is concentrated, that much is certain. I will have every man understand that." He nodded in agreement with himself. "But once we have balled our fist, I intend to wield it."

The old man's mood lightened again, but Longstreet could not shake his growing alarm. The old man wanted a fight. Say what he might, he loved it. But they had to fight wisely now, so far from home. The army could not afford another bloodletting like Chancellorsville. Not even one called a victory.

Porter Alexander had come to him that morning not to tell stories of big yellow dogs and amusing little girls, but to express his concern about their stocks of high-explosive shell. "There's enough for one real battle and to cover a march," Alexander had told him. "But we won't have a round to spare."

"Perhaps you and I are too prone to worry, Pete," the old man said, reading his mind again. The use of his nickname startled Longstreet. Lee was a formal man on all occasions.

"Here we are," Lee continued, "worrying ourselves over grand strategy, and you know the last thing I heard from Powell Hill?" He shook his head slowly, as if at a child's antics. "General Heth asked if he could go fetch some shoes. It seems the men have more immediate concerns than a pair of somber generals do."

"Well, I'd rather have a thousand new pairs of shoes than a thousand new rifles myself," Longstreet said, "and that's the Georgia truth. If Hotspur Harry can bring in a load of shoes, boots, or ladies' slippers, I'll tip my hat to him."

Skirmishing raindrops reached them. They rose together and hastened under the fly before Lee's tent.

"I told General Hill I had no objection, to act at his discretion," Lee went on. "As long as no one brings on an engagement, he understands that."

"Did Hill happen to say where his men intend to go hunting for this treasure?" Longstreet asked. "I have half a mind to force-march Hood over the mountains and beat them to it."

The volleys of rain grew heavier, thumping the canvas, trying to break through.

"According to General Heth, the shoes are in that crossroads village east of Cashtown." Lee's expression tightened in consternation. "I know the name full well, but it eludes me."

"Gettysburg," Longstreet said.

Ich habe das verdammte Regen zum kotzen satt," Bettelman cried in a tone of glorious outrage. *I've had enough damned rain to make me puke.*

His nearby comrades laughed, despite the torrent pounding them. Bettelman's outbursts of indignation at every aspect of army life were so dramatic and sudden that that they enlivened the grimmest march. And this march was wretched.

"An hour since, you complain about the heat," Heisler reminded him. Shaking the wet from his neck and face, he added, "You want to be cold. You get rain. Now you don't like the rain."

"It's the mud I don't like," Bettelman replied. "I am not made for the insane life of a soldier. I'm a watchmaker. I am not made for this."

But he *was* made for it. Corporal Friedrich Schwertlein had seen Bettelman stand on the field of Chancellorsville, as steady as the statue of a warrior, face blackened with powder and jaw set, firing calmly into the Rebels as they came on screaming. The regiment had stood its ground, even after Colonel Krzyzanowski ordered them to withdraw. They had stood, and fought, and bled as the army collapsed around them. Only to read in the newspapers that every one of the Germans, "the Flying Dutchmen" of the Eleventh Corps, had run away, a vile disgrace to the Union. But the 26th Wisconsin had not run. Not even when half their number lay dead and bleeding, with fires devouring the brush around them and the Confederates hurling themselves forward through the under-growth, maddened by the unexpected resistance. Schwertlein himself had stood his ground as well. Telling himself, *Rastatt nie wieder!* Never again a surrender such as Rastatt.

Rastatt was far away now. Across an ocean. Fourteen years gone. But the fight was the same. Prussian princes then, slavemonger aris-tocrats now. Another desperate battle to save a republic. Another chapter in the universal struggle for freedom.

Fritz Schwertlein certainly did not consider himself a national-ist. The day would come when nations would disappear in the rec-ognition that all men were brothers. Yet, it burned in him, as it did in every man still marching under the regiment's colors, to hear all Germans derided as cowards. In the battle each man sensed ahead, it would not be "Rastatt never again!" but "Never another Chan-cellorsville!" This time, it would be different, their reputation would be redeemed.

The rain halted as suddenly as it had begun, leaving a mire through which the men had to struggle. Some lost their shoes and cursed, while others fell out to remove and save their footwear. More than a few already had collapsed from the heat and strain. The march seemed endless.

"Wie weit noch?" Bettelman whined. How much farther?

Roused by the question, Heisler asked Schwertlein, "Do you think we are in Pennsylvania, Fritz?"

"No," Schwertlein told him. "Emmitsburg is in Maryland. We have not come to Emmitsburg. After that is Pennsylvania."

To their rear, a commotion rose. Horses complained and hot voices commanded: "Give way there! Get out of the way!"

Accustomed to their fate, Schwertlein and his fellow Germans stepped to the side of the road, seizing the excuse for a few minutes' rest. Their clothing steamed.

As the limbers, guns, and caissons neared, the soldiers stepped back deeper into the brush. Even so, great splashes of mud reached them. Low Irish by the look of them, the gunners ignored the foot soldiers as they whipped their horses through the clinging slop.

"If they stick and ask me to help, I don't help them no more," Bettelman muttered. Then he reconsidered and added, "Perhaps I am better to be an artilleryman? To ride so? Better than this *verschweinte Infanterie*."

The last caisson sloshed by, leaving knee-deep traces and long puddles amid the slime. Some fellow attempted to raise a song, but the mood was too disheartened. With the rain blown off, the heat punched back through the trees that lined their route.

Lieutenant Trenk rode up and dismounted beside them. He always walked with the men, mounting his horse only when he needed to reach regiment or brigade headquarters in a hurry. In the 26th, officers and men saw each other differently. Some had fought with Sigel all the way to Freiburg in '49, and so many of them had been driven into exile after the failed revolutions in the Germanies that most viewed rank as a necessary evil on the path to a utopia of equals. They were not Prussians, that was the thing, but men from Baden and Hesse, from the Palatinate or the Lower Rhine. They could march as well as anyone and fight better than most. But they were *civilized* Germans, not slaves of the *Junker* tyrants beyond the Elbe.

"*Was neues, Herr Leutnant?*" Heisler asked. "Any news?"

"It's true about Meade. He's in command now."

"Another Englishman. So I think we lose again," Bettelman commented.

"Well, don't say that to Colonel Kriz," the lieutenant told him. "He doesn't like talk of losing. And he'll be riding up the column in a little while. *Halt's Maul, ja?*"

"*Der Kriz* is a good man," Bettelman said. "I think he is really German, not a Pole."

"Bettelman thinks every good man has to be German," Heisler put in.

"The Poles are a mixed-up bunch, though," the lieutenant observed. "You have their minor noblemen like Kriz, their *szlachta*. Some of them are educated men. And they're brave beyond imagining. But the peasants live like animals, and they make no effort to improve themselves."

"Spoken like a true Hohenzollern," Schwertlein told him. "I should run up and ask the band to play the '*Hohenfriedberger.*'"

"The Lion of Rastatt roars!" Lieutenant Trenk laughed. "Come on, Fritz. You know what I say is true."

Schwertlein hid the sudden wound he felt. He had not been a lion at Rastatt. Not at the end, when the garrison surrendered and he hid in a woman's cupboard while the Prussian officers rounded up the revolutionaries they later would shoot in a ditch below the walls. He had fought until that hour, though, in his angry, amateur's way. It was only at the end that his nerve had failed him.

Trenk's mockery was meant in fun, of course. He knew only that Schwertlein had been at Rastatt, nothing more. The two men had befriended one another in their early days of exile in Milwaukee, before either realized that he had become American in his heart. Trenk, an advocate back in Konstanz, had been struggling to read the law in his new home, while Schwertlein, the younger by three years, had not yet found his vocation as a journalist. They had shared their dreams of a free, universal society, as well as the inevitable nostalgia of the immigrant, but not every detail of their pasts had come into the open. In America, you could edit your previous life like a newspaper article.

When the regiment mustered in, the men had voted for Schwertlein as their lieutenant. But before a single shot was fired, he had proven inadequate to the task, an eternal observer of men, not a leader by nature. They had voted for him only because they had known his name from his newspaper columns. Trenk became the lieutenant and he stepped down to corporal, an arrangement better suited to them both. The embarrassment had been fleeting.

"Anyway," Schwertlein said as they marched along, "what does

it matter? German, Pole, American? The only identity that matters
is whether a man stands for a better world, or defends the old order.
Krzyzanowski fought for a better future in Poland, and he fights
for the same thing now."

"Our corporal's reading us one of his columns," Heisler joked.

"Scheisse," Bettelman called out. "More artillery comes."

But it wasn't another column of guns and limbers. It was only
their brigade commander, Krzyzanowski, creating the uproar behind
them. Lean and almost comically elegant, he sat, straight of spine and
smiling, on a white horse that pranced even in the depths of mud.

But Schwertlein remembered Krzyzanowski at Chancellorsville,
riding just as erectly amid the madness, wielding his saber to direct
men where to aim their fire or halt for another volley, a knight
strayed into the wrong century, a hero out of Schiller. Colonel Kriz,
too, had felt the sting of injustice, after he and two of his regiments
had held the line for the better part of an hour, letting the artillery-
men save their guns, as an entire corps collapsed around them.

As the colonel neared, some men in his path took up a song in
Krzyzanowski's honor:

> Was gestern recht war . . . für den Rhein . . .
> ist's Heute nicht auch . . . recht für Polen?

Other voices took it up, organizing themselves in song. Despite
the slaughter at Chancellorsville, they still had men in the ranks
from a number of singing clubs back in Milwaukee. Schwertlein
sang, too, in a baritone honed on Schubert's *Lieder* in his family's
parlor in Mainz.

> What once was justice . . . for the Rhine . . .
> is it not just . . . today for Poland?
> Should Poland not be . . . theirs, but mine . . .
> a country we have . . . merely stolen?

> Have you forgotten . . . our own plight . . .
> All you profound . . . thinkers so hallowed . . .
> Should Poland not . . . be free by right . . .
> And free of Prussians . . . with their gallows?

The colonel acknowledged the song with a grin that lifted the wings of his mustache. Riding along, he paid a succession of salutes to the men he soon would lead back into battle. His war was theirs, theirs his, a struggle not only against Confederates or Prussians, but against all the world's princely houses and potentates, Russian, Austrian, Ottoman . . . Their fight was waged to break the chains that bound men oceans apart. The difference now was that they had a genuine army, not just a rabble with shotguns, scythes, and rusty swords from attics. They had an army, and a free land worth defending.

When the colonel had passed from sight, though, all the high emotions vanished with him. The men went back to the muck and the murderous heat.

"War is shit," Bettelman said.

He rode into the confusion in a rage. Rain pounded. Headed in conflicting directions, the wagons and their teams blocked all the streets. Officers barked, but the teamsters only shrugged, waiting for someone else to put things right. The guns, the infantry, all the rest of Slocum's Twelfth Corps could not get through the infernal muddle. Everything was falling behind schedule.

"*You*, damn you," Meade barked at a private hunched on a wagon with the reins slack in his hand. "Who do you belong to?"

The soldier was little impressed with the drenched old man before him. He just shrugged. Meade wanted to have him arrested, but retained the presence of mind to grasp that the teamster's removal would mean an abandoned wagon.

"I asked you which unit you're assigned to, you sonofabitch," Meade barked.

The boy shrugged a second time, but said, "Third Corps, I guess."

Sickles. That whoremonger bastard. His trains had no business in Middleburg, or anywhere near it. The last of them should have passed through hours before.

Meade yanked his mount around and worked his way back to the captain in charge of his escort.

"*You*," Meade said. "Have your men open these streets. Whip man and beast, if you have to."

The captain saluted, but looked dazed by the maelstrom. Every-

one in sight appeared half-drowned, and the crawling chaos around them stank of wet wool, wet horses, and waste. The captain went to work, though, waving the leading men of his squadron forward.

Meade rode over to General Hunt, who had sheltered under the wooden awning of a shop to light a cigar. Meade dismounted, tied Old Baldy to the nearest rail, and stormed up the steps, spurs clanking.

"It's Sickles," he snapped. "Again. The man takes nothing seriously but his debauchery." He whisked some of the water from his uniform, a useless effort. Too hot for an oilskin, he had made the best of it and now he was soaked.

"Storm's passing," Hunt said calmly. "That should help."

"It's not the storm. It's Sickles." Meade went back into the slackening rain to fetch pencil and paper from a saddlebag. Waving away a cigar, he wrote against the flat of a door frame, giving Sickles the very devil.

Out in the main crossroads of the town, the jumble of wagons had begun to move. But not quickly enough for Meade. The army was a vast animal, hard to manage and always ready to stray. As he moved his headquarters forward, he had ridden along choked roads, often taking to the fields to speed his passage. The journey had led him past countless mired wagons and caissons with broken wheels, past knots of arguing officers and sergeants with their vocabulary ablaze. And, always, the endless columns of regiments came on, men marching in their undergarments in the killing heat, kerchiefs trailing behind their caps, and many of them as barefoot as the Confederates. With his telegraphic communications cut by Stuart's raiders, he had nonetheless tried to get a message through by courier, asking not for reinforcements—he knew there were none—but for a shipment of shoes, if shoes were available.

As for Stuart, Meade refused to take the bait and chase him across Pennsylvania. Let Pleasanton and his cavalrymen fend him off as best they could. The thing now was to concentrate the army, not weaken it. Stuart was, in the end, more nuisance than danger. And Meade wasn't certain he minded having Lee's cavalry separated from the rest of the Army of Northern Virginia. If Stuart was raiding in the east, he wasn't scouting in the west. Meade couldn't understand the logic of what seemed to him a folly, but he meant to take advantage where

he could. He had sent Reynolds a message to ensure he was pushing Buford's First Cavalry Division forward as far as Gettysburg.

Lee was at Chambersburg. He knew that now. Rumors put some of his men across South Mountain . . . although that could have been warmed-over talk from Ewell's passage the week before. Or it might be a token force meant to cover the passes. Or a sign Lee's entire army was on the move again. He needed more information, much more, if he hoped to shape the campaign to his own advantage.

Finished with the note to Sickles, Meade turned to Hunt. "Find Sickles. Give him this. Damn it, I know you're a busy man, Henry, but he won't take anything seriously unless he hears it from the mouth of a fellow general. Give him this note, and tell him I'll be damned if I let him afflict this entire army with his slows. He needs to keep to his march schedule. It's not a damned suggestion."

Hunt didn't protest at being handed a courier's mission. And Meade didn't worry about diverting the man for a few hours. As chief of artillery, Hunt was thoroughly competent. Meade trusted him to do all that had to be done in his sphere of action.

But just as the artilleryman had flicked the stub of his cigar into the mud and started off, Meade called, "Hunt?"

"General Meade?"

"When you cross Pipe Creek, see what you think of it as a defensive position. For the entire army, I mean. It looks all well and good on the map, and I've got Warren inspecting the length of it, but I'd appreciate your view on the subject. An old gunner's opinion."

Hunt saluted, a bit carelessly, and moved for his horse. He wasn't careless when he placed his batteries, though. If Hunt blessed a position, it would be a sound one.

The sun tore through. The ill-tempered weather went from bad to worse, humid as a swamp. But the road through the town had opened. Regiments from the Twelfth Corps began to stream past.

The men did not cheer him. He didn't think they even recognized him. Anyway, some would have preferred to have Reynolds, others would have liked McClellan back. Even Hooker still had partisans in the ranks.

Well, they didn't have to love him. They just had to fight.

THREE

Y our soldiers certainly do seem full of fight," Arthur Fremantle, captain and lieutenant colonel of Her Majesty's Coldstream Guards, announced to the gathered officers. Pleased with himself, as always, he nodded under the lantern's light. "Fine chaps, if a bit wild."

Longstreet understood what the Englishman meant: The men of the Army of Northern Virginia were undisciplined and ragged. Impressive specimens in their way, but not to be measured against Her Majesty's finest. Fremantle didn't understand that there were forms of discipline that had nothing to do with parades.

"They'll fight," Longstreet agreed. He balanced his plate of stew on one knee to reach into his boot and scratch his leg. He hoped he hadn't picked up poison ivy again. Or the camp itch.

"Yes, sir, fight they will," Tom Goree put in. "Take a right pleasure in it, some of them. All's we can do to stop them from gutting, cooking, and eating the Yankees they knock down."

Goree had attached himself to Longstreet during the journey from Texas to Richmond at the outset of the war. He looked like a cleaned-up Comanche. A fine example of a Texas gentleman, Goree was fit to be trusted with a lady's honor, but not with a sharp knife. Give a Texan a knife, Longstreet thought, and he can't help using it on something.

"In all seriousness, Lieutenant Goree, one finds their morale remarkable," Fremantle continued. "All in all."

"Haven't et so good in all their lives," Goree explained. "They weren't so pleased with things last winter. Were they, Moxley?"

"Wasn't all that pleased myself," Moxley Sorrel said. "Any more of that stew, John?"

"Jupiter's saving a little for our European friends," Fairfax told him. "If they haven't gotten themselves bushwhacked by some Pennsylvania *Hausfrau*."

"All right," Sorrel told him. "I know you'd be mortified, were guests to judge a Fairfax inhospitable. Next time, though, tell that darkey of yours to buy an extra hen wherever he steals them."

Longstreet focused on his plate. He wasn't in a talking mood, not even with men he liked. Lee was on his mind, not some bothersome Englishman. He had not been able to get the old man to pledge to let the Federals attack. Longstreet knew Lee well enough to sense what he kept inside, and what Lee held back worried him. The old man loved to go right at his enemies, to tear into them and have done with it. The restraint of Fredericksburg had been a fluke, a matter of numbers so lopsided and a defensive position so tactically immaculate—along with a fool for an opponent—that Lee had been obliged to wait for the Federals to come at him. And that had been the right thing to do. It almost always was now. The killing power of massed artillery and rifled weapons was hurrying the age of the bold charge to an end. A fool could see it. And if your enemy would not oblige by attacking you, then you went around him, unhinged his position, and forced his hand. It wasn't an age of war, but one of slaughter.

Longstreet also had begun to see that, for all Lee's protestations to the contrary, the old man really didn't want advice. Not from him. Nor from anyone else. Lee wanted his views confirmed. Unlike Jackson, with his mad eyes and his Bible, the old man was not immune to vanity. Behind that beautiful gentleman's armor, Lee was as human as any man. And very much alone in the midst of his army. He didn't value Longstreet's suggestions about the campaign, but needed someone to talk to, a set of ears.

"Am I mistaken," Fremantle asked, "or is there rather a divide between this headquarters and General Lee's?"

Longstreet looked up sharply. How had the man sensed that?

Fremantle hadn't sensed anything. He'd just noticed the obvious. "I mean to say," the Englishman continued, "that it rather strikes one how General Lee surrounds himself with Virginians. While you, General Longstreet, gather in officers from the other states. Cavaliers and Roundheads, would you say?"

"Fairfax over there is a Virginian," Longstreet said. "And single-handedly responsible for providing proper vittles to this headquarters. We always keep a tame Virginian around to rally our eats." He wiped his beard. "And to see to our table manners."

"Even when there's no table," Sorrel said, joining the merriment. "John's straggling on us, he forgot the napkins again tonight."

"Colonel Fremantle may have something of a point, though," Fairfax suggested, "about the Roundhead business." Fairfax was ever the man to ease another's conversational blunder. "After all, my family aligned with Parliament until the regicide." He reweighed his proposition, then added, "Of course, I'd tend toward putting the Roundhead label on the Federals, I think. They certainly have the self-righteousness . . . and the deplorable sobriety. I don't think anyone here's guilty of the latter." He smiled. Fairfax was a master of smiles. "Anyway, Colonel Fremantle, not all of my fellow Virginians are shining Cavaliers." His smile turned sly. "Except General Pickett, of course. He's one Cavalier who shines himself three times a day."

Longstreet guffawed. "Poor George. Best leave him alone, John. Given that he isn't here to defend himself." He laughed again, though.

Goree looked up, sniffing the air. "He ain't? I swear I can smell his cologne water. Of course, he wears enough so's you'd smell him the other side of the Mississippi."

Longstreet felt compelled to explain to Fremantle that the joking was in good spirits, that all present had a high opinion—or a tolerably high one—of George Pickett. He didn't want an outsider to misunderstand their ways.

But Fairfax spoke first. "Before we break out the elixir that soothes the soul, Colonel Fremantle, I must assure you that we'd tease George Pickett exactly the same way were he among us. He's a fine soldier, and a brave man. Just a trifle lavish with the pomade."

The oldest of the circle, Fairfax was more the staff's master of household than a soldier. He, too, had attached himself to Longstreet early on, asking nothing in return. Longstreet enjoyed the man's company, as he did that of all the men he had allowed to remain by his side.

"But don't it seem odd," Fremantle pressed on, deaf to the subject's sensitivity, "that General Lee, in command of this rather . . .

geographically complex army . . . surrounds himself exclusively with Virginians?"

"I'm not a Virginian," Longstreet said.

"Yes!" Fremantle pounced. "Exactly so, sir! And you're over here, while General Lee dines across the road with his staff." Belatedly, he picked up the undercurrent. "I say, have I raised an indelicate subject?"

He had indeed. There was great resentment in the army about the preferments given to Virginians. Longstreet was the odd man out. But it did not bear talking over with a foreigner.

Horsemen drew up in the shadows. Scheibert, the Prussian observer, and Ross, his Scotland-born Austrian counterpart, made their way through a squadron of moths maddened by the lantern. Lawley, the fellow from *The Times* of London, trailed in after them. Most men had at least one quality to recommend them. The newspaperman didn't.

"Find us any Yankees?" Goree asked.

"No," Scheibert said, dusting off his uniform frock coat. "They are not showing themselves, the Unionists." Dueling scars shone white on his browned cheek. "But I must say to you something about the people here. You must not judge Germans by their unfortunate example. They have fallen from the race and do not even speak properly."

Ross, the Austrian officer, took matters more lightly than the Prussian. "Anyway, they haven't a great deal to say. Except that they're rather frightened of your 'Louisiana Tigers.'"

The two European officers made an odd pair, evidently hating each other to the point of declaring war—or perhaps fighting a duel—yet doing everything but the most private things together. Longstreet figured that neither wanted to let the other out of his sight.

"Gentlemen," Fairfax announced, "our menu this evening offers a dish affectionately known in this army as *poulet militaire*. Or chicken stew. Of which there may be a portion or so remaining, if you'd care to go see Jupiter. . . ."

Ross pinched one end of his perfect mustache. If the Prussian paraded dueling scars, Ross suggested that he had left a few slashes on Viennese hearts. "Oh, we've eaten, thank you. These Pennsyl-

vanians may speak poorly"—he glanced at his Prussian colleague—
"but they do cook well enough." He rubbed his hands together, as
if recalling a delectable romance. "We had quite a peasant feast,
actually, *ein echten Bauernschmaus.*" His seductive smile widened.
"No surprise that these Yankee Dutch girls are so fat, the way they
tuck in. A fellow would rather fear one as a lover."

Longstreet reached down to scratch his leg again. There were
nights when the unwitting minstrel show that Scheibert and Ross
performed entertained him. This was not such a night. There was
too much on his mind, too many things remained unknown.

Why hadn't they encountered Yankee cavalry? Surely Stuart
hadn't drawn off all of them with his antics. Brandy Station had
been a revelation. The Federals were learning. It took two years to
make a cavalryman, according to military lore. Now the boys in
blue had had their two years.

Longstreet could not believe they weren't out there, horsemen
in the dark, closer than Lee believed.

Determined not to be relegated to a minor role, Fremantle
edged closer. Since he wore only civilian clothes, the observers in
their traveling-circus uniforms kept their distance. But he wasn't the
sort of Englishman to quit the field.

"Lieutenant Goree claims you spent some years in Texas, Gen-
eral. I myself entered the Confederacy through Texas, you know.
Rather a swashbuckling place . . . one finds the people quite forth-
right." The Englishman glanced at Goree. "But charming, of
course." He turned back to Longstreet. "How did *you* find it, sir?"

Texas. Ft. Bliss. The post had been well named. He and Louise
had never been as happy anywhere else. Later on, Albuquerque had
not been bad, even if shadowed by the coming war, but El Paso and
Ft. Bliss had given them wondrous years. The summer days scorched,
but gorgeous nights redeemed them. And no post he knew had ri-
valed the place for comradeship, even between the officers and se-
nior enlisted men. Few in number, the wives of all ranks had shared
in the post's society, while the old Mexican families, with their
public dignity and polished silver buckles, had opened their doors
to everyone. He had not expected that, only a decade after a war
had raised a foreign flag above them. There had been a storybook
goodness to the place, a whispered magic, and it had softened him.

He recalled one winter morning when he led out a patrol in the brilliant chill, with the sky overhead as clear as a maiden's conscience. He had raised up his eyes to the mountains ahead, thinking that it was a strange thing to be so happy.

"I liked Texas all right," he told Fremantle.

They had been so in love, despite a loss, and the world had been sweetly, safely routine, interrupted only by an occasional march into the wilderness to show a band of Comanches or straying Apaches that the U.S. Government took an interest in their behavior.

Then secession had come, with its confusions. His choice of sides had never been in doubt, but nothing was sweet or safe or routine any longer. In the war's first winter, scarlet fever killed three of their children. Louise waited on the far side of a river of sorrow now, and he knew not how to bridge it or where he might ford it. On learning the children were ill, he had rushed to Richmond, only to sit at home with the curtains drawn, neither he nor his wife able to rise from their grief to attend the burial. So the little ones entered the winter-hard earth alone. He understood war and its savagery, but not the death, so senselessly, of his children.

In his bleakest hours, Longstreet saw God as a murderer.

Sergeant Blake watched the Bunyan twins straggle in. Night had preceded them, but the regiment's camp lay just beyond the crest of the mountain their march had climbed and the sky overhead held a last hush-a-bye glow. If you knew a man well enough, you could make him out at a distance in such light.

The Bunyans were strange boys, oxlike and quiet, who kept close to one another. Blake had tolerated it when James, the twin with longer hair, fell out and his brother, John, abandoned the march to stay by him. Another time, with another man, Blake might not have been so kindly. But there was something about the Bunyans that didn't bear interfering with.

It was odd, what knocked a man down. The 26th North Carolina had endured many a tougher march, and the regiment had been rested before this one. The heat was cruel, and the route wound uphill, but the distance was short compared to the efforts they had endured of late. And neither Bunyan had ever quit a march before. Yet, this time James had begun to fail early on, dropping at last by

the roadside, to the jeers of passing comrades. Sometimes, a man was just weak and there was no reason.

The twins affected a manly jauntiness as they approached the embers of the cook-fire. They were good boys, ashamed of straggling.

"Lookee," Cobb cawed, "it's the Bunyan girls come calling!"

"Shut up, Cobb," Art Peachum said.

Despite the attempted bravado, James still walked with a weakness the dark wouldn't hide.

"Sit on down," Blake told the twins. "There's ham and beans."

"Likker, too," Cobb said. "Maybe Sergeant Blake will join you for a snort after your eats?" He cackled, ever pleased at another's misery. "Oh, I done forgot. Sergeant Blake don't let liquor pass his lips. I wonder why that is?"

"You can just shut up," Peachum told him a second time.

Blake turned to Jack Ireton, sensed close by. "Corporal Ireton? Call out a detail and gather up canteens. Start with the Bunyans' there. Fill them at the well up top."

"If it ain't drunk dry," Ireton said. It was an observation, not a protest. The army had emptied a number of wells down to their muddy bottoms, much to the dismay of the local farmers.

"You all right, James Bunyan?" Blake asked.

"He's all right now," his brother answered for him. When the two boys came down from the hills and joined up, a wag had nicknamed them "Pilgrim" and "Progress," but the labels had not stuck, except in memories. Blake, too, had been given a nickname. Besides the inevitable "Quaker." For a brief time, he had been known behind his back as "Lost Lenore," until the men agreed among themselves, without much talking, that it went beyond the bounds of fair amusement.

"I didn't ask you," Blake said to the private. "I asked James."

"It was just a dizzy spell, weren't nothing," an unsteady voice reported across the thickening darkness. No one wanted light badly enough to restoke the cooking fire in the heat.

"Going to have to carry us smelling salts for these girls of ours," Cobb announced.

This time, everyone ignored him.

The Bunyan twins were anything but girlish. Hulking—

although not as tall or strong as Blake—they had defied their father to come down from Hawk's Hollow and put on gray coats. Old Charlie Bunyan and his elder boy, Reese, went off to join the Federals. Last time anyone back home had heard of them, they were riding with a bad lot in western Virginia. When newspaper folk wrote high laments about brother against brother, they didn't know how rough things got in the hills. Blake didn't doubt but that the Bunyans would kill their own kind, if the chance came. Kill, then mourn.

A jug of farmhouse whiskey made the rounds. No one passed it to Blake. They knew better. Cobb needled him briefly, but the other men let things be.

There was no fairness to any of it. Blake had become a sergeant not because he was too hard-raised to skedaddle at New Bern, but because he was the strongest man with the biggest fists in the company. And there was no sense to those endowments, since, after his grandparents sent him down from Virginia, most of the work he had done had been in Mr. Curran's store, while each of the men gathered by him had fed themselves and their kin by working fields on which a low-country planter would not have wasted one nigger. They had toiled, while he, at most, shifted sacks of flour. Yet, he could have beaten any man in the company in a fight. It never had come to a test, but they all sensed it, these lean men with muscles of harness leather.

The camp conversation shifted toward home, as men compared the mountain on which they sprawled to the highlands they knew, insisting the resemblance was uncanny. But that was a lie, if one they yearned to believe. In Pennsylvania, even the mountains promised a fertility that would have been the envy of any bottom-land farmer in North Carolina.

For his part, Blake had no wish to be back home. Not anymore. The store, which hard work and Mr. Curran's age—and kindliness— had made half Blake's when he was twenty-three, meant nothing now. He had labored toward a dream of respectability. But, thanks to one wretched, accidental meeting, that dream was dead.

Masked by the dark, Blake allowed the hard expression he kept up to twist into bitterness. The truth was that his dream had died before that. The men over whom he had charge had joined because

they believed in something, even if they were not certain what it was. No slaveholders, they had come down from the glens as their ancestors had, as if at a war horn's call. Men who sat so near him their smells had names—Tam McMinn, Hugh Gordon, and Pike Gray—had rallied to a cause they could not have explained had they been granted eternity to find words. And he, Thomas Fox Blake, had joined for a woman.

He had been a fool from the start, he saw that now. But Lenore Hutchinson had been favored not only with beauty, she was the daughter of a family of high position, by mountain standards. Calling upon her at her square-built home, he had known desire, but saw respectability. And she had preferred him over his closest rival. He was sure of that. But Lenore never spoke it out loud, for Rafe Granger wore a name still better than hers, even if rumor held that Rafe had already ruined his health as surely as his father had ruined the family fortune. And the Granger boy had time for courting, all the live-long day. Lenore had turned down each of them in turn, enjoying their pain while hinting that, in time, they might ask again. Then the war came. Rafe Granger rode off to join a cousin's cavalry troop in Virginia. Blake enlisted to match his rival's gesture.

Not six months into the war, Lenore had wed a banker down in Raleigh, a man who found his duty closer to home. A year thereafter, Mrs. Curran wrote Blake that Lieutenant Rafael Granger had fallen during a cavalry raid in the Valley. And Mrs. Lenore Bascombe had given birth.

And here he was, on the eastern side of a Pennsylvania mountain, waiting to take the lives of other men.

As the men went hunting sleep in the won't-quit heat, Colonel Burgwyn came by. What light remained in the heavens caught the gleam of boots shined by his nigger. When the colonel made the rounds, a fight was coming.

Blake both admired and resented Burgwyn. He admired the young man's flawlessness, his perfection in all things, and the grace with which he demonstrated his bravery. Although he was a North Carolinian, Burgwyn had graduated, young, from the Virginia Military Institute, where he had studied under Jackson and learned his soldiering. After General Pettigrew, Burgwyn was reckoned one of

the smartest young men in the South, as clever of mind as he was princely in his carriage, and the regiment was proud of him. The only time any of the men had seen him shaken had been on the march north, when they made camp on the Blue Ridge on a site that was home to a congregation of rattlesnakes. A soldier had killed a snake over five feet long by the colonel's tent and it clearly troubled Burgwyn just to look at it. But the colonel had steeled himself to take the dead serpent in hand and pretend to admire it.

For all that, Blake could not help feeling that the twenty-one-year-old colonel had known privileges untoward in their extravagance. Blake knew jealousy cheapened a man and he fought it. He even had learned that, to the low-country gentry, the Burgwyn family was of little consequence, as well as suspect for its Northern ties. Yet, when it came down to it, Burgwyn was unmistakably an aristocrat, and Blake wasn't. A Quaker upbringing, Blake recognized, did not suffice to master the heart's spite.

After his customary pleasantries, repeated company by company, the boy-colonel grew serious. "You'll get the formal orders down through your officers, but you might as well hear it now: We're to be prepared for an early march. And we'll march light. You're to leave all knapsacks and blankets for the trains to gather up." He paused, an actor performing. "There's a battle waiting down in those plains we saw from the mountaintop. We cannot know precisely where or exactly when that battle will come, but we all know it's coming."

The men murmured in agreement. It was a manner of saluting, of acknowledging the colonel, despite the darkness. Blake was glad that Cobb kept his mouth shut.

"Now, I've heard the same ribbing you have," Burgwyn continued. "Our brethren sometimes belittle us because we haven't had the privilege of sharing in every one of those battles in which they've triumphed. They even poke fun at our new uniforms." He paused to reset his voice, boy-orator as well as boy-colonel. "It's true that our duty has led us elsewhere at times . . . but those labors, too, were of the first importance. Still, I know such mockery can sting."

When Burgwyn cleared his throat, the sound came as sharp as a gunshot. "That mockery will soon end. The Twenty-sixth North

Carolina will shatter any doubt as to its valor. I know every man among you will do his part . . . to bring glory to his regiment and to the good old North State."

Had the men not been weary, or if they could have seen the colonel's face, his zeal might have penetrated them. But no cheers answered his speechmaking, only another round of good-natured murmurs, as if the men were sending off a child tasked, just before bedtime, to recite a poem for company.

Accustomed to a richer response to his oratory, the colonel seemed unsure of himself. He lingered.

At last a voice—Hugh Gordon's—called out, "Don't you worry none, Colonel. We'll whip the Yankees proper for you."

A few more brisk assurances came out of the darkness. And that was all. Blake was baffled by the mood, the unusual lack of connection. He knew these men were spoiling for a fight.

Perhaps, he thought, the whiskey had been just enough to dull them and not enough to quicken them again.

Instead of moving on to the next group of soldiers, the colonel called, "Sergeant Blake? Is Sergeant Thomas Blake there among you?"

"Yes, sir," Blake answered. He rose and stepped through the thickening darkness, careful of sprawled men.

When he closed on Burgwyn, the colonel asked, "Stroll with me for a minute?"

"Yes, sir. Colonel Burgwyn, I can assure you that the men of this company are ready to fight. They're as willing as any men on earth."

"I know that, Sergeant," Burgwyn said softly. "I know that." A half-dozen years younger than Blake, he sounded like a father. They reached the road and turned down the slope. Blake waited for the other man to speak.

Black clouds advanced below armies of stars.

"I'd like to hear your side of a matter," the colonel said, "before I carry it any further. Before I do anything officially."

The incident at Culpeper Court House leapt to mind, the hot shame of it. The thought that Colonel Burgwyn knew enraged Blake.

"I'm told," Burgwyn continued, "that you have experience with accounts. That you're quite the fastidious bookkeeper."

Blake felt relieved and drained. "I suspect, sir," he said, struggling to mask the quiver in his voice, "that some of my old customers have been talking on me. A man had to keep clear ledgers back home, if he wanted certain folks to pay their debts."

"Well, we're all paying greater debts now," the colonel said. "I need a new man for regimental headquarters, someone who can keep up with the required reports, with muster figures, pay arrears, all of it. I hoped . . . that I might interest you in that."

"No, sir."

The bluntness startled the colonel. He stopped walking, then turned back up the slope. After giving way to a mounted provost guard, the colonel said, "I suppose you want to be with your men. In the battle ahead. That's commendable, of course." He sought convincing words. "But the thing is I need a man I can depend on. Families need to know what's happened to their loved ones, if they're dead, wounded, or missing. The army needs this figure, the government that one . . ." He laughed, but there was no heartiness in it. "One thing I've learned, Sergeant Blake, is that an army's largely what it is on paper. Can't I persuade you?"

"No, sir."

Burgwyn stopped again. Blake sensed that they would part now. Some things were clearer in the dark than in the light.

"I could order you to do it," Burgwyn said. But he laughed again. The sound was as soft as rustling leaves. "Many a man would leap at the chance, you know. A regimental clerk need not go forward."

"I wouldn't do it, sir. Even if you ordered me to."

"That verges on the insubordinate," the colonel noted. "But may I ask why? Why is it that a man won't seize such an opportunity? Comradeship? Pride? His sense of a greater cause? You've been offered a chance to cheat death, you know. Yet, you declined. Why is that?"

"Fighting's all I have left," Blake told him.

A ghost in the darkness, Cobb appeared. A shadow, a voice.

"Din't I tell you? He has the mark of death on him, sure as a hoor takes your money. You just tell me you don't feel it, Quaker.

Go on." He snorted. "You going to lie? The way you been lying? About who you are?"

"We all have the mark of death on us," Blake said.

Cobb cackled. Blake smelled his reek.

"Your Quakers say that?" the foul little man asked. "That what they say? That the Lord has us all marked down for death? Something like that? That's not what I'm talking about. And you know it."

"You're the one who doesn't know what he's talking about." Blake didn't have the heart for a fight, though. Something nameless weighed on him. "Go off to sleep now. Git."

To Blake's relief, the creature moved away. But Cobb wasn't finished.

"Maybe," he told Blake in parting, "if you're right close when the Yankees kill him, you can snatch those pretty boots off him." He laughed. "Be a tight fit. But you could always sell 'em."

Blake found his way among the scattered soldiers. Some snored, while others moaned at luckless dreams. Unable to sleep, a few played cards by candlelight, silent but for the percussion of the deck. He came to his spot, or near enough, took off his shoes, rolled up his tunic, and lay down on his back.

Sleep flirted and fled, a cheat. Like Lenore. "Lost Lenore." He wondered if he had come so far down that he would be capable of killing her. He disbelieved it, but the fact that such a thought could taunt him chilled him. Was it truly about bad blood? Was there a contamination, not of the body but of the soul, that a father could pass down?

His father. Drunk and dead in a ditch. Nor was "dead in a ditch" a mere expression. They found him on a winter's morn, frozen like a wet coat forgotten outside during a freeze. He was told that his father had been a handsome man, but that was not part of Blake's collection of memories. He could almost grasp the beauty his mother was reported to have been, but even that required additions of fantasy. Small children do not see their parents so.

He knew the story, for his grandparents, good Quakers, had wielded it as a warning to him.

Thy father drank. He drank away all his gifts, and the Lord had

blessed him with many. He broke the hearts of his elders. Thy father was already given to drink when he took thy mother, our daughter, unto him. He had long deserted our meetinghouse, he was a creature plunged into sin. Then he took her, an innocent child, in the night, and only the Lord can say why thy mother went with him. Of course, he couldn't support her, Thomas. Or thee. He was a feckless man of degraded habits. So thy mother came home to us. With thee. And we took her in. And thee. Despite her sins and defiance. For she was humbled then, humbled and starving. And thou wert thin and pale as a leaf of paper. Dost thou recall what happened next, Thomas? We know thou dost. We know. And thou knowest. They found thy father dead. He lay in a gully in Leesburg, face buried deep in filth, as close to Satan's abode as he could get. Could any man sink lower? Abandoning wife and child for a bottle of whiskey? Abandoning the Lord and all His mercies? And then thy mother, who would not repent of the sin of taking him unto her, died of the cholera. It was a terrible death, it was a judgment. The wages of sin are death, Thomas. Dost thou understand that?

Loving in their black-cloth way, his grandparents scrutinized him for signs of weakness, but he revealed none. He excelled at his schoolwork, even though he was beaten by the schoolmaster, another excellent Quaker. He was beaten not for what he did, but for who he was. For learning his lessons more quickly than the children of honest parents. Quakers did not believe in violence, but Mr. Harding had beaten him until he could not rise under his own power.

Perhaps it had been the beatings that made him strong. At fourteen, he could have killed the schoolmaster with his bare hands. But he never considered doing so. He accepted his punishment, as if there were justice in it, after all. But his schoolmates were another story.

That fall, on an apple-frost day, the teasing refrain of "Drunk as a monkey and dead in a ditch" was repeated a time too many. He did not behave with the restraint asked of a Quaker. He set upon the largest boy, a Presbyterian sent to the school because it was free, and beat him nearly to death. None of the other students, full of catcalls minutes before, dared intervene. Tom Blake,

the drunkard's son, put his fists to Master Robert Knox so fiercely that he broke his jaw and ribs. The boy had to lie abed into the new year.

His grandparents sent him down to North Carolina, to fellow Quakers. Mr. Curran, white of hair, had put him to work in the store, watching him carefully and locking him into his bedroom when it was time to sleep. But that was all right. No one knew about his father there, so there was no trouble. And the Currans took him to their hearts, the truest Christians he had ever known. They even bore it when, at his maturity, he told them he could no longer go to their meetinghouse, that it wasn't in his heart. Even after that, Mr. Curran rewarded him by making him part owner of his store. It was a business where no man was cheated, but each man was held to account. Even as Blake grew ever taller and brawnier, as if under a magic spell, the mild work suited him. He looked like a blacksmith, but reveled in pen and ink.

He had nursed so many hopes. And, unlike many a man, he had been willing to work to fulfill them. His energy was boundless. Within himself, he sensed he could do anything. He would make men respect him. He would *earn* their respect. He would become the pride of his community. He would be envied.

Even after war's trickery began, he nurtured his dream. After his love married and he learned more about himself than a man should know, he had kept up his hopes for honors. Cobb was right: He *had* dreamed of becoming a lieutenant and then a captain, as battles took their toll of other men.

Then, on the night they camped near Culpeper Court House, a courier had come by, seeking a drink of water and directions to General Heth. The horseman was the boy he had beaten nearly to death. He recognized Blake immediately. After a moment's shock, Lieutenant Knox grinned mightily. In a ringing voice, he cried, "Well, if that ain't Tom goddamned Blake, the town drunk's boy! This where he ran away to?"

Blake had only turned away, hiding his face, as Adam had done from the Lord on the flight from Eden. He knew then that his dreams were at an end. He had been put in place forever, and the society in which he moved, even that of the stone-pegged hills,

would never let him be anyone else. He would never be an officer, not if the war lasted a century. Were he to prosper and grow rich hereafter, he would still be "the drunkard's son."

But he had one thing they could not take away. He had the war.

He dreamed of the golden fields beyond Roznowo. He knew that the old manor house stood just behind his back, shaded by great trees as old as time. Mesmerized by the shimmering world before him, he could not turn. Wheat rose above his father's knees as they walked the fields together. The northern sky was a peerless blue, and his father's hand was powerful. But he could not see his father's face. The man looming so tall was both real and a shadow. A voice called to them. It belonged to his wife, but that couldn't be. Even in his dream, he knew that his wife could not be present with his father. He had been happy in the dream at first, nearly ecstatic, but confusion marred it. His father had vanished and he could not find his wife, who was lost amid the boundlessness of the fields. He turned around at last to take his bearings, unsure if he were still a boy or grown. The manor house was gone, everything was gone, except the fields of wheat and rye and barley that stretched to infinity. He ran and ran, but could not find a refuge.

Colonel Wlodzimierz Bonawentura Krzyzanowski awoke with a sense of immeasurable loss. The dream had been so rich and deep that it took him a moment to grasp hold of reality. He was not a child now, but a man. His wife was real, and she was in Washington. His father was long dead, the estate long since sold off to pay the family's debts. His father had fought under Napoleon to revive the Polish state, had served on the plague-ridden march to Moscow and the horrid retreat, had given all he had, including his slight wealth, for his dream of Poland reborn, and he had failed. He had died in his son's sixth year, killed by the sale of his ancestral home at the demand of his Poznan creditors, the firm of Wolff, Falk and Levin Koenigsberger.

His dream of the fields beyond Roznowo had haunted Krzyzanowski for as long as he could remember. Those images had pursued him until he no longer knew if they had ever had any substance in reality. The real fields were not endless, of course, although they had stretched far across Pomerania's flatlands. Did he remem-

ber the manor house correctly? Was the image of his father but a fantasy?

The lands girdling Roznowo beckoned him, not the Prussian-regulated streets of Poznan, where an aunt and uncle had raised him along with their own brood after his mother left him, the least healthy of her children, at their door. He had spent most of his life, in Poland and then in America, in cities. Yet, his dreams always returned to rye and barley.

He realized that he had been weeping. Tears often came when he dreamed about his father. He possessed not even a token of the man now, not a saber from Napoleon's wars, not a button, not a signature on a countersigned paper acknowledging his debts. A world had vanished, its joys hunted to extinction.

His father had died in 1830. The next year, Poland rose again, defying the Russians, Austrians, and Prussians who had enchained her. But the powers aligned against the Poles proved invincible again. Uncles Bogumil and Nemezy, brave men in the family tradition, disappeared into prison. Poverty crept up to their door and slipped in through the windows. Still, his aunt and his last free uncle did as much for him as they did for their own children. So he could grow and make his own futile gestures.

He had been studying mathematics at the Lycée of St. Mary Magdalene when the next Polish rising came, in 1846. For two years, he had lived a secret life as one of Mieroslawski's underground supporters. But Prussia's agents knew all. The revolt failed everywhere, most bloodily in Ruthenia, where the Austrians turned Pole against Pole as the Swedes had done two hundred years before. By the time Krakow's revolutionary government fell, ending yet another dream of freedom, Krzyzanowski was a refugee, keeping low in Hamburg, on his way to exile in America.

His waking dream since then had been to return one day and liberate his country. But the struggle for freedom ran deep in his blood, far deeper than borders could limit. When the slave states seceded to maintain their realm of bondage, he had rushed to New York to raise a volunteer regiment of Polish and German exiles. He endured the infernal politicking for military appointments and the stealing away of recruits by other regiments better supplied with bounty money. He was ready to sacrifice all to show his gratitude

to the land that had given him freedom. He was prepared to give his life. Yet, even then he had believed that, one day, he would return to his true fight. In Poland.

He rose from command of a regiment to that of a brigade, riding in front of his ranks, not to their rear. The blood of generations of Polish officers ran in his veins, of winged hussars and Turk-slayers. He had been born to the ways of the battlefield.

Yet, even when his soldiers fought with valor, credit was given sparingly, if at all. The newspapers ridiculed their accents and exaggerated their supposed peculiarities, inventing slurs. Foreigners could not possibly be as brave as the native-born. The winter before, his promotion to brigadier general had been denied after a congressman joked that he wasn't going to make a general of any man whose name he couldn't pronounce.

But that humiliation's impact had been slight compared to what Krzyzanowski discovered about himself as winter muddied its way into spring. Another revolt had broken out in Poland. He had always promised himself that, when the time to fight came again, he would return to the land of his birth. But when the revolution finally erupted, he found that his world had changed. His life was here now, on this soil. His family was here. And the war in which he led a brigade was a war that might be won, not another hopeless, romantic gesture. With or without him, he knew the Poles would lose. His destiny lay here, in this new land.

Then came Chancellorsville. A dozen generations of his ancestors warned him that the corps' flank was exposed. General Schurz saw it, too. But General Howard, another Bible-bound American Englishman and as proud in his way as a Prussian, dismissed the idea as nonsense: The Rebels were on the other side of the army and the Eleventh Corps might not see action at all.

With General Schurz's quiet authorization, Krzyzanowski did what little he could. When the Rebels came on, howling like Tartars, his 58th New York, his Polish Legion, and the 26th Wisconsin, the Germans of the Sigel Regiment, were positioned to face them at the Hawkins farm, an island of blue soldiers engulfed by a vast gray sea.

Two regiments could not hold back an attacking army—or halt a fleeing one. His men stood their ground anyway, surprising even

Krzyzanowski with their courage. As figures in blue fell rapidly in their slaughter pen, he had needed to plead with the 26th Wisconsin to fall back before it was too late to save the regiment. The Germans had been unwilling to leave their wounded, unwilling to stop killing those who had killed their own. Madly outnumbered, his two dying regiments held for nearly an hour, at a dreadful cost. And as they withdrew, in good order, they fought on for another hour, halting to make successive stands, while thousands of others ran to save their lives.

The newspapers ignored their heroism, writing that the "immigrants" were all cowards.

As he lay in the dark, Krzyzanowski swore he would prove them wrong.

FOUR

June 30

G od awmighty," Pike Gray said. "What time is it?"

"Time to get up," Blake told him. "Regimental muster. Out on the road."

The soldier rose from his sodden blanket. "They letting us time to boil coffee?"

The wetness in the air fell between a drizzle and a mist. Harder rain had soaked them in the night. Ghosts moved among the trees and became men.

"Just bind up your bedroll and get out on the road. We're to march immediately."

But they didn't march immediately. The end-of-month muster was fraught with coughs, complaints, and curses in the darkness. After its completion, officers repeated the order to pile their knapsacks and blankets for the wagons to collect. Any man too ill to march hard was to stay behind.

Few chose to do so.

Talk went around that a big fight lay ahead, chased by a rumor that Grant had been thrashed at Vicksburg and was in retreat. That meant a victory in the days ahead might end the war.

Standing in the mud of the pike as the first light reached them, men ate what they had in their haversacks. Word came down that the march had been delayed again. They could build breakfast fires by the roadside, but had to be ready to fall in at a call.

A tease of rain swept over the trees, coming to nothing. Soldiers coaxed fire from wet sticks, drawing more smoke than flame. Still, the smell of boiling coffee reached Blake and his men.

"Probably just for the officers," Art Peachum said. A barrel-chested man with scrawny haunches, he was fair-minded and gen-

erous for most of his waking hours, but not in the morning. "Their niggers probably been keeping wood dry for 'em."

Billie Cobb conjured a hint of flame from wood chips. Quiet this morning, as if dreams had oppressed him, he let the other men watch as he worked. Miraculously, the breadth of the fire increased.

"You ain't completely useless, Cobb," Hugh Gordon told him.

Cobb just cackled his little laugh. Flames snapped.

"Who's got the kettle?" Peachum hollered. But the Bunyan twins had already fetched it from the stacks of packs and blankets.

"Probably tell us to fall in, just when she's ready to boil," Ollie Wright said. Wright was a man rarely noticed, who slipped around the back of things. Asked once why he rarely said anything, he answered that he rarely had anything to say. Folks left it at that. The army taught most men to get along.

They weren't a pretty sight that morning, though. For all their new uniforms, the men looked bedraggled in the seeping light. The rain had glued down Tam McMinn's red hair below his kepi. A good-tempered team of human oxen, the Bunyans slumped against the same wet tree, shoulder near to shoulder. Wright and Ireton crowded near the fire, as if the slight flames might dry clinging garments. Eternally disheveled, Cobb looked little worse than the rest of them now. Misery evened men out.

The fragrance of coffee soon caressed them all.

Lieutenant Devereaux came by, drawn by the aroma. Not all of the officers had darkies to look after them.

The officer attempted to lend his visit weight. "Orders from division," he told them. "General Heth wants the brigade to search a town down yonder for supplies. Shoes, mostly. We're just to go there and come back, not stir up a fight."

"The Yankees might have something to say about that," Cobb told him. He lifted his face and grinned hideously. "Can't you feel 'em out there, Lieutenant? They got to be in a killing mood, with us tramping on their shit-pile."

The lieutenant stiffened. "Oh, I believe we can take care of any Yankees we encounter."

Somebody had to say it, so Blake did: "Cup of coffee, sir?"

Devereaux smiled. "Why, I call that generous, Sergeant Blake. Don't mind if I do."

There was time enough to finish one pot and then another. The men had soldiered long enough not to press their luck beyond that. Except for those taking care of private matters in the woods, they were ready the instant the order rang out to fall in and march down the mountain. The others would catch up quick.

The rain had ceased, but the clouds hung so low it seemed a man could stretch on his toes and touch them. Had he tried, the infernal mud would have pulled him back down.

Enough men, horses, and guns had passed over the road in the preceding days to make it a mire. Blake slipped and landed rump-down in the slop, keeping his rifle above him. Mud stew shaped his trousers to his legs when he rose. It added weight.

The other men laughed, but their mirth was no more than a token. Even Cobb refrained from mocking remarks. Before they were off the mountain, every man felt the strain in his ankles and knees.

"This just ain't no pleasure," Pike Gray said. "No pleasure at all."

"Know what my favorite part of all this bumming about was?" Peachum asked. "Crossing the Potomac. Suited me just fine, it truly did. Tearing off every last rag, belly on down, and letting that cool water come on by."

Hugh Gordon whistled. "Wasn't that a sight to see, though? A whole bare-assed brigade. Blessed thing that there wasn't no ladies present."

Cobb fired off a laugh. "Maybe they would've enjoyed it. Get to do some comparing, size things up."

"Shut up, Cobb," Peachum said.

Cobb hooted in his broken-throated way. "You don't think the ladies take an interest? Think they're all pretty statues, set high up to decorate a house? That what y'all think?"

"Cobb doesn't know any ladies," Corporal Ireton said. "Never did, and likely never will."

At that, Cobb fell silent and marched apart without leaving the ranks. It was told on him that he'd had a wife he doted on, but that she'd run away some years before.

"I expect we've all known a lady or two," Blake said. "Cobb included." He turned the conversation. "You, James Bunyan. You feeling right today?"

"Fit as a fiddle, Sergeant. I just—"

"Then pick up your feet. You're plowing a row, boy."

"Yes, Sergeant Blake."

They entered a tidy settlement, but the band had not been sent up to play this morning. That told the men things were serious indeed.

Word came down the line that the place was called Cashtown. A fine-looking tavern graced the busy street. Officers milled in front of it. Rain teased.

Beyond the town, soldiers from other brigades pecked at camp duties, standing down for the day and leaving the marching to Pettigrew's lot. Farther on lay fields of wheat and oats that begged to be harvested as soon as the weather dried. For all the talk of battle, the world seemed sweetly calm.

The column halted. The march did not resume quickly, but the men were not allowed to fall out on the roadside. Captain Carr rode forward, then returned. Word filed back that they'd reached the forward picket line and General Pettigrew was dickering with the commander about something. Beyond lay an unknown world and, somewhere, an army clad in blue.

When the march began again, the rain did, too.

Meade stepped out of the tent. He had dressed down Butterfield again. The man could not keep up with the new regimen. Nonetheless, Meade's confidence had grown. The army, like an unruly child, just needed a firm hand.

He could feel the blue beast out there, drawing itself together, the various corps approaching positions from which they could march quickly to the battlefield he chose. Since taking command, he had been pleasantly surprised at the support from his corps commanders, who so recently had been his peers. Even Sickles appeared to be showing more vigor.

The trick of it was to keep control, to avoid treating the corps as loose odds and ends, as Hooker had done at Chancellorsville. The army had to fight as an army. Its parts had to converge toward one goal.

A few raindrops fell, dull thuds on Meade's slouch hat. But it was only a skirmish, not an attack.

General Hunt, the army's chief of artillery, rode up, followed by

two aides in gunner's jackets. Soldiers hastened out of the way of the hoof-splash.

"Well, Henry?" Meade asked as Hunt tossed his reins to a captain just out of the saddle.

Face spattered with mud, Hunt got right to the point. "The Pipe Creek line's the true place, you were right. The south banks generally run higher and steeper, and the bridges are easy to cover. Plenty of fords, but they'll slow an attacker nicely."

"General Warren's of the same opinion," Meade told him. "I've sent him back out to survey specific positions."

Hunt pulled off his riding gloves and wiped his eyes. "Damned good place to fight, sir. If we can bring Lee to attack us on that line, it could be Fredericksburg in reverse. And we'd be well positioned for a pursuit. Lee would have no recourse but to retreat due west. And he couldn't defend those passes, they're easy to flank. He'd either have to stand and fight again, or risk what remained of his army in a pell-mell run."

Meade nodded. "The trick is drawing him back into Maryland. But I think it can be done."

"Any further word on Lee's position?"

"Still stretched out on the roads. Buford reported infantry and artillery west of Gettysburg this morning. Hill's men." Meade sighed. He'd had only brief snatches of sleep since assuming command and felt bone weary. But there was no time to rest. "As soon as I learn more details of the ground from Warren, we'll get orders out. If Butterfield's up to the simple task of copying. But plan on the Pipe Creek line for your guns, Henry. Meanwhile, Buford can watch Hill, and John Reynolds can move the First and Eleventh Corps to Gettysburg tomorrow to cover our flank. While I move the rest of the army into position."

Hunt pulled his riding gloves back on, another tired man. But a game one. He'd be off now to inspect his ammunition trains.

"Headquarters staying here?" the artilleryman asked. "This where I'll find you?"

Meade shook his head. A few drops of rainwater fled his hat brim. "I've ordered a move to Taneytown. I want every subordinate able to reach me quickly. I won't have the dilatory communications we all suffered under Hooker."

A serious man, Hunt surprised Meade with a smile. Perhaps he was thinking fondly of his guns. "We'll fight at Pipe Creek, then?"

"Pipe Creek," Meade assured him.

Lee read the dispatch the courier had delivered, then raised his eyes to Longstreet and to Hill.

"They chose George Meade, not Reynolds," the old man said. He seemed uncharacteristically surprised. And not especially pleased. But, then, he had been out of sorts for days. Waiting with growing impatience for Stuart to materialize. The staff's jollity earlier that morning had been a mild rebellion against Lee's dourness.

"Well, that's fine," General Hill said. Despite his grin, the gaunt Virginian looked uncomfortable in his own skin. Afflicted. Clots of brown hair rested on his shoulders and the red calico shirt he affected made him resemble a scarecrow. But his eyes burned. "Meade's an engineer. He'll be timid."

"He wasn't timid at Fredericksburg," Longstreet said.

"I'm an engineer myself, gentlemen," Lee reminded them. "Perhaps you will not abuse the discipline too harshly."

Longstreet thought that would close the topic, but Lee mused, "General Meade will commit no blunder in my front . . . and if I make one, he will make haste to take advantage of it."

"We'll lick George Meade," Powell Hill said. He was a valiant, volatile man.

Lee half-turned away. "I *must* know where those people are. I must know what Meade intends." He wheeled on Longstreet, ignoring Hill. "It's taken two days for us to learn this news about General Meade. Of what else are we in ignorance?"

Say it, Longstreet thought. *Go ahead. Admit that Stuart has let you down. Get it off your chest.*

Lee mastered himself and addressed his next words to Hill. "General, I must know immediately, if you find those people to your front. Meade may not move swiftly, but he will move surely."

"Nothing out there but a few militia," Hill assured him. "Been quiet."

Lee dropped the dispatch on a camp desk set up in the open air. "Those people will be fighting on their own soil now. That cannot help but steady their morale. When we find them, we must defeat

them without delay. They must not have further opportunity to rally."

The old man turned to Hill again and continued. "We cannot afford chance encounters, General Hill. No one is to bring on a general engagement until this army is concentrated. When our blow lands, it must be sudden, and it must be decisive."

Longstreet chose not to speak. He had made his argument for choosing good ground and forcing the Federals to do the attacking. And he would make the argument again. But not in front of Hill. He could not be frank in front of the other man.

Hill adjusted his spattered britches, bothered by what they contained.

"In two days' time," Lee said, as if to himself, "this army will be together again. Then we shall see to those people."

As they marched beyond the picket line, a Virginia regiment joined the column behind them. The pike led through more good country. Rain kept flirting. The pace General Pettigrew set the brigade went hard.

"Swear to God, I smell Yankees," Peachum said.

"That's just old Cobb there," Ireton told him.

Cobb didn't respond beyond rubbing the sores on his nose. He was still sour. Blake wondered what else there once might have been to the man. Besides the woman who had run off long ago. There were blank pages in Cobb's history.

After covering several miles, the column halted again. A courier galloped past, headed rearward. It was impossible to move fast enough and far enough to avoid all the mud kicked up by his mount's hooves.

"Sumbitch," Cobb said. Evidently, he was speaking again.

Minutes later, a civilian on horseback followed the courier's path, though at an easier pace.

Blake saw Lieutenant Colonel Lane, the regiment's second in command, trot back to confer with his company commanders. Lane was a hard man, with no time for nonsense. He looked hacked from oak, then painted in shades of brown. He was not a high gentleman born. Blake trusted him.

A minute later, Lieutenant Devereaux appeared to tell the men they could fall out. The company had to send out pickets, though.

"Time enough to cook coffee, sir?" Tam McMinn asked.

"Wouldn't risk it," the officer said.

"What's holding things up, Lieutenant?" Peachum asked. He dug into his haversack for a cracker.

"Spy fellow claims there's Yankees ahead, next town yonder."

"Told you I smelled 'em," Peachum crowed.

"Lot of them?" Blake asked.

The lieutenant shrugged. He was the decent son of respectable parents, nothing more. Not among the highly favored, although better born than Lieutenant Colonel Lane. "We have orders not to get ourselves in a fight. That's all I know."

Peachum looked up at the sky. "Well, now, I guess we can just stand here and get rained on."

But the courier retraced his route, horse lathered, and the column quickly re-formed. The eastward march continued. Every man paid more attention to the flanks now. Watching for a glimpse of a blue uniform. Weariness faded. Senses peaked.

No Yankees appeared. No shots rang out. Rain fell again.

" 'Least it keeps things cooled down," James Bunyan said.

They passed another tavern, this one set on a ridge where country roads joined. The column descended the slope and compressed its files to hurry over a bridge. A narrow creek had overrun its banks.

Just short of the next crest, the column halted again.

"Just one time," Pike Gray said, "just once, I wish I could be an officer up there on a fine, high horse so I'd know just what the devil's going on."

"Get shot right off it, too," Cobb told him.

Lieutenant Devereaux wheeled his mount from a group of officers and raced back along the column. Yanking back too hard on the bit, he reared up short of Blake.

"Sergeant Blake! Take out skirmishers! Right and forward. Honor to the Twenty-sixth!"

And the boy turned away again, without having said how many men were to go. Blake culled a dozen and waved them out along the edge of a woodline, then pushed on into the trees. On either

side of him, men checked their weapons as they walked, then trailed their rifles to load them with dry powder.

Blake's senses burned bright. The rustle of the column off to his left fitted into a box, letting him hear the other, nearer sounds. Wet brush stroked him, briars went ignored. It was ever a wonder to him how the mind ranked dangers so finely, concentrating mightily on survival.

The trees weren't thick enough to hide a man. No birds sang.

He kept a watch on the men beside him, but they knew their work and maintained their intervals. Some crouched like hunters, while others walked upright and strained to see ahead, but all of them moved silently. The wet earth smelled of rot.

They climbed through the grove. Their silence grew wintry, the stillness of men intent on killing game.

The trees didn't thin, they just stopped. Every man paused before breaking from the concealment. The crest of the ridge lay just a dash ahead. But no one had a mind to run.

Blake stepped out into the open, going cautiously at first. Other men took his lead. A crow's abrupt complaint startled them all.

They had moved at an angle and, looking left, Blake saw that they had only come parallel with the head of the column. Other skirmishers had been thrown forward, too. He reached a narrow lane that traced the crest. A few hundred yards northward, General Pettigrew sat on his mount, surrounded by his subordinates, all of them focused on a distant scene.

Blake followed their line of vision.

Before a cluster of fine brick buildings, blue-jacketed cavalrymen watched the men in gray who were watching them. Some of the Yankees remained mounted, but others had their boots on the earth, carbines ready.

Blake waved his skirmish line forward, down a mild slope of wet wheat. A column of Federals trotted out from the town beyond the near buildings, reinforcing their comrades. They did not appear alarmed by the Confederate presence.

"Those ain't no militia," Pike Gray said.

"Keep moving," Blake told him, trying to pitch his voice just right. "No talking."

This was it, then. How it began. Again. A few men against a few

men. Would it remain a minor skirmish? Or lead to a fair battle? It hardly mattered to him and those beside him. As they descended the slope, headed toward the flank of the Union horsemen, they moved at the edge of the world.

A courier broke from General Pettigrew's side and cantered down the ridge toward the skirmishers. Blake signaled to the men to halt where they were. Some knelt down, half-disappearing into the wheat. Clutching their rifles.

The rider reached them, a lieutenant Blake didn't recognize. The officer eyed Blake's chevrons.

"Withdraw your men, Sergeant," the lieutenant told him. "Fall back on your company. Orders are to reverse the march immediately." He spurred his mount back toward his brother officers.

"Take a shot?" John Bunyan asked as the hoofbeats faded away. "I could drop one of them blue-bellies from here."

"No," Blake said.

Brigadier General James Johnston Pettigrew was born on July 4, 1828. His family possessed wealth and social prominence that reached from their North Carolina plantation southward to Charleston and northward to Philadelphia. Handsome and brilliant, Pettigrew graduated first in his class at Chapel Hill at the age of nineteen, received a prized appointment as an astronomer at the Naval Observatory in Washington, and soon discarded a position that slighted his genius. He read the law in a gentlemanly fashion, in the office of Charleston relatives, and took that city's society in thrall. He traveled to Europe, twice, and privately published a handsome account of Spain. A former superior called Pettigrew "the most promising young man of the South."

But Pettigrew felt a lack in his lustrous life: military glory.

An eager member of the Charleston militia, he applied himself to the study of military science. In the course of his European sojourns, which included earning a law degree from Berlin, he first attempted to join the Prussian army, but royal officials found his interest suspect. He later sought to attach himself to the French army as it marched to face the Austrians in Italy, but the Battle of Solferino ended that war before he could find a suitable place among the officers of Napoleon III.

After returning to Charleston with fewer laurels than hoped, Pettigrew became the colonel of the First Regiment of Rifles, the most fashionable assembly of militia companies. After unsuccessful efforts to cajole the surrender of Ft. Sumter, he faced a setback when General Beauregard's arrival trimmed his authority. South Carolina seemed not to value his services sufficiently, so he acquired the colonelcy of the 22nd North Carolina. Within months, President Davis bowed to society's dictates and personally pressed Pettigrew to don a brigadier's star. After a polite interval of reflection, Pettigrew accepted.

His reputation grew, but not to the heights of fame scaled by other men. Opportunities for glory flirted, but then fled. Thus, on a gray afternoon in a Pennsylvania hamlet, James Johnston Pettigrew was dismayed by the reaction of his division commander to his report.

General Heth frowned and said nothing. In the street, commissary wagons roiled the mud.

"The Union army is at Gettysburg," Pettigrew repeated. "I refrained from an attempt to enter the town, sir, in accordance with my instructions not to precipitate a battle. But there can be no doubt that the Federals are before us."

"The Hell you say," Heth told him.

It long since had struck Pettigrew that Heth, although a Virginian, was not quite a gentleman.

"We observed their cavalry for nearly thirty minutes," Pettigrew continued. "Their behavior suggested a larger force nearby. I believe, sir, the Yankee army is to our front. General Lee must be informed."

Heth shook his head. "Shit for the birds, Pettigrew. There's nothing out there but militia. You're seeing hants."

James Johnston Pettigrew was mortified. He knew what he had seen. And he was not accustomed to being called a fool, if not a liar. Before the war, such treatment would have merited a visit from his seconds.

"Some of the men reported hearing drums, sir," he pressed on. "Drums would, of course, mean the presence of infantry."

"I know what goddamned drums mean."

Appearing behind the trail wagon of the train, General Hill,

the corps commander, came on at a trot, followed by his retinue. Spying the division and brigade commanders in consultation, he reined in his horse and dismounted.

"Get your new shoes, Harry?" he asked Heth.

Heth grimaced and rolled his eyes heavenward. "Not by a damned sight. General Pettigrew here didn't see fit to enter Gettysburg. He reports"—Heth curled his lip—"the presence of Yankee cavalry. Not farmers on mules, the real thing."

A. P. Hill snorted. He looked pained, his tall frame cramped up. There were personal matters that did not bear discussion, indelicate considerations, Pettigrew understood. The general's long, greasy hair repelled him, too.

"Well now," Hill said, "I've just come from General Lee." He picked at his calico shirt as if hunting a louse. "His staff puts the Yankees down in Maryland. Haven't even struck their tents." He smirked. "Scared, most like. Got a new commander. George Meade, the glorious builder of lighthouses."

"How current is the staff's information, sir?" Pettigrew asked.

That annoyed Hill. "Current enough, I expect."

"I told him it had to be militia," Heth explained, as if Pettigrew were no longer present. "Just farmers got up to parade around on their mules, then run like Hell."

"With respect, sir," Pettigrew said, "the cavalrymen we saw were not about to run away."

Hill shifted from one leg to the other, as if feeling the need to relieve his body. His tone grew conciliatory, though, indulging a child. "Well, now . . . we all know it's easy enough to get excited. Everybody's looking forward to a fight, not just you, General Pettigrew. Get excited, your eyes play tricks."

Suppressing his sense of ill-treatment as best he could, Pettigrew turned and waved to his aide-de-camp, who had kept a respectful distance across the road.

"Captain Young!" he called. "Come here."

Young had served under Hill during the Seven Days. Hill knew him and liked him. Perhaps the corps commander would listen to Young.

The captain sloshed across the ravaged street, high boots and spurs digging deep. It was hard to move with dignity.

The young man saluted the generals as he approached, tilting his saber out of the mud with his other hand.

"Captain Young, would you please report what you saw on the ridge before Gettysburg today?"

"Yes, sir. Good afternoon, gentlemen. Immediately to the west of Gettysburg, we observed Union cavalry vedettes. They moved in good order and were reinforced with additional elements as we watched."

"Militia. On mules," Heth said.

Young's expression instantly grew wary. But he, too, had seen what he'd seen. "I didn't judge them to be militia, sir. They appeared extremely well-drilled."

Hill nudged a torn-up clot of grass with his toe. "I cannot believe that any portion of the Army of the Potomac is up. A patrol, maybe. . . ."

"Goddamned militia," Heth insisted. "Nothing but."

Hill thought about it. "Most like, Harry, most like." He inspected the weather, judged the hour. "Find out in good time, I suppose."

"Well, if there's no objection, then," Heth said, "I'll take my division tomorrow, go to Gettysburg, and get those shoes."

Hill pulled at his trousers and shifted his weight again. "No objection," he said. "None in the world."

Heth's irritation had not been quelled, though. Rather too loudly, he said, "I'll put Archer's brigade in front this time. He won't shy." The division commander turned his eyes on Pettigrew. "That will be all, sir."

Pettigrew saluted and plodded off through the mire, flushed and humiliated. The suggestion that want of valor had deterred him from entering Gettysburg was as unbearable as it was unjust. His orders had been clear: He was not to bring on an engagement. And the Federal cavalry had been right there in front of them, for any man to see.

General Heth would learn who was brave and who was not.

Pettigrew snapped his horse's reins from the orderly sergeant's hand. Leaping into the saddle, he took care, even now, to show a good seat. His aide aped his every gesture.

Pettigrew did not turn his mount eastward to where his brigade

had camped, on picket duty for the corps that night. Instead, he rode for General Archer's headquarters. He felt it his duty to pass on to his fellow brigade commander all that he had seen, not only regarding the Union cavalrymen, but the problem of the terrain, the way the ridges running perpendicular to the pike offered a succession of fine defensive positions to a skillful enemy. He would not bear the blame for any blunders tomorrow. And instructing Archer was the honorable thing.

When the two riders had put a safe distance between themselves and their superiors, Captain Young drew his horse close and said, "I'm left in a spirit of unbelief, sir. At the obstinacy of our generals."

After riding a stretch in silence, Pettigrew told the younger man, "I fear that many beliefs will be changed tomorrow."

Morgenrot! Morgenrot!
Leuchtest mir . . . zum frühen Tod . . .

Schwertlein struggled to ignore the song the regimental *Liederkranz* had begun across the camp. Its sentimental morbidity repelled him:

Crimson dawn! Crimson dawn!
Comes the night . . . and I'll be gone.
Soon you'll hear the trumpets calling,
Then you'll see the bodies falling,
And my short life . . . will be done.

The men sang it because the hated Prussian army had forbidden it. They sang it because they liked the yearning melody. And they sang it because they were hopelessly sentimental, even in the depths of war. Sentimentality was a German disease, Schwertlein decided.

He was tempted to clap his hands over his ears. But that would have made it hard to write the letter.

His words had to be stripped of clumsy sentiment. He did not want sympathy. He wanted far more than that. When the time came.

Footsteps climbed the steps to the porch, but Schwertlein refused to look up. A shadow invaded the cast of lantern light, falling on the page, on his unfinished sentence.

"Another article for the newspaper?" Heisler asked.

"Yes," Schwertlein lied. He surrendered and raised his eyes. His friend did not look well.

"It's dry here," Heisler said, glancing around the porch. "I'm surprised the officers haven't taken it."

Schwertlein shrugged. "They're over at the academy, with the Sisters. So I'm allowed my porch." He leaned back on the rough-hewn chair, inspecting his comrade while bantering. "The farmer's an old widower. He was surprised I had the manners to ask if I could sit here. He expected us to just take what we want."

Heisler smiled, if not strongly. "He may find that some of his chickens have joined the regiment."

"Sit down, Josef," Schwertlein said. He blotted the paper and folded it over. "Tell me what's wrong."

"Nothing," Heisler answered. Too quickly. "Absolutely nothing. I just . . . I've written a new poem. I thought you might read it and give me your opinion."

Schwertlein turned an amused expression on his friend. "Always, we go through this . . . you worship your Heine as the god of poetry, and I hand the laurels to Goethe. Our tastes are as different as wine and beer."

"Heine's the voice of freedom."

"Of sentimentality and sensation. Goethe's the better poet. Disciplined, precise . . ."

"Goethe was a reactionary, a hireling of the *ancien régime*."

"And a better poet."

"And I will never be even as good as Heine. I understand. But . . . will you read this, Fritz?" Heisler drew a paper, folded square, from deep in a pocket.

Schwertlein accepted the poem in the best spirit he could muster. Heisler loved poetry, but poetry did not love Heisler. He had no gift, only an impulse that burst into awkward rhymes.

In the ring of yellow light, to the sound of distant singing and insects in multitudes, Schwertlein read the words entrusted to him. The poem was not as long as most that issued from Heisler's pen. But that was not why Schwertlein looked up so sharply.

He peered into his friend's eyes. "So much darkness? Why?"

Rump perched on the porch rail, Heisler looked off at the

campfires protesting the darkness. "I didn't really come about the poem."

"What then?"

Still searching the darkness, Heisler said, "I'm afraid."

Schwertlein gave a snort. "We're all afraid."

His friend shook his head. "It's different this time. I feel something. Always . . . I've always been able to put these thoughts into this pocket and those thoughts in that pocket. You know what I mean. A man thinks about things. But he doesn't truly think about them. The mind accepts terrible things, because such things are only to happen to other men." Weeping as gently as a child, he found the wherewithal to meet Schwertlein's eyes again. "I have always known that I would go home one day, that I would return to Marthe. *Und die Kinder.* But now . . . this time . . ."

"It's the damned singing. It's morbid."

"It's not the singing."

"And there's the rain, the mud, the heat. It would wear down any man."

Drying his eyes with his fingertips, Heisler shook his head. "Do you know what I'll regret? Apart from never seeing Marthe and the children again?" He raised his chin, showing a good profile and the edge of a bitter smile. "I would have liked to write one truly great poem. To leave one poem behind . . . that would rival your Goethe. Only one, and I would be content."

"You'll live to write many more poems."

"You can't know that."

"And you can't know that you won't."

A moth struck the lantern's glass and exploded.

"Sometimes . . . a man knows a thing," Heisler said.

"*Quatsch!* Rubbish!"

Heisler only shook his head again.

"If the sun shines tomorrow," Schwertlein told him, "you'll feel better. Wait and see. And then we can all complain about the heat again."

"Fritz? I'm not so foolish as you think. I know the poem isn't any good. But I'd like you to keep it. And there's something else. A favor. Please. No matter what happens to me . . . write and tell Marthe I didn't suffer, that it was all clean and good. Spare her."

"I can't listen to this. You're talking nonsense. *Reine Scheisse.*"

"But promise me you'll write to her."

Schwertlein laughed a single, hard syllable. "And what if I'm the one who dies?"

"It won't be you," Heisler told him. "I can tell."

"No! You listen to me." Schwertlein's voice rose. "You *don't* know what tomorrow will bring. None of us knows. Damn it, man . . . think like that and you *will* get yourself killed. But you don't know a thing about any of this. Nothing. And you're talking absolute nonsense."

"We'll see, Fritz, we'll see," his friend said resignedly. "I'll leave you to your article now."

And Heisler left the porch. In moments, the darkness had swallowed him.

Schwertlein tried to return to his letter. He was writing to Maria Schenk, the woman he had loved for almost a decade, although it was not yet the time to say it aloud. Or write it.

They had met on her wedding day, at the fest following her vows. A torrent of fire had passed between two souls, a sense of mutual shock, of immediate and immeasurable sorrow that things were as they were and irremedial. No poet would ever put that succulent horror into words. As he watched her later that afternoon, across the gay crowd in that hall, he wished he had died at Rastatt rather than live to meet this wife of a minor friend. For her part, Maria fought not to look at him again, but even as a new bride she had failed in her duty.

When they met over the years, on the street or at a charitable affair, they could barely speak complete sentences to one another, settling for a minimum of courtesies. They both *knew.* They had known from that first instant that life had played a terrible trick on them and their fate was cast in iron. There was no recourse for decent people.

Her husband had died in camp, of measles, in February. Cautiously, they had begun a correspondence, dealing, at first, with the mundane matters that followed Heinrich Schenk's death. But when those things were settled, neither had broken off the correspondence. She wrote to tell him the news from home, as a sister might.

He answered by describing as much of the war as he thought decent: not least, that the accusations of cowardice lodged against all German soldiers after Chancellorsville had been a calumny.

Now he hoped to nudge their exchanges to a deeper intimacy. No article he had ever written, not even the chapters of his unfinished book, had ever demanded such precision of language, such care. He feared that one wrong word might ravage the future of which he dreamed. And of which, he was convinced, Maria dreamed, too.

Men feared different things. But all men feared. Poor Josef, with his sudden *Werther* morbidity, dreaded the coming battle, although he had always been as brave as any man. Schwertlein's own terror was of a life lived in loneliness, without the only woman he ever would love.

How lives changed, as the fires of youth burned down! He still dreamed of the world revolution, of justice and equality for all. Rastatt would always be there, with its dead. It was a dream no Prussian fusillade could kill. He clung to those youthful visions of a world purged and perfected.

But he worried that, if forced to choose between the revolution and his love now, he'd choose Maria. Whose hand he once brushed lightly in a shop.

Schwertlein could not write. Safe words refused to come. He longed to pour out his heart. But that would never do. Every turn of phrase had to be measured.

In the devious way the mind tricks a man, he thought of his father and mother. What kind of love had they shared behind their propriety? Had he been oblivious to a mighty passion? It was hard to imagine such things, of course. No child credited his elders with such feelings. Yet, now he conjured hints of mutual tenderness out of the sternness with which they had faced the world.

He recalled the parlor, *die beste Stube,* in their home in Mainz, where his father served the archbishopric as an overseer of property accounts. Only to have his treasured son flee the university to join a revolution that called for an end to ecclesiastical property. The room had been savagely cold in the winter, except on Sundays, when the tiled stove was lit and the family gathered together in

dreary reverence. At last, the rich smells of dinner would seep in, assaulting the solemnity. He had hated those endless afternoons as a boy, but now they seemed of inestimable value.

Mainz. With its hideous cathedral, its red stone the color of enfeebled blood. The city lived in its alleys, not at the altar. There had been sugared almonds at *Karneval* and sweet wine from the vineyards that stretched from the river into the hills. He recalled the smell of printer's ink and the curses of laborers, market wives all peasant slyness, and priests going round in pairs like God's policemen. He could see the barges on the Rhine and his mother at home with starched lace at her neck, her posture that of a guardsman, her heart that of a saint.

All gone now, all gone.

In the distance, the tireless singers, perfect marksmen in their harmonies, told of a lover who promised to return when it snowed red roses and rained cool wine. A forlorn village beauty replied that it never snows roses or rains down wine. She knew that he never would come again.

"Farewell, my treasure!" they sang. "Farewell, my love!"

Schwertlein could not finish the letter. Safe words refused to come and he no longer trusted his pen. With a groan he would have judged sentimental in another man, he folded the paper and pocketed it, rising to seek out his blanket. There were rumors of an early march in the morning.

The letter could wait, he told himself. There would be time tomorrow.

PART
II

THE DAY OF THE SOLDIERS

AFTERNOON, JULY 1ST

1. Krzyzanowski's Brigade, with 26th Wisconsin on right flank
2. Barlow's Division
3. von Amsberg's Brigade
4. von Steinwehr's Division, XI Corps reserve
5. 26th North Carolina attack
6. Iron Brigade

KEY

Infantry
Cavalry
Line of attack
Attack continue
Path of retreat

All locations approximate
Artillery not shown

FIVE

July 1, Morning

The march came to a halt amid a muddle of commands. Overhead, rain clouds threatened, but held their fire. It was not yet nine, but the heat added weight to knapsacks and wet the men's faces with sweat.

"This is a thing I cannot understand," Bettelman said. "We march around and around. And why? If we stayed in one place, the Rebels would have to come to us, and we could spare our legs." Rueful at the world's resistance to logic, he snorted.

Laughing, Schumann told him, "Maybe the generals think of more important matters than your legs." A master carpenter back home, Schumann appeared to be in fine spirits, having rejoined the regiment the day before. Luck had spared his life, after his wounding at Chancellorsville. "It's not so bad, Leo," he told the watchmaker. "Smell the fresh air! Gulp it, man! In the hospital, I am always thinking I would give my life to breathe clean air again. For just one day." He splashed through a thickening puddle. "The stink is the worst thing. They scrub and scrub, but you smell the rot always."

Lieutenant Trenk rode down the column, pausing by Schwertlein. "First Corps' wagons are blocking the road. Another godless mess. Colonel Boebel's ridden forward to see what Kriz means to do."

"And he'll find that Kriz has gone off to see what Schimmelpfennig and Schurz are going to do," Bettelman put in. "Your watch keeps better time now, *Herr Leutnant?*"

Trenk nodded. *"Ja, Leo. Danke. Bist ein echter Meister."*

"Somebody in this army has to fix things properly," Bettelman continued. "Perhaps I should join the quartermasters and ride always on a wagon and make things go better?"

"I thought you were going to join the artillery?" Heisler said. It was his first comment of the morning and Schwertlein was glad to hear the bantering tone.

Bettelman made a dismissive face. "*Ach,* the cannons are too loud, I think."

Orders snapped down the column. Soldiers reordered their ranks. Trenk turned his horse and left them.

A quarter-mile on, the men of the 26th Wisconsin followed the rest of their brigade and turned from the road. Stepping over a knocked-down fence, they trampled a broad wheatfield as mounted officers ranged among the stalks. From a low rise, the blue columns of the Eleventh Corps stretched as far ahead and behind as a man could see.

The clouds opened their barrage while the men were in the open.

"Close up," Schwertlein ordered, testing his corporal's authority. "Close up now." His friends chose to obey him, although there was grumbling enough.

The column found another road, but the deluge had turned it into a trough of mud. Orders came back, barked through hammering rain, to increase the pace to a quickstep. Men stumbled in the mire, then ran crazily to catch their companies. The landscape rose into low hills studded with boulders.

Schwertlein kept an eye on Heisler, who had been so fatalistic the night before. The schoolteacher and would-be poet looked normal, to the extent the downpour allowed a man to judge.

They slogged up another country lane between a gauntlet of drooping trees, then struck open country again. Ahead, they spied sunlight beyond the walls of rain. That, too, spurred them forward.

At a fork in the road, Colonel Krzyzanowski sat astride his white horse. Erect as ever, the little officer smiled and saluted their colors, then waved to Lieutenant Colonel Boebel. With his finely trimmed mustaches and goatee, Kriz seemed wonderfully unperturbed by the rain.

"There go my boys!" he called out in perfect German. "The heroes of Chancellorsville! My own boys!"

Dozens of voices responded with the colonel's most notorious and frequent command: *"You must speak English now!"*

Wet as river rats, the soldiers laughed. The colonel grinned and

held up a hand, palm out, admitting he'd been caught. The battled-down ranks cheered him as they passed. The downpour stopped abruptly, surrendering to the sun.

But the silence the rain left behind uncovered another sound. In the distance, Schwertlein heard the thump of cannon.

Just proud as peacocks, ain't they?" Cobb said. "Like they're riding off to the fair."

Limber and gun after limber and gun, caisson after caisson, Pegram's artillerymen clattered past the picket line, leading Archer's brigade toward Gettysburg, the town where the Yankee cavalry had been the day before.

"They're confident enough, that's for damned sure," Corporal Ireton said. "Whoever heard of putting guns out front like they was cavalry?"

"Maybe the Yankees run off? After they seen us yesterday?" James Bunyan said.

"I wouldn't count no blue-bellied chickens just yet," Pike Gray told him. "Those Yankees didn't look in no running mood to me."

"Maybe they got orders," James Bunyan said. "Maybe they were ordered back."

Cobb cackled. "Sounds like old Progress ain't in a fighting mood today."

"Man's got a right to think, ain't he?" John Bunyan said, defending his twin brother.

Cobb enjoyed the testiness. "We're all privates here, boy. Except Sergeant Blake there. Wouldn't want to forget him. And Corporal Ireton. And privates ain't supposed to go thinking on things. Plays Hell with whatever the officers got in mind. Hell and a spit, boy, they don't even want sergeants thinking overmuch." Smirking, he looked at Blake. "Do they now?"

Cobb had picked open one of the pustules on his nose. It had bled onto his cheek and down into his beard. He had not washed his face to cleanse himself. To Blake, the man looked like a leper from the Bible.

"No, sir," Cobb went on, "all they expect folks like us to do is line up all polite and tip our hats and say, 'Better take your shot now, Billy Yank, 'cause I'm a-going to shoot you, if'n you don't.'" He

gestured toward the infantrymen following the artillery out on the pike. Then he bore down on the Bunyan twins. "Ain't no general going to weep over you and there ain't going to be no fine words in no newspaper. Only folks going to weep over you are your kin. And they'll get over it."

"Shut up, Cobb," Peachum said.

But something had stirred up Billie Cobb more fiercely than usual. He turned on his comrade in arms. "You always tell me to shut up, Artie. Know why that is? Do you, now? You don't like the truth of this world, that's all. Tell me one word I spoke is a lie, just one word of it." He spit yellow filth on the ground.

Hugh Gordon broke the bitter mood. "Looks like those clouds are pulling off south. Going to be a right scorcher."

On the pike, the long lines in gray flashed bits of color where men had chosen civilian shirts over nakedness. Officers of the waiting 26th North Carolina called in the pickets. Lieutenants gathered companies together as their captains assembled near Colonel Burgwyn and Major Jones. Blake couldn't see Lieutenant Colonel Lane, the regiment's second in command. It unsettled him. Lane was the one who had his confidence, a tough weed, not a flower. Blake wanted him present.

Davis's brigade followed Archer's down the road. By regiment, the army was turning the mud of the pike back to dust.

"Let's go now," Blake called. "Move sharp. Form up. Hugh, you go fetch Tam. He's over calling on his cousin."

After a detachment had been culled to guard the wagons and the musicians had been subtracted to serve as stretcher bearers, the regiment mustered eight hundred men to go forward. The knapsacks they had just gotten back from the wagons the evening before were piled up again and ammunition was counted, cartridges checked for moisture. When they moved out by column, bringing up the rear of the brigade, the air was as thick and hot as a low-country swamp. It was just nine o'clock.

They had not marched a half-mile when they heard cannon.

"Guess them Yankees didn't run off, after all," Cobb announced. Smiling his blackened smile, he added, "Good thing, too. The killing spirit's on me, boys, and I'm looking to have my fun."

From Cobb, it wasn't a brag. The man meant every word, Blake

knew. Cobb took pleasure in hurting all things that lived and thrived, and cared not for the censure of God or man.

The rest of the men remained silent as they marched. The entire column had tensed, merged into a single beast. As the artillery duel continued up ahead, enough guns came into play to announce that this was more than a skirmish.

Playing cards lay strewn along the road now, discarded by men who suddenly feared the Lord. Even Cobb turned silent. The route began a gradual ascent. Feet kicked up dust. Some men drew neck rags up over nose and mouth, but most just sealed their lips against the grit.

They heard small-arms fire, rippling volleys, and the peck of lone shots. The first wounded man staggered rearward, cradling his shredded arm. Ahead of the column, smoke curtained the low horizon.

More wounded men materialized, some helped along by shirkers. Suddenly, there were dozens of them edging both sides of the road. The worst cases came on stretchers. Most of those men were silent or moaning low, but a few screams pierced the thunder of the guns. Two bearers shed their burden in a field, arranging their newly dead comrade as if in sleep, then turned back toward the fight with their bloodied canvas.

As the regiment hurried up the grade at quick time, Blake recognized the ridgetop tavern they'd passed the day before. Colonel Burgwyn waited beside it, watching as his regiment caught up with him. Broad-shouldered and bullish, Lieutenant Colonel Lane sat his horse next to Burgwyn. Blake was glad to see him.

A bearded soldier using his rifle as a crutch limped away from the battle. Powder-blackened, his face wore a fixed grin. As he passed the men going forward, he called out, "You're in for it now, fellers, you're in for the devil. Them Black Hats are out there, mean as cottonmouth snakes." His laughter was worthy of Cobb.

An artillery shell struck the road in front of the regiment's colors. Blake could not see if men had fallen, but the banners remained aloft. Colonel Burgwyn rode out to urge the lead company forward.

Atop the ridge, twelve-pounders had been placed in battery on either side of the road. The cannon spit flame and recoiled. Their

crews rushed back upon them, some of the men stripped to the waist and gleaming as they swabbed the barrels and loaded the next charges.

Yankee rounds burst in the fields and screamed overhead. Someone ordered the regiment to march to the left, but Colonel Burgwyn spurred his horse into the field in front of the column, pointing rightward with his saber. The colors wheeled and the regiment followed, crossing the road onto the flat of the ridge behind the guns.

"Think any one of these sumbitches knows where we're going?" Cobb asked after leaping a roadside ditch.

"Straighten your ranks," Blake ordered. "Maintain your file. Keep moving."

General Pettigrew galloped up on a handsome dapple gray. His aide, Captain Young, trailed behind him. Pettigrew paused in midfield to speak with Burgwyn and Lieutenant Colonel Lane. The cluster of officers seemed bound to catch the eyes of the Yankee gunners.

Blake wondered if the stream down in the hollow before them was still overflowing. Probably not, he decided. Not much rain in the night. They'd get across that quick enough. Beyond lay the woods through which his skirmishers had moved with ease the afternoon before. Things were different now. Yankees would be in those trees.

General Pettigrew gave a command Blake could not quite hear, but Colonel Burgwyn rode closer to the men and gave it again: "Twenty-sixth Regiment . . . by the left flank!"

Around them, the entire brigade began to deploy. Burgwyn rode down the length of his regiment and back again, red sash trailing. He had put on a fine uniform for the day.

"Ain't he just too pretty now," Cobb said. "Up on that fine horse of his. Yankees going to pick him right out as the prize of the litter. Ain't that so, Sergeant Blake?"

Blake didn't respond. He concentrated on getting his small piece of the regiment into its proper place in the forming lines.

Facing eastward in double ranks, the men got their clearest view yet of the fighting. Smoke hazed the line of the streambed. Stumbling figures emerged from the dirty mist, wounded men missing weapons or caps, some bloodied visibly even at a distance. On the

slope of the opposing ridge, which ran parallel to the high ground the regiment occupied, drifting clouds of gunsmoke revealed swarms of blue-clad infantrymen, then hid them again. The Yankees were drawn up in yellowing fields and amid groves cleared of underbrush. Many wore tall black hats.

The cavalrymen appeared to have withdrawn, replaced by those dense blue lines and batteries of guns at deadly intervals. Only here and there could Blake make out knots of men in gray on the far slope. But the smoke settled in the low ground concealed much, he told himself. Things got confused, when you saw only a piece of them. The fight might not be going all that badly.

"We going in, do you think, Sergeant Blake?" James Bunyan asked.

"When it's our time," Blake told him.

He noticed something wrong, though. The withdrawing men he had thought all wounded harbored many in their midst who appeared unscathed, still clutching their weapons. Some stopped and turned to fire into the smoke, while others plodded back up toward the road down which they had marched. Defeated.

Blake said nothing. But he was not the only one who saw it. They were witnessing the end of something, not a beginning. The morning's attack had failed.

Small bands of men coalesced in the fields below them, coming together as if to divide their shame. Blake saw no colors held high, no officers attempting to rally their men. Things looked worse and worse.

"What's happening?" James Bunyan asked. The boy was jumpy as a colt. "Why are they coming back like that?"

"Yankees gave 'em a whupping, that's why," Cobb said. "Archer's fellers never were no good."

"Maybe you can show them how it's done," Blake told him. Instantly, he regretted having spoken.

Cobb was delighted, though. "Well, now, that's just what I aim to do, Sergeant Blake. Soon as all those fine gentlemen with their plumes and sashes make up their minds about it."

With the attack turned back, the Union gunners shifted their efforts to the new battle line atop the ridge before them. Shot

screamed overhead. Other rounds splashed the slope to the regiment's front. The Federals were bracketing their target.

In the next company, a man toppled forward into the grass. Blake assumed the heat had brought him low, but someone called, "Sharpshooters!"

Another man fell, spewing blood.

Heedless of the danger, Colonel Burgwyn cantered out in front of their ranks and called them to attention.

"Regiment . . . about-*face*," he commanded.

The company officers echoed him.

"Forwaaard . . . ," Burgwyn called.

Again, his subordinate commanders repeated the order.

"March!"

Glad to move off the exposed crest, the soldiers stepped out sharply. A man might desire to go in one direction or the other, but nobody cared to serve as a do-nothing target.

The colonel halted them just behind the ridgetop, forty paces from their former position, where trees broke up a meadow. Some of the men had shade. Blake's people didn't.

Lieutenant Colonel Lane rode along the line, telling the men to lie down in place, sparing them from all but a direct hit by plunging fire.

Just as Blake dropped to the earth, an artillery caisson to the regiment's left exploded, shaking the earth beneath the soldiers' bellies. When he looked up again, Blake saw writhing horses whose legs kicked at nothing and heard their bewildered whinnies. A bareheaded sergeant walked down the harness line, shooting each beast in turn.

"Think we'll just quit this one?" Peachum asked him. "Pull on back and wait till we have us a bigger club to hand?" He wasn't afraid, just figuring things out.

Lifting his face from the spikes of hot grass, Blake saw the regiment's officers, still on horseback, conferring as calmly as if on a parade ground. Colonel Burgwyn shone like Ivanhoe.

"No," Blake said.

Lee found General Hill hunched in an ambulance in Cashtown. It took Hill a moment to realize who was before him. He clambered down awkwardly, dressed only in his shirt, trousers, and boots.

"Are you in health?" Lee asked. Powell Hill's scarecrow flesh was the color of bone.

"Yes, sir. Just a morning distemper. That's all."

"Can you explain the firing I hear?"

Hill shook his head, struggling through a cloud. "Not completely certain what that's about. Told Harry Heth to find out what's ahead of him. He knows . . ." Hill jerked up a hand to scratch his scalp. "He knows he's not to bring on an engagement. Orders were to report back immediately, if he came up against Federal infantry . . . anything but their cavalry."

The distant cannonade did not sound as if it were waged against a few horsemen. Lee struggled to maintain a proper tone. "Are you certain you are fit to command your corps, General?"

Hill straightened. The message had begun to penetrate. Lee could not offer sympathy. Sick or well, men had to do their duty or pay the price. Hill would have to rally and do his.

"I'm fit, sir. Fit and ready. Just a touch of something. It's let up now."

"Don't you think, General Hill, that your place might be forward at such a time?"

"Yes, sir. I was just about to go."

"I must understand what we have before us, General," Lee told him.

"Yes, sir. Going to look into it myself." Drawn by Lee's presence, Hill's staff had gathered round. A. P. Hill turned toward the nearest man. "My horse. Get my horse. Where's my horse?" His voice grew testy and color returned to his face.

An aide hurried up with Hill's coat and hat, but the horse did not appear.

"I must wait here, General," Lee told him, "until the rest of my staff comes up. Then I shall join you. For now, though, I must stress again that I cannot have a general engagement. Not until this army is concentrated and we know the disposition of those people. Do you understand me, sir?"

Hill's long, limp hair seemed a dead thing, but sparks enlivened his eyes. Hill was good in a fight. Battle brought him to life. That was why Lee had given him a corps. The problem was that Lee did not want a battle. Not yet.

Led by an orderly, Hill's horse appeared. It looked considerably more robust than its master.

"Go now," Lee said softly, "and see what General Heth has made of things."

As Hill gained the saddle, it was evident to Lee that the man was suffering. But he would have to bear it through the day. Duty cared not for the body's tribulations.

Major General A. P. Hill saluted and spurred his horse. Soon, he was lost to sight amid an army hurrying forward.

They saw the town ahead. It lay under drifting smoke. Lieutenant Colonel Boebel bellowed the order to advance at the double-quick.

"*Mein Gott!*" Bettelman cried. "I can't, I can't!"

But the watchmaker could, and he did. Groaning.

The regiment had covered at least a dozen miles in haste, through drenching rain and mire, then under a punishing sun. For the last three-quarters of the route, there had been no pause for rest. Canteens were empty, gullets were dry. Schwertlein could not remember a harder march. Yet, surprisingly few men had fallen out. Spirits had quickened at the sound of the guns.

And the regiment's shirkers were gone now. The men marching beside him had suffered wrongs after Chancellorsville that this day might redress. Nor did they want their comrades' disapproval. No man sought death, but fate would have its say. There was nothing left but to fight.

The road led up a slope toward a cemetery. The town grew across a broad swale to the left. Its nearest streets teemed with blue-clad columns, with guns rolling forward and caissons jangling rearward. As the regiment trotted closer, ambulances became distinct from commissary wagons. Lightly wounded soldiers made their way back from the fighting on their own, some walking in pairs, as if another's strength might keep death from surprising them. Officers shouted, their purposes uncertain. A dog howled.

Across broad fields, through buildings and trees, Schwertlein could make out stretches of the battle line to the west. The army had made its stand along a ridge. As the road climbed, he saw the orange belch of cannon in the distance, followed by black bursts that thinned into gray.

Up on the cemetery hillock, officers huddled, watching the fighting across the roofs of the town. Schwertlein recognized the corps commander, General Howard, behind a pair of field glasses. He was a man who cared more for his Sundays than he did for his soldiers, and who made his disdain for all things German apparent. As Schwertlein sweated past on the road below, the general lowered his glasses and spoke to an officer beside him. Schwertlein would have liked to hear what was said.

Couriers galloped off from the cemetery, headed in every direction. Guns unlimbered below the gravestones, establishing a rear line of defense. Regimental flags from von Steinwehr's division were recognizable only because the color bearers waved them to call in stragglers. The air, poisoned with gunpowder, hung dead.

As the regiment forced its way into the town, struggling to close with the rest of the brigade, the commotion of a hurrying army raised a din to rival the blast of the guns. Lieutenant Trenk rushed rearward, face set below his kepi. This time, he did not pause to talk, did not even see his friends from home as he passed them.

A chaos of soldiers, wagons, and batteries rushing forward or being withdrawn clogged up the streets. Citizens on their doorsteps or leaning from windows cheered on their saviors. Those who had flags waved them, pretty girls, children, old men, and double-chinned wives. Their clamor lifted hearts and lightened feet.

Upon realizing that the regiment passing before them was filled with Germans, the citizens divided their cries, the English-speakers sticking to their hurrahs as local Germans yelled themselves into euphoria in dialect as thick as pea soup. The men of the 26th Wisconsin had not been cheered so handsomely since they marched to the Milwaukee railyard to join the war.

Struggling to force a passage for his wagon, an Irish teamster called out to them, "Jaysus, haven't we handed the Johnnies their arses this fine day? You nivver seen such a drubbing as we've handed them. . . ."

It seemed to be true, and wonderful. In the town square, where a cannon had spun off a wheel, a company's worth of Confederates stood somberly, all the defiance crushed out of them, waiting to be escorted rearward as prisoners. A few men in gray still looked

fierce-eyed upon the world, but others, glad to be done with the war, strode deeper into Yankeedom on their own.

Stripped of their canvas, a pair of wagons nudged past with butchered soldiers. It seemed there were not ambulances enough. Some of the wounded moaned, some begged for water. Others were dead, gone over in the short trip back from the battle line. One wagon trailed blood through its planks. Here and there, a gore-spattered head retained its cap, bearing the circular First Corps badge. A burned man wore the last bits of a gunner's jacket. His body shivered vigorously, but his eyes were already dead.

"It may be over before they send us in," Schumann said. Panting and gleaming with sweat.

"*Herrgott* be merciful and let it be so," Bettelman muttered, forgetting his vigorous atheism.

Another contingent of prisoners, ragged and clotted with blood, passed toward the rear. A gray-clad lieutenant wept as he stumbled along. Rushing out to block his path, a burly civilian waved his fist and cursed. A Union captain sent the man back to his house, but the fellow shrieked further insults from his doorway.

The prisoners walked on.

For all his professed hatred of those who had forced war upon the country, Schwertlein empathized with the captive soldiers. He had never been a prisoner, but he knew only too well how men felt when they gave all they had, yet were condemned to failure. War was a sorrier business than storybooks told.

After executing a column-right, the regiment marched between storefronts for a stretch, then passed brick homes again. As lovely as daffodils, two blond girls rushed out with buckets of water. Other civilians, young and old, distributed loaves of bread and even sausages.

"You know what that means, Fritz?" Schumann asked knowingly.

Schwertlein nodded as they pushed along, their pace reduced again by jostling confusion. "We'll be on the flank. If the people still have food to give away, we're the first ones down this street."

"*Genau,*" Schumann agreed.

To their left, the artillery continued its work, but the rifle fire had lulled.

"Maybe it truly is over," Heisler said. His voice sounded brittle now.

"Get yourself some water," Schwertlein told him, mustering all the authority he could.

The houses thinned, giving way to narrow orchards and broad fields beyond. Lieutenant Trenk galloped past again, going forward this time. His horse spewed green foam from its mouth.

The blue serpent of men wound from the road into a grove of apple trees. Despite the grunting artillery fire from the ridge to the west, the world seemed oddly peaceful. Exhausted men foresaw the order to rest and dropped to the ground the moment the column halted. Some slid off their remaining equipment before collapsing, while others folded into themselves as if shot. Dappled with light and shadow, devout soldiers knelt and prayed the *Vaterunser*. The regiment's militant freethinkers let them be. It was not a day for teasing.

They had given all the vigor they had to the march. It seemed as though no man could go a step more. But Schwertlein forced himself to remain standing, looking about for Sergeant Arnold or one of the other noncommissioned officers from the regiment.

He was about to order Heisler to help him gather canteens when orders rent the air: *Up. Get up. Stand to.*

Corpses rose, groaning, cursing, stretching wretched backs and stiffened limbs.

Sergeant Arnold appeared and called the roll, even as stragglers found their way to the ranks. Astonishingly, only three of the men who had answered up that morning were missing now. A hard man, Arnold announced that those three would be marked as deserters.

Knapsacks were gathered by company, but when the musicians and the last wagons went to the rear, the knapsacks remained on the ground. The officers expected to hold their line.

Schwertlein felt his stiffened garments rub. He needed more water. He needed rest. They all did. The battle *had* to be over. He didn't see how such played-out men could fight. The spirit was willing, willing and more, but the flesh had been blown to Hell by the brutal march.

Dismounted for the present, Lieutenant Colonel Boebel stepped

out in front of the regiment. He looked like a pastor about to call down hellfire.

Boebel moved the regiment into the sunlight, leaving the welcome shade to align the 26th with the rest of Krzyzanowski's brigade in a great square of companies. Their footfalls trampled oats and wheat, the sound queerly massive before it came to a halt. Then the entire brigade marched forward to a reserve position at the right-rear of its sister brigade, von Amsberg's. Barlow's division had passed and formed in the open fields on the corps' right flank. Shouted orders, the clank of metal, the rustle of thousands of uniforms, the squeak of leather, and the *plonk* of bouncing canteens summed to a thing strange and mighty.

Exhausted as their bodies were, the visible power of the army, the blue ranks long and deep, with colors held high by the dozen, stirred the men. The cannon fire in the west had slackened, in a sulk. It seemed to them that the day was already theirs.

John Reynolds had told the captain he sent as courier to kill his mount, if necessary, but to lose not a second in reaching Meade. And it was well he had done so.

All morning, the situation had developed swiftly as Meade paced, pondered, and fretted, with Buford reporting Confederates not only to his west, along the Chambersburg Pike, but several miles to the north of Gettysburg as well. Buford had engaged troops from A. P. Hill's corps, forces his cavalrymen could only delay, but he also had reported Reynolds just three miles distant.

The next courier had come from Reynolds himself. A slight officer, little larger than a jockey, delivered a message scrawled in the saddle: "The enemy are in strong force . . . I will fight them inch by inch, and if driven back into the town, I will barricade the streets and hold them back as long as possible."

That was Reynolds, through and through. If Gettysburg was a proper place to give battle, John would recognize it and buy the time the army needed to concentrate. If the ground proved unfavorable, he'd cover the army's flank while the right wing withdrew to the Pipe Creek line. Reynolds also had identified high ground near Emmitsburg, where the Confederates could be further delayed, if need be. The man was thorough, a rock for the entire army.

Butterfield, on the other hand, had fallen behind again and been chastised again. The circular with the Pipe Creek plan had gone out only that morning, when it should have been distributed by midnight. Pipe Creek remained Meade's preferred battleground, but he recognized that Lee and the press of events would have their say. He did not intend to blind himself with his own grandiose schemes, as Hooker had done.

Meade believed in engineering. There was beauty in it. Not merely in the finished structures, calculated to their perfect degree as to height, width, weight, and stress, but in the clarity of the process, the sublime predictability. If forced to offer his ideal of beauty, he would have cited not a woman, but the tall and slender lighthouse at Barnegat Bay, his masterpiece.

Yet, he had fought long enough now to recognize that an engineer's training took a commander just so far and no more. The blueprints for battle rarely matched the result. What little he had read of Jomini impressed him not a whit. Interior lines might offer a great advantage to a commander sound in his judgments, but designing campaigns based solely on perpendiculars, obliques, and angles was the labor of an ass. The engineer might pick the ground, choosing it wisely, but then the human beast leapt into the business. In war, clear thinking laid a fine foundation, but battle was captive to the foibles of man.

Still, good ground mattered, of that Meade had no doubt. He only wished he knew more about the terrain at Gettysburg. He still had not a single map that satisfied him. The decision to give battle or not depended on John Reynolds' judgment now.

Meade had sent additional messengers to each of the corps, altering their movements, alerting them that their plans could change again, hurrying Sedgwick, redirecting Slocum, getting Hancock in pocket, always seeking to cover the possibilities of the day. Sickles was moving in the proper direction to support Reynolds' fight, if need be. And Howard would be up right behind John, his lead elements probably on the field by now. So Reynolds would have two corps on hand, with two more corps available by evening.

But was Gettysburg a worthy place for a *defensive* battle? Meade's stomach complained of acid. He had turned down an offered mid-day meal, unable to eat a bite. And he was tired. He yearned for a

night of sleep. Standing with his coat draped open, as was his practice in hot weather, he felt bent, despite his good posture.

If only a portion of Lee's army presented itself, Meade was ready to pitch into it and let the defense be damned—as he had written his wife in a fit of bravado. Otherwise, he wanted Lee to be the attacker. But he did not want Lee deciding where the attack would come.

Had *Lee* chosen Gettysburg?

Meade ached for another message from Reynolds, with more details. Surely, John would have matters in charge by now?

At least the pressure was off of Harrisburg, and it no longer seemed Lee might dash for Philadelphia. Now it was all about choosing a battleground and forcing the other man to slip into error.

Pacing before his headquarters tent, Meade fought the impulse to mount his horse and ride forward, to see the situation at Gettysburg himself. But that would be folly. He was no longer a mere division or even a corps commander. He had to remain where his orders could reach each of his subordinates promptly, and where their reports could find him without delay. He burned to be at the front, but had to keep to his place at the army's center.

It was all a damned bit harder than it looked.

Turning back to the tent, he thrust in his head and snapped at Butterfield, "Has my report to Halleck gone off, or not?"

Butterfield had taken his blows already and declined to be further annoyed. "It's gone," he said.

"The order to Sedgwick to close on the army?"

"Hours ago. We spoke of it, General Meade."

"Hancock?"

Butterfield looked suitably put-upon at last. "You spoke to him yourself. Not an hour ago. Was there something else?"

"Has his corps closed in its entirety?"

Butterfield drew out his watch. "Perhaps not fully."

"Find out," Meade snapped.

Hancock's visit had buoyed him for a time, although the doubts of the day soon set back in. Win Hancock would have liked to be forward in Reynolds' place, Meade knew. The man loved a fight. Meade would not have trusted Hancock to plan a grand campaign, but there was no one better on a battlefield.

Well, Hancock would get his chance, whether at Pipe Creek or at Gettysburg. Or somewhere in between. Meanwhile, Hancock had placed his headquarters a few minutes' ride away, on the other side of Taneytown. With a short rest, his Second Corps could be on the march again, if needed. Meade applauded himself for the manner in which he had drawn the army together. Only Sedgwick remained worrisomely far from the likely battlegrounds.

Despite himself, Meade smiled. Thinking of Win Hancock. The way the man left every button of his tunic undone but the top one, since, fighter or not, his belly had pushed aggressively to his own personal front. He looked a grand man in the saddle, though. Inspiring. Meade knew that, in a matter of hours, Hancock would come to him with some excuse to ride forward, to get into the scrap at Gettysburg, with or without his corps. And Meade, like a parent, would have to tell him no. He could picture the scene as almost a comical one, as if Hancock truly were no more than a child. "You must stay with your corps, Winfield!" "But . . . but I don't *want* to. . . ."

"No more messages from Reynolds?" Meade asked Butterfield. It was a foolish question and both men knew it.

Butterfield shrugged, no longer concealing his exasperation. "You would've seen the man before I did. I haven't left this tent."

Frustrated that he had no further excuse for anger, Meade stepped back into the sunlight. It was beastly hot with the rain blown off. "Damn it," he said to no one in particular, "where's young George gotten to?" Then he raised his voice: "Where's Captain Meade?"

No one replied. All in the vicinity did their best to evade the general's eyes and scurry along. Yes, they knew damned well he was in a mood. But what had Frederick the Great said? That soldiers should be more afraid of their officers than of the enemy? The staff of the Army of the Bloody Blue Potomac needed a touch more of that. Hooker's damnable legacy of slovenliness. No engineer would have tolerated it.

Old Frederick knew a damned sight more about war than that bugger Jomini, so adored by Little Mac.

Even as he thought these things, Meade knew he was being unfair. The staff was doing all it could. It was too small. As if they

were still fighting in Mexico, puny army against puny army. So much needed to be changed. If he survived in command, he would build the army a proper staff at last. If . . .

Why didn't Reynolds send more details of the fighting, damn him? Meade needed facts. He had an army to move, and the move had to be in the proper damned direction. He could not afford to confuse his corps commanders with an endless succession of countermanded orders, making a worse muddle than that idiot Burnside.

With a start, Meade wondered if, before long, another general would be damning him for an idiot.

With Gettysburg fourteen miles off, he could not even hear the battle's noise. For all he knew, there had only been a skirmish, over now. Or there might be a significant encounter still under way. Buford had made it sound as though there were plenty of Rebels to chew on.

The point was not to be the one who was chewed.

He needed to know, needed to know. It was John's *duty* to send regular reports, damn it all, and not just have a grand lark chasing laurels.

Meade had expected better of Reynolds. He really had.

He spotted his son returning from the grove that masked the latrine. His temper was such that he was prepared to tear into the boy anyway. How could he expect to know what the army was doing, if he didn't even know where his son was? Instead, Meade stuck his head back in the tent.

"Send a message to Pleasanton. Urgently. He needs to keep this headquarters informed, blast him. I need to know if Ewell is headed for Hanover, or if he's descending farther to the west. You saw Buford's report. Tell Pleasanton if he can't do the work, I'll find—"

Meade heard the hoofbeats of a hard-driven horse. He rushed back into the open. It was all he could do not to run to meet the courier. Coming from the direction of Gettysburg.

Surely he would learn now what Reynolds thought of the ground and the force before him. Enough to enable Meade to make the fateful decisions that must rest upon his shoulders. He took the old maxim to heart: It was almost impossible to recover from flawed dispositions at a battle's outset. Whose dispositions would prove flawed, his or Robert E. Lee's?

The horse was spent and the rider looked no better. Meade recognized Major Riddle, one of Reynolds' men.

Foot catching in a stirrup, Riddle almost toppled backward. Meade was about to upbraid the man for his clumsiness. Unbecoming to an officer, even a worn one.

Then Meade saw the man's face.

It can be difficult to tell the difference between tears and sweat on a drained man's features.

Riddle failed to salute. He looked distraught, shocked. Ill. His mouth opened. With difficulty. As if the jaw had been clenched too hard and too long, until the human mortar hardened.

Gathering himself, the major said, "General Reynolds is dead, sir."

SIX

July 1, Early Afternoon

Why don't we attack?" James Bunyan asked. Lying amid the ranks that stretched down the field like ready-made corpses, the twin fidgeted, a child afflicted with worms. "How long they going to keep us a-laying here?"

"Long as they want," Cobb said as he rolled to one side. He had picked open the sore on his nose again. "Got to give the Yankees a fair chance to get themselves fixed up and ready."

"It just don't make no sense," the boy said.

"The generals know what they're doing," Blake told Bunyan, Cobb, and all the men sprawled around him. Although he was not certain of that himself.

"I didn't see that many Yankees when we was up top there," Peachum put in. "Seems like we ought to get things done with. While there's not so many of them."

Cobb delivered his customary cackle. "Plenty of them for Archer's boys, seems like." Flies adored him.

Blake wondered if he should ask the captain for the let to send a detail to fill canteens. Even lying still, a man felt the sun's punch. And there'd been some whiskey early in the morning, although Tam, Hugh, and the others had tried to hide it. What helped at dawn took its revenge at noon. They'd all be raw with thirst.

As the sun peaked overhead, the fight faded into a dull exchange of artillery, the way two weary but well-matched brawlers kept slopping occasional punches toward one another. Blake understood the men's impatience, felt it himself. They were willing to fight, they were ready. But waiting gnawed at a man. Didn't make a fellow afraid, but left him a bit less steady. And it gave the wrong sort of man too much time to think.

He couldn't figure the delay himself. He even agreed with Cobb. There were Yankees aplenty on that other ridge, but not so many that a big brigade like Pettigrew's couldn't whip them. Surely the generals had a greater plan, a scheme invisible from his crushed-grass bed. Perhaps they were waiting for still more brigades and divisions to come up, to deliver a mighty blow. But it did seem to give the Yankees the same opportunity.

"These damn ants," Jack Ireton said.

Cobb hooted. "Be worms at you soon enough."

Sometimes Blake wondered why the men lying beside him fought at all. Not one man in the company held slaves, not even the officers. Nor did they have much else. Other than their pride. Of course, that was part of it, the war did give them something, making something of them for a time, spiriting them away from their poor-white work, hard debts, and bent-bone children. He'd heard many a time that this was a rich man's war and a poor man's fight, but Blake suspected that was the way of every war. True, some young bucks from high families went off to display themselves. But men of fortune who'd already had their waistcoats let out a time or two found good reasons aplenty to stay at home. Like Lenore's banker.

Lenore. When he thought of her now, he was brutal. Given the chance, he would not be a gentleman. He would hurt her. Damage her. With all the anger he had taken to that swamp girl whose pap was willing to see himself off for an hour or two if money was in prospect. She had borne his assault in silence, as if used to it, then told him, "You come around again, Mr. Soldier. You come on anytime."

But he had not gone back. He had gone to her on a rumor of availability, fleeing the regiment's low-country camp in the twilight, bursting with rage at the news of Lenore's marriage, her betrayal. Delilah had done less, he told himself, cursing his beloved as a cold whore. And the girl had been waiting by candlelight for custom, in a cabin rancid with body smells and spoilage. Afterward, sick-souled, he had feared terrible consequences from entering her stinking body, but none afflicted him. Thereafter, he remained chaste of women, giving himself to the war and the war alone. But he dreamed of hurting Lenore, of degrading her, of winning her.

I am no longer to be trusted among decent folk, Blake told himself.

Cobb fetched up a garter snake and bit it in two, letting the severed ends dangle, twitch, and spurt. Black-toothed and grinning, he chewed as if he had taken in a mouthful. James Bunyan sat up, crawled back a few feet, and retched.

"That there snake a close relation, or distant?" Peachum asked Cobb.

"Yankee branch of the family," Pike put in.

"Well, better a goddamn family of snakes than rabbits," Cobb answered, spitting. He was done playing with the halves of the serpent and discarded them. "Plenty of rabbit in some of these here Bunyans. Snake was headed for James there, ready to swallow him whole."

John Bunyan leapt up, fists ready. Quick of body, Blake pulled him back down. The steadier of the twins landed with a thump.

"Take it out on the Yankees, boy," Blake told him. "Cobb isn't worth it."

"That's right now, that's exactly right," Cobb added. "Any man with Quakers up his tree can see it plain. Man ain't worth a turd if he ain't got a name, if he ain't somebody. You tell them how it is now, Sergeant Blake."

In the distance, drums pounded. But whose?

Blake knew where his hardened heart had gone, but not where the thoughts of the other men had strayed. He even suspected, for the first time, that Cobb might have set about something with good reason. James Bunyan was failing, although the boy had never malingered before. Better for him to burn into a fury, no matter its cause, than to lie there thinking too much about what lay ahead. And if it angered his brother, too, that harmed nothing.

It still bewildered Blake how men could downright hate each other, yet fight to save not themselves but men of whom they'd had the blackest opinion but minutes before. James Bunyan might think of shooting Cobb, rather than a Yankee, but he would not do it. Instead, he would kill the Yankee who lunged for Cobb. Even the Bible didn't explain such things. Lenore was in it, in many forms. But Billie Cobb was absent.

When the order came to rise, all else would be forgotten and

the men would go forward as one. James Bunyan would go, and Cobb. Peachum and Ireton, Tam McMinn and Hugh Gordon, Oliver Wright and Pike Gray. Eight hundred of them would rise, straighten their ranks, and step out forward. Some few might falter on a given day, but they would be as nothing. The men who lay beside him now, dusting off ants and trying to coax last sips from dry canteens, would do their duty, even if unsure to whom or what or why that duty was owed. He knew they would fight and believed they would fight well. Because, in the end, fighting was one thing a hurt man could believe in. For all the filth and horror, it was pure.

Blake looked forward to it. Not because he hated Yankees. His hate was less discriminating than that. When he'd taken that girl on her cob-filled mattress, he had almost closed his hands around her neck and tightened them. Instead, he had plowed her mercilessly, intent on inflicting pain that oldest of ways, summoning death with the deepest of all desires, determined to hear her scream. But she had said nothing, barely moaned, and let him do what men did. Perhaps, he thought, he should have killed her father. Did that toothless whoremaster also count as a son of the Glorious South? Blake figured people were people, wherever birth placed them. Today, men who knew nothing meaningful about one another would slaughter each other over accidents of geography. Say what they might in the grandest of words, there was no virtue in it. But killing Yankees was deemed a good thing, and he was good at killing. Nothing made him feel better than fighting. He had not made that girl-child scream, and the creature had even bidden him return, sickening him. But he could make Yankees scream.

The problem wasn't getting men to kill. It was getting them to stop.

Now and then it confused him that he felt so little fear. It seemed almost a madness as he watched himself pass through the days. He even tried to talk himself into a dread of what might happen to him in battle. But he couldn't make it stick. He'd seen enough to know the horrible wounds a man could suffer. Yet, he was more impatient than poor James Bunyan, or Peachum, or even little Cobb, to stand and go forward.

There's something wrong with me, he told himself. I'm as ugly

inside as Cobb is outside. How could I believe in a God, if he made me like this?

Blake never had high thoughts. "Dixie" was as foreign to him as China. He felt a bothered closeness to the back hills of North Carolina, and the northern poke of Virginia still held him in a dark thrall. But neither piece of dirt was worth the dying. Where was the glory in fighting for fields that could not feed their owners? Blake took no interest in gallant, glorious gestures.

But he was interested in killing. It made him feel clean.

It's a dirty business," Major General Winfield Scott Hancock told Meade, "when you lose a man like Reynolds."

But Meade, who had ridden Hell-for-leather to Hancock's headquarters—leaving his escort to gather and catch up—understood what filled the Second Corps commander's mind. Hancock cared about Reynolds' fate and had counted the man a friend. But Win would have gone through a gauntlet of corpses to get into the fight.

And Hancock understood why he had come, although Meade's purpose had not yet been spoken. Meade was tempted to tease Hancock a bit. But there was no time for nonsense.

Reynolds dead. The news had shocked Meade. His first thoughts had veered near panic. Reynolds had been his crutch. Next, a wave of sorrow had crashed over him for the man who was no more. But the queer feeling that arose thereafter filled Meade with new vigor: He must depend upon himself now, and he suddenly felt capable of doing so. It was almost as if Reynolds' death had freed him.

Meade had seen at once the order in which things must be done. And he meant to do them.

He had shouted in to his chief of staff that Reynolds was dead and Hancock would go forward. After ordering young George to follow with his map, Meade had galloped off with only one alert aide beside him, leaving his escort of wellborn Philadelphians scrambling for the glade where their horses were tethered.

"Win," Meade said, "you'll take command at Gettysburg. As soon as you can get there. Your authority on the field will be absolute. Absolute, mind you. You will command in my name any troops that reach you. Only Slocum will rank you, once he arrives." Meade paused. "I have to keep my headquarters here through the

day, I see no alternative. By night, we'll know whether I should join you, or if it's wiser to pull back to better ground."

It was more than Hancock had expected. Instead of a chance to land in the fight, the fight had landed on him. At first, he was flummoxed. Then he said, "Howard's senior to me. So is Sickles, if he gets there first. They may buck."

"And I'm damned well senior to both of them," Meade snapped. "I've been empowered to make any changes I see fit."

Hancock looked both eager for the task and skeptical of the army commander's authority.

Meade reached for his coat's inside pocket and produced the letter he kept close on his person. Halleck as general-in-chief and Stanton, the secretary of war, had given him the authority he now claimed. The president would sustain his decisions on officer appointments.

"Well, those two sonsofbitches won't be tickled," Hancock said. The man had a soldier's heart, but a sailor's mouth. *Not* a true Philadelphian. "Especially Dan."

"Sickles will do as he's told, or he can take himself back to the lobby." Meade considered the generals with whom he was cursed. "Howard will be glad to hand you the responsibility. And if you do well, he'll be glad to claim credit afterward. Damn it, Win . . . I need you to get there as fast as you can go. If you think the ground and our position is better than Pipe Creek would be, if Gettysburg is the place to fight, advise me and I'll order up the entire army."

Hancock thought about that. "So . . . I'm to choose?"

"You're to advise me. The decision will be mine. If it's the wrong decision, it will rest on my head, not yours."

"I didn't mean it that way."

"It doesn't matter how you meant it. There's no allowance for personal feelings now, including mine. We're in a pinch, with John Reynolds gone. God knows what Howard's gotten up to in the meantime. Nor will Doubleday do for First Corps. We can only hope the division commanders act well on their own." Meade's thoughts turned brutal. "The wrong men get killed, Win."

Big, stout, and as impressive as man-flesh could be, Hancock nodded his head, then took off his slouch hat and wiped his forehead.

"I'll have to put Caldwell in command of my corps," he said.

"No," Meade told him. "I want Gibbon."

"Caldwell's senior."

"And Gibbon's the better man. For God's sake, Win . . . Caldwell's pride doesn't matter now. Blame me, when you tell him. I don't give a damn who likes me and who doesn't."

"Gibbon, then."

"And get this corps ready to march again. Even if Gettysburg isn't the place for a battle, I don't want Lee gobbling us piecemeal. If we must withdraw, I intend to execute a careful retrograde, not a bloody damned rout." He turned toward his son, who waited past a cluster of just erected headquarters tents, chatting with the captain of Meade's bodyguard. "George," Meade called with a wave, "bring over the map."

His son dashed forward, bearing a roll wrapped in oiled cloth.

"Win, I haven't got a decent map to give you. This is the best I have. It's the only one of any use, and it isn't much."

Hancock calculated for a moment, then said, "I'll take an ambulance forward. I can study the map and write orders for Gibbon and the corps while I'm under way. The horses can trail. I'll mount and ride the rest of the way, once I've got things gripped."

Meade considered the soldierly figure before him, broad of girth but well able to carry it off. Hancock was almost as handsome as John Reynolds, and even more eager to join the fray.

That last thought brought Meade up short.

"If you want to go up in an ambulance, I don't care," he told Hancock. "Just don't come back in one."

Colonel Krzyzanowski longed for a mug of cool beer. As he sat astride his horse, flanked by the war-shrunken regiments of his brigade, he watched the empty fields before him and slipped into a reverie. The war was long over and he was a prosperous man. His soldiers gathered to honor him at a grand reunion, where they celebrated the exploits of their youth. It was a daydream to which he often fled, and the party was always held in a German *Bierkeller,* the songs ever those his Germans sang in camp, melodies less antic and yet less mournful than the songs of his Polish childhood. A mug of beer would have been welcome in the cloudless afternoon.

Confederate guns had appeared on a hill to the left, enfilading the Eleventh Corps' drawn-up divisions until answering batteries rolled up and responded. Then there had been an ill-managed attack below the same hill, an odd sort of stumbling forward by men in gray that had met with a sharp repulse. Some of von Amsberg's men had been drawn into the fight and seemed to have won through. Firing lingered on well to the left, but did not sound especially threatening . . . although Krzyzanowski understood that what a man could not see for himself was not to be trusted.

Except for enduring the brief artillery bombardment, his own brigade had not been engaged and the tedium of waiting had returned. Krzyzanowski did not doubt that more Rebels were out there, some of them to his front, marching or already mustering beyond the fringes of trees, hidden by the low ridges and marshy swales. Streams cut the land, unseen until you blundered into them, as he had noted on the brigade's march north. The landscape could be an enemy in itself, good for a bad surprise.

While he believed that he sensed an enemy presence not yet visible, he knew, too, that he was cursed with an imagination common to his old countrymen, ever afflicted with visions of misfortune. Understandable, of course, given how often misfortune had been Poland's lot. But battles went to those who kept their heads. So he watched, and waited, suppressing emotion, but reasoning that there had to be a Confederate force before them, or the Rebels to the west would have withdrawn after the beating they'd taken that morning. Fond of the theater, Krzyzanowski doubted that he was attending a one-act play.

Then he saw a thing that shocked and appalled him. Right flank and forward, at least one brigade of Barlow's division had begun to move. Heading away from the rest of the Union line. Barlow's skirmishers had engaged stray Rebs on a rise far in front of their lines, but the annoyance didn't merit such a response. Yet, there it was: Barlow's entire division seemed to be shifting forward and right. Aides rode across the fields to post as guides, and batteries rattled forward, all shouts, whips, and hooves. Passing their rifles to comrades, soldiers dashed ahead to tear down fences. Regiments swept past a burning house at a run. Barlow's intent seemed to be to re-anchor his defense upon that knoll.

It was madness. A fool could see it. Reduced to two divisions on the battle line, with von Steinwehr held in reserve behind the town, the Eleventh Corps was already spread thin. Straining to cover the northern approaches to the town—a fan of roads—the corps also had to hold fast to the flank of the First Corps, whose battered divisions held the western ridge. Barlow was being an ass, unhinging the entire defense and begging the Rebels to flank him. Beyond Barlow's right, there were only a few Union cavalrymen. Now the corps' center began to break open as well.

With eyes inherited from centuries of soldiers, Krzyzanowski understood Barlow's thinking, faulty though it was. It was the sort of decision a well-meaning captain might make. Possessed of more pride than judgment, and scornful of experienced German officers, Barlow was a man whose view of the universe reached no further than his own division. The bump of earth toward which his troops were advancing might have served as an artillery platform for an enemy attacking him. Taking it gave Barlow high ground of his own, so moving forward seemed the obvious thing to do. Obvious, and blind to the greater purposes of the army and the day. The movement was amateurish. Selfish. *Stupid.*

The Polish colonel touched his horse with the edge of his boot heels, gently and just right. The animal understood him and didn't need the application of spurs. At a canter, the white horse carried him over the field, heading toward General Schimmelpfennig, who had taken the division after General Schurz moved up to lead the corps. Even before Krzyzanowski's men had fired a shot, there had been a plentitude of confusion, as General Howard took overall command of the field on Reynolds' death.

Krzyzanowski had been sorry to hear that Reynolds had fallen. The man had a fine reputation throughout the army. But such events were the stuff of war, and mourning must wait on battle. He was more concerned about the living Oliver O. Howard's role as the senior man present now, although the Virgin alone knew where he was. He had ridden past perhaps an hour before, and that was the last the Eleventh Corps had seen of him. Was he back on the graveyard hill behind the town? Where he might not see Barlow's folly? Did the man, in fact, command anything?

From Krzyzanowski's sister brigade, Colonel von Amsberg had

also ridden up to confer with Schimmelpfennig. With at least a regiment already engaged, von Amsberg gleamed with sweat, but his uniform remained in perfect order. The two were speaking German, hotly, as Krzyzanowski joined them.

"Der verdammte Arschloch!" Schimmelpfennig bellowed. *"Dieser Englische Scheisskerl! Gassen laufen soll er! Was macht der Idiot?"*

The general was not happy with his fellow division commander.

"We're in the shit now," von Amsberg told Krzyzanowski. "That supercilious horse's ass is exposing both his flanks. He's breaking the whole damned line." His horse bucked slightly and von Amsberg tightened his grip on the reins. "This is going to be one bloody mess."

As Barlow's lead regiments reached their forward positions, small-arms fire erupted on the far right.

"Move your brigade up to where you can support the blasted fool, if he needs help," Schimmelpfennig barked at Krzyzanowski. "Then wait for my order."

Lee sat astride his horse, watching the battle dwindle toward failure. Those people still held the formidable ridge that stretched across his front, and flanking efforts had failed. He could not see beyond the high ground where the blue line had been refused, but reports were not encouraging. It was a bad day that cried out for redemption.

Not one of the staff officers present said a word to him and they kept a broad silence even among themselves, ears cocked to the ebb and flow of war. Lee had masked his anger as best he could, commanding himself to keep his voice even and his facial features placid. But the men who knew him felt his cutting mood.

He was furious with Harry Heth, who had behaved impetuously, as a mere captain hungry for glory. No matter the man's excuses and explanations, the fact was that Heth had ignored his orders not to bring on an engagement. When Lee had arrived on the ridge, only to find that two brigades had been shattered, his human impulse had been to admonish Heth severely. But a commanding general had to be more than human. And Harry was a good man, gallant and brave, a wellborn Virginian. It would not have done to upbraid him in front of others.

Still, it had been a struggle to show restraint. Oblivious to Lee's mood, Heth had pestered him for permission to send in his un-committed brigades, those of Pettigrew and Brockenbrough. Heth was anxious to redeem himself after the morning's debacle. But the army did not exist for personal use. When Hill failed to deny Heth's request himself, Lee had told Heth directly that there would be no attack until he knew more of the enemy.

Hovering in the background, young Pettigrew had looked crushed when Lee spurned the proposed attack. Although not a Virginian, the man had good bloodlines and behaved with proper form. Pettigrew led the army's largest brigade, and Lee expected him to acquit himself handsomely when the time came.

But the time had not yet come.

The morning's bleak defeat bit into Lee. His temper flared as he thought about it anew. He had arrived on the ridge only after pass-ing a widening stream of wounded, and those men had been de-jected, not defiant. Some wounded men would always claim the worst had befallen the army, of course, but when the day ran well, others capable of speech would call out as he passed that the Yankees were "a-running," or that "we're pushin' 'em, General Lee, we'll whip 'em for you." But those men walking rearward in the rising heat had whipped no one. They had been whipped themselves.

It rankled.

Still, the urge to regain the advantage was insufficient reason to stoop to folly. Lee had to be patient for an impatient army, hard though it was. Fresh hope had flared, as word came from Rodes and Ewell that they were approaching from the north, with Early near. But Rodes' initial assault, visible at a distance through the smoke, seemed to have been blunted.

It was not a good day.

And where on earth was Stuart? Lee had never needed his eyes and ears as much as he felt the need now. Where could the fellow be? Had he lost his senses? Was Longstreet right that the man had grown vanity-addled, seeking an exploit to cancel Brandy Station? Never had a trusted officer let him down so badly, with the poten-tial for such consequences for the army.

It was vital, of course, to conceal the depth of his concern from

those about him. The army must not know how blind he felt, but must see him in full confidence.

Lee stiffened his perfect posture in the saddle.

He wished to confer with Hill, but could not spot the man now. If an opportunity did arise to reverse the day's defeat, Hill must be ready to seize it. Lee wished to make clear, though, that nothing more would be done without his order. There had been blunders enough. The army's reputation must not be further tarnished, those people allowed no additional cause for confidence.

A captain approached on foot, bearing items wrapped in cheese-cloth. He was a new man on the staff and, to Lee's dismay, the fellow's name had fled him.

"Will you take some refreshment, General Lee?" The captain looked up expectantly.

Lee waved him away. "This is not the time." He caught another officer signaling the captain to take himself off. Which the fellow soon did.

What was Rodes about up there? Was it going to be another piecemeal slaughter on the far end of the ridge? Couldn't Ewell control his corps? Was there a single capable general on the field? It burned in Lee that, according to reports, General Archer had gotten himself captured. *That* would be a fair prize for those people. Better had Archer died a worthy death.

Where had Hill gotten to? He wanted to speak with Hill.

Coat patched charcoal with sweat, Harry Heth rode up. He wore a hat clearly too large for him, padded out with rags or the like, and Lee felt compelled to speak of it. Generals could not afford to appear as buffoons.

But that, too, must wait. For a private moment.

Gasping, as if his horse had ridden him, Heth said, "Rodes is heavily engaged, sir. Had I better not attack?"

"No, General Heth," Lee told him. "Must I repeat that I am unwilling to bring on a general engagement today?"

"But Rodes, sir? His attack will fail if he goes unsupported."

Lee's demeanor turned chilly enough to freeze the afternoon. His expression did not alter, although his color warmed. In a steadied voice, he said, "I have given you my decision, General Heth.

Longstreet is not up. For all we know, those people may have their entire army present. Good day, sir."

Hangdog, Heth took himself off.

Better, Lee consoled himself, to have men too enthused about giving battle than men who would hold back. Yet, so much had been lost in so few months. Men meant to command divisions had risen to lead corps because they were the best of those who remained. Others, such as Harry Heth, who led brigades to splendid effect, were elevated to fill divisional commands before they were fully ready. Colonels who had not yet completed the school of the regiment had to take brigades into battle. And Jackson was gone, the greatest loss of all.

Longstreet was strong and dependable, but he did not see that the army's strength was its valor, the shock of its attack. The Army of Northern Virginia, *his* army, could not fight too often or too long on the defensive. It must strike, impressing its will upon those people. It was a sword, not a shield.

Yes, blood would be spilled in pressed attacks. Did Longstreet think him such a fool as not to understand that? Lee harked back to Mexico, to the bloodshed at Molino del Rey. Men had drawn the wrong lesson, too focused on that engagement's casualties and unable to grasp its subsequent effects. What Lee had noted was how those hours of ferocity had eased the assault on Chapultepec and the battle for the causeways. That sacrifice of American lives made the Mexicans lose heart.

The cost of stunning an enemy was immediate, but the dividends endured. Why did Longstreet refuse to understand that?

The best of the men left to Lee, Longstreet had sulked of late. So determined was he to force Meade to attack first that Lee was weary of hearing it. Yes, if the situation was propitious, Lee would take the defensive. But if those people seemed likelier to yield to a sharp attack pressed home, he would deliver it. Longstreet made too high an ideal of Fredericksburg. Not every one of those people would be as inept as Burnside. Meade would not make such errors.

The trick to beating George Meade, Lee judged, would be to hit him very hard and so swiftly that the need to make quick decisions would overwhelm him. Meade would be attentive to details, so he would have to suffer an avalanche of them on the field of

battle. An engineer understood an engineer, after all. He needed to make Meade think too much and do too little when every moment mattered. Unbalance him, then keep him off balance. Hit him hard, and keep hitting. Prevent him from gripping the situation and turning it. That would be the way to defeat George Meade.

And when you beat the man, you beat the army.

For all that, their first encounter had not been promising, thanks to Heth's blunders. While Hill, incommoded, had lingered in the rear. It scorched Lee's pride to recall how he had indulged them. An excursion for shoes, indeed. A lark and a folly. . . .

Yet, those fateful shoes had mattered enough to the men who had marched off to get them. What was *his* merit, finally, as a general at the head of a shoeless army? If he could not clothe these men who did all he bid them? After all, the Duke of Marlborough's victories had been those of a quartermaster. Still a mere John Churchill, he had seen to it that new shoes awaited his soldiers along his line of march. But Lee had men who had gone without shoes for months. At Chancellorsville, he had hoped for a Blenheim, but ended with a gory Malplaquet.

Each time Lee visited Richmond, he heard the Confederacy creak a bit more loudly. Despite the resolute parties—which he declined to visit, pleading duty—he detected a growing hollowness as well. The mistress of the grandest house no longer served the delicacies that, last year, had been essential, and mourning garments robbed the streets of color. For his part, President Davis grew unreasonable . . . although Lee would never have breathed it to any man.

And his army walked barefoot.

A mighty victory was needed. Not a mere stab, but a deathblow. Only then would there be hope of English intercession, even were it merely to impose peace. The spirit of the North had to be crushed along with its army. Those people had to be brought, at last, to reason.

One smashing victory now might save it all.

A seasoned battlefield hunter, Lee's senses quickened. He saw before he saw. Rising in the saddle, he peered northeast. There was value in Rodes' actions, after all. In the abrupt ways of battle, matters had turned. Lee sensed it as much as observed it. Rodes was

properly at them, taking ground. A corner of the blue line was dissolving.

Now. Now was the time to hit them.

Heth had seen it, too. He rode hard toward Lee.

Lee held up his hand: *A moment yet.*

Hill appeared, as if summoned.

Lee studied the far field a swallow longer, then turned to Powell Hill. Careful of the chain of command, he said, "I believe the time has come for General Heth's division to go in, if you would order it."

SEVEN

July 1, Midafternoon

The soldiers of the 26th North Carolina stood at attention in two long ranks behind the crest of the ridge. Blake's company had been assigned to the second line, right of center, giving the men a splendid view as Pettigrew's and Brockenbrough's brigades formed for the attack. No enlisted man spoke now, not even Cobb, and the Union cannon on the far height had gone silent. The stillness was thick as raw cotton.

File closers dressed the lines until they were perfect enough for a parade ground. Lieutenant Colonel Lane waited just behind the regiment's right wing, where Blake could sense his reassuring presence. Colonel Burgwyn, who had dismounted for the charge, impulsively leapt on his horse again and rode down the line, sash trailing as he called out encouragement to his men.

Blake felt the raw, taut life of the soldiers near him: Cobb plank-thin and small . . . Peachum short, too, but barrel-chested over his starvation haunches . . . gaunt Jack Ireton with his corporal's stripes and gambler's eyes . . . and the beef-slab Bunyan twins, a human wall. Plagued with freckles and moles, red-haired Tam McMinn was the tallest among them. He stood shoulder to shoulder with Hugh Gordon, who looked part Cherokee, but insisted he wasn't. Pike Gray would have preferred to be forward with the skirmishers—he liked the independence of the work—but had accepted his lot, standing straight as a well-made post between Hugh and Methuselah-bearded Ollie Wright. Blake wondered, with a calmness that teased his conscience, who among them would die or fall wounded and maimed.

The sun gilded the stillness. A faint breeze touched the colors,

but could not stir them. Their own cannon ceased bombarding the opposite ridge.

Colonel Burgwyn dismounted again and sent his horse to the rear. The boy-colonel looked striking, almost beautiful, as he strode through the regiment's ranks. His young face was newly shaven, his mustache pomaded. Blake waited for a curse from Cobb, but it did not come this time.

"Colors, forward!" The command rolled down along the line of regiments. The 26th's color guard stepped out, halting where all the men of the front rank could see it.

"Load!" The order rippled outward from the vicinity of the pike and General Pettigrew, but Burgwyn's men already had done that.

"Fix bayonets!" Thousands of men in two brigades scraped metal over metal. The sound was of myriad whetstones briefly worked.

"Shoulder . . . arms!" The second word, bellowed by every officer down to captain, came out "hahhhms."

Off to the left, in Brockenbrough's brigade, a drum began beating. The 26th had sent its musicians to the rear.

Two birds rose from a thicket and raced off.

The men waited again, wet of forehead beneath their kepis and brimmed hats. Feeling the uncompromising hardness of rifled muskets against gray wool and flesh, they knew what the next command would be.

"What are they waiting for?" James Bunyan asked, voice barely a murmur.

No one answered him.

The next round of commands came not from their officers, but from the rear, upsetting the order of things. Pender's men were forming up to follow them. To come forward over their bodies and finish the job.

A fly settled on Blake's cheek. He tried to shoo it by wincing, but the creature would not leave him. In a black moment, he imagined that it last had rested on a corpse, perhaps down in the streambed. Still he did not raise a hand to swat it.

Worse things waited than flies.

He felt a touch of James Bunyan's impatience now. Why, indeed, were they waiting? Blake itched to get into the fight, to end this infernal delay and get to where he could become fully himself again,

to pass beyond the need for further commands from other men, to thrive, however briefly, in the whirlwind.

The drumming on the left flank ceased. And then the great command came down from some mortal god, echoed by General Pettigrew and his fellow brigadier, then by their regimental colonels and, in turn, by the captains:

"Divi-*zhunnn!*"

"Bri-*gade!*"

"*Reg*-iment!"

"Compan-*eee!*"

"For'*erd!*"

"For'*rud!*"

"For'*id!*"

"For'*ward!*"

"March!"

The drumming started up again as the color guards and the two endless ranks stepped toward the crest of the ridge. The skirmishers moved out with their weapons up and ready, but all those behind them marched with their rifles shouldered, as if passing in review. Two long fences of bayonets shone high.

"Close up, close up!" The voice was overeager. The men did not need to be badgered now. That would come later.

The second line followed the first at a hundred paces and Blake's heart stirred at the spectacle. The first rank passed through a thicket of trees, parted around a battery, then came together again, dressing on the colors. Beyond the flat of the ridgetop, a split-rail fence marked property. The line broke to scramble over it, knocking down rails and re-forming at the quick. Beyond lay a long, declining slope sown with oats. Bayonets flashing above them, the men in the first rank descended toward the creek.

The color bearer of the 26th waved his blood-red flag, then stilled it again. Thousands of footfalls shushed through ripening grain. Swarms of insects rose from the stalks as boots, worn shoes, and bare feet trampled their world. With the sun passed behind him, Blake could see the Yankees even more clearly than in the morning, before Colonel Burgwyn moved the regiment behind the ridgetop. There were plenty of Federals in a high field to the left by a house and barn, but the blue-bellies who awaited the 26th remained

partly concealed by the grove that reached down to the thickets and brush of the streambed. No great expanse, the field down which the men from North Carolina marched seemed endless.

It surprised Blake that the Yankee artillery didn't open up. No sooner had the thought reached him than he heard the roar of guns. Blessedly, there were no cannon posted straight ahead of the 26th North Carolina. Their ranks went untouched, even as other regiments growled for revenge as they suffered.

Blake and his men scrambled over the fence's remains and quickly rejoined their line. Lieutenant Colonel Lane's booming voice ordered the second rank to resume the advance.

And then, with both lines still descending through the oats, Colonel Burgwyn's voice passed on a command shouted down from brigade:

"Charge!"

The soldiers let go a piercing Rebel yell, all yips and wailing cries, nightmare voices of banshees keening in Ireland's hills and misty creatures warning intruders in Scotland's wildest glens. Wonderful and terrifying, their noise propelled them forward.

No man ran, but the pace quickened sufficiently for calls to ring out: "Close up, close up, dress on your company, dress on the colors, close up!"

Staring down through the regiment's first rank, Blake fixed on the chest-high growth that blocked the way to the streambed, then barricaded the far bank below the enemy.

That's where we'll get it, he thought. *They won't be able to hold off firing before that, but that's where they'll really give it to us. While we're fussing on through those thickets. And down in that creek.*

A soldier broke from the front rank, running forward. A Company F man, Blake judged by his position. The soldier stopped amid grain that brushed his crotch, leveled his rifle, and fired toward the Yankees.

The half-hidden Federals ignored him.

Those Black Hats, Blake thought. *They've been around the courthouse square in a buggy a time or two. They know their business. They'll wait.*

But Blake was at least half-wrong. The front line had taken but another dozen steps when a snake of flame flashed from the woods

beyond the stream. The report of the volley followed in a trimmed second.

The range was long, but a few men crumpled along the forward rank. Blake glimpsed a gray-clad corpse in the oats, almost underfoot, a wide-eyed boy killed that morning. Flies rose from his face as the soldiers approached, but one stubborn insect clung to a bloodied ear.

Cobb broke out of the line just long enough to kick the corpse's head with perfect accuracy, crushing the bug with the rock-hard ball of his foot.

"Do the same for me, I expect," he said.

"Halt!" Colonel Burgwyn cried. The front rank stopped at a step's delay. Lieutenant Colonel Lane held up the second line.

"Colors, six steps to the rear! First rank, ready! Aim! *Fire!*"

The effects of the volley disappeared into the woodline across the creek. Without waiting for the command, the men reloaded.

"Colors, forward!" Burgwyn cried. "Regiment, shoulder arms! Forward at a quickstep!"

A Yankee volley exploded from the cover of the trees. A few more men went down. But the men in gray and blue were not killing close. Yet.

Roughening their alignment as they hastened over the morning's strew of dead and sun-punished wounded, the men in the front rank neared the streambed thickets.

The Yankees gave them another volley.

This time, the 26th was in range. All along the first line, men contorted, performers at Death's circus. Some crumpled in upon themselves, clutching lead gifts to their bosoms, while others raised arms heavenward. A few just dropped, sacks of flour kicked from a wagon.

"Close up, close up! Dress on the colors!" The voices calling out grew urgent now.

The men up ahead shoved their way into the thorns and wild shrubs blocking their way. Another volley punched into the first rank as it struggled toward the creek.

The colors fell. A moment later, they rose again. The new bearer waved them with an angry passion. Clustering together, the crush of men in the brambles made perfect targets. Without slowing the

second rank to maintain the proper distance, Lieutenant Colonel Lane dashed forward to help Burgwyn and Major Jones put things to right.

As Blake and his men hastened forward, watching the butchery unfold before them, Yankee artillery opened an enfilading fire from the high ground near the pike. It gashed through men caught in the thicket. Bodies tumbled, burst, dissolved. Spraying blood wildly, limbs leapt into the air.

"Close up, close up!"

"Git through there, damn you!"

"Yea, though I walk . . ."

"Look what they done to me . . . Lordy, look at my legs!"

"Out of my way, you crawling piece of nigger-shit."

"Dress on the colors, men, dress on the colors."

"Oh, my God . . . oh, my good God . . ."

The thicket looked like a henhouse after a vixen went through it. Only feathers were lacking.

Beside Blake, the mortified voice of James Bunyan asked, "We got to go through that?"

"Hope you done said your prayers last night," Cobb told him.

"Shut up, Cobb," Peachum said. His voice arrived in a shout.

"Just keep moving," Blake ordered. He needed to hear his own voice, to know it was ready and strong. No one was shirking. Every soldier had ceased to exist for himself alone and belonged to a greater creature that tugged him forward. Even James Bunyan did not falter a step.

The colors dropped again, only to rise like the dead on the Day of Judgment. Closer to hand, Lieutenant Devereaux flashed his sword, imitating the regiment's captains. To Blake, the boy looked scared somehow, yet he got out in front of the line as if he were downright impatient to get at the Yankees.

The Federal cannon let loose on the second line as it neared the briars. Another volley leapt out of the trees beyond the stream.

Ollie Wright cried out. The shocked sound carried no intelligible words. He dropped his rifle and ran forward, waving an arm to hail an invisible friend. Red wet pulsed through gray cloth below his shoulders. A lot of blood had burst out of him at once, like a strung hog cut open wrong.

Wright collapsed before them. Pike Gray broke ranks to rush toward his friend, but Blake collared him. "Get back in line, Pike. He's gone."

"First of many." Cobb laughed.

The mood hardened. It was one thing when other men died, even those with faces you knew well enough to nod to as you went about your business. But Wright had been one of them.

Ahead, the slaughter in the brush continued as the Yankees fired at will. But Blake saw heads and shoulders disappearing willfully now, as men from the first rank leapt down into the creek's bed. Going forward, still going forward.

Colonel Burgwyn paused, waving his sword, trying to bring the companies back into line. His mouth moved, but the din was too great for Blake to hear him. Lieutenant Colonel Lane remained upright as well. He was shoving men forward through the underbrush, while barking at others as soldiers fell around him. The regiment was crowding together, converging toward the colors. Blake spotted Major Jones just in time to see him drop backward in a half-somersault. But the major got back on his feet and went stumbling about, patting himself for wounds. He looked whole, but stunned.

All bulk and black fury, Lane ran back toward the second rank, halting just before Blake and his men. Walking backward in front of them, he called, "You git on through them goddamned briars, hear? You just git the Hell on through 'em, and don't you stop."

His coat was porcupined with thorns and splashed with other men's blood.

Then they were in the underbrush amid a madness of bodies. Agonized cries rose from underfoot. Nature's bayonets, long thorns ripped flesh. Pike Gray paused to fire, taking revenge on all the world.

"Keep on going," Blake screamed at him. "You can't hit a thing from here."

Instead, something hit Pike as he lowered his rifle. A dark comet, a piece of shrapnel or solid shot, streaked past Blake's snout so close he felt hot wind. It disintegrated Pike's head in a cloud of blood. For a moment, the headless body wiggled like a drunk whore dancing. White bone poked the sky between the monstrosity's shoulders. Then the ruined meat just folded up.

"Keep going," Blake yelled. Looking around him, he saw that both of the Bunyan twins were with him, stink near. Beyond them, Tam McMinn towered above the shrubbery, but somehow had managed to bloody his face with scratches.

Blake glimpsed Lieutenant Devereaux in the maelstrom, only to see the boy yank himself down in the brush, a child playing hide-and-go-seek. Blake was unmoved, didn't much care if the officer was just plain quitting or if he'd been hit. He had not expected much beyond tomfoolery from the lieutenant, and the hard thought crossed his mind that things might go better without him.

The colors fell by the streambed. Again, unseen hands raised them.

"Dress on the colors, rally on the colors!" Blake saw Colonel Burgwyn on the far bank, miraculously untouched but for muddied boots, waving men up from the creek. He held his sword in one hand, a pistol in the other.

Slopped and bloodied, men dashed past the colonel, anxious to gain good footing on solid ground. Beside Burgwyn, a soldier clutched his neck and tumbled backward into the water.

Order reemerged before Blake's eyes, as the remnants of the first rank formed up in the thinned-out brush and saplings across the creek.

But men seemed to fall as fast as they got into line. It was pure murder.

Thorns tore at Blake, but he thrust his body onward. He could not have spent a full minute among the brush and briars, but it seemed to have been hours. All through the trial, he kept watch on the men given into his charge, so much so that he stepped smack into the bowels of a human carcass.

He pulled back his shoe lightning fast, as if he had stepped on a rattler. But the slime of man-guts wet right through to his skin. Looking down, he recognized the dead soldier's face: one of the color guard.

Then Blake and his men were down in the creekbed, slipping from the muddy bank and splashing into the mild current, struggling to keep their footing on round, wet rocks. Blake welcomed the water as it washed over his ankles and licked his calves, scouring off the grease of another man's death.

Tam McMinn paused in midstream, methodically raising his weapon, seeking a target above him, scanning the trees. He took his time, as if tracking lazy squirrels. Perhaps the feel of the water had pleased him too much, the caressing womanness of it, the chill a seduction, and he just did not mean to go on.

The man's unearthly stillness announced madness.

"Tam!" Blake shrieked. Too late. The tall man convulsed and fell to his knees, dropping his rifle, bewildered.

The stricken man mouthed words. Astonished that his life had come to this. Then he puked blood and dropped facedown in the water.

"Go! Go, damn it! Get on up there! Climb up," Blake hollered. His men did what he ordered, clambering up the slick bank. Seconds along the streambed had slowed to hours.

Demonically agile, Cobb used his rifle's butt to vault himself up. Gaining firm ground first, he howled like a wolf.

Blake scrambled up wet clay and into more briars. But the band of underbrush was narrower on this side. The trees, with their hope of cover, loomed ahead.

He could not see the colors or Colonel Burgwyn now. Smoke pestered his attempts to peer into the grove. Men in gray ghosted before him. At times, he believed he saw figures in blue a short pitch up the slope. But the powder clouds had grown thick enough to turn men into phantoms.

Lieutenant Colonel Lane materialized from the man-made mist, cursing at everyone to get on up the hill and into ranks. Blake could not see a line, but trusted that it was there. Beside him, Cobb yipped with glee as he dashed forward.

The dead, the wounded. They lay so thick it seemed impossible that anything much was left over from the regiment. Yet, all around Blake, gray-clad soldiers hurried forward. Some of them screamed in naked anger as they struggled through the last briars and into the trees, but others were silent, already resigned to the grave.

The Bunyans were with him. And Cobb, grinning and howling, a fugitive from an asylum. Hugh Gordon. Jack Ireton. Somehow they held together. Then they found themselves on a ragged firing line that melded the survivors of the first rank and second together. The wasp-zip of bullets passed impossibly close.

Men had countless ways of reacting to a bullet's strike, all of it part of a crazy dance, black witchery.

Blake could see the Yankee line now. Up the slope, between the trees. The Black Hats were shooting down at them, potting vermin. Some of the men in blue taunted and cursed their antagonists. Blake aimed and fired without conscious thought, seeking targets more quickly than the mind's knowing could follow. He believed he had brought a man down, but anyone on the line could have made the shot. Beside him, big James Bunyan snapped his ramrod in two and stood staring at it, as if no stranger event had occurred since Creation. Blake paused in reloading long enough to reach out and shake the boy hard.

"Get one from a dead man, damn you."

But James just stood there dumbly as his brother fired uphill by his side.

"Curse you, James Bunyan, you—"

A round entered the side of the boy's face and burst out the opposite cheek, expelling teeth, bone, pulp. James just stood there, dumbfounded, unsure of what had come over him, an ox whacked with a plank.

His brother saw that James had been hit and broke off his own reloading. Staring helplessly.

"You just keep on killing," Blake screamed at him. "I'll fix this."

But it couldn't be fixed. How could it be fixed? He wanted to slap the boy's ruined face, to force him to keep fighting, to reverse time, to make things be as he wanted them to be. There were too many men down now, James was needed.

Clubs thumping a sack, two more bullets entered James Bunyan. But he still did not go down. The wrecked jaw sought to move. Bovine eyes filled with tears, whether of pain or rage. He reached out his hands, expecting to cradle an infant. When he realized that he could not speak, he bleated like a baritone sheep and struck the air with his fists. All that in seconds.

"Nothing to be done." That was Cobb. Beside Blake. "Git back to killing yourself, Quaker."

A stream of blood had found its way through James Bunyan's ruined throat. It pulsed lazily. The boy reached for Blake and fell.

The line was moving. Forward. Up the hill. John Bunyan bel-

lowed, but did his duty and left his brother behind. It surprised Blake, who had expected John to quit the fight right there and cling to his brother.

A volley crashed through the trees. Wood splinters flew.

Regaining the firing line, Blake, Cobb, Bunyan, and Ireton mingled with men from another company, little more than a grab away from the colors. Hugh Gordon was missing and Blake had no idea what had become of him. What was left of the regiment unleashed another, wilder Rebel yell.

The blue line receded, stepping backward through the smoke. Leaving plenty of Yankee bodies on the ground, Black Hats scattered around them. Then the 26th's line stood at last among Federal corpses and the beseeching wounded of the other army.

The colors drooped, but did not fall, as a wounded man passed them on. Blake's ramrod was so slick with sweat he could hardly grip it to ram home a cartridge and ball. Cobb, too, struggled with his rifle. His hat was gone and his black madman's hair framed a face ghastly with pleasure.

"Volleys, give 'em volleys," a voice demanded. Blake thought it was Lieutenant Colonel Lane giving the command, but could not be sure. The noise engulfing the firing line was deafening. "Close up, and give 'em volleys. Rally on the colors."

Blake slipped on blood-greased bark and tumbled forward, landing on a dead Yankee. He got the full scent of the man—tobacco, sweat, and death—as his face scraped on bloody blue wool. A hand yanked him backward, upward. It belonged to Cobb.

"Don't you go quittin' on me now, Quaker." Grinning black-mouthed. Behind him, Jack Ireton wore a terrified look, as if Blake falling were the worst thing that could happen.

"Just slipped," Blake shouted above the rifle-spatter. "Get back in the line."

Other men had filled in the gaps between them and the regiment's flag.

Unbloodied, unstained, Colonel Burgwyn appeared beside them, an apparition from a better, cleaner world.

"Advance, men!" he cried. *"Advance!"* Then he was gone again.

The Yankees had re-formed farther up the hill. An organized volley stopped the 26th cold. For an eternity, two rough ranks

faced off, with barely ten yards between them. Each side fired as swiftly as its soldiers could reload. It seemed a miracle that any man, on either side, remained standing.

Lieutenant Colonel Lane replaced Burgwyn's presence among them.

"We're pushing them," he called out, "we're pushing them back! Git on up that sonofabitching hill!"

They edged forward. A few feet at a time. Over the Yankee dead. Adding their own casualties to the wastage.

Entering a cloud of smoke, Blake and his men found themselves enshrouded in a storybook spell. Separated from the world they knew. Blinded. Impossibly lost.

"Any man seen Colonel Burgwyn?" Lane's voice called through the miasma.

"I don't see shit."

"That you, Clarence?"

"Oh, Jesus! Mother! I'm hit!"

"He's over yonder, on the left somewheres."

"Keep on moving, damn you!"

"Advance! Forward, men!"

"Water, for the love of God!"

"I'm shot."

"Keep moving! Lookee! They're breaking!"

Emerging from the drift of smoke, Blake saw the Yankees all too close and with horrible clarity. The Federals weren't breaking. But they were pulling back, keeping the best order they could as they fired on the move, blue-clad men pitching forward on the slope, as if leaping at their enemies as they died.

Primitive. The word struck Blake, a mental bullet. *We're nothing but fancied-up animals, that's all we are.*

In a window of quiet, a matter of hardly a second, Blake heard men panting and crying. He imagined he could hear blood pumping from arteries, lungs bubbling, guts slithering down the hillside.

He and his men were near the colors again. An officer ran by, just behind the firing line—what remained of it—and ordered everyone to close on the banner.

The officer didn't belong to the regiment. He was a captain from the brigade staff, Blake believed. He had no place here, but

the fool was running right out ahead of their line of rifles, yelping like a boy devil. Near him, the colors fell again. The officer swooped down and lifted the shot-through flag above his head, delighted by life and everything in it. He waved the battle flag so madly Blake heard cloth snap. The idiot was daring the Yankees to shoot him.

They did. The captain bent over, clutching his abdomen. The flag slid from his hand and fell, then the officer dropped on the flag.

Another officer rushed forward. Despite the man's black-stained face and the pillows of smoke between them, Blake recognized Lieutenant Wilcox from Company H. He rolled the fallen staff officer from atop the flag and lifted the banner high. It was bloodied with dark patches now.

"Come on, men!" Wilcox yelled, so piercingly that the whole field must have heard him. He thrust the standard forward, climbing the hill. All those who remained alive and capable followed him.

Then Wilcox fell, too. Sliding to his knees, he released the flag to use his hands to search his wounded body.

Soldiers surged past the lieutenant. No one wanted to touch the flag now. Raising it was a death warrant, executed immediately. As for Blake, he was more interested in killing Yankees than in pretty gestures.

He fired into the blue line up the hillside, wonderfully satisfied to feel his rifle's kick against his shoulder. But as he paused to reload, he saw Colonel Burgwyn, sword held at waist level, running toward Wilcox and the discarded flag. As Blake fitted a fresh cap to his rifle, Burgwyn took up the flag in his left hand, lofting it. The staff had been shattered halfway down, so the colonel stretched to his full height to let the banner be seen. A sublime boy, he ran forward.

Blake heard Burgwyn cry, "Dress on the colors, men, dress on the colors! Tar Heels to me! Come on, boys!"

Blake thought the Yankees surely would bring him down. But Burgwyn paused abreast of Lieutenant Cureton, mouthing an unheard command. The lieutenant waved a private forward to take the flag from the regiment's commander.

Then Lieutenant Colonel Lane appeared, too. And things seemed all right. Lane and Burgwyn paused to exchange words. Blake

lifted his rifle, aimed into the blue mass, and fired. A man dropped at his shot.

But as he reached for another cartridge, he saw the new flag bearer stumble and fall. Blake looked toward Burgwyn, fearing the colonel would be mad enough to take up the banner again. But in that instant, Burgwyn jerked and wheeled about, drunk at a country dance.

He fell. Lane knelt beside him.

And Blake heard Cobb's laughter.

"Move fast, Quaker, if you want them boots."

Turning to knock Cobb down, Blake saw Jack Ireton seated on the ground, playing with the red, white, and gray spewings of his belly the way a child plays with a wonderful new toy.

Perhaps it was the sight of the colonel falling. Or maybe it was his recognition of the hard death awaiting Jack Ireton. But Blake felt a new fury. And Cobb wasn't target enough for it. Bloody-faced and merry as a farm boy at the fair, Cobb was fighting the war by his own rules. Blake decided to let the devil be.

"Come on," Blake called to the two men who remained by him. And they went forward again, Blake, black Cobb, and empty-faced John Bunyan.

The old verse, queerly applicable, leapt to his mind, a substitute for thought: "Surely, I come quickly . . ."

That's right, Billy Yank. I'm coming for you. Quickly.

Lieutenant Colonel Lane stormed by, his anger borrowed from Kings or perhaps Joshua, nothing New Testament about it. "We're going to give them sonsofbitches the bayonet," he shouted. "Shoot 'em in their bastard guts and give 'em the damned bayonet."

The tattered clans of the regiment's companies began to howl. The shredded line straightened remarkably, the men wild as pent-up hounds about to be loosed on their quarry.

Sharp to the left, two lieutenants, Cureton and Blair, were practically wrestling over who would bear the flag next. In charge of the regiment now, Lieutenant Colonel Lane descended upon them.

He tore the flag from Blair's grip, speaking words no one but the two lieutenants could hear. And Lane dashed forward himself, flaunting the short-staved banner.

For an unearthly moment, Blake saw Lane rimmed by sun-

light, as if he had been chosen for a miracle. The smoke had concealed how near they had come to the far edge of the wood, to the top of the ridge, to what must pass for victory. They were almost there.

Waving the broken flagstaff, Lane bellowed:

"Twenty-sixth! Follow me!"

Fewer than a hundred men remained to drive home the attack. But hundreds more, ghosts now, filled out their ranks. A last, triumphant Rebel yell soared above torn treetops.

The Yankees were pulling back again, abandoning the grove. This time, their order was broken. They stumbled rearward in huddled groups, pausing to fire, outraged at being bested. But others in blue just ran now—not many, but enough to distract their remaining officers from the fight. Sergeants shouted, mouths wide, but their voices could not compete with the tumult of war.

Blake rushed forward, bayonet ready for man-flesh. Cobb kept up to his left, John Bunyan to his right. The three of them, and dozens more, surged toward the crest of the ridge, howling like demons.

Surely, I come quickly . . . The words became a chant inside Blake's head, inextinguishable, resounding. *Quickly . . . I come quickly . . . new heavens, and a new earth . . . quickly . . . I come . . . quickly . . .*

They have no place in me, Blake told himself, attempting to resist. *These words are not my own. Mine own. Thou, thee. Quaker talk.*

Surely, I come quickly . . .

You are your father's son. Reciting scripture blasphemously in your drunkenness. But you are drunk on blood . . .

Led by Lieutenant Colonel Lane, they burst from the trees into the dirty sunlight of the battlefield. Even now, not all of the Yankees were ready to quit, but anyone could see that their defense was finished. Now it was just about stubbornness and spite.

Lane turned to his ruined regiment, shouting, "Come on, boys! Come on!"

A Yankee bullet caught him in the mouth.

Blake's heart plummeted, even as hatred quickened him body and soul, lawless, delicious.

"Sumbitch," Cobb cried, "those sumbitches." It was as much emotion as he had ever shown.

Captain Brewer of Company E, one of the last officers still on his feet, took up the bloodied banner.

He did not have to shout to rally the men. They rushed after him screaming and howling. They were attacking the Yankee army with fewer men than the regiment's smallest company had counted an hour before.

Still beside him, John Bunyan seemed unaware that a bullet or sliver of shrapnel had scraped his scalp, painting the left side of his head and neck crimson.

Flesh wound, Blake decided. *Or the boy wouldn't be standing. Head wounds are always bloody. Means nothing, most like.*

Blake needed someone other than Cobb to survive with him.

He fired his rifle into the chest of a Yankee who had appeared not five feet in front of him. Too late, Blake realized that the man wanted to surrender.

Didn't matter, anyway. Didn't matter.

Surely, I come quickly . . .

But then, as at a command, all quickness left him. A collective will pulled up the attack's survivors atop the ridge, stopping them among clots of contorted bodies garbed in blue. The men still alive from the 26th North Carolina were spent and done, there was nothing left in them. If the Yankees had pushed back now, they might have redeemed themselves.

But the Black Hats continued to fall back, small clusters of them, moving down through a swale and carrying off those of their wounded who could limp along or cling to a tent-mate's back. They were drawing off toward a Yankee battery and more troops formed up on a ridge at the edge of the town.

We can't, Blake thought. *We just can't go over there. Too many of them. We just can't.*

A mighty, magnificent cry broke just to his rear. The Rebel yell. For an instant, Blake went chill with the thought that it really was the ghosts of the regiment's fallen.

Instead, it was the men of Pender's division, fresh as daisies, coming up behind them to finish the charge.

Blake sat down on the ground. Only by propping himself up with his rifle could he stop himself from pitching out flat. He did not

remember deciding to sit down. He had just done it. Men in gray and various browns swarmed past him.

"God awmighty," a fellow sergeant told him as he passed by, "you boys *done* something. God awmighty, you sure done something. . . ."

Then the first line of Pender's men went down into the swale. Soon, the second line passed. The men cheered the milling survivors of the 26th and their ruined flag.

Somewhere up ahead, cannon opened again. But it no longer mattered.

Blake sat. Smeared with blood and pus, Cobb had taken a place beside him. Befuddled and gory, John Bunyan got as far as his knees and stayed that way, kneeling the way an ox would. They were surrounded by dead and terrified wounded men. All in blue uniforms. One man seemed to be trying to speak to Blake, to ask something of him, but Blake could not understand. The fellow might as well have been a Chinaman.

. . . and a new earth . . . a new earth . . .

The last firing moved off toward the town, leaving the moans of gut-torn men, of men bleeding to death from limb stumps, of men whose lungs had been gashed, or whose spines had been cracked without enough force to kill them then and there.

The field stank.

Slowly, Blake looked around for an officer. He saw none.

Using his rifle as a crutch, he rose. Amazed that he could stand, that he was whole.

"Come on," he told Cobb and John Bunyan. "Gather up ammunition from the dead. This isn't over."

"Sumbitch," Cobb whispered.

EIGHT

July 1, Midafternoon

Get those fences down!" Colonel Krzyzanowski ordered, gesturing toward the broad fields stretching across his brigade's front and on the right flank.

Colonel Robinson and Lieutenant Colonel Boebel saluted and rode back to their regiments, leaving Krzyzanowski in midfield with his two aides. Hastily formed work parties rushed forward as the uproar of combat intensified. General Barlow had gotten himself into a deadly pinch. Krzyzanowski could not make out all of the details, but the volume of fire was alarming. The terrain beyond Barlow's awkward line obscured the Rebel positions and the size of their force, but it was clear that the situation was grim.

A dog straining on a leash, the Pole awaited orders to advance the final distance into the fight. He knew those orders would come. But why not now, while there was still a chance to eke things out? If that fool Barlow had to be rescued, the time was now. Krzyzanowski would have preferred an attempt to re-form the corps' defense on the original line near the town, but feared that it already had grown too late.

Abruptly, the Confederate cannon shifted their fire toward Krzyzanowski's lines again. The guns had reappeared in their former positions on the high hill to the left. And there were more of them now. As he turned to gauge the effect on his brigade, a row of men in the 82nd Ohio disappeared in a smear of blood.

The battle noise notched up again.

He considered ordering the men in the ranks to lie down, but decided against it. In the confused combat unfolding on both his flanks, seconds might matter. There were times when men had to die,

and he had to make them do it. That, too, was in his blood. But it was bitter.

He put the side of his boot heels to his mount, sparing the creature the bite of his spurs again. At a canter and followed by his aides, he traversed his brigade frontage, the better to see if the skeletal 75th Pennsylvania had finished aiding the effort to block the Rebel probe of the corps' center.

The regiment's commanding officer, Colonel Mahler, had performed heroically. With his horse tumbled atop him and the beast kicking in agony, the injured officer had risen to his feet again, refusing to go to the rear. With the help of one of his staff officers, Mahler had hopped back into the fray like a fellow in a sack race, cheered on by his Pennsylvanians.

Those boys were all too few, but they were fighting on their home ground. Krzyzanowski understood. Their hearts were in it. They'd give a good account of themselves and their company-size regiment.

Yes. Good. Mahler and his men had contained the thrust and were returning to their place in the brigade reserve. Krzyzanowski rode no farther, but turned his horse again. "Come on," he called to his aides, two enthused young men.

On the right, billows of smoke obscured all beyond the firing line of Barlow's forward positions. That was where Krzyzanowski's worries lay. He pulled up his mount before his 119th New York, trying to hear acutely, to judge the course of the hidden fighting from the intensity and direction of the firing. But there was too much noise, too much confusion. The constant report of the guns, along with the incessant rifle volleys, jumbled the world.

The Eleventh Corps' own batteries dueled with the Rebel artillery on the high hill again. Dilger had repositioned his guns adeptly, the man was brilliant. That much of the fight seemed subject to control, if things did not worsen. The Pole trotted over to his right flank, to his Wisconsin Germans, the Sigel Regiment. Along with his beloved Polish Legion, the 58th New York, they had made a stand at Chancellorsville as heroic as any action he had ever seen. Only to be included in the battle's general shame, in the accusations of cowardice delivered by distant voices. Nor had the failed

generals risen to defend the honor of men who had died for their errors.

The 26th Wisconsin would be the first to catch it, if Barlow's front collapsed or his flank was turned. Shrunken though it was, he wished his Polish Legion could be with him today. Every man would count on this field. But his 58th had been ordered to detached duty, leaving only a handful of its men on the field, positioned between the New Yorkers and the Wisconsin *Deutschen.*

Lieutenant Colonel Boebel, an old revolutionary, rode out to meet him. Shells burst near enough to shy their horses, but both men were confident riders. Krzyzanowski's aides moved off to give the commanders privacy.

"Well, Hans," Krzyzanowski called over the roar, "you'll be in for it soon enough."

"Too damned soon, I am thinking. Young *Meister* Barlow's made a barnyard slop of it. If the Secessionists don't turn his flank, they have no brains at all." At the report of a shell, his horse pranced. The German tightened the reins.

Krzyzanowski understood what his subordinate was thinking: *Chancellorsville again. Except this time we made the same mistake in broad daylight, when we had the choice right in front of us.* But the Pole would not, could not, say it. Chancellorsville would not be mentioned, not by him, not today. He had to appear confident, not only willing to fight, but ready to win. The art of command had a great deal to do with convincing lies.

Boebel spoke again. "I think I would as soon shoot this Barlow as any of the Rebels."

Krzyzanowski smiled bitterly. "Better not, Hans. General Howard adores him. Barlow speaks prettier English than you or me." The Pole's expression lifted one wing of his mustaches. "The boy even looks like an Englishman. The way he pouts. Even when he isn't pouting."

That was as far as Krzyzanowski would go to criticize a superior, even the dreadful Oliver O. Howard. He remembered Howard's condescension in the last fateful hours before Jackson struck at Chancellorsville, the obstinate refusal to shield the army's flank, despite mounting indications of an attack and the pleas of his foreign-born subordinates. The Pole remembered all that. And his dead.

Finished with the work of dismantling the fences before them, Boebel's men hurried back to their places in line. Krzyzanowski had wanted the fence-line to their right torn down as well, but the sergeants in charge of the details had left the work incomplete.

Everyone had nerves now. The men were impatient for action, for collective motion, for anything but this awful waiting in the vale of artillery fire. Krzyzanowski understood the soldiers he commanded, sensing each shift in mood, the slightest change in spirit. Nonetheless, any slighted task annoyed him. All of the fencing should have been pulled down.

He nearly chided Boebel, but it wasn't the proper time. The man didn't need pestering. More important matters lay ahead than fences. And no matter how skillfully and promptly he and his regimental commanders made their decisions and gave their orders, graver errors awaited them.

Battle was a litany of mistakes. The goal was to take fewer missteps than your enemy. Krzyzanowski had seen enough of war to be skeptical of the claims made for dead heroes. Perfection took no part in any war, and even the greatest genius needed luck. Wars were won not by the most competent army, but by the least incompetent on a given day. You did your best, praying that you and those above and below you bungled less than the men on the other side.

And there already had been bungling enough. Beyond his brigade's right flank, wounded men streamed back from Barlow's lines, not a few of them helped along by comrades glad of an excuse to leave the fight. Most of Barlow's men held on tenaciously, but their exposed position was impossible.

It was always like that: There were always madly brave men, as well as inventive cowards. The only time he had seen men fight without a single one running to the rear had been at Chancellorsville, when his own two regiments had made more of a stand than he'd asked or expected. To get them to withdraw and save the remnants of themselves, he had needed to do everything short of dragging each one off by hand. He had never seen men fight so. Only to be humiliated by newspapermen who had never smelled a battle.

Beside him, Boebel looked careworn and worried.

"Sieht nicht besonders gut aus, Herr Oberst." It doesn't look particularly good, Colonel.

"*Naja,*" Krzyzanowski answered, "*die Soldaten kämpfen aber richtig. Auch für den blöden Barlow.*" *But those soldiers are fighting well. Even if it's for that fool Barlow.*

They often slipped into German as tensions rose.

Suddenly, cannon opened up, battery after battery, from the right. With a mortified look, Boebel saluted and hurried back to his regiment. Krzyzanowski could see only the muzzle flashes through the smoke, not the guns themselves. But the Confederates now had the entire corps in a crossfire.

As he stared into the fire-specked clouds, he felt his face go pale.

Following orders, he had moved up his brigade to a position from which he could advance rapidly to buttress Barlow's line, if that was the decision of the generals. But through all of his brigade's evolutions, he had hoped against hope that Barlow's men would beat back the Rebels long enough to let them withdraw to their proper position, denying the corps' flanks to the encroaching enemy. If he were ordered to back up Barlow now, it would uncover the corps' center. And there was already a quarter-mile gap on the corps' left, between von Amsberg's men and the First Corps on the ridge off to the west. Its casualties unreplenished and stripped of a division, the Eleventh Corps was simply too small to defend the extended frontage: They offered little more than a glorified skirmish line. And Barlow had worsened their situation immeasurably. The Confederates had their choice of weak points to strike.

The corps' line would not be restored. The fact sank in with finality. And the fight, when his turn came, would be a damned melee.

Krzyzanowski stood in his stirrups. Straining to see through the smoke and muddle on the right flank, where the crisis was impending. Still unable to distinguish the Confederate positions or numbers, he could not anticipate the most effective way to deploy his regiments. It would come down to hasty decisions in the murk of smoke and noise.

Signaling to his aides to remain in place, he rode forward a few yards, back turned to the men under his command. As ever when combat was imminent, he folded his hands on the pommel of his saddle and closed his eyes for stolen seconds to beg the Virgin for grace and courage. At that moment, he saw an ancestor, leopard-

skin over his gleaming breastplate and sword in hand, leading his winged hussars against the Tartar onslaught. The Black Virgin shone above him, she would always be with Poland. And Poland was wherever her sons fought. America, too, was Poland. The land of his birth wasn't only a plot on the map, but a faith, an idea, a willingness to struggle against hopelessness. His forebears had stood by Potocki amid disaster at Korsun, when the Commonwealth was under siege by traitors, and led banners of hussars under Sobieski, when the Polish king drove the sultan's janissaries from Vienna. His ancestors had marched to Moscow not only in 1812, but in 1612 as well, then saved their homeland from a Swedish king deemed invincible.

Now *he* was here, on a field far from Poland, in Poland's endless heart.

Krzyzanowski straightened himself in the saddle, touched a mustache tip, and turned from the past to the present. He wheeled about to judge the damage done by the artillery enfilade: Not yet so bad, not so very bad. The Confederate gunners were still seeking the proper range. The drifting smoke cut both ways. And his men were stalwart, if weary.

What of the Rebels across the field? Were they weary, too? How long had their march been to reach this place? Krzyzanowski understood that only the prospect of battle had revived his men. But such energies could be fragile. How long would their strength last? Longer than that of the Rebels? Of such things, too, were victories and defeats made.

A rider approached at an all-out gallop. Coming from the corps rear. It would be an order from General Schurz, the acting corps commander.

Instinctively, the Pole turned away from the courier to scan Barlow's lines again. Yes. He could see it. The great crumbling had begun. Undercut by folly, valor succumbed. The barrage unleashed by the newly emplaced Rebel cannon had signaled a renewed attack by their infantry.

In the middle distance, he spotted gray patches amid the blue now.

"General Schurz's compliments, sir," the major panted. He held out a written order. Schurz was a fine soldier. He gave orders in

writing, whenever possible. Protecting his subordinates, not himself.

"What does it say, Gerhard?"

"You're to move to General Barlow's aid. Without delay. In the manner you see fit."

"And the corps' line? The center?"

The major shook his head: He didn't know about that. Such decisions were not his to make.

Krzyzanowski tucked the order into his pocket. He had known what it would say. He nodded to the major, releasing him. The officer pulled his horse about and raced back toward his duties in the rear.

"Sasha!" the Pole called to his senior aide, Captain Maluski.

The aide drew closer, followed by Lieutenant Brueninghausen.

To his regret, Krzyzanowski could not take the time to put his own orders on paper. "The Eighty-second Ohio advances with its left flank on that road, maintaining contact with von Amsberg's right, but refusing the brigade's flank, if pressed. The Seventy-fifth will move forward immediately at a right oblique and establish a line of battle two hundred yards behind Barlow's left. Clear?"

"Yes, sir."

"Then *go*."

Maluski whipped his horse like a demented Cossack.

"Wash?"

"Sir?" Lieutenant Brueninghausen asked.

"The Hundred Nineteenth New York advances at the oblique, echeloned twenty-five yards behind the right flank of the Seventy-fifth Pennsylvania. They'll guide on the Pennsylvanians. Understand?"

The lieutenant nodded, fighting to master a horse disturbed by the growing roar.

"Wait a moment."

Struggling with his mount, the lieutenant turned his face to the colonel again.

"You will then ride to General Schimmelpfennig and request a battery, or even a section, to go into position in front of those big buildings on the right, where Barlow's men are falling back. We'll use the guns as a pivot, if we're forced back ourselves. Do you have all that?"

skin over his gleaming breastplate and sword in hand, leading his winged hussars against the Tartar onslaught. The Black Virgin shone above him, she would always be with Poland. And Poland was wherever her sons fought. America, too, was Poland. The land of his birth wasn't only a plot on the map, but a faith, an idea, a willingness to struggle against hopelessness. His forebears had stood by Potocki amid disaster at Korsun, when the Commonwealth was under siege by traitors, and led banners of hussars under Sobieski, when the Polish king drove the sultan's janissaries from Vienna. His ancestors had marched to Moscow not only in 1812, but in 1612 as well, then saved their homeland from a Swedish king deemed invincible.

Now *he* was here, on a field far from Poland, in Poland's endless heart.

Krzyzanowski straightened himself in the saddle, touched a mustache tip, and turned from the past to the present. He wheeled about to judge the damage done by the artillery enfilade: Not yet so bad, not so very bad. The Confederate gunners were still seeking the proper range. The drifting smoke cut both ways. And his men were stalwart, if weary.

What of the Rebels across the field? Were they weary, too? How long had their march been to reach this place? Krzyzanowski understood that only the prospect of battle had revived his men. But such energies could be fragile. How long would their strength last? Longer than that of the Rebels? Of such things, too, were victories and defeats made.

A rider approached at an all-out gallop. Coming from the corps rear. It would be an order from General Schurz, the acting corps commander.

Instinctively, the Pole turned away from the courier to scan Barlow's lines again. Yes. He could see it. The great crumbling had begun. Undercut by folly, valor succumbed. The barrage unleashed by the newly emplaced Rebel cannon had signaled a renewed attack by their infantry.

In the middle distance, he spotted gray patches amid the blue now.

"General Schurz's compliments, sir," the major panted. He held out a written order. Schurz was a fine soldier. He gave orders in

writing, whenever possible. Protecting his subordinates, not himself.

"What does it say, Gerhard?"

"You're to move to General Barlow's aid. Without delay. In the manner you see fit."

"And the corps' line? The center?"

The major shook his head: He didn't know about that. Such decisions were not his to make.

Krzyzanowski tucked the order into his pocket. He had known what it would say. He nodded to the major, releasing him. The officer pulled his horse about and raced back toward his duties in the rear.

"Sasha!" the Pole called to his senior aide, Captain Maluski.

The aide drew closer, followed by Lieutenant Brueninghausen.

To his regret, Krzyzanowski could not take the time to put his own orders on paper. "The Eighty-second Ohio advances with its left flank on that road, maintaining contact with von Amsberg's right, but refusing the brigade's flank, if pressed. The Seventy-fifth will move forward immediately at a right oblique and establish a line of battle two hundred yards behind Barlow's left. Clear?"

"Yes, sir."

"Then *go*."

Maluski whipped his horse like a demented Cossack.

"Wash?"

"Sir?" Lieutenant Brueninghausen asked.

"The Hundred Nineteenth New York advances at the oblique, echeloned twenty-five yards behind the right flank of the Seventy-fifth Pennsylvania. They'll guide on the Pennsylvanians. Understand?"

The lieutenant nodded, fighting to master a horse disturbed by the growing roar.

"Wait a moment."

Struggling with his mount, the lieutenant turned his face to the colonel again.

"You will then ride to General Schimmelpfennig and request a battery, or even a section, to go into position in front of those big buildings on the right, where Barlow's men are falling back. We'll use the guns as a pivot, if we're forced back ourselves. Do you have all that?"

"Hundred Nineteenth advances right oblique, guiding on the Pennsylvanians, twenty-five paces behind their right. Any available cannon to those buildings."

"If the general has any guns for us, stay there and guide them into position yourself. If he doesn't, ride on to General Schurz and ask him. Now *go!*"

The boy's mount was only waiting to be unleashed. It carried him off powerfully.

Krzyzanowski turned his own horse toward Boebel and his Wisconsin men. He was not hopeful that Schimmelpfennig or Schurz would find a battery or even a section of guns for him, but he had asked, anyway. There were times when a single twelve-pounder changed the course of a fight. You asked, you hoped, you fought.

"Hans?" he called above the roar.

The big German waved his head up and down in acknowledgment in substitute for a salute.

"How many men mustered today? Four hundred?"

"Three."

"Well, the fight's on your shoulders. And theirs. And let the devil lick our asses for dinner. When the Hundred Nineteenth goes forward, you'll follow, guiding on their right. They'll make an oblique movement toward those Confederates. Watch your right. Refuse your flank, if necessary. Don't wait for my order. Use your judgment. *Klar?*"

"*Jawohl, Herr Oberst.*"

Boebel looked off to the right, inspecting the vast stretch of the battlefield his whittled-down regiment faced. The German fixed his attention on the broad smoke-swathed vacancy Barlow's advance and collapse had uncovered. At least two brigades of Confederates could get through that gap, if they had the men present and saw the opportunity. And they would see the opportunity. No half-capable officer could miss it. The only question was whether the Confederates had the men present to seize their chance. It looked and sounded as if they did.

The German's eyes met Krzyzanowski's. They were both thinking the same thing: This has the makings of a colossal, stinking, steaming shit.

"Do what you can, Hans," Krzyzanowski told him.

The lieutenant colonel's eyes had darkened to a combative shade. "Oh, we'll make those pigs squeal, before they take over *this* barnyard."

To the left, the two men saw the 75th Pennsylvania stride forward, the miniature remains of a valiant regiment. Bayonets fixed, the 119th New York followed on the right, in echelon. The voices commanding them carried only faintly on the acrid air, as if the shouting officers were already ghosts.

Krzyzanowski kicked his horse into motion, letting Boebel get on with leading his regiment and aiming for the rear of the 119th, seeking a vantage point from which he could observe the advance of the 82nd Ohio, whose few hundred men had to hold the division's center.

He now had a frontage to defend that would have taxed a full-strength division. And barely 1,200 men under arms to cover it, hardly more than the strength of a regiment in the war's first year. The 75th Pennsylvania had only 158 men in the field, less than the tally of two Confederate companies. . . .

A massive Rebel yell, a scream from Hell's depths, soared above the roar of the guns and the crackle of rifle fire. The Pole yanked his mount around again.

And there they were, coming on at a dogtrot. The line of men in gray seemed endless as it crushed Barlow's right and swarmed past it. As Krzyzanowski watched, the entire Union line before his turning brigade began to unravel.

Some of Barlow's companies and a few shredded regiments maintained their integrity as they withdrew, fighting for every step. But the Rebels seemed to be everywhere. They were pouring around Barlow's left now, too, headed straight for the heart of Krzyzanowski's brigade, while still more swept down the road toward the 82nd Ohio, a mighty gray torrent that seemed unstoppable.

Unflinching, his own men went forward in handsome ranks, rescuing at least the appearance of order amid the growing chaos. A detail of soldiers ran forward to tear down another neglected section of fence.

On the right, waves of Confederates bounded up from a depression, rising from the earth itself, from graves. They came on at a near run, flaunting their red banner with its blue diagonal cross.

It looked to Krzyzanowski as if the entire Rebel army were upon them.

The veterans of the 26th Wisconsin changed front crisply, as men fleeing Barlow's debacle ran past and through their ranks. Even then, islands of men in blue fought on, firing as rapidly as they could into the gray sea flooding all around them. Barlow's men had deserved a better general.

What made one man stand and another run?

Krzyzanowski applied his spurs for the first time, racing forward to halt the 119th New York and the Pennsylvanians where they were, to prevent a gap opening within the brigade, in addition to those on the flanks. But Mahler of the 75th, already badly injured earlier in the day, had seen the danger and wheeled his men into a fighting line. The 119th had followed suit.

His own deployed regiments and long fingers of smoke blocked his view of the 82nd Ohio. He would have to trust their situation for now.

Glancing to the rear, Krzyzanowski prayed that he would see a battery rushing forward. He needed guns, needed them *now*, with even Barlow's cannon overrun—would the Rebels turn those guns on his own men?

On the right, the Wisconsin Germans unleashed a powerful volley, a great, ragged bark. A few stubborn packets of Barlow's men had halted by his soldiers, lending their lives to the fight, unwilling to quit even now.

It all went so fast, so terribly fast.

Even at Chancellorsville, he had never seen such masses of men in gray. The trees and undergrowth had limited visibility on that other field, and the fighting had been close and vicious. But now, whenever the smoke tore, he saw Confederates coming on in hordes worthy of the Tartars against whom his ancestors had lowered their lances.

Bayonets would have to do.

All of his regiments were delivering volleys now, all of them steadfast. He spurred his mount over to his brigade's left, galloping through the litter of fleeing soldiers and ambulatory wounded.

To his horror, he saw that von Amsberg's men had been driven

back hard on that flank, opening yet another gap in the line. Now it was his own 82nd Ohio that was vulnerable to envelopment.

He cursed Barlow and cursed him. He cursed Howard. Cursed himself. Cursed history and fate, the earth and sky. His own brigade had been thrust into a salient by General Schurz's belated, hopeless order, but without even the benefit of the scrap of high ground that lured Barlow to his fate.

That was the lesson handed down through countless generations: The *husaria* always closed ranks and never opened a gap for the Tartars to wedge in among them. But today his army had opened up one gap after another.

Captain Maluski caught up with him.

"Orders, sir?"

"The Eighty-second Ohio must refuse the brigade's left flank and hold as long as possible."

Having just returned from that regiment, Maluski looked doubtful.

"I know, Sasha, I know," the colonel told him. "I see the gap from here. We just have to do what we can. And fight like beasts."

Krzyzanowski rode back along the rest of his line, shouting praise at his men, assuring them that they were giving the Rebels better than they got. But the sight of men twisting and dropping, and the sound of pain-addled screams, left him doubtful of his claims.

A boy stumbled past him, a hand over each eye, watering the field with blood.

How could there have been such a blunder? Not just Barlow, as bad as that was, but sending a battered corps to hold back what looked like the bulk of the Army of Northern Virginia? Didn't the high generals back in their headquarters know anything? Where was the sense in this?

The Rebels were killing flies mired in honey.

Well, the sense was in the fight itself. Even a hopeless one.

His men howled throatily at the Confederates, as if curses could kill. Their volleys brought the Rebels up short, forcing the gray mass to form a firing line, here fifty, there seventy yards distant. The Confederates seemed unwilling to press any closer, as if surprised at this unexpected resistance after they had collapsed the Union line.

"Give it to them, boys, give it to them!" Krzyzanowski yelled.

The problem was that there were ever more men in gray joining the other firing line. Hordes. Tartar hordes.

Krzyzanowski dug his spurs deep into his horse's belly. *Fear me, darling, not them.* He rode hard for the 26th Wisconsin, a slender belt of blue resisting a vast gray body. Boebel was the key man now.

The Pole looked right. Still no sign of a battery, not a single cannon. While the Rebels seemed to have dozens of guns available to them. Dozens, and then dozens. Shells landed everywhere.

The shortest way to the Wisconsin line led over a lateral fence that had not been dismantled. His horse had jumped higher obstacles.

Galloping madly through the flush of wounded men blundering rearward, he spurred his mount again. It rose and flew over the fence, its rider masterful in the saddle.

But a swarm of bullets stung the white horse in midflight and it landed crazily, rearing again, shrieking, then coming back down on one foreleg that snapped away, tumbling its rider to the rock-hard ground.

The last thing Krzyzanowski felt before losing consciousness was the slam of the horse's skull landing on his ribs.

*D*er Kriz ist gefallen!"

"I saw them pick him up. He isn't dead."

"They always pick up colonels, dead or not."

"He isn't dead, I tell you. *Gestorben ist er nicht!*"

"Look to the front, damn it," Corporal Schwertlein ordered, loading his voice with all of the authority he could muster.

"*Doch*, which is back, and which is front now?" Schumann joked ruefully. The Confederates seemed to be everywhere.

The soldiers of the 26th Wisconsin called hot-voiced to one another, firing as they spoke, attempting vainly to open holes in gray ranks close enough for men to read the expressions of the men trying to kill them.

"*Mit oder ohne,*" Bettelman said matter-of-factly. "With Kriz or without him, we're in the sewer now."

Lieutenant Colonel Boebel had been struck down as the regiment moved into action, shot in the leg, then, as he struggled to rise, hit again in the same leg by a piece of shell. The regiment's commander had been dragged off with bone revealed and the use-

less meat of the leg trailing behind, calling orders until he broke off
in midsentence. Then Major Baetz, the next in command, had gone
down. Lieutenant Young was killed and Lieutenant Grode toppled
over. The Rebels were taking aim at every officer. Yet, the officers
of the 26th kept stepping forward.

The Rebel line advanced in a bending wave, its rough-clad sol-
diers firing as they came on.

"*Scheisse, Scheisse, Scheisse,*" Bettelman said. "Shit, shit, shit." De-
spite his language, the watchmaker's voice was now the calmest
among them, its tone more melancholy than alarmed. Bettelman was
an odd one, Schwertlein thought. Judging by his comportment in
the rear, you would assume him to be the weakest man in the com-
pany on the battlefield. Yet, he always stood firmly in the front line,
working his rifle as intently as if repairing the innards of a watch.

War revealed men.

Another Rebel volley flamed and crackled. Lieutenant Stein-
meyer dropped face forward in the trampled grain. But Schwert-
lein's old friend Lieutenant Trenk remained unscathed. He had taken
up a fallen soldier's rifle and joined the line.

Men fell, men fell, men fell. Another round of solid shot tore
through the ranks, spraying the air crimson. Other men's blood
whipped Schwertlein's face. Yet, those to whom his heart was
bound had escaped the Rebel fire until now: Leo Bettelman, with
his watchmaker's daintiness and a mammoth wife in Milwaukee;
Schumann, the master carpenter, just recovered from his wounds;
Josef Heisler, a would-be poet and family man meant for peace; and
Hannes Trenk, his first friend in America, a fine and honorable
man endangered now by the rank upon his shoulders.

It seemed impossible that the Rebels had not surged forward
and overrun them. Schwertlein could see the rage on the blackened
Secesh faces, smell it in the air as it thickened the gunsmoke. He
finished reloading, raised his rifle, took aim, and fired again. The
man he had singled out arched backward, mouth opened in a cry
that never sounded.

What sort of man had he been?

Mechanically, Schwertlein began to reload. In a fit of insanity,
Otto Schumann embraced him, pulling him toward the ground.

"*Otto . . . zum Teufel . . .*"

His friend's dead eyes and drooling mouth fell against him like a lover's.

As Schwertlein fought to stay upright, Schumann's corpse slipped away. A force greater than a rifle ball had torn his chest apart. He struck the earth like a heavy, spineless doll.

Slopped with Schumann's blood, Schwertlein went back to reloading. Screaming as his hands did their duty methodically. His fingers quaked, but he rammed the bullet home.

An eye for an eye, he thought. He repeated the words inwardly, turning them into a mad child's singsong: *An eye for an eye, an eye for an eye, an eye for an eye . . .* He raised his rifle and felt its punch-back against a shoulder already bruised.

The Rebels were drawing hopelessly near, lapping around the regiment's flanks like floodwaters.

Captain Fuchs ran along the rear of the rank, in command of the regiment now. "Withdraw while firing . . . maintain your ranks. Rally beside those buildings. Keep up your fires . . . steady, boys . . ."

As the shrinking regiment withdrew, maintaining its order stubbornly, the right flank of the retreating New Yorkers jostled into the Wisconsin left, drawing officers desperate to untangle them. The 75th Pennsylvania either had moved off in another direction, or had disappeared from the face of the earth. The Ohio men might as well have been in Africa.

"*Scheisse, Scheisse, Scheisse,*" Bettelman muttered. *Shit, shit, shit.*

Lieutenant Trenk laughed wonderfully and called out, "*Nein, nein! Schiesse, schiesse, schiesse, Leo!*"

Shoot, shoot, shoot!

"Shooting in the shit," a neighboring voice replied.

They fought their way backward, leaving ranks of dead and twisting comrades on the worthless ground where they had stood. Still more soldiers dropped as the regiment worked toward the illusory shelter of stout brick buildings, the town's farthest outpost.

The only reprieve they got was from the Rebel guns. The Confederate infantry had come so close that their cannon on the right flank had to shift to targets in the rear. The guns shot their projectiles over the heads of the soldiers of the 26th, separating them from the town that waited beyond another open field.

The New Yorkers had pulled away again, fighting their own

battle-within-a-battle. Hoarse now, Captain Fuchs kept shouting orders. A few surviving sergeants did their best to maintain a coherent firing line, but all around them the corps had come apart, its regiments dwindling to companies and dissolving.

All of it infuriated Schwertlein to the brink of tears. Chancellorsville again. Would this, too, all be the fault of the "Flying Dutchmen"? Certainly, native-born Americans, fine men such as General Barlow, would bear no blame.

His rage made him fight all the harder, more careless of death than he had ever been.

Lieutenant Maschauer dropped his sword and pistol, clutching himself and wobbling rearward like a drunken man about to vomit. Captain Fuchs seemed to have vanished into thin air and Captain Domschke took up the task of holding the regiment together.

They stopped to make another stand by the brick buildings, fighting amid the wreckage of other regiments. Some hard men from Barlow's disaster rallied near them. And the 119th New York had reappeared. Schwertlein believed he even saw the colors of a resurrected 75th Pennsylvania, although a mere handful of soldiers stood around them.

The former editor of a rival newspaper to Schwertlein's, Captain Domschke cursed the Rebels with language that would have embarrassed bargemen on the Rhine. He even managed to make the men laugh, a drink of fresh water poured over the mind.

In a milder moment, the captain shouted, "Give it to those slave-fucking shit-boys, drop them like cowshit, like turds in a teapot, and send the rest of those piss-cutters back to the clapped-up whores who dropped them out of their asses like a French fart. Shoot off their cocks and tell their girls it's bratwurst. Then shove it up their assholes for good, old Wisconsin!"

It was as if the captain had unleashed a decade of editorial frustration.

Still wielding a rifle like a private, Lieutenant Trenk, who had shared Schwertlein's hardscrabble early days in America, flung away his weapon and sat down. As if he had decided to pause for a rest. His hat had dropped away, exposing crinkled blond hair. A thin ribbon of blood strained from his mouth.

"Hannes!" Schwertlein cried. *"Hannes!"*

His friend did not respond. His eyes were open, but still. Leo Bettelman reached out and moved Trenk's shoulder. It woke the lieutenant, who looked up at them with an eerily peaceful smile.

"You go on. I'm going to rest now." His voice was hard to hear.

Schwertlein and Bettelman tried, awkwardly, to lift him up. Trenk shook his head. "I want to rest now. They aren't animals. They'll care for me."

"You've got to get up. Help us, Hannes."

"Let me go. It hurts." He smiled faintly, spreading the blood on his chin. "We'll meet when the war is over."

There was no time, no time. *"Hannes!"*

"I'm going to rest now," the lieutenant told his friends.

Bettelman gave up and went back to firing.

"At least lie down," Schwertlein cried. "So you won't be hit again. Lie down."

"*Ja. Ach, ja.* I'll lie down, Fritz. *Danke.*" He slipped into the grass.

Perhaps the wound wasn't a bad one, Schwertlein told himself. Perhaps they would meet again . . . perhaps . . .

He reloaded and fired.

A messenger galloped along their mockery of a line, not pausing to risk his life as he shouted the order: *"Retreat! Back to the town! Retreat!"*

Still cursing magnificently, Captain Domschke ordered the men to withdraw firing again. An open field stretched between them and the first houses and outbuildings. Its expanse seemed as broad as the fabled prairies of the West, the empty lands that lay open beyond the settled territories. Schwertlein had hoped one day to cross those endless plains. But not this one.

As they began to withdraw, a line of Rebels saw their chance and rushed toward the dying 26th. Sergeant Major Metzel splashed back against Sergeant Arnold, the two of them the last visible remnants of a noncommissioned officer chain of command. The two men fell into a trampled bed of grass. By the time Arnold tried to rise, the Rebels had surrounded him.

Captain Domschke's voice was missing now, replaced by the rasp of Captain Fernekes.

"Rally to the colors!" the captain cried. "Stay with the colors!"

Those colors fell, not for the first time, but were promptly raised again.

"Stay with the colors," Schwertlein repeated to his own dwindling band. He was unsure of how loud his voice was now. His parched mouth was fouled with the taste of gunpowder, his canteen emptied hours ago. But there was no time to pause for a swallow, anyway.

As they struggled backward across the endless, boundless field, the Confederates swarmed in ever greater numbers, enclosing them on three sides and surging to close off the fourth. The regiment began to break apart. A few men ran, then more. But even in that hellish field, most of those still able to fight balled about the colors, firing in every direction except straight into the rear. Elsewhere on the field, other clots of blue put up futile resistance.

Schwertlein wondered how many men had spilt their blood on him. He was caked with it, drenched, fly-bait. His hands were so slippery with sweat and gore, his ramrod tried to leap away as he jammed it down the barrel. He was shaking, too. But he was not going to quit. Damn them all. They could kill him here. But he was not about to run. Or raise his hands, as other men were doing across the field.

A rump of the regiment made it to a makeshift line on the edge of the town. A few fresh, or nearly fresh, companies rushed forward.

Too little, Schwertlein realized. And too late. Still, he was glad to see them.

The survivors' backs were to an orchard. The same one in which they'd paused on their arrival? Schwertlein couldn't tell, it didn't matter.

The line they had joined fell back again, crumbling.

Wonderfully, bewilderingly, the regiment's survivors found themselves behind a solid firing line. Schwertlein could not have explained how they had gotten there.

Drained. Panting. Bodies impoverished with sweat, uniforms chalked with jagged lines of salt. And smeared with blood. Faces masked by powder stains. They still had the regiment's colors.

Schwertlein realized that, in his group of perhaps three dozen soldiers, not an officer remained.

Surely, some still lived? There had to be more left of the regiment

than this. Over the last, frantic hundred yards of their retreat, the remaining ranks had splintered and diverged. There had to be more of them out there, more soldiers, more sergeants, more officers . . .

Closer to the rifle volleys than a high officer should be, General Schurz trotted by. He looked pained by all the world. Captain Winkler rode beside him, equally glum.

Schwertlein called out to the captain, who had served with the regiment before being lifted into a staff position. Winkler was a good officer, one of the best.

Other men spotted him, too. They added their voices to Schwertlein's one-man clamor.

Winkler recognized the colors, the men. His face took on an expression of disbelief, whether that they were so few, or that any remained alive.

After speaking a few words to Schurz, Winkler steered his mount over to them.

"Die Offizieren sind ja alle weg, Herr Hauptmann!" Bettelman explained. *The officers are all gone.*

Hopelessly German even now, the men could not imagine fighting without an officer to lead them. They crowded around Winkler's horse, begging him to take command of the fraction of a company left of their regiment.

Their pleas caught fire in Winkler.

"I must ask General Schurz," he told them. "Give me room . . . give me room, men!"

He turned his horse and spurred it back toward the general.

Schwertlein and Bettelman watched him go, with Josef Heisler standing just behind them. Schwertlein turned to the would-be poet.

"How goes it, Josef? *Alles in Ordnung?*"

Heisler shrugged, but said nothing. His face was blank.

"You can write a poem about all this, after it's over," Schwertlein told him. "Your masterpiece."

Bettelman snorted. *"Ja, ja . . . die Kunst ist lang, und kurz ist unser Leben . . ."*

Heisler nodded and repeated, in English: "Our life is short . . ."

"This is no time for Goethe," Schwertlein snapped at Bettelman. "Dear God in Heaven . . ."

"You don't believe in God, Fritz. So why call on him? Why do I do it myself, I wonder? The old fellow's insidious, taking advantage of us the way he does."

But Schwertlein, throat raw and mouth burning, had no interest in debating theology with the watchmaker. He just wanted to pull Heisler through the day, to save that one life now. To prove that the man's dark fantasies had been wrong. He worried more deeply about Heisler than he did about himself.

Captain Winkler trotted back toward them. Wearing a grin. If leaving the general's staff to take command of thirty or so men was a demotion, he didn't show it.

Winkler formed them up, just to the rear of the desperate struggle beyond the orchard. Before they could move, a stray bullet hit a soldier in the arm, splitting the bone. Winkler ordered him to make his way back to the hill beyond the town. Then he led his little band, with its torn colors waving, back to a white cottage where the town began.

Other elements of the brigade had gathered there.

"Hurry," Winkler ordered. "At the double-quick. We're going to make a stand."

The captain knew more of the situation than they did, Schwertlein assumed. But before they could find a place in the ragged line, blue-clad fugitives fled past them again. The new line, the fresh regiments, had not held.

"Here they come!" someone shouted.

With an unearthly howl, a Rebel regiment surged toward them from the right. No matter where they tried to make a stand, the Confederates swept in around them, behind them, appearing everywhere.

"Regiment!" Winkler barked. "Left into line, wheel! Guide on me!"

His commands were interrupted by a massed volley from the gray line.

"Retreat!" someone shouted from another unit. Others took up the cry.

"Who said that? On whose order?" Winkler demanded. None of the men beyond his own small band paid him any attention.

The captain looked ready to kill any living thing before him, friend, foe, or neutral. His forlorn-hope command had not lasted long.

He ordered his men back.

But they had not gone far among the fugitives and wounded before they found a remnant of the 119th New York defending a street a block inside the town. Winkler ordered his soldiers to join them. Schwertlein recognized at least one 75th Pennsylvania man, too. But the 82nd Ohio seemed to have been swallowed whole.

With a peculiar rage born of weariness and shame, the men fired into the gray attackers funneling into the street. Truthful or not, some men called that they were out of ammunition and made for the rear.

"Maintain your line," Winkler called. "Don't worry about which regiment you're in. Just keep firing."

But the captain's voice had grown desperate. Anyone could see that the street could not be held.

From nowhere, a caisson materialized, belatedly fleeing the Rebels, dashing in between their barefoot skirmishers. Despite hunching low, the driver fell to a shot.

The caisson careened wildly toward the remnant of Krzyzanowski's brigade, doing what the Confederates could not.

The team of horses crashed into the rank of blue-coated soldiers, breaking it utterly. Men shoved, tripped, and leapt sideward as they fled from the maddened beasts and the crippling wheels. In the chaos, a soldier from the 119th New York accidentally shot Heisler in the head.

You must go to the rear!" General Schurz told him. "You can't even stand up straight."

A broken army retreated around them, crowding the street.

Krzyzanowski looked up at the mounted man and shook his head. "I have to find my brigade."

"Don't be insane, Kriz."

Madness had overtaken the town's center. While struggling to save as much as possible of the corps he'd inherited, Schurz had found Krzyzanowski limping forward, sword in hand.

"I will not desert my brigade."

"You're wounded. For God's sake, look at you!"

"I have to find my brigade."

Schurz looked away. "You don't have a brigade, Kriz. It's gone."

"I'll find what's left of it."

"Listen to me! Your men gave a good account of themselves, they were heroic. But it didn't go our way. Now we have to rescue what we can. The survivors of your brigade will need a commander. Back there, on the hill, not here. All you're going to do is get yourself captured. If not killed."

"Maybe killed. Not captured."

"Don't be so damned Polish. This is a time for common sense, not romantic gestures."

"Sometimes gestures are more useful than sense." He winced as his smashed ribs bit into his body again. As General Schurz looked down from the back of his impatient horse, Krzyzanowski spit up more blood.

"I don't have any more time," Schurz told him. "I order you to go back to the cemetery. Take the mount from the first healthy officer you find."

"No."

"Damn you, Kriz, I'll have you court-martialed."

Krzyzanowski smiled. "I thought I was going to be captured or killed, sir?" And the crippled colonel turned his back on the general to push his way into the wreck of a terrified army.

He limped. Wheezing. Coughing and suffering lightning bolts of pain. Hatless and missing a shoulder board, he set his face in the fiercest look he could conjure and held his sword ready as he twisted himself forward. The effect was strange and wonderful: Almost biblically, the sea of frightened men parted before him. Everyone feared a madman.

It couldn't end like this, that was the thing. Not with this vast giving up, this flight that lacked even the dignity of a surrender. It broke his heart that he'd been carried from the field, only to wake in a genteel parlor with hammer blows inside his head and invisible spikes driven into his left side. He told himself that his ancestors had fought for hours and days in worse condition. But he wondered if that were true.

A soldier jostled him. The pain-lightning shot through his chest again. The Pole stumbled to the nearest wall to steady himself and coughed up a dark ball of blood. The mortal meat was not having its best day.

Then he shuffled around a corner and met the most thrilling sight of his life: In the town square, amid tipped wagons, crawling wounded, and scattered corpses, the flag of the 119th New York stood defiantly beside a pair of cannon blasting the Rebels.

He recognized powder-blackened faces in profile, men from the 119th and his other regiments, fighting on as the rest of the army fled.

Krzyzanowski attempted to raise his sword, but the daggers where his ribs had been resisted. He called out through bloody phlegm, but could not be heard.

A big sergeant, wild-eyed and running, knocked him to the ground. Not one of his men, thank the Almighty. Krzyzanowski struggled back to his feet. In the worst pain of his life.

As the Pole approached the handful of stubborn warriors, a corporal who had turned to reload called out, *"Es ist der Kriz! Der Kriz ist wieder da!"*

Soldiers looked right and left until their bloodshot eyes discovered him. But he saw, too, how their expressions wavered as they watched him struggle forward, a bent-over creature.

A sergeant with a bloodied scalp saluted.

Krzyzanowski corrected his posture as best he could to return the salute. And he found his voice again.

"Dress on the colors, damn you!" he shouted. *"This isn't a Russian whorehouse!"*

And Wlodzimierz Krzyzanowski went back to war.

Schwertlein and Bettelman had become separated from the remains of the regiment. There were no longer explanations for such things: The world just did as it pleased with the day's survivors. A storm of humanity battered the town, which had seemed so small that morning, but had since become a boundless maze of dead-end streets and alleys blocked by Confederates. There was no sense to the place now: A street remained in Union hands, with clusters of soldiers still fighting, while the next lane, closer to the supposedly safe side of town, was packed with Rebels herding Yankee prisoners.

They had seen panicked officers ride their own men down, while others gave up their horses to the wounded. They had watched as a soldier was trampled to death by a blue mob, but other soldiers paused to aid wounded men whose names they would never know. Cannon fired down streets. Before one house, a woman shouted imperiously that they should all stop shooting, because they were destroying private property.

As they reached the end of another useless street, Bettelman said, *"Scheisse."*

Giddy, Schwertlein laughed. "You need to expand your vocabulary, Leo."

"What are you laughing about? Good God, Fritz! This isn't funny."

A gang of soldiers had rewarded themselves with liquor as they waited, weapons discarded, for the Rebels to round them up.

Even then, Schwertlein could hear that there was still fighting in the town's guts. But he had answered to the last orders to withdraw. Now the events around him seemed a grim comedy.

In an oddly quiet lane, he and Bettelman shied from a wide-eyed corpse in blue. Someone had already stripped off the boy's shoes and turned out his pockets.

They stumbled back into the retreating stream and plodded along in what the mass of men deemed the right direction. All too soon, an eruption of firing on the left led to cries of "We're surrounded!" and another panic. Made cowards by the day, men ran, heedless of the direction.

Some men still held their rifles, though. That was something. Schwertlein and Bettelman had theirs.

The street rose. From a low crest, Schwertlein saw a pulsing blue river ahead. The mood was very different now from the buoyant spirits they'd felt just hours before, when the townspeople cheered them as saviors.

Artillerymen trying to save their guns lashed out with whips until those on foot threatened to shoot them. Firing broke out directly ahead, followed by the inevitable cries of "The Rebels!"

"This won't work," Schwertlein said. "Come on."

"No more alleys. No more streets that end in brick walls."

"Come on. I order you."

A soldier jostled him. The pain-lightning shot through his chest again. The Pole stumbled to the nearest wall to steady himself and coughed up a dark ball of blood. The mortal meat was not having its best day.

Then he shuffled around a corner and met the most thrilling sight of his life: In the town square, amid tipped wagons, crawling wounded, and scattered corpses, the flag of the 119th New York stood defiantly beside a pair of cannon blasting the Rebels.

He recognized powder blackened faces in profile, men from the 119th and his other regiments, fighting on as the rest of the army fled.

Krzyzanowski attempted to raise his sword, but the daggers where his ribs had been resisted. He called out through bloody phlegm, but could not be heard.

A big sergeant, wild-eyed and running, knocked him to the ground. Not one of his men, thank the Almighty. Krzyzanowski struggled back to his feet. In the worst pain of his life.

As the Pole approached the handful of stubborn warriors, a corporal who had turned to reload called out, *"Es ist der Kriz! Der Kriz ist wieder da!"*

Soldiers looked right and left until their bloodshot eyes discovered him. But he saw, too, how their expressions wavered as they watched him struggle forward, a bent-over creature.

A sergeant with a bloodied scalp saluted.

Krzyzanowski corrected his posture as best he could to return the salute. And he found his voice again.

"Dress on the colors, damn you!" he shouted. *"This isn't a Russian whorehouse!"*

And Wlodzimierz Krzyzanowski went back to war.

Schwertlein and Bettelman had become separated from the remains of the regiment. There were no longer explanations for such things: The world just did as it pleased with the day's survivors. A storm of humanity battered the town, which had seemed so small that morning, but had since become a boundless maze of dead-end streets and alleys blocked by Confederates. There was no sense to the place now: A street remained in Union hands, with clusters of soldiers still fighting, while the next lane, closer to the supposedly safe side of town, was packed with Rebels herding Yankee prisoners.

They had seen panicked officers ride their own men down, while others gave up their horses to the wounded. They had watched as a soldier was trampled to death by a blue mob, but other soldiers paused to aid wounded men whose names they would never know. Cannon fired down streets. Before one house, a woman shouted imperiously that they should all stop shooting, because they were destroying private property.

As they reached the end of another useless street, Bettelman said, "*Scheisse.*"

Giddy, Schwertlein laughed. "You need to expand your vocabulary, Leo."

"What are you laughing about? Good God, Fritz! This isn't funny."

A gang of soldiers had rewarded themselves with liquor as they waited, weapons discarded, for the Rebels to round them up.

Even then, Schwertlein could hear that there was still fighting in the town's guts. But he had answered to the last orders to withdraw. Now the events around him seemed a grim comedy.

In an oddly quiet lane, he and Bettelman shied from a wide-eyed corpse in blue. Someone had already stripped off the boy's shoes and turned out his pockets.

They stumbled back into the retreating stream and plodded along in what the mass of men deemed the right direction. All too soon, an eruption of firing on the left led to cries of "We're surrounded!" and another panic. Made cowards by the day, men ran, heedless of the direction.

Some men still held their rifles, though. That was something. Schwertlein and Bettelman had theirs.

The street rose. From a low crest, Schwertlein saw a pulsing blue river ahead. The mood was very different now from the buoyant spirits they'd felt just hours before, when the townspeople cheered them as saviors.

Artillerymen trying to save their guns lashed out with whips until those on foot threatened to shoot them. Firing broke out directly ahead, followed by the inevitable cries of "The Rebels!"

"This won't work," Schwertlein said. "Come on."

"No more alleys. No more streets that end in brick walls."

"Come on. I order you."

Bettelman shrugged and followed him.

Schwertlein believed that he had a sense of which way to go now. He thought he had recognized a number of buildings from their triumphant morning passage. Even if he was deluding himself, it gave him a renewed purpose.

More shooting broke out behind them. They heard the pleas of men trying to surrender. Catcalls and cries of triumph followed in the accents of a different army.

"You know what I would like now?" Bettelman asked him.

"To be home with your wife?"

"That's asking too much. I'd settle for a glass of Baden wine. And a nice onion tart."

"You're mad."

It was Bettelman's turn to laugh. "We're all mad today. You, me, everybody. You saw it. What was the sense in all that? Trenk, Heisler, Schumann . . ."

"You should have stayed home and fixed watches."

"*Einverstanden!* Agreed! But I was a fool. Like you. Now here we are. Don't *you* feel like a fool this lovely afternoon?"

At the moment, Schwertlein felt nothing but shame and madness. Plus the determination not to be made a prisoner.

A door opened and a white-haired man leaned out. Except for the woman concerned about her property, he was the first civilian Schwertlein had seen in the course of the retreat. All of the houses, except those requisitioned as hospitals, were shut up tight now.

"That way . . ." The man pointed. "Keep going. Down there. Left at that white house. The path leads into the fields."

He disappeared again. A lock turned.

Schwertlein and Bettelman did as the old man bade them. And the fellow had been the best of Good Samaritans. In minutes, they emerged into a meadow ripe with manure. Hard to the left stood a big red barn. Beyond it, the landscape rose sharply.

On high ground studded with cannon, orderly ranks of blue-uniformed infantry awaited the day's survivors. Other regiments, unbloodied, hurried up a road that traced the ridge. Guided by the shouts of confident officers and with battle flags flying, columns wheeled into pastures to extend the Union lines.

"It looks as if we haven't had enough," Bettelman said.

NINE

July 1, Late Afternoon and Evening

Blake tried to talk himself into elation, but it just wouldn't take. He liked to fight, and he liked to win. But this day was a bitter depletion.

Part of it was just the lack of water, he figured. As he strode back from the chaos of the town beside his comrades, he felt that slow-me-down hint of dizziness that came from neglected thirst on a hot workday. Maybe, once he got his fill of water, his spirits would lift.

"Soon as we get back in them woods," Billie Cobb said, "I'm going to take me a shit."

Blake pictured Cobb squatting among the corpses, the wounded. Cobb wouldn't care, either. His was a sensible approach to life for a soldier, but Cobb's actions were not the deeds that made it into the history books featuring heroes. Blake remembered, back at school in Waterford, reading about George Washington, who clearly had not had to move his bowels a single time in his life.

Then Blake thought about the knights in armor in a picture book his mother had given him and which he had hidden from her Quaker folks. What the devil had those fellows in iron suits done, when the need came upon them?

For the first time in hours, Blake smiled. But there was no happiness in it. Just contrariness.

At the behest of some officer well to the rear, the remnants of the 26th North Carolina had been ordered into Gettysburg on the tail of Pender's men. Knock Jones, the major who had been only third in command that morning, was now the senior officer in the regiment. A mustached plug of a man, Jones had formed up his weary men in column, then led them into town, where the ruckus

sounded like dogs loosed on a prayer meeting. The order to enter the town had been a fool's doings, since the streets were already crammed with men in gray and the only visible Yankees were prisoners shuffling rearward. Old Knock, who was twenty-two or so, didn't quite know what to do or to whom he was meant to report. Eventually, he just turned the men around, marched them back to the edge of town, and waited.

With the afternoon's heat and smoke congealed on everyone left alive, a rider worked his way along the pike to tell them that General Pettigrew had ordered his division to fall back to the other side of the creek, to the groves and fields they had occupied in the morning. Questioned sharply, the courier said that, yes, what he had said was correct: General Pettigrew had the division now. General Heth had been wounded in the head.

"Glad he wasn't hit where it might've done him a hurt," Cobb observed.

Then Major Jones led them back the way they had come, through fields upon which the density of dead and wounded increased sharply as they climbed back up the ridge their charge had won.

Surrounded by battle's leavings, Blake felt bone weariness and a closing of mental shutters. And thirst. Thirst, as if his insides were shriveling.

They didn't march, but trudged back to the scene of their triumph like a pack of country folk coming home late from a cockfight a county over. Knock Jones halted them just where their attack had lost its drive. When the major first tried to speak, his voice would not emerge. His throat was dry, too.

"Y'all listen now," Jones managed to tell them. "I know you got kin or friends down in those woods. Go find 'em, but don't dawdle. Take the wounded on back, but there'll be no burying of the dead right now. That'll come. You just get our wounded and take them on back. Then the regiment's going to muster where we lay down this morning, when we were waiting to go. And I don't want any man disgracing this proud regiment by wandering off. You do what's right, hear? Now fall out and get to doing."

Blake figured Jones himself was anxious to find out if Colonel Burgwyn had been killed or only wounded. The two had been close, David and Jonathan.

Lugging their rifles and slumping to the last man, the survivors of the 26th descended into the grove where the day's butchery had been done. It didn't take long for men to start calling out names or dropping abruptly to their knees. Some men shared what little water remained to them—if any—with Rebel and Yankee wounded alike, but most ignored the cries and pleas of their enemies. It wasn't viciousness. It was necessity. The way a man saved family before he did strangers.

Cobb stepped away to have himself a squat between two dead Yankees.

"I don't care what the major says," John Bunyan declared. "I'm going to bury James." They were the first words the twin had spoken since they had left the ridge.

"Just hush," Blake told him. "We're going to take James with us, like he's only wounded. And we'll bury him back yonder, where it's clean."

The twin went down the hillside in long strides, an inner compass guiding him to the spot where his brother had fallen.

Blake found Ireton, guts strewn and dead. Flies feasted. Blake couldn't watch. He went down the slope after John Bunyan. Cobb buttoned his trousers and followed.

They could have hopped down the hill from corpse to corpse, but that wasn't enough to shock Blake. What made him shudder was the speed with which the bodies had been stripped of anything valuable. He understood taking shoes, although he wasn't keen on trying on a dead man's footwear himself. But here trousers had been stripped off and shirts torn from men who were not even dead, but only wounded and quivering. His Quaker kin did not have a realistic view of mankind.

Ahead of them, John Bunyan pulled up, yanked back by invisible reins. The boy stared around himself, scrutinizing the aftermath of slaughter, then the earth itself. He turned to Blake and Cobb.

"He ain't here."

"Calm down now," Blake told him. "You sure this is the spot?"

"He was right here. I *know* it. Right here."

"Maybe wild pigs et James," Cobb said.

The twin lunged for him, but Blake was quicker, inserting himself between them. "That's just Cobb."

John Bunyan seethed. Knuckles bloodless on his rifle.

"Damn you, stop and think," Blake told him. "Nobody carried him off. You just stop and think."

The new idea sank in. "He's only wounded."

The possibility was difficult for Blake himself to accept, given the other twin's multiple wounds and the way the boy had gone down like a drained hog. But he could see no other explanation.

"That's right," Blake told John Bunyan. "Nobody was about to lug James off. Now put on your thinking cap. Where would a wounded man take himself off to from here? If he could?"

A few trees and a dozen bodies over, a voice cried out one raw word of discovery: "Ezra!"

John Bunyan took on a trying-to-think look, but the boy's mind had slowed to a crawl. There was too much freight in that wagon's bed today. He shook his head. Heavily, reluctantly.

"That creek down there," Blake told him. "Water."

The twin took off at a run. Blake and Cobb walked after him.

"Just getting that boy's hopes up," Cobb said. "God's a mean sumbitch."

The formulation slapped Blake. He could never have said such words, not even now. But he had felt them. Often.

"You seen him, Quaker. That big lummox had more holes in him than a nigger's longjohns. Even if he's still alive, it won't be for long."

"Maybe it'll be for long enough."

Cobb cawed a laugh as they parted to pass beyond a mound of bodies. "You think they're going to have them some frilly, store-bought good-bye, Quaker? Out of one of them illustrated week-lies?" He spit, but there was no wet. "James Bunyan's just dying twice over now. What good's it going to do that brother of his?"

They walked down the hill past their own strewn dead, ignoring the torments of the Yankee wounded, loyal only to their battered clan.

"Folks need to say good-bye," Blake said. "It comforts them."

"Naw," Cobb responded. "They don't, and it doesn't. Folks just do what they think they're supposed to do, no matter how it pains them." He cackled. "Don't it never strike you, Quaker, how the Yankees cry their eyes out over some whipped nigger they dreamed

up, then go to church and worship the sumbitch who does all this? Don't that seem like pissing in the whiskey jug to you?" They worked through the trampled thorns by the water and Cobb said, "Look at that."

James Bunyan had dragged his butchered carcass down the hill into the pink and brown water. Reunited, his brother sat with him in midstream, cradling his torso on his lap, disfigured head to his bosom.

"You're going to be just fine, James, just fine, just fine . . ." The unsavaged twin rocked his brother back and forth. Even from the bank, Blake could see that James had suffered not only the three wounds he had witnessed, but others as well. The portion of his uniform that lay in the water had turned charcoal and maroon, but the big chunk of meat John held against him was sheathed in blood in various stages of drying. It looked as though pranksters had drained buckets of blood from other wounded men, then poured them over James.

"Ma's going to tend you," John Bunyan said, almost singing. "They're going to send you on home, and Ma's going to see to you. She'll have you back behind them mules come autumn, if not sooner . . . just you wait . . . and Rachel, she's going to cry her eyes out from pure happy to see you coming up the hollow . . . they'll all be shouting for you, James, shouting and dancing, just to see you come on home . . . you're going to make me all jealous . . ."

"That boy's dead," Cobb said. His voice was quieter than usual.

"Well, we're not going to tell John that. You understand me, Billie? Let him have his grief his own way. He'll figure things out. Then we'll see about the burying."

Cobb didn't answer directly. "Ought to look round for a new hat. Never will find mine again, not worth the bother. You think wearing a dead man's hat would be bad luck, Quaker?"

"If God's the way you say, it doesn't matter. Come on, let's get started."

They splashed into the stream, its waters drawn from a slaughter-house. Blake knelt down on the streambed stones, close enough to confirm that Cobb was right.

James Bunyan was dead.

The still-living twin looked up, expression as earnest as any

Blake could remember. More earnest, even, than his mother's looks had been when she clutched the last thing she possessed in her soon-to-end life, which had been him. He had not been allowed to see her after the cholera came over her and her Quaker parents moved her to the barn so she would not infect the house with her puking and shit-ting. Blake was glad now that he had been deprived of the sight of her dying. That was one wise thing his grandparents had done, no matter their reasons. Better to remember her faded beauty and beaten-down voice, rather than filth and delirium.

God wasn't what Cobb called him. Describing God took big-ger, harder words.

"We got to get James on back to the surgeons," John Bunyan said. "We got to hurry on now."

"Sure enough," Blake told him, "that's what we're going to do. Where's your rifle?"

"Yonder." He pointed at the bank.

Blake turned to Cobb and held out his own weapon. "Here. Take this. And fetch his."

"Nope," Cobb said.

"Damn you, you'll do—"

"Nope. You're the sergeant. I figure that makes me the body-toter."

Blake looked at little Cobb, then at the big, death-heavy body in the stream.

Cobb understood and said, "I'm tougher than you. You're stronger, all right. But I'll last. And you're the sergeant. Wouldn't want old Knock to think we was ignoring military courtesies, would we?"

So they went, John Bunyan stepping backward, slipping amid the round wet rocks and then on the bank-slime, lugging his brother's body under the armpits. Cobb followed, holding the corpse beneath the knees.

"You get tired, you tell me," Blake ordered.

"I won't get tired, Sergeant Blake," John Bunyan said. Then he spoke, in soothing murmurs, to his brother again.

Snake-strike close, a voice called, "Sergeant Blake? *Sergeant Blake?*"

Blake turned. Amid the ruined brambles, Lieutenant Devereaux

struggled to lift his torso. Blooms of blood had spread over thigh and forearm.

"Help me."

Blake's first instinct was to stop playing along with John Bunyan and tell him and Cobb to pick up the lieutenant. But there was something going on beyond the brush that changed his mind.

"You put your brother down for a minute," he told John Bunyan. "Put him down gently now. And wait for me." To the lieutenant, he said, "We'll get you on out of here, sir. Just hold on a little longer."

He laid down two of the three rifles he lugged, keeping his own. And he marched out into the field where the slaughter had begun just hours before.

Scavengers were robbing the dead and wounded. Three of them. Shameless and unconcerned in the afternoon light.

Their pockets bulged.

He came close enough to draw the interest of one of the looters, who paused. The other two kept on mining pockets. A wounded man struggled faintly to resist.

"You," Blake said. To all of them. He raised his rifle in their general direction, holding it just shy of his shoulder. In their greed, the three men had laid their own weapons aside.

All three of them rose now. Sizing him up.

"You need to stop what you're doing. Right now." He cocked his rifle. "And empty out your pockets."

Bearded and ragged, the men straightened in defiance. One hitched up his trousers.

"You ain't no sergeant of ours," the rear man said. "So git along."

Blake turned his rifle toward the speaker. "I pull this trigger, it won't matter all that much whose sergeant I am."

Instead of cowering, two of the men edged closer. The third kept still.

"Now, I ain't got my letters all that good," one of the men told Blake, "but I've got my numbers. And one shot from you still leaves two of us. That means at least two of us four are like to stay right here with these poor folk." He smiled, snaggletoothed. "How you like that figuring, Sergeant Whoever-the-Hell?"

Blake saw Cobb before the men did. Cobb had worked around

behind them. With a bobcat leap, he left the concealing greenery and slammed his rifle butt into the side of the rear man's head. Shutting his iron-hard foot over the fallen man's throat, he locked his weapon against his shoulder before the other two scavengers had time to turn.

"Why don't y'all tell Sergeant Blake there about them numbers again?"

If the men had been little impressed with Blake, they took Cobb a great deal more seriously. Kind meets kind, Blake thought.

"We were just minding our own business."

Cobb let go one of his mocking laughs. "Mighty fine business, too."

Other men with more honorable concerns emerged from the creekbed, bearing their wounded blood relatives or blanket-mates. In the opposite direction, a band of litter bearers appeared, returning to their duties from a field hospital. Plenty of company now.

"Empty your pockets and go," Blake told the robbers.

One of the men snickered. "You wouldn't shoot a fellow soldier, Sergeant."

Cobb spoke up. "He might, or might not. But me, I set myself a goal of killing five men today, and I'm only certain of four. So you git. And take this turd of yours with you." He removed his bare foot from the soldier's throat and the man moaned. Just for good measure, Cobb punched his heel into the man's ribs.

Blake hailed two sets of stretcher bearers. They weren't the regiment's Moravian musicians performing their alternate duty, but they responded. He led them into the brambles.

The first two bearers took up Lieutenant Devereaux, who groaned as they lifted him onto the bloody stretcher and carried him off. But when the other bearers moved to shift James Bunyan, one, a red-haired boy, said, "This here fella's dead."

John Bunyan sprang up and broke the bearer's nose, knocking him several feet backward.

"Stop it, damn you!" Blake ordered. His throat felt torn.

John Bunyan looked at him. Trying to remember who this man was and why his voice carried authority.

"James ain't dead," he proclaimed.

The two men stood frozen as the unmolested stretcher bearer

tended to his comrade. They waited long enough for flies to find them. Then they stood there a bit longer.

At last, John Bunyan tightened his eyes on Blake's. "*You* tell me. I don't trust that Cobb. Or them folks. You tell me if James is . . ."

Blake knelt down. He took theatrical pains over the body, checking for a pulse in the ruined neck and at an unblemished wrist. He dropped his ear against the boy's blood-encrusted chest to search for a heartbeat. Then he brought his face close to the horror that remained of James Bunyan's jaw, testing for breath.

He was careful to stand up and slip into a ready stance before he spoke.

"He's dead. I'm sorry."

John Bunyan didn't wail or cry. Nor did he lash out this time. He just nodded. Looking away from Blake, away even from the big carcass that had been his twin brother.

"I guess I knowed," he said mildly. Then he added, "Ma'll take it well enough. She's the strong one. But this is going to ruin Pa, just ruin him. It don't matter about him riding with those bushwhackers. James was still the apple of his eye."

From mild, the twin eased to docile. He looked again at Blake, then at Cobb, and back to Blake. "Can we take him on, though? I don't want to leave him here like this. I want to be able to tell Pa I buried him proper."

Blake held out his rifle to Cobb. "My turn to carry."

Colonel Burgwyn was dead and Lieutenant Colonel Lane was set to die. They heard the news as soon as they reached the much-diminished crowd of sprawled and sitting men behind the tavern ridge. Blake asked for Major Jones. He didn't want to seem defiant on such a day and hoped to get permission to take James Bunyan off a little ways and bury him. But Knock Jones had gone to pay his last respects to Colonel Burgwyn.

Blake remembered the colonel soft-voiced in the night, not two full days before, as Burgwyn had tried to make a bookkeeper of him. The boy had risen to a man's place well enough. And he had paid the cost. With many another.

Two other survivors from the company joined the burial party without being asked. After a testy exchange with some artillery-

men drawn back into the reserve, a gunner lieutenant ordered his men to loan Blake and his companions a pick and two shovels.

"Just bring 'em back," the lieutenant said.

Blake nodded.

As his death thickened, James grew heavier. They carried his body back through a swale, then angled away from the road to escape the screams from a field hospital.

"Only thing meaner than a red-haired woman's a surgeon with a saw," Cobb said.

"Now that's a plain fact," Corny Wright, one of the helpful pair of volunteers, confirmed.

"Just hope somebody'll have the decency to bury me apart, when my time comes," the other man, Charley Campbell, said. "I just can't take to the idea of being thrown in a pit with folks I don't know."

"And shallow enough for dogs to have a chew," Cobb put in, offering them his lopsided cave of a smile.

"We ain't going to bury James shallow," John Bunyan said. Blake caught the sudden fear, the dread, in the boy's voice.

Before Blake could speak, Cobb told the twin, "No, we ain't. No Yankee hound's going to feast on one of our'n."

"Digging's a calming thing, anyhow," Corny said. Cornelius Wright was a blacksmith, famed back home for making up in skill what he lacked in muscle. Charley Campbell, who had sworn off liquor young to please his mother, had doled out whiskey in his uncle's tavern. Charley had been renowned for never touching a drop to his lips.

Blake understood what the two men were about. They had lost their campfire-mates that afternoon. They needed to belong again, to enter a new family within their greater clan. So Corny and Charley had leapt to make themselves useful. It was fine by Blake, who knew neither man was trouble. But he needed to make sure no lines were being crossed.

"I didn't see Sergeant Dunlap back there where we're putting down," he said.

Corny grunted. "Yankee peckerwood shot him between the eyes."

Weary men, they slowed almost to baby steps as they took the body up another hillock. On top, Blake said, "We'll stop here."

Charley sighed. "Be easier to dig, we was to put him in bottom-land."

But Blake wanted to do this one thing right and proper. For John Bunyan. Who would be needed in the coming days. For John, his ma, the sister, and the worthless other brother who'd gone off with his pa to ride with Yankee bushwhackers. And he wanted to do it because it put some rightness to the day.

"This a good enough place?" he asked the surviving twin.

John Bunyan said, "Over there's better. By them trees. So he'll have shade."

Blake expected a crack from Cobb about dead men not having a particular need for shade, but it didn't come. Maybe Cobb was just too worn out to keep up his meanness. But the filthy little man with the ruined nose had been all right that day. Not least with the scavengers down by the creek.

Nor did any man complain of the additional labor of digging where there would be roots to hack through. They were too weary to protest against much of anything. They were willing—even Cobb was—to let Blake decide things.

Conscious of the need to return to what remained of the regiment, Blake paced out a length of earth where the falling sun threw shade, but the roots might not be so bad.

"Look here, John," he said to the twin, who stood, still bewildered, over his brother's body, "this strikes me as a fine spot. He'll have the morning sun to warm him after the night, and shade all afternoon to keep him cool. Think this would be agreeable to your kin?"

Gone inward again, the twin nodded, but said nothing.

Aching to belong, Charley and Corny did more than their share of the work, going at it hard until Charley's muscles shook visibly. John Bunyan replaced Charley in the hole. Except for Cobb, they were young men all, but looked of middle age.

"You get out of there, too, Corny," Blake told him, taking off his coat. "You've done your part."

Jumping into the rough-made hole, Blake thought how odd it was that he'd never contemplated the prospect of being laid in a mass grave himself. He'd thought about dying and had not been

much troubled by the possibility, but the thought of lying forever crushed against or under another man's rot queased him.

Tired, he thought. We're all tired. Deadly in need of water.

"You, Charley Campbell," he said. "If you're rested enough, you gather up those canteens and go on over and see if that farm-house can spare a little water without asking Yankee dollars for it."

The barkeep did as bidden, promptly, moving as fast as a man tired to failing could make himself go, heading across a half-mile of fields.

They all need to belong, Blake thought, heaving up another shovel load. Even Cobb, in his way. Why don't I feel it? Under all the yes-sir-no-sir, why don't I feel that need?

Pausing to rest his weight on the shovel, Blake asked, "Deep enough?"

Tight beside him, John Bunyan stopped digging. Blake had grasped that, if he didn't put a stop to things, the boy would bur-row right on through to China.

The twin peered over the lip of the grave and beyond the cluster of trees. To the west, shadows deepened on the mountain the army had crossed to come to this place. Then the boy looked at his worn shoes and Blake's.

"I reckon."

"Dog nor man won't get him down that deep," Corny assured him.

"Anyway," Cobb added, "dogs'll have easier pickings after today."

"He'll still be here, you ever want to bring family back," Blake said.

For a long moment, they listened to the slackened gunnery in the east, beyond the corpse-laden ridges and the town.

Another chill thought pierced Blake.

"The Yankees aren't leaving," he said.

"How's that?" Corny asked. Every man among them had believed this battle won and done.

"They aren't leaving. Just listen. Listen to how quiet it's gotten."

"It ain't quiet," Cobb said. And he was right. Desultory firing continued. With the shovel-blade-on-stones digging done, the shrieks from the field hospital back along the pike carried over, too.

"Not quiet. Just quieter."

He saw the realization dawn on Cobb. But the little man's ravaged face went blank again.

"If the Yankees were running, we'd be on them," Blake explained. "There's light left. We'd be after them like hounds on a three-legged fox. And we'd hear it."

"After we whipped them like that?" John Bunyan asked. His voice was near despair. "We're going to have to fight them again? *Here?*"

Blake shrugged. "Somebody will. Maybe not us." Through a fine field of oats, Charley Campbell strode toward them. Laden with their canteens. Blake promised himself, swore to himself, that they would be full of cool well water. "All right. We need to bury James and get on back."

So they laid him gently in his grave in a Pennsylvania field, and they shoveled in the dirt again as the living brother watched. Used to makeshift, backcountry doings, Cobb fashioned a cross by deep-notching a fallen branch and forcing a stick down into it horizontally.

He held it out to John Bunyan. "Put this in the ground there, boy."

The cross got the twin thinking. "We need to say some words. Some scripture."

Blake could have done so. He could have spewed out chapter and verse until morning. But he did not want to do it. Not that. He feared the words would come fouled from his mouth. The dead boy deserved a sincere voice at the last.

"My Bible's in my knapsack," Corny said. "Wherever that happens to be."

Charley came up with the canteens. Blake heard water sloshing. Charley grinned, let the canteens settle to the ground, and drew a roll of pressed meat and a loaf from under his jacket.

"They would've give me the parlor furniture and at least one of the children, they're so scared."

Take. Eat. Drink. This is my body, and this is my blood . . .

"Know any Bible words by heart, Charley?" Blake asked. Offering the man a chance to come another step closer to his new family.

Charley thought it over, then said, "Not the right ones, I reckon."

Let down at the last, John Bunyan looked like a beat-on pup. Resigning himself, Blake took a long swallow of the finest water he had ever tasted and prepared to speak the words that had to be said.

Before Blake finished drinking, though, Cobb stepped up to the head of the grave and straightened himself behind the cross he had fashioned.

The foul little man spoke in beauteous mimic of a preacher for whom the Word itself was wine:

And when all the children of Israel saw how the fire came down, and the glory of the LORD upon the house, they bowed themselves with their faces to the ground upon the pavement, and worshipped, and praised the LORD, saying, For he is good; for his mercy endureth forever. . . . Then the king and all the people offered sacrifices to the LORD.

Cobb poured a brief stream of water onto the grave, then continued, "Lord . . . we commend unto you your poor servant, this fine boy, young James Bunyan, who never hurt nothing or no one he wasn't made to by the ways of this world, who strayed not into temptation, but done his duty to God and man, and loved his kinfolk. We ask, Lord, that you take James to your bosom, where he will shine as true as he done upon this earth. And we ask your mercy, Lord, on those James left down here amid trial and tribulation, when his enemies and thine slew him. Their wickedness has lifted him on high, above this vale of sorrow and into your grace. Amen."

"Them words do?" he asked John Bunyan.

The twin nodded his contentment.

And they went back across the ridges and through the swale, past the calling of the men on the surgeons' tables, and they returned their borrowed tools to the artillerymen.

"Huh," a black-eyed sergeant said. "Never thought I'd see you boys again."

"Thank you," Blake told him. It seemed a time for civilities.

They ate as they walked, selfish, knowing that to share further would break this bond of complicity and help no one. By the time they reached the spotty grove and backslope where the 26th North Carolina mourned, they had almost missed the muster.

The regiment had gone into the attack with 800 men that morning. Just 212 answered when the roll was called. Blake's company had begun the day with 89 men. Only 19 remained alive and whole. Nor had their supply wagons appeared. So the rest of the men had not even the small, wonderful portions Blake and his soldiers had enjoyed as a funeral feast.

Up the ridge a throw, by the tavern pump, men lined up for water.

"I can go this time," Corny said. "I don't mind standing a wait."

"Later," Blake told him. "And we'll draw straws." It was his way of welcoming the two other men closer. Close enough to have something a man might depend on.

Campfires came alight in the gloaming. There was as yet no food for the regiment to cook, nor even coffee, but the fires had another purpose, intended to fend off the spirits that had followed the ancestors of these men from moors and fens, from brutally enclosed pastures and wild, bare mountains, following them across the great water and into new moors and glens, then following them here, to this place of death, relentless and mocking.

A captain none of them recognized came by. His uniform had not been disturbed by the day's events. The sword he wore looked sure to have been the gift of a wealthy father.

The officer stopped before them, a wonderfully self-confident young man. Handsome enough to trouble a rival beau.

"Come now, boys . . . not enough strength left to build yourselves a fire?"

"Ain't no food to cook," Cobb told him.

"Too damn hot," Charley Campbell said.

The officer was nonplussed. After regrouping, he attacked from another angle.

"Well," he said, "I can understand that . . . if you're weary, I suppose." He tried for a jocular tone. "We're all pretty tuckered out, indeed we are. It's been quite a day. Your regiment did magnificent service, though, simply magnificent. And it did not go unnoticed. Do you know what the message said that General Pettigrew sent to Colonel Burgwyn?"

"Before he died?" Blake asked. "Or after?"

"Before," the captain said hastily. "I'm sure it was before. I understand that your colonel didn't . . . that he didn't perish immedi-

ately. But don't you want to know what General Pettigrew said? About all of you?"

Charley Campbell, whose tavern work had taught him to deal with a great assortment of men, said, "Be good to hear it, sir. Why don't you tell us?"

Cobb guffawed.

In a voice clipped back, the officer told them, "General Pettigrew said—and these are his exact words, mind you—that your 'regiment has covered itself with glory today.'"

"That's right nice," Cobb said. "Got any tobacco?"

When Longstreet rode up, the old man was engaged with correcting and signing orders. Surrounded by Taylor and his other staff men, Lee stood behind a table that had been dragged outside and placed under a tree. He nodded toward Longstreet and briefly raised a hand, a gesture at once of greeting and a signal to be patient.

Tired and stiff, Longstreet swung out of the saddle, landing so flat-footed that it jarred his spine. He had spent the day hurrying McLaws and Hood through the mountains toward the gun-thunder. Pickett still trailed the army, ostentatiously enthused about battle and full of excuses why he didn't move faster. When Longstreet had seen that he could do no more in the rear, and after a tease from Hood about trying to outshine Jackson, he had ridden on to Gettysburg. His own staff followed after, dogged by the English varmint, Lieutenant Colonel Fremantle.

What Longstreet saw along the way and heard at brief stops on the pike had troubled him. He had never encountered such a mix of the triumphant spirit of victory and the desolation of commanders who had lost much of their commands. One of Heth's staff officers had confessed to casualties of 75 percent in some regiments, with entire brigades broken. Those were numbers the South could not replace. Heth himself had been wounded, his division passing to Pettigrew. Longstreet thought of Pettigrew as the "Dancing Master," but he was fair-minded enough to recognize that the man displayed more sense than Harry Heth.

Yet, if some officers appeared stunned by the day's costs, others were jubilant, yapping about destroying a Yankee corps in "the

most gallant charges ever a man did see." And for all the wounded
streaming rearward or laid out in the fields by the surgeons' butcher
shops, it did seem that the Federals had suffered a far worse day
than the Army of Northern Virginia.

Done was done. Longstreet worried about what would come
next.

His staff men had a good sense of when to leave him alone and
they held back now, tethering their horses in the shade of a proud-
got-up building that clearly belonged to some form of institution.
Longstreet patted Hero's wet neck, getting the horse-smell the way
you never quite did in the saddle, then took a long swig from his
flask. The horse shook his head, sneezing, and clopped a half-step
backward. Longstreet steadied the creature and drew out his field
glasses. At a nod, Tom Goree came up to lead off the mount. Fre-
mantle had to be restrained from leaping forward with more of his
pestering questions.

Longstreet walked a dozen paces beyond the cluster of build-
ings on the ridge and out on a rough-kept lawn. He didn't use the
glasses at first, but took in the entire sweep of the landscape. The
town filled the left side of his span of vision, but on the right a shal-
low cradle of fields separated him from the Federals, who were
gradually filling in lines along a low ridge a mile away. But the fea-
ture that seized his attention rose behind the town.

He raised the glasses. The hill was a graveyard domain, crowded
now with living men in blue. As he watched, Union soldiers filtered
back from the town, singly, in pairs, or in clusters, few of them run-
ning and some pausing to fire rearward, no longer under concerted
pressure from his own kind. Their destination was a low stone wall
lined with their fellows.

That wall should have been taken. Longstreet could not under-
stand why the assault had stopped short, why Hill had not pushed
right through the town to the high ground, once he was well at it.
Hill, with his ruined loins and fevered eyes. Lee, too, had been
present. Why hadn't *he* insisted on driving the Federals hard, when
Hill wavered? That was, after all, the old man's fashion in a fight,
that excited and merciless appetite of his for the kill at the end of
the hunt. What had happened?

Longstreet understood the many ways in which attacks just

come to a stop all on their own, running out of go. But this case looked to him like inattention.

With every passing hour, that Federal position was only going to strengthen. Already, the hill wore a fiery tiara of cannon. It was the finest position the Army of the Potomac had occupied since Malvern Hill.

Was that all for the better, though? Would the inherent superiority of Meade's position deter the old man from fighting on the aggressive? Would he see the light at last?

Steadying the glasses, Longstreet scanned the emerging Union line from the gun-encrusted skull on the left, down along the declining ridge, past the last infantry regiment to arrive, and on to where cavalry pickets had pushed out into the fields and meadows. Beyond them, the landscape sank obscurely, only to cast up a pair of smooth-top hills. The hill farther to the south was notably higher, but more thickly wooded and less useful to artillery. The low hill was key.

If Meade had the men present and the common sense to occupy those hills by the next morning, his line would not be turned upon that flank and on this field. In that case, the old man would have to listen to reason and agree, at last, to slip deep behind the Union left, settle on good ground between Meade and Washington, and force the Union commander to do the attacking.

Longstreet surveyed the ridge again, guiding the tunnel of sight past galloping couriers and fresh regiments arriving, drawn back to that gun-clad cemetery. He watched as caissons delivered more ammunition. Small blue figures stocked shot near the guns. Other artillerymen, stripped to the waist, dug out sheltered positions for their cannon. Below them, foot soldiers in blue urgently added height to stone walls and built up fence-lines with planks and dirt. On a promontory below a brick gatehouse, a battery line flamed and recoiled, firing northward. Toward Ewell's men, that would be, had to be.

Why hadn't Dick Ewell run right over that hill, before the Yankees had a chance to fortify it? The man had Tom Jackson's men under his command, for God's sake. They would've done it on a dare.

It sank in that, if everyone present had lacked the sense to take that position today, it would not be taken. The *only* possibility was to go around Meade.

Finished with the pen-and-ink work of command, the old man joined him on the lawn.

"I wonder, is General Meade on the field today?" Lee said.

Longstreet saw an opening. "Must be. That's a position an engineer would choose. You would, sir."

Lee didn't take the bait.

"Well, George Meade's trapped himself good and proper," Longstreet went on. "You can see he's concentrating as fast as he can. No, sir, we could not call the enemy to a position better suited to our plans. All we have to do is file around his left and secure good ground between him and his capital."

The old man's complexion pinked and he reared back his head as a horse will. Pointing toward the Federal position, he said, "If the enemy is still there tomorrow, we must attack him."

The old man's blood was up, it was all too plain.

"Well, if he *is* still there," Longstreet said, "it'll be because he's anxious that we should attack him . . . a good reason, in my judgment, for not doing so."

Lee stared across the fields. Shadows lengthened toward the Union lines.

"It would be folly to assault that cemetery, the way they're building up," Longstreet said. "Just look at it. If it was to be done, why wasn't it done today? Before they all piled in. Count the guns up there."

"I have given General Ewell," Lee began, "permission to outflank that position this evening, if practicable."

"Ewell's not Jackson," Longstreet said.

Go ahead, Longstreet thought. Say it. Tell me that I'm not Tom Jackson, either.

"He will do his duty."

Like Stuart? Longstreet almost said. The gay cavalier was still absent, perhaps in Maine by now. "Sir, you said you didn't want a battle . . . not one like this . . . where Meade has such an advantage, where you don't have proper information . . ."

In the town, sporadic shots crackled, but there was no meaningful action.

"General Meade," Lee said, "has tolerably good ground. We have this army. And it cannot be defeated."

Longstreet turned sharply, as if assailed by a madman. He was about to speak, to protest, when Lee's unexpected paleness stopped him cold. The old man's face was greased with sudden sweat.

"If you will excuse me, General Longstreet?" Unsteady, his eyes were already fleeing, before his feet could act.

The old man hurried off, moving much more rapidly and with far less grace than was his habit. Longstreet understood. Lee's guts were in rebellion again, a situation that always unsettled and angered the old man, part embarrassment at the human condition and part outrage that his own body would be disobedient.

It was not a good situation. The day's win, costly though it had been, had gotten the old man's blood up. Now he was going to be sick-cranky and stubborn as a mule, too.

It cannot be defeated. Longstreet felt stricken by the remark, as if hit by a spent ball. The army had never taken the field that could not be defeated. Especially if its generals believed it could not be defeated. Look at Xerxes . . . the French knights at Agincourt . . . Charles XII . . . Napoleon . . .

Longstreet raised the glasses to his eyes again. If Ewell was going to outflank anybody, he had damned well better do it soon. As Longstreet watched, another Federal regiment crested the ridge in the distance, coming on in columns of companies to extend the line behind still more stone walls.

Madness.

Or was it, Longstreet wondered, just plain pride? The sort of I-won't-give-one-inch-damn-you pride that had led South Carolina out, followed by the rest of them. To what extent had Lee succumbed to the siren song of glory? Seduced by the mighty victories to his credit? To what degree had all of them succumbed? Had they been numbed by their triumphs?

Pride comes before a fall. There never was an army that could not be defeated. Never. Longstreet could not recall hearing Lee or any other man utter such dreadful words until this hour. It put fear in him.

The old man returned to his side, better composed.

"My apologies, General. An indisposition." Willing to repair the breach between them, Lee attempted to lighten the exchange. "Speaking of indispositions, I see that our English friend remains attached to you."

Longstreet waved his head back and forth like a flag of surrender. "If I hanged Colonel Fremantle from an apple tree, he'd use his dying breath to give me a lecture on pippins."

"Well, don't hang him. That man may prove worth an army and a fleet."

Longstreet didn't believe that, either. The British were not coming in. The more he heard of Fremantle's blabber, the more he was convinced of it.

"We won a victory today," Lee said. "Those people held an initial advantage. But we overcame it. Perhaps if Colonel Fremantle witnessed a still-greater victory?"

"And we might give him one. If you issue the orders tonight to move around Meade's flank. George Meade's got his whole army headed this way now. He'll have a devil of a time turning it around. We can upset his plans, unbalance him . . . make him fight to his rear. . . ."

"We won a victory today," Lee repeated. "If Meade is determined to fight here, we shall win a greater victory tomorrow. This army will not fail us." The old man stepped closer, looking into Longstreet's face. "I cannot withdraw from a victorious battlefield. The men would not take it well."

"The men who wouldn't take it well are dead, sir. Heth's division's gutted."

"And those people have lost two corps. They will be demoralized. They will fight less well tomorrow than they did today."

Escorted by Taylor, Lee's ever-alert familiar, a courier approached. The old man faced the intruders.

"From General Ewell, sir," Taylor said.

"Is General Ewell attacking?" Lee asked, before hearing the message. "Has he found an opening on the flank?"

The courier, a staff officer Longstreet did not know, saluted and said, "General Ewell's compliments, sir. He asks for support, if he's to make an assault."

Disappointment lowered the old man's face. Had he been in full health, he would not have let another see such emotion. After a moment's contemplation, Lee told the staff officer, "General Hill's corps is in some disarray. His men have had a hard fight. I will look into the matter, but cannot promise General Ewell additional sup-

port." He paused again. "Emphasize my order to your general: He is to attack, if practicable."

The courier saluted and strode off. Taylor eyed the two generals, then followed the courier. He had read the atmosphere.

"Jackson would've just done it," Longstreet said. "He wouldn't have sent a courier. Ewell's looking for an excuse not to attack."

"General Ewell will do his duty."

"That may be, sir. But he isn't going to attack that hill or anything else tonight. I'd bet my command on it." Then something snapped inside Longstreet and his voice grew more heated than ever it had in the presence of Robert E. Lee. "If we have to take that . . . that hill . . . do it now, sir! Do it now, with every man available! Or set this army on the march around Meade's flank. Do it now, or the price tomorrow will be higher than this army can afford."

Lee let his subordinate calm himself, then said, "You told me yourself that Meade holds a strong position. This is not a time for hasty measures, General Longstreet. We will act tomorrow, when your corps is up and we can execute an attack that will trap those people and destroy them." The old man's body quaked again, but Lee, inhumanly disciplined, quelled the tremor. "How far back is General Pickett? Will his division be available?"

"He won't arrive until late tomorrow. Too late for the day's fight. It's hard to move this army on one road."

"Then we shall make do with Generals Hood and McLaws." The old man considered Longstreet in the slanting, gilded light. Judging. "I know you will not let me down."

TEN

July 1, Evening into Night

The corpse grabbed him again. Schwertlein froze in midstride. He shut his eyes, then opened them. Odd wisps lingered in the evening air, but Otto Schumann was gone.

Of course he was gone. He had never been present. Schumann was dead. Lying out there. Amid the rest of them.

Schwertlein sucked in the gunpowder air. Sweat had burst from his body at the sudden hallucination. He had *felt* the dead man's embrace, fresh and immediate. Schumann had clutched him precisely as he had done on the battlefield. No. *More* intensely than that. The slain man's arms had wrapped around him more completely and had been unwilling to relinquish their grip, their last clutch at life. Gruesome and terrible, Otto's face had pressed to his own.

"Fritz!"

Bettelman had paused to look back at him. As Schwertlein met the watchmaker's bewilderment, he watched his friend change into Schumann's corpse.

"Fritz? What is it?"

Then Schumann was gone, completely, and the world appeared as it was supposed to be, as normal as the rattled aftermath of battle would concede. A soldier toting a case of cartridges jostled him: "Would you be getting out of me way then, ye great dumb Dutchman?"

Between the gravestones, men grunted, complained, worked, laughed, wept, stood to their posts, or, searching, called out the names of comrades the day had devoured. *Survivors.* Amazed to find themselves so few, astonished to find themselves so many.

Bettelman stepped back to stand in front of him, eyes shifting

from surprise toward alarm. "Are you all right? You're pale as a corpse."

Schwertlein forced a smile. "I'd be in the right place."

The watchmaker did not appear convinced that all was well, but shrugged and said, "Come on. They can only say no."

The 26th Wisconsin had nothing to eat. Water was to be had from a pump up the hill by the cemetery gatehouse, but the men had lost their knapsacks after grounding them at the orchard, and their commissary wagons had disappeared. Other units that had been in the fight that day were as hard-used as the 26th, but the newly arrived regiments at least had the contents of their packs to sustain them. Still others, fresh from the rear, cooked meals in cauldrons.

"Come on, Fritz," Bettelman repeated. "I tell you, I fixed watches for some of them. When we were in winter quarters at Stafford Court House. More than one of them owes me still."

Clammy after his explosion of fear-sweat, Schwertlein followed. The distance was not far enough to mark them as absent from their place of duty in the line. Not amid the ongoing confusion. And he was as hungry as Bettelman. He could not recall ever being so hungry.

Maria. Had it been only the night before when he had sat on a farmer's porch, agonizing over cautious hints? What could he write to her now? That they had been defeated and humiliated again, but, great good luck, he himself had barely been nicked? Oh, yes, his dearest friends were dead or abandoned to the Rebels. But he was fine, just fine, in excellent health and spirits . . . his uniform was only a little dirtied . . .

Maria. Unreasonably, the image of her left him nauseated, sick at something about himself for which he knew no name. It was as if he had become smaller as she watched, as if she had spurned him harshly from afar, from across a gulf so vast that he could not call out to defend himself, across a chasm so monstrous that he would never reach her again.

Was he truly alive? How certain could a man be of that, after all? Was all of this a *Totentanz*, a dance of death, around him?

Before he indulged himself in a personal missive to Maria Schenk,

it would be his duty to write to another Maria: Maria Schumann, the carpenter's wife, a woman he knew only from the homely musings of her fallen husband. And he would need to write, hardest of all, to Josef Heisler's Marthe. To beautify Josef's death, just as requested. To lie. To the wife the teacher and would-be poet had idolized.

Her name conjured a line from Faust, spoken by Mephistopheles to Marthe, the incidental procuress: *"Ihr Mann ist tot und lässt Sie grüssen."*

Your husband's dead and sends you greetings.

It had always struck Schwertlein as the cruelest of all the cruel lines in the play. Yet, it never failed to draw a laugh from the audience. Especially when the devil was played with skill.

"Please, Leo. A minute," Schwertlein said to the watchmaker's back.

Bettelman halted again. His eyebrows arched quizzically.

"I feel dizzy."

"You must drink water, Fritz. You're always telling the rest of us to drink water."

"I can't drink anymore."

"You must."

Dutifully, he took a swig from his canteen. But water was not the problem now. He sensed Schumann out there in the dying light. Moving parallel to him. Waiting to spring. To clutch him again.

Schwertlein broke into another sweat. He had imagined the dead man's face against him, kissing him as a passionate woman would.

How could it be so real? Otto was dead. He was not here. He was *dead*. Lying in a field beyond the town.

Otto scooted off to hide again. It was a child's game played in Hell.

Schwertlein knew it was an illusion. But it was the same as being in a dream that he knew to be a dream, yet could not escape.

"Can we sit for a bit?" His corporal's rank was meaningless. Little Bettelman led now. Trailing a strange, entranced creature in a soiled blue uniform.

Schwertlein dropped on his backside, resting against his rifle. Leo took a place nearby, bracing his back with a tombstone. In the half-chaos, no one paid them any attention.

"It's Otto," Schwertlein said. "He keeps coming back. Right in front of me. Grabbing me. The way he did . . ." He closed his eyes, saw Schumann, and promptly widened them again. "When I see him, his face is right there, his eyes. Right against mine. As if . . . as if he's about to kiss me . . . *es ist doch grausam* . . ."

"You're dreaming on your feet. It's been a bad day."

"I know I'm dreaming. I mean, I know he isn't real. Of course he isn't. But I see him anyway. And when I do, he seems impossibly real. . . ."

"It's odd," Bettelman said.

"What?"

"I thought you'd be mourning our poet friend. Or worrying about Hannes Trenk, whether he's still alive. And here you are haunted by Schumann. You weren't even close to Otto."

The fresh night swarmed around them. "It's the *way* it happened. It was . . . almost as if his life were trying to enter mine, to take refuge inside me, to hide and go on living. I could feel his fear of dying. I could smell it."

"He was already dead. I saw it. It was only the way getting hit turned him around. A freak thing."

"I felt what I felt."

Bettelman raised his eyes to the thickening sky. "You're thinking too much, Fritz. Just be glad we're not prisoners. Or worse. You just need sleep."

"Here?" He gestured at the imperfect lines of headstones, some already broken off or toppled by gun carriages.

"A man can sleep anywhere."

"*If* a man can sleep. You're right, though. It would make more sense if I thought about Josef or Hannes. Maybe they're waiting their turns." He stared at the trampled grass, at a past tableau. "Josef came to me last night. I was writing, I didn't want to be bothered. But he insisted. You know what he told me?"

"That he was going to die?"

"He told you, too?"

"No. We were close friends, but in a different way. He was depressed, though. Any man could see it. We've both seen men like that before. They know."

"That's nonsense. And I told him it was all nonsense." Schwertlein rested his head against the wood of his rifle. "He asked me to write to his wife. To tell her it was all tidy and clean."

"Will you?"

"Write to her? Of course."

"Tell her it was all tidy and clean."

"It was his last wish."

"She won't care, you know."

Schwertlein woke from his exhausted melancholy. "She's his *wife*, Leo."

The watchmaker moved his foot out of the path of a trio of soldiers. "You didn't know Josef Heisler before the war. I did. For you, he was only a wartime friend. I knew him much longer. And I advise you not to mourn him too excessively." Bettelman paused to select his next words. "The thing is . . . his death was not so unfortunate. In fact, I think he was lucky. Oh, don't look so shocked, Fritz."

"Josef loved life."

Bettelman shrugged. "But life did not love him. It's as you told me once, when we were joking about him and his mooning about. You said that he loved poetry, but poetry didn't love him. He was just the kind of poor, kindly fool who isn't loved back by those he picks to love." The watchmaker leaned toward him. His face was earnest in the softening light, with no trace of cruelty. "Perhaps this day has spared him much disappointment, a great deal of heartache. He wished to be a great poet, but had no gift—it didn't take a scholar like you to see it. He read his poems to me, too. He bored everyone with them. He was a man whose dreams soared above his abilities. What good ever comes of that? Do you think he was destined for joy, Fritz? And the poor fellow's wife took other men into her bed. Not from grand passion. From habit. I never believed that woman had a soul, only her appetites. Josef's children don't look a bit like him."

Schwertlein would have preferred that all of this had gone untold, that Bettleman had remained the whining clown to whom all were accustomed. The day had stripped away more than the regiment's knapsacks.

"None of that makes his death a good thing," he told the watchmaker.

"You think not, Fritz? This war solves many, many problems, not just slavery or questions of government. How else explain men's eagerness"—he swept a hand across the antic scene playing out in the frail light—"for all this?"

"You really are a cynic," Schwertlein said. "Only of a higher order than we realized. A cynic's cynic."

"No, I'm a watchmaker. I'm interested in how all the little wheels and cogs and hammers function, individually and together. But I have no time for sloppy rhapsodies and romances about wheels and cogs." He used his rifle to lever himself to his feet. "We need to get moving, *Herr Corporal*."

Schwertlein rose obediently. They passed through a Walpurgis of campfires and contorted faces, of bedeviled horse teams, whips, and elusive laughter. At last, Schumann said, "Him. Over there, with the blond beard. I fixed his watch and he still owes me for it."

The two of them stepped slowly toward the fire. Men with their coats off sat back from the heat, eating stew from tin plates. The scent of coffee spiced the aroma of meat.

"That smells good," Bettelman said.

Fire-licked faces turned toward them.

"I'm Leo," Bettelman continued. "Remember me? I fixed watches for some of you. In the winter. I thought, perhaps, my friend and I might get a plate of food? All outstanding debts canceled in full!"

A slab-faced man addressed himself to Schwertlein's sleeve stripes, rather than to Bettelman.

"Germans?"

"*Ja*. Twenty-sixth Wisconsin."

"Then you just get the Hell out of here. Men that don't fight don't eat."

There was food, after all. Not much, but better than none. When Schwertlein and Bettelman returned to their regiment's portion of the line—hardly more than a company's frontage—they found that someone had delivered and cracked open two barrels of hardtack. There was no coffee.

Rifles laid ready against the stone wall, they sat down on a bump of grass by the road that pierced the line. Schwertlein wished

he at least had the tin cup that hung from his knapsack, so he could dip the hardtack in water to soften it. Some Confederate had it now, along with a tattered copy of *Phänomenologie des Geistes* and one good pair of socks.

He broke off a piece of cracker, put it in his mouth, then filled his mouth with water. A man did the best he could. Beside him, Bettelman simply chomped away.

From their position, they could look far to the west, over a finger of houses and outbuildings that stretched southward from the town and past the arc of Rebel campfires to the outline of the long mountain. As late as it was, a glow still gripped the ridgetops: The light was reluctant to die. As Schumann had been, in the instant of his death.

"I should not have spoken as I did about Heisler's wife," Bettelman stated abruptly. "That was wrong. It isn't my affair. This is why I only joke and do not talk seriously. When I talk so, I become wicked. I'm sorry."

"I didn't know any of it, Leo, I had no idea. The way he went on about her, she sounded half St. Ursula and half Venus." He watched two soldiers engaged in horseplay, wondering where they found the strength. "She must be an attractive woman, if not a good one."

"She has her appeal. To plenty of men. The appeal of a woman who has two children behind her, but no obstacles in front of her skirts. I don't know if Josef ever truly saw her as she was, even the way she looked, or if he simply created a Marthe in his mind and took it for the real one. What did he need, really? A dream-woman to whom he could address his poems. That's all." Bettelman sighed. "Here I am, speaking ugliness again. It's just that I always resented her flagrancy. And poor Josef was so unsuspecting, so simple. We belonged to the same *Turnverein,* although there was always more jabbering than gymnastics. That's how we met." Bettelman smiled at a recollection. "Josef was a lovely person, only . . . inadequate. Not just to Marthe Heisler and her sort, but inadequate to life. The truth is, I pitied him. Like an ailing cat you find at your door."

The watchmaker shifted his seat, arching his small spine. "Let me give you my best advice, Fritz, advice from the heart: Marry a

big, fat woman who can cook. One who won't have men knocking at your kitchen door when they think you're away for an hour. One who feeds you well because she's grateful. And because she wants to feed herself well, too. That's been the secret of my happiness."

Bettelman gestured to the left. Schwertlein's eyes followed. Colonel Krzyzanowski was conferring with his surviving officers by a campfire. Normally as straight up and down as a rifle barrel, the Pole was bent at the shoulders, pressing his left side with one hand as if stanching the flow of blood.

"Look at Kriz," Leo said. "He's in a bad way. But the fool won't take advantage of it. He has a wife and brats, too. And I hear he had a thriving business in Washington, selling crockery and the like. He could go home. He's done his part. He could take advantage of his misfortune and turn it into the best of luck. But he won't. The fool."

"Would you?" Schwertlein asked.

Behind them, the voice of the eternal sergeant barked at laboring soldiers to deepen a shit trench.

"Yes. Without a second thought. If I had such a wound. When I complain on the march, I'm never joking. I'd go home and count my blessings."

"What if you could just go home? Without a wound? Just walk away."

"That's different."

"Why?"

"Even watchmakers have their pride."

A cracker fleck had wandered up into his nose and Schwertlein sneezed. Recovering, he said, "I don't think any of us will be allowed much pride after today."

"Fritz! Forget them, would you? They didn't know, they weren't there. And they need someone to blame. Tonight they have their stew, tomorrow we'll have ours." He murmured a sound meanly related to laughter. "They couldn't very well blame one of their own kind, after all. That *hochwohlgeborener Arschloch* Barlow, for example."

"I hate the injustice of it. After how we fought. . . ."

"And you'll write a proper account of it all for your paper. To set the record straight."

Schwertlein waved that away. His arm was darker than the

gathering night: The summer day continued its rearguard struggle. "It won't matter what I write. It'll reach them too late, after everyone's cast their views in iron. The New York City papers will write that the 'Dutchmen' ran again. And the Chicago papers will repeat what New York decrees. And the English-language papers in Milwaukee will delight in passing on the word about the husbands and sons of their German neighbors."

"The truth will come out in time. It always does."

"That's a lie! Leo, that's as great a falsehood as a man ever uttered. The truth is what the strongest voices say it is."

To their left, a line of skirmishers bounded over the wall and trotted down the slope to the nearest buildings. Order was returning, measure by measure.

"Tomorrow will be an interesting day," Bettelman said, changing the subject. Their roles had reversed, with Bettelman now the optimist, while Schwertlein wallowed in doubt. "I hope the damned Rebels will only let us sleep. That's all you need, Fritz."

Bettelman hadn't felt Schumann's embrace, though. He hadn't known that near-kiss or felt the smear of gore. He had not gotten that last horrid breath in his nostrils.

Schwertlein dreaded sleep. Schumann was lurking out there. Waiting. If he saw and felt the corpse slap against him so vividly while awake, what would it be like when he lacked the defense of light and the armor of reason?

"They didn't know." On a scraped tongue, Schwertlein tested the words Leo had offered him. "They weren't *there*."

"At least," Bettelman said, "the whole army isn't running away this time. Who knows what tomorrow will bring?" He broke off another piece of the flinty cracker.

"I've never had the desire to kill men before," Schwertlein said. He wasn't certain he was speaking to Bettelman any longer.

"But you have it now? A desire to kill?"

Schwertlein didn't answer. He stared at the last hint of light over the mountain. He watched it die. Clouds were pressing in, felt as much as seen. *Your husband's dead and sends you greetings.* He imagined himself touching the breasts of the woman he had loved so long in secret. Pawing her with hands covered in blood.

"Damn it again!" the watchmaker cried. His trill of pain was so

sharp that, for an instant, Schwertlein thought his friend had been hit by a sharpshooter.

"Damned crackers!" Bettelman explained. "I just broke a tooth."

At noon, he had still hoped to fight at Pipe Creek. By six, he'd decided to move the army to Gettysburg. Now, at ten, he finally felt able to leave for the field himself. As soon as Butterfield finished the last dispatches for him to sign.

It had taken the devil's own determination to remain at his Taneytown headquarters, where he could not even hear the dueling cannon and remained at the mercy of intermittent couriers who often bore contradictory scrawls from generals on different portions of the field. He had wanted to rush off, to see the situation for himself. But he was not going to repeat Hooker's error and let the army commander's purpose go unanswered: He meant to lead all of his army, not merely the portion engaged.

Orders had to go to every corps, some countermanding earlier directives. Command relationships needed to be resolved, priorities assigned, roads allocated. Who should march first along *that* route, the next increment of the artillery reserve or an ammunition train? Or was the road best cleared to hurry on a division? Commissary wagons, ambulance columns, missing signal elements . . . it wasn't as damnably simple as the stay-at-home politicians and the newspapermen assumed.

Reynolds dead, John Reynolds dead. That news had been followed by his dispatch of Hancock to take temporary command of the field, but no sooner had Win rolled off in his ambulance than guarded reports that reeked of a bloody mess began filtering in, followed by Buford's chilling note that there "seemed to be no directing presence." Later, word came that Hancock had propped things up, leading to a brief sense of relief—which ended again when Hancock's less-than-manly assessment of possible courses of action arrived in the evening:

> *The battle is quiet now. I think we will be all right until*
> *night. Then it can be told better what had best be done. I think*
> *we can retire; if not, we can fight here, as the ground appears*
> *not unfavourable with good troops.*

What kind of pussyfooting was that? ". . . the ground appears not unfavourable . . ." Meade understood, of course. Hancock was a lion on the battlefield, but he wasn't going to put himself in a position to be blamed for a defeat, if one was coming. All the responsibility would be on Meade.

He was disappointed in Hancock's lack of manliness, though. He already had accepted that defeat, if it came, would belong to him alone. He could see it already: If the army emerged triumphant, the generals and colonels would squabble over whose bold action made the decisive difference. Let things go poorly, and there'd be no chests thumped to claims of "*I* made the fatal mistake."

"George, see if General Butterfield has those papers ready for me to sign. The man's slower than a Spaniard repaying a debt. And ask if anyone's found my spectacles yet."

He needed to get to Gettysburg now, to see the ground for himself. If the clouds blew past, there would be a good moon later, enough light to let him judge the terrain's potential. And he wanted to hear from Warren, his fellow engineer, a man who saw the details other men missed.

Out on the road, an endless column creaked by. An army's march was marked by a queer disturbance of the air, something more than a collective breath or the obvious concert of noises. There was a life to it that evoked no comparisons. Even more than battle, the march was the essence of the soldier's world.

He had longed to implement his scheme for the Pipe Creek line, but the day had a will of its own. The army had to go to Gettysburg. That did not mean, even now, that the army would remain there for the campaign's climactic battle, but it had become unthinkable to withdraw his two battered corps, even had Lee been willing to let them retreat without further molestation.

The thing of it was, Meade understood, that the army could not bear another episode of quitting. To flee Gettysburg in the stink of defeat would have broken its last morale. He would have to put up at least enough of a fight to call it a drawn match before he could withdraw to give battle elsewhere. And there still was the possibility that he could concentrate his army more swiftly than Lee, after all. The Confederates now on the field might be overconfident. What if he slammed into them with two corps and staged a double

envelopment with the remainder? Would the ground allow him to do that? Yes, the dispatches had informed him that he held the high ground. But how high? How expansive was the position? Could the flanks be anchored securely? If forced to defend, were his lines of fire strong enough to sweep the advancing enemy? He needed to know these things and many more, but still possessed no good map.

"Sir?"

"What is it now, George?"

"General Butterfield's ready for you."

"Oh, is he? General Butterfield's ready for me? Well, I suppose I'd better snap to. Hadn't I?"

"It wasn't like that, sir. I spoke poorly."

"Oh, I know Dan Butterfield, don't think I don't. Where is the man?"

Meade entered the headquarters tent, impatient to be gone and ready to leap on any fault he could find. But he found none, other than a few misspellings by clerks assigned to the copying work.

"This penmanship's hardly legible," Meade said.

"The men are tired, General Meade," Butterfield said.

"Damn it to Hell, I'm tired, too. Which one of us hasn't slept in three days?"

Butterfield shrugged. "That would be pretty well everyone."

"Me, that's who. The army commander. Because I have to check every damned clerical nook and cranny and do all the work myself."

He knew he was being unfair. He knew it all too well. But he could not stop himself. He really did need sleep. But there would be none again this night.

Butterfield took the rest of his licking in silence, unwilling to give Meade the argument he craved. The army's commander scrawled his name on the last order.

"These need to go out immediately. I don't care how many damned horses you kill. Or couriers, either. No more overnight delays, the way you did with Pipe Creek."

"The orders will go out immediately. If you'll allow me?"

Meade stalked off. "George, is my horse ready? Who has my horse? And get my other spectacles from my tent. Is the escort mounted?"

But before the commander of the Army of the Potomac could

make his way to his horse, riders hurried into the headquarters camp.

It was Hancock. With Warren. Their appearance startled Meade. For a moment, he feared disaster had overtaken the army, that the two men had fled the field.

But as the generals stepped into the cast of a lantern's light, their faces wore no hint of panic.

They spotted him and saluted.

"Hancock? What are you doing here? And you, Warren?"

"Thought you might want to hear more than we could put in writing," Hancock said. His voice was good, strong. "Slocum's up, he's taken command. Need to look in on my own corps, too. So you don't court-martial me for dereliction of duty."

"It's been a devil of a day," Warren, the chief engineer, said. A lean man with a cavalry mustache, Warren had the bearing of an English squire and the eyes of a bird of prey.

"It's been a *shit* of a day," Hancock said. "And I need to piss like the horse that drank the creek dry. My kidneys aren't what they used to be." He tipped his fingers to his hat again. "If you'll excuse me for a moment, General?"

As Hancock disappeared into the darkness, Meade asked Warren, "How bad is it?"

"Bad. But not irretrievable. Lee had a nasty morning of it himself. His numbers told, though."

"Is his whole army up?"

"I can't say. There were enough of them to swarm us on both flanks. Hill's up, his entire corps. Ewell appears to have two divisions present. No one knows for certain about Longstreet."

"Sharpe places him in the rear of the army, strung out behind Hill. But he may have reached the field already."

Warren took that as a proposition. The man even smelled tired, reeking of a long day in the saddle. "I doubt Longstreet's up. Or they would've tried to take the high ground while they had us reeling. And they didn't. They ran out of fight in the town."

"How good *is* the ground?"

"Good. What I saw of it. Defensible. Better than the ground Lee holds. Although his isn't bad: low ridges, with open fields between us. He has the town, but it's no help to him. He couldn't launch his

main attack through those streets, he wouldn't have space to debouch and form for the assault." Warren paused to take out a cigar. Striking a match, he caught himself and offered a cigar to Meade.

"No. Thank you."

Narrowing his eyes at the first bite of smoke, Warren said, "Howard may have made a royal mess of everything else, but he got that one thing right: He saw the good ground right off. Kept von Steinwehr's division on it, with enough guns to hold. May have cost him the fight north of town and most of his corps, but old Oliver bought us a day."

"How many men did we have on the field when you left?"

Warren blew a gun-cloud of smoke and said, "Couldn't say with any precision. They were still streaming in. Enough to eke by for now, I think."

Meade nodded. "If the ground's good, and Lee spares us the morning . . ." He tallied the march tables in his head again. If Sedgwick drove his corps hard, the entire army could be unified by the next evening. Should his own inspection of the ground confirm that Gettysburg was the place to give battle, so be it.

Hancock reappeared. Despite his bulk and weariness, the man was as jaunty as a lieutenant. He clapped his hands together and announced, "Makes the night lighter and the day brighter."

"Win, that had to be the longest piss in military history."

"Hard ride. I've been holding my fire."

"G.K. tells me that Howard at least saved us good terrain."

"That he did, our Ollie O. And I expect he prayed on it, before he made up his mind. Divine inspiration, no doubt. Last I saw him, he was having a delightful supper in the cemetery gatehouse, while they carried in wounded men on either side of him. Model of Christian charity, our Ollie." Hancock considered his tone, then changed it. "Hard day for the poor bugger, actually. Did his best, I suppose. Division commanders did what they could, but it looks to have been a brigade and regimental fight. And most of them *did* fight, don't think the Rebs got off cheap. And we've got ground I wouldn't want to attack, if I was in Lee's bright and shiny boots. Although I suppose we really should thank Buford for that, as much as Howard. And John Reynolds, bless him." He lightened again, refusing to be dragged down by the day's tribulations. "It

true that Buford's Comanche-mad over you jumping up Custer and Farnsworth to brigadier?"

"I did not inquire as to General Buford's opinions on the subject," Meade said.

"Buford can be cantankerous," Warren put in, "but he doesn't hold a grudge past the next cigar. I'd worry more about Judson Kilpatrick taking it out on Farnsworth."

Meade noted his son standing off with his horse, wary of interrupting. There was no time for army gossip now.

"Well, gentlemen," Meade declared, "I think I'd best be off to see our battlefield. Win, you'll want to rejoin your corps, keep your boys moving. They'll have eternity for sleeping." He turned to Warren, whose cigar flared to light his hawk's eyes. "I'd welcome your company on the ride, G.K., but if you need to rest your horse . . ."

Warren shrugged. "You won't be doing much galloping, the road's packed up. Brutus and I can limp along well enough."

Meade waved his son toward them. Young George held up his spectacles.

"This army's done limping," Meade said.

PART
III

THE DAY OF THE GENERALS

AFTERNOON/EVENING, JULY 2ND

1. Kershaw's Brigade
2. Barksdale's Brigade
3. Law's Brigade
4. Wofford's Brigade
5. Supporting attack by
 Anderson's Division

6. Meade's headquarters
7. Union troops hasten to
 re-establish line
8. Sickles wounded
9. Krzyzanowski's Brigade

KEY

▰	*Infantry*
▱	*Cavalry*
→	*Line of attack*
┅►	*Attack continues*
∿►	*Path of retreat*

All locations approximate
Artillery not shown

ELEVEN

July 2, Early Morning

His thoughts were not soldiers and refused to be disciplined. During the wearisome ride to Gettysburg, Meade's ruminations had strayed to his father. Richard Meade had died, a broken man, at fifty years of age, hardly older than Meade now was himself. Trusting his fellow man had been the elder Meade's mistake.

Born in Cádiz on New Year's Eve 1815, George Gordon Meade missed his family's glory days. His father had grown wealthy as a Philadelphia merchant based in Spain, a country the older man loved. During the Napoleonic occupation, Richard Meade had lent his fortune to the Spanish crown to fund its desperate struggle against the French. When the monarchy was restored at last, his father's reward was prison for requesting the repayment of his loans.

First, the Spaniards cheated Richard Meade, then, when diplomacy freed him, the United States Congress cheated him as well. The remaining years of a bankrupt life had been spent in vain attempts to recoup lost wealth, with the family struggling to hold its social position. Upon her husband's death, Meade's mother had grasped West Point for a gentleman's education free of cost, only to feel mortified when her son embraced a military life.

Now here he was, filthy and worn, in a cemetery gatehouse surrounded by an army he commanded. The odd thing was that the specter of his father had not left him wary and fearful, as it usually did. Rather, he saw a grand hope for redemption: Fending off Lee would secure his family's place in Philadelphia for generations.

"It was a relief," General Howard said. His pinned-up right sleeve dangled. The oil lamp pulsed. "I can't *tell* you what a relief it was. Lee should have pressed his attack. I really am not certain we could have held."

Old cigar smoke and sweat thickened the air.

"But he didn't attack," Meade said. "And you held." Drained but determined, he looked around the candlelit room at the corps commanders present: Howard, Sickles, and Slocum, the latter just dismounted and in the door. Hunt, his chief of artillery, sat in the shadows. "What do you think, gentlemen?" Meade continued. "Is this the place to fight a battle? If the army comes up?"

"I am confident that the army can hold this position, General Meade," Howard continued. Enthusiastically Christian, Howard was mannerly, narrow, and courageous. "As soon as Slocum arrived, we were all right." The Eleventh Corps commander, who had been through a bitter day and had not slept, caught himself: "And General Sickles made a difference, of course. His presence."

"Slocum?" Meade asked. "What do you think?"

"We can fight here. If we defend and let Lee come on."

Slocum's appearance on the field had been unforgivably tardy, but Meade saw no use in admonishing him now. Slocum was a careful man, allergic to every risk, but assigned a position to hold, he'd cling to it stubbornly.

"Sickles?" Meade asked the man's opinion for courtesy's sake.

"Oh, my boys are up for a scrap. We'll give Bobby Lee a time of it."

Disregarding the politician's bravado, Meade straightened his back to stretch out the saddle pains. There would be more time on horseback before the dawn. And thereafter.

"Well, I'm glad to hear you say so, gentlemen. I've already ordered the other corps to concentrate here, and it's too late to change." He stepped to the local county map spread upon a table. A treasure procured by Howard, the map was useless for terrain, but it laid out the roads in detail. "Look at this."

The corps commanders and Hunt crowded around.

"There's our problem." Meade pointed to the black line of the Baltimore Pike. The road ran just in front of the gatehouse, then off to the southeast behind the army's right flank. "That's the only road to our rear that's properly made. I just came up the Taneytown road. It's too raw to support this army, should we be forced to withdraw. And all the other routes are in Lee's hands or between our armies." Ambushed by a yawn, he mastered himself

and scanned the weary faces. "Were you General Lee, what would you do?"

"Cut that damned road," Slocum said. "I can hold him off, though. If he doesn't swing wide to the east."

"He'd be a fool not to try to cut it," Meade said. "That's plain as day."

"There's rough ground on that flank," Howard put in. "All hills, trees, and rocks. It would break up an attacker's formation. When they probed us, they didn't get anywhere."

"They came through the woods at Chancellorsville well enough," Meade said, and Howard was chastened. "Lee likes flanks." He turned to Slocum. "At first light, I'll have Warren join you for a scout. An attack by your corps and the Fifth—once it's up—would correct our line. Push it out from the pike, give us some depth. I'll expect your opinion promptly, John."

"What about *my* flank?" Sickles said. "The Taneytown road's just behind me. It's rough, but it ain't useless. And there's the Emmitsburg road to my front."

Meade shrugged. "Just relieve Geary when it's light and take your assigned position. Hancock will fill in the line between you and Howard. When Win comes up, tighten your front."

Even as the chains of exhaustion tugged him, Meade almost smiled. "This doesn't seem a bad position, gentlemen. We have the advantage of interior lines, and the rest of the army's nearby." He glanced at his chief of artillery. "Hunt's reserve is in route, and I mean to let his gunners earn their keep. If Lee spares us till noon, he'll have a fight on his hands." Meade grunted. "And if he waits any longer, he's a fool."

Meade felt compelled to see more of the ground before he rested. Flanked by his son and Captain Paine, one of Warren's engineers, he rode far enough to the east to mark the wall of high ground shielding the Baltimore road. The wooded crests could not be explored on horseback in the dark, so he turned and clopped through the graveyard again, then followed the southward decline of the ridge amid the embers of campfires left to themselves. Off to the west, across broad fields, the enemy's fires smoldered in the moonglow.

What if . . . what if he could *defeat* Robert E. Lee? Not just

fend him off, but actually whip him? What if he really could do it? They all had gone in awe of the man, all of their careers, admiring the dashing hero of Cerro Gordo, then fearing the invincible figure in gray who beat every challenger. Even Antietam had been no more than a bloody, clumsy draw. Every real soldier knew it. But what if *he* were to be the one to defeat Lee? Might that not soothe his father's ghost at last? Such a victory would mean more than a strengthened social position. It would be a triumph.

Meade felt a new confidence, an emotion so strong he worried it might be lunatic, born of sleeplessness. He had resolved not to make mistakes in confronting Lee. But that was not enough. Not losing didn't mean winning. He wouldn't have another Chancellorsville, but he didn't want a second Antietam, either. He wanted to *win*.

Lee would take the aggressive, that was clear. Fredericksburg notwithstanding, he always did. Lee would strive to land early blows, to stun him, then punch through while he was reeling. The trick would be to keep his lines snug, with deep reserves behind them. Let Lee punch through one line and meet another.

So deeply did he sink into his thoughts that the cries of the wounded might have been nightbirds calling. As Old Baldy threaded his hooves between the lines of sleeping men and slumping sentinels, the ground sought to trick the commanding general's eyes. But Meade understood the secrets of the earth. An engineer's mind was good for that, at least. Ahead, to the south, the black bulk of the smaller and greater hills, first glimpsed on his ride from the rear, anchored not only his proposed line, but the entire landscape. The moonlight made dark, earthbound clouds of groves, but the wide grain fields and water meadows shone silver, their patina deep where the land folded down and rose again, bright along the crests of the low ridges between the armies. He would need to see it all again, in the merciless light of day, but this stretch of his line appeared made for concentrations of artillery and volleys at maximum ranges.

"George?" he called.

His son rode up beside him. "Sir?"

"What would you do, if you occupied this ground?"

Captain Meade hesitated. The general sensed the boy's reluc-

tance to be caught out in some elementary error. In the distance, a sentry fired at a spook. But neither army was willing to be roused. Not yet.

At last, his son told him, "I'd wait and hope the enemy attacked me."

"Exactly."

The hand shook him again. *Hard.*

"General Meade . . . Father . . ."

"What is it? Is Lee attacking?" Lifting his head from the tabletop, he registered the dread in his own voice.

"No, sir. Everything's quiet. You wanted to be awakened."

Meade shifted his bones in the chair. "What time is it?"

"Three thirty. As you asked."

Meade remembered something. "George? I thought I ordered you to get some sleep?"

The guttering candle sparked. Through bleary eyes, he read his son's amusement.

"They were all afraid to wake you, sir. They asked me to do it." George held out a steaming tin cup. *Coffee.*

Meade smiled, too. Despite the fierceness of his hour of sleep, he had roused sufficiently to see the humor. "Old Snapping Turtle" indeed.

Acrid, the coffee pierced him. "Thank you, George."

"Sir? Your party's ready. General Hunt and Captain Paine. General Howard wants to ride along, too, if that's all right."

Meade grunted. "I thought the man would be dead to the world. After yesterday."

"And Cadwalader's found a shanty just behind the lines that we can use for your headquarters. It's close to the center and right, and not far from the left flank, either."

Brilliant quicksilver, the coffee shot through his body to his soul. "Good, good. Fine." He was astonished to find that his buoyant mood endured. He had half-expected to wake and discover that his confidence had been a hallucination.

What if he *could* beat Lee?

He rose and felt the old saddle-bite in his loins and along his thighs. More riding ahead. He needed to see if the ground looked

as fine at first light as it had in the darkness. He didn't want to be carried along on other men's enthusiasm.

Emerging to join his reconnaissance party, he visited the outhouse at the yard's end. Overused by the soldiers, it was vile.

Liberated from the filthy enclosure, he gulped mild air. The darkness had already softened to Quaker gray. Old Baldy nickered as Meade approached and he stroked the animal back along the jawline, then down the neck. "You miss your rest, too. Don't you, boy?"

Meade hauled himself into the saddle, suffering the awful impact of groin on hard leather. War demanded a seasoned mind, but wanted a youthful body.

"Shall we, gentlemen?"

They rode first to the nearby guns, whose muzzles pointed northward. An alert sergeant snapped to attention and opened his maw to wake his fellow gunners. Meade hushed him.

"Let them sleep," he told the man. "Until your captain calls."

The artillerymen had dug out positions for their cannon, then improved the entrenchments with planks and firewood. To the north, the ground dropped steeply into the shadows, toward the Confederates. The height on which Meade paused was the keystone of the defense, but only the brave and foolish would assault it.

By the time the party reached the hill to the east, the troops were stirring. A first bugle blared, then another. Drums responded. The terrain grew rugged, challenging the horses. The soldiers in position along the crest and above the ravines had done what they could to make their front formidable.

"You," Meade called to an unbuttoned major. "Have your men deepen those earthworks. And those firing pits."

Surprised at his business, the major saluted above a dangling pink pennant. Thereafter, Meade led the way back across the low interior ground to the ridge that ran south from the cemetery. He was gaining a sense of how the position fit together and wasn't displeased. In oyster-shell light, the party trotted past grumpy rows of regiments standing to. The moonlight had not deceived him the night before: Even allowing for dips and swales, the ridge that would form the center of his line offered commanding positions for massed artillery.

"Not bad for your guns, Henry," Meade called over his shoulder to General Hunt.

"Best damned ground I've seen," the artilleryman answered. "Sweep the damned place clean." Hunt sounded almost jolly.

As if insulted by the gunner's words, a section of enemy cannon blasted the morning. Distant and invisible, they seemed to be firing at nothing.

"Twelve-pounders," Hunt remarked. No Union guns replied.

As they rode along the lowering ridge, Captain Paine sketched a map of the terrain, marking the positions Meade chose for each of his corps. It was the captain's one remarkable ability, that gift of wielding pencil and paper in the saddle as ably as if at a draftsman's table.

Weary and worn though he knew himself to be, Meade felt invigorated. The morning offered up a marvelous spectacle, if one with a deadly purpose: this good ground; *his* soldiers waking upon it; the rest of his army hurrying toward him; the bugle-bitten morning air; the restoked campfires and busy men around them; and the metal snap of stacked arms retrieved by those who would wield them this day. He felt thousands of souls emerging, one by one, from the sullenness of the soldier's dawn, through blade-sharp coffee that sliced down the throat, and into the confidence of men massed, armed, and ready. Those romantic fellows with their poetry never grasped the seductive force of routine.

Ahead lay low ground, the position's weakest stretch, marshy and tree-addled. The lines of fire were limited here, but if it was a challenge to defend, it would be equally hard to attack. And it had to be held, for beyond it lay the two hills. Even in the still-poor light, Meade saw that only the nearer, lower height mattered. Its western slope had been timbered, scalped raw, and it begged for a battery to be wrestled to its crest to face the enemy. He assumed Hunt saw it, too. As for the farther, higher hill, it was thick with trees and worthless. His left flank depended on that first, sugarloaf-shaped promontory. Sickles just had to sit on it and not budge.

It was enough. Meade had seen what he needed to see. He pulled up his horse and began to turn about.

"Have all that, Paine?" he asked the sketching captain.

"Yes, sir."

"Good. Let's go."

"General Meade?" Howard asked. "Would you care to call on Sickles? While we're here?"

Meade did not wish to have his good mood spoiled. "Sickles has his instructions. He just needs to do what he's told."

Ascending the ridge again, they had no trouble finding the shack selected for Meade's headquarters. A squat white-painted building not a quarter-mile behind the line of troops, it bustled with orderlies hurrying to unload the headquarters wagons and put up the staff's work tents. A picket fence had been knocked down along half its length, a small garden looted and trampled. The headquarters guard, a troop from the 6th Pennsylvania Cavalry, lazed in a roadside meadow, brewing coffee. Meade smelled frying ham.

Behind the busy road, a red sun rose. Its rays turned the mists in the low ground to bloody gauze. The sight stopped Meade and held him. He felt a power, an essence, for which he possessed no words. A page had turned in the heavens, but he could not read the script.

Mastering himself, the commanding general turned back to his duty, calling for coffee as he marched into the shack.

Butterfield, his chief of staff, and the adjutant, Seth Williams, were at work in the cabin's main room. Meade took the sketched map from the engineer captain and laid it on a table.

After explaining how he wanted the arriving corps positioned, he told Butterfield, "The ground's good enough, but I'm concerned about our right. The Baltimore Pike's crucial. I've ordered Slocum and Warren to weigh an attack to shield the road. Two corps, I'd think. If an attack's practicable. The rest of the line would remain on the defensive."

"That's Ewell's corps in front of Slocum. Jackson's men," Howard explained, telling Meade what he already knew. Howard always had a note of the schoolmaster in his voice. Meade wondered if the man had delayed rejoining his corps because he awaited praise for yesterday's work. Given the losses, laurels were hardly in order.

"Better Ewell than Longstreet," Meade said. "Changing the subject, gentlemen: Hill and Ewell were in yesterday's fight, so we may assume that Longstreet's corps will lead Lee's attack today. And Lee *will* attack. He didn't march all this way to watch a pa-

rade." He drew out his watch, but didn't really look at it. "We just need a few more hours." He looked around. "Where's Pleasanton?" He wanted his chief of cavalry.

"He was here when we arrived," Butterfield said.

"I want to see him." Meade spotted an idle lieutenant. "Find General Pleasanton. Tell him I want him immediately. Then fetch Colonel Sharpe." He turned back to his chief of staff. "Get tracings of Paine's artistic masterpiece out to all the corps. Sign them for me. As soon as that's done, draw up a plan for an orderly withdrawal of the army, as a contingency. If things don't go our way, I'm not going to have another shambles like Chancellorsville. I want every corps, division, reserve element, trains—all of them—to know which route they're to follow and their order of march. Designate alternate rear guards, depending on whether we have trouble on the right, left, or in the center. Make sure Patrick and his provost men understand the plan in detail."

Before Butterfield could pose any questions, an artillery captain— one of Hunt's men—plunged in through the doorway. Undaunted by the assembly of generals, he touched the brim of his kepi without breaking stride. When he spoke to Hunt, his voice was too guarded for Meade to hear.

"Speak up, man," Meade snapped. "What's the problem?"

General Hunt answered for the captain. "Sickles left his artillery ammunition in the rear. The train hasn't even reached Emmitsburg."

"That son—"

Meade caught himself. It would not do to damn a corps commander in front of so many subordinates. But Sickles was going to catch Hell after the battle.

"It's all right," Hunt said. "I keep an extra reserve for times like this. We'll get him through the day." Hunt looked annoyed, though.

Meade regained his composure, if not the full flush of his earlier mood. What the men around him needed now was confidence. In him, in themselves. Whippings could wait.

The morning grew up around them, its hours and minutes crowded with decisions great and small. General Newton came in, stinking of horse and bleary-eyed. But willing. Meade had ordered him up from the still-distant Sixth Corps to command the battered

First. Doubleday's pride would be wounded and Meade knew he would make another enemy by not sustaining the man in Reynolds' position. But it could not be allowed to matter. He needed the strongest generals he had in command of his corps this day. Newton was a fighter. And a fellow engineer.

Glad for the excuse to flee the cigar smoke and regain the morning air, Meade led Newton up the ridge to explain the army's position and his role. The sun already had weight.

"Doubleday outranks me, you know," Newton said as they strode toward the cemetery.

"My worry, not yours," Meade told him. "Abner will sulk, but he'll lead his division well enough. The man simply isn't meant for higher command."

"Not completely sure I am," Newton mused.

"You'll have to be."

A bullet passed between them with the sound of tearing silk. Meade glanced about angrily. "Somebody's being damned careless."

But a newspaperman—worse, a New York newspaperman—rose from behind a tombstone and dashed toward them. "General, General!" he cried. "There's a sharpshooter down in that steeple! Down in the town!"

Meade and Newton withdrew. Quickly.

"Well, that's a first," Newton declared as they put the crest behind them. "Saved by a newspaper fellow. Who risked his own neck."

"Nonsense," Meade said. "He knows no honest Rebel would waste a ball on him."

The generals laughed. But Meade was already done with Newton and drafting a dispatch to Washington in his mind. The triumvirate of Halleck, Stanton, and Lincoln had to be fed and pacified, if he was to have the freedom to fight Lee his way.

What was he forgetting? He had to be forgetting something, there was so damnably much to be done. He demanded of his mind that it be thorough, but his faculties wanted rest.

All of it had to be done by strength of will.

By the time he saw Newton off and returned to the headquarters, Howard had gone back to his corps, but Hancock had arrived, belching and barking, compounded of piss and vinegar. "Damned

inhospitable," he told Meade. "I expected a proper breakfast, after all that. You're letting me down, George."

"Just make sure we don't end up eating crow, Win," Meade said. "Butterfield explain where you're to go in?"

"Gibbon's bringing the men up. I see you've got me playing governess to Sickles on my left."

"He shouldn't need much minding today. He just has to hold his position. I don't see the left as the threatened flank just now." Meade considered the problem one more time. "If I'm wrong, I can bring up the Fifth Corps and use Sickles as a pivot. He'll be all right. Humphreys and Birney are both good men, they'll handle their divisions properly."

Hancock grinned. "You're just partial to Humph as a Philadelphia man."

"As you claim to be yourself," Meade shot back.

"Not the same, though. What the Hell ships did his grand-daddy build? The *Constitution* and what the devil?"

"The *Constellation*. There's no harm in coming of good family, you know. Gives a man a standard to live up to."

"Well, hats off to Bobby Lee, then. He's got more family history than the tsar of all the Russias."

"Not," Meade said, "a Philadelphian, though."

They both laughed.

"What's so funny?" Henry Slocum asked. Back from their reconnaissance, he and General Warren had tied their horses beside the house. They both appeared bewildered to find Meade in such good spirits.

"Old George here was explaining to me why Marse Robert ain't a blue blood," Hancock told them. "No Philadelphia ties."

"Well, G.K. and I wouldn't know about that," Slocum said. "We're both brown-dirt New Yorkers."

"You and Dan Sickles."

"City man," Slocum said. "Doesn't count."

"Well, what do you think, Henry?" Meade asked Slocum, bringing the conversation back to business. No matter the course he chose to pursue, an infernal amount of work remained to be done. "Can you attack to advantage?"

Slocum shook his head. With a stand-by-me glance at Warren,

he said, "We'd be damned fools to attack over that ground. Too broken up. Creek to get across, then God knows what. Be impossible to hold an attacking force together. If a regiment maintained its alignment for three hundred yards, I'd call it lucky."

Disappointment hit Meade. He had hoped for an opening to strike Lee first, to impose his will on the giant figure in gray. But this wasn't about what he wanted to do. It was about what needed doing. If the ground was bad, he would not attack over it: *Make no mistakes that can be prevented, and do not surrender to impulse.*

"G.K.? You agree with Henry?"

"I'd rather see Lee attack up those hills, than us attack down and start uphill again. Troops up there are dug in nicely enough. Lee comes at us that way, it'll be Injun-mean, but he'll have the worst of it."

Meade nodded. "He'll want that road. He *has* to see it."

"Well, he won't get it, George," Slocum told him. "We can *hold* that ground. Just let him try and take it."

"We should watch our left, too," Warren said. "Remember Chancellorsville, how Hooker kept looking east, because that's what made sense? Damn it, we *saw* Jackson moving west, but wouldn't credit it. Because it didn't fit the picture we'd painted for ourselves."

Meade was annoyed by the implied comparison of himself to General Hooker, but he suppressed the emotion. *Let the man say what he has to say,* he counseled himself. He could almost hear his wife's voice speak the words.

Warren shook his head at his recollections, then returned to the present question. "Lee may risk the bad ground and hit us on our right, but he's got better space for maneuver on our left, out beyond Sickles. The Baltimore road may not loom as large to him as it does to us." Warren's face twisted, lifting his thick mustache on one side of his mouth and lowering it on the other. "What I *can't* figure out is why he hasn't hit us already. He must know our last corps haven't come up."

"Maybe Longstreet's not up, either," Hancock put in. He looked at Meade. "I agree with G.K. Watch the left, as well as the right. Bobby Lee has a logic all his own."

"The left's sound," Meade declared. "All Sickles has to do is maintain his line and hold on to that first hill. I don't think that's

asking too much." Suddenly, though, he felt a new need for certainty. "George!" he barked. He didn't look around, but expected his son to be near. And the boy was.

"Sir?"

"Ride down and make sure that General Sickles has taken up his position."

Longstreet sat on a fallen log, with two sick men beside him. Lee was downright fidgety, his bowels still out of temper. As they studied the map that lay on the ground before them, the old man glanced around like a woman worried about mice getting under her skirts. Beyond Lee, gaunt Powell Hill looked like Death's calling card.

Lurking at a respectful distance, Harry Heth was the target of one of Sam Hood's rare but potent diatribes. Struck in the head by a spent bullet and saved by the paper padding in his hat, Heth still had the wobbles and wasn't fit to resume division command. But he wanted to be in on things. They all did. Hood looked ready to fight whoever came to hand, blue or gray.

Earlier, when he and the old man had conferred alone, Longstreet had raised the prospect of a wide turning movement once more. Lee had been brusque, barely controlling his anger. He had made it clear that he wished to hear no more of grand maneuvers.

The old man just could not resist a fight. But, God only knew, Lee had been right before, Longstreet cautioned himself. Perhaps Meade and his command *would* fall apart at a serious blow. . . .

Longstreet wasn't convinced, though. His presentiments shaded dark. The Yankees had taken a beating the day before, but their army had not turned tail. Meade was not faint of heart. And the thumping Hill's divisions had given the Federals had punished the Army of Northern Virginia, too.

The old man was ruthless in his pursuit of victories. Which was fine, up to a point. But the butcher's bill could not be paid out endlessly. The casualty lists in the Richmond or Charleston papers had a finality to them that only a fool would ignore. Sometimes, he wondered if Lee truly grasped that the soldiers who loved the old man so unreservedly, with such blind trust, had flesh-and-blood lives of their own.

Longstreet was a soldier. He understood that men had to die in war. But he deplored the waste of life he had witnessed. Modern weapons raised the cost of gallant charges to forbidding heights. This was no longer a matter of pikes and harquebuses, nor even of flintlock muskets. Artillery and rifled weapons were devastating— not for the generals who still made a god of Napoleon, but for the men in the ranks who followed their orders. War excited Longstreet, but slaughter appalled him. And the deaths of his children had made him treasure life.

Where would this end?

Fighting off a sulk, Longstreet could do no more than hope for the best. He feared that the combination of a bad stomach and vanity did not bode well for Lee's judgment on this day.

Bad bowels led to bad decisions. That was a story as old as war itself. Longstreet wanted to believe that Lee was regaining his strength. Although he remained unsteady under watchful eyes, at least the old man did not need to excuse himself as often as he had the evening before. He did not look as though he'd slept much, though. Lee was tough as hickory, but the tree was old.

Longstreet took a stick to the map before them. "That road. And that one. If Meade brings up his entire army, he won't have much in the way of lines of retreat. Now, if those roads were cut . . ."

"Interior lines, though," Powell Hill said. Even his voice seemed skeletal. "Meade's got that advantage."

"I'll speak with General Ewell about the matter," the old man told them. "When we have settled things here." He raised his face, peering above and beyond the town, searching the terrain that he couldn't quite see. "I understand the ground's irregular in front of General Ewell's corps. And the town itself won't do for an attack."

"Ewell can't just sit there with a third of the army," Longstreet said. "If he could just cut that one road, get around in back of them . . ."

Nettled again, Lee said, "I do not foresee any portion of this army 'just sitting,' General Longstreet. But I'm inclined to make our main effort on our right and the enemy's left. If Captain Johnston makes a favorable report."

Johnston, one of Lee's staff engineers, had been sent off while it

was still half-dark to feel Meade's southern flank, to see if it extended as far as the two hills that blocked the horizon.

"Think they're all up?" Hill asked. Speaking across Lee to Longstreet.

"Nope. But they're coming. How fast . . . your guess is as good as mine." Longstreet gazed across the broad fields to the right. The blue lines on the ridge had lengthened since he had first observed them the evening before. "Looks like Meade might have some fight in him."

"General Meade will be methodical," Lee snapped. "I expect that. But let us hope that he will also be predictable."

Wearied of Harry Heth's impenetrability, Hood sauntered over to his superiors. He touched the brim of his hat, acknowledging Lee's authority.

"Been looking at those Yankees up there," the Kentuckian said. "Done set themselves up nice. Half of me wants to have at 'em . . . but the other half's wondering if it wouldn't be prettier to let them come on down and attack us."

Longstreet was grateful that Hood had said it. But the old man wasn't pleased. Lee thought of Hood in terms of fierce attacks.

The old man stabbed a finger toward the blue lines. "Meade is *there*. If we do not whip him, he will whip us. We will not surrender the initiative to those people, General Hood. We will attack them."

An odd thought struck Longstreet: Was it about *Meade*? Was Lee insulted that he'd been offered no grander opponent? Carefully hidden from the world, the old man's pride could take peculiar turns.

Hood caught the queerness in Lee, too. Longstreet saw the Indian-fighter wariness come up in the other man's eyes. Then the thump and clatter of mounted men arose behind the tree trunk where Lee had centered his command.

Hood peered into the morning. "Just the Army of the Grand Coalition," he reported. "Damned circus."

Lee looked up sharply. He did not countenance swearing.

Hood missed the cue, his grimace didn't alter.

The old man said nothing.

Longstreet gestured to Moxley Sorrel to come to him.

"Keep them off us for a while yet," he told his subordinate. The "Grand Coalition" consisted of the international observers and a few newspapermen.

"Yes, sir," Sorrel answered. But his disappointment was clear. He, too, wanted to listen in on the generals' deliberations.

Another, more welcome party rode in afterward. It was Captain Johnston, Lee's engineer, and his scouts. He'd been gone for hours.

Johnston looked bright-eyed: dusty, sweat-greased, and pleased with himself.

The captain approached, saluting and righting his sword belt. Boyishly enthused, he halted before the generals, waiting for a word from the old man.

Lee pointed at the map. "Report, sir. Tell us what you have found."

"They're not *there*," Johnston said. Instead of indicating his discovery on the map, he gestured diagonally across the fields, toward the two round hills. "We were right *there*, on the slopes of those hills. And there wasn't a Yankee in sight, not a single one."

"Did you get there?" Lee asked in a tone of disbelief. "I can't believe Meade would leave those hills unoccupied."

"New in the job," Hill put in. "Right about now, George Meade's likely feeling overwhelmed as a one-armed rat-catcher."

But Lee focused on the captain. "You can *assure* me that those people are not on those hills?" He pointed toward the heights himself, still unconvinced.

"Sir, there was nobody up there. That's the plain truth." Johnston knelt before the map. After orienting himself, he guided their eyes with a finger. "And here. This road, the one from Emmitsburg. We rode right up it, as far as a peach orchard. About here. Map doesn't show it, but there's a low ridge."

"You got that far?" Lee asked, still incredulous.

"Yes, sir. And the only Yankees we saw were four cavalry strays."

"And you saw nothing of their army? Heard nothing?"

The captain shook his head. "No, sir. Not down there."

"And you're certain you reached *those* hills?"

Johnston looked unjustly accused of fibbing. "I don't know where else we could've been."

The old man turned to Longstreet. "Surely you see it, General? Our plan is made for us. Your corps will assault their left." Lee traced a line on the map again. "Directly up this road."

"We could go deeper. Get in behind them."

"No. Right up this road," Lee said sternly.

"I only have two divisions present, sir. Pickett won't be in until late in the day. And Hood's still missing Law's brigade. Law's marching in from New Guilford." He looked at Hood, the only like-minded man present. But Hood could not help him.

"It will be enough," Lee said. "We must strike those people swiftly. Before General Meade corrects his error. General Hill will cooperate with you." Lee's demeanor altered: His decision had been made, the time for discussion was at an end. "You'll roll up his flank. If practicable, General Hill will then strike the center. And since General Ewell seems unwilling to visit me, I shall visit him. Perhaps he can demonstrate on General Meade's right, confuse him and keep him from bolstering his left." Lee stood. "Ready your troops, sir," he told Longstreet. "We shall finish this business today."

Behind Lee's back, Longstreet raised his eyes to Heaven. But all he saw was the varmint of an Englishman, Fremantle, up in the high branches of a tree. Whether the ass had climbed up there the better to see the Yankees or to eavesdrop was open to question.

Before his orderly could bring up one of his horses, Lee's departure was delayed. Laff McLaws, Longstreet's other division commander on the field, rode into the headquarters. He guided his horse right up to the fallen tree. A man of prosperous physique, Laff didn't care to walk more than he had to.

Longstreet felt sick at heart. The whole situation baffled him. He couldn't believe those hills were undefended. From what he knew of Meade, the man would not be such a fool. For that matter, he wasn't certain that he believed half of Johnston's report.

He did not want to attack. He feared it. And James Longstreet did not fear many things.

His dread bloomed into anger: Why was Lee doing this? At what cost to his corps? None of the possible explanations soothed him. The old man's back was up, and that was that.

Thick as a well-fed bear, McLaws dismounted. Puffing.

"Ah, General McLaws," Lee said. "Please join our discussion. You're something of the subject of it."

McLaws saluted, big beard pulling at his chubby face.

The generals gathered around the map again. Speaking to McLaws, Lee said, "You and General Hood will take your divisions into the attack on our right and the enemy's left. Meade has made a grave error, and we will not forgive it." He took up his stick again, then traced a specific attack route. "I wish you to place your division across this road, and I wish you to get there, if possible, without being seen by the enemy. Can you do it?"

McLaws looked at Longstreet, bewildered that his corps commander had been cut from the chain of command.

Longstreet nodded, but fumed. The situation was intolerable. He himself was the man who should give orders to McLaws.

"Well, I know of nothing to prevent me," McLaws told Lee. "Of course, I'd like to have a look at the ground myself, take out a scout."

"No, sir," Longstreet interjected, voice edged like a weapon. "I do not wish you to leave your division." He knew even as he spoke he was being unfair. But he was smoldering. Leaning over the map, he contradicted Lee. "*I* wish your division placed *so*."

"No," General Lee said. His voice was cold, not loud. "I wish it placed just perpendicular to that."

Befuddled by the contest of wills into which he'd blundered, McLaws turned to Longstreet again. His plump face shaped a plea. "I need to have a look at the ground, then. I could go right now, be back right quick . . ."

"You will remain with your division," Longstreet snapped. The man had already been tardy once today, he reasoned. But anger, not reason, had spoken.

"Now lookee there," Hood cried, stealing their attention. He pointed across the fields. "More goddamned Yankees."

TWELVE

July 2, Morning into Afternoon

Jesus weren't no fool," Cobb declared.

Blake looked up from the corpse whose belt he was tugging off. He and his men had been ordered to retrieve items useful to the army and stack them by the roadside. Before laying the bodies in the trenches others were digging.

Meeting Blake's stare, Cobb grinned, black as perdition. The little man had been distant throughout the morning, but seemed more himself now. Among the dead.

"Reckon he wasn't," Charley Campbell agreed, just to pass the time. "Likely right smart."

But Cobb wasn't finished. "Matthew 8:22. 'Let the dead bury their dead.' Show you why he might've been minded that way." He tromped on a blue-clad corpse's belly. The Yankee farted monstrously.

"God awmighty, don't *do* that," Corny yelled. "The stink's high enough."

"Prettiest gal you know, she'd let go the same perfume," Cobb said. "Let her lie dead in the sun, she'd stink right up. Lace dress, ribbons, and all." He tapped the Yankee with his toes, playful, threatening. "That there's just the incense leaving the temple of the flesh."

"Well, let that temple be," Corny told him.

Cobb returned to Blake's unbroken stare. "Don't it strike you funny, Sergeant Blake? I mean, it's downright unfair. How one dead man just looks like he's having a sleep under a shade tree, while the next feller's all bloat and stink and rot and maggots, after a single night. The good Lord does play favorites. Don't he?"

"Dead is dead," Blake said. He bent again to his labor, yanking

the belt and cartridge box free. The corpse had stiffened. Empty hands clawed the air.

"Sure now . . . you don't believe that," Cobb said, winking as if they shared a mighty secret. "Some of these boys must be up there on clouds of cotton, singing out to harps and heavenly trumpets, with niggers washing their feet and serving them beefsteaks. Ain't that how it is, how it's supposed to be?"

Blake considered the profile of the next corpse up the slope. The side of the Yankee's skull had burst outward, leaving an eyeless gash. If Blake had any faith left, it was dying. As surely as the bodies on that hillside were quit of life.

It was so strange: Other men found God in war's commotion. Sunday meetings weren't enough for them. They sang hymns in the middle of the week, in camp or on the march, and scoured their Bibles by firelight for comfort. Men hid in different ways, it seemed to Blake.

He wondered about Cobb now. Since the burying of James Bunyan the evening before, curiosity had begun to nibble at him. There had to be more to the man in that foul carcass, its stench worse than a number of the dead. Blake didn't believe that God had made Cobb what he was. There had to be flesh and blood in his ruination, some earthly tale.

A detail of soldiers came along for another load of corpses. One man had found a wheelbarrow, but most lugged soiled litters. They did not have to bear their burdens far. The low ground behind the creek, with its softer earth, sufficed for the ditches filling with gray-clad bodies. Yankees were left to themselves and the raccoons.

Up on the ridge, where McLaws' men—Barksdale's brigade—had come up and were having a rest, the 26th North Carolina's band began to play. "Camptown Races" fought the rattle of skirmishing in the distance, then the musicians blared out "Bonnie Blue Flag."

"Ain't that a comfort?" Cobb snickered. "Takes a feller's mind right off of everything."

Ever the good-tempered barkeep, Charley Campbell said, "I don't mind it."

"Queer, though," Corny put in. He raised his snout, as if catch-

ing a higher scent. "Thought sure they'd be fighting proper by now. All that marching going on. But it don't sound like much of anything to me."

"Takes time for all those generals to figure out how to kill them the most men," Cobb explained, "Yankees and our'n alike. Glory runs neck and neck with the casualty lists, if you ain't noticed. They'll want to outdo whoever went at it yesterday." He looked around at the human wreckage, the pants shit through in death and the dried blood gravy. "Show what fine, brave gentlemen they are."

"We won yesterday," Corny said. His voice was sullen. He'd clearly had enough of Cobb and his teasing.

"Now, that's a plain fact," Cobb agreed. "We just whupped the piss and pride right out of the Yankees, and that's a God-honest fact no man can dispute." He grinned. "Why don't you ask that dead boy you're fiddling with how he feels about it?"

"That's enough now," Blake said. His tone made it clear that Cobb had reached a limit.

Yet, Blake could not but feel the rightness in what Cobb said. He had waited for the customary elation victory had delivered in the past, but the joy had been unwilling to appear. The one brief rise in spirits Blake had known had come that morning, when a Moravian from the band mentioned seeing Hugh Gordon the afternoon before, bloody down one side but alive, walking back up the road over which they had marched. Blake would have liked to search the field hospitals for him, but orders had come down to tend to their dead. So the regiment's survivors gleaned the fields, leaving back ashen officers and Colonel Burgwyn's nigger. The darkey wept inconsolably.

Blake tossed his harvest of belts and leather boxes atop a fresh pile the others had begun. Just up the slope, a dead man in blue still wore a good pair of shoes. It seemed a wonder they had not already been taken. The brogues looked about Blake's size, and he was tempted. His left sole was worn beyond fixing, and the right had a hole down front. But he could not make himself do it, could not take from the dead. He asked himself if he was just embarrassed at the prospect of being seen, and smiled grimly. Cobb would never let him forget it, if he took those shoes. That much was certain.

But there was more to it. The thought of slipping on a dead man's shoes chilled him unreasonably.

Blake moved along.

The dead came in all God's varieties, favored and shunned. Cobb had that much right. A few had bloated already: the carefree who went into battle with full bellies. Others remained lean, as in life, but their limbs skewed like the branches of stunted trees. Some intact faces were boyish, angelic. Others had glimpsed an eternity of torment. Then there were men with no faces at all, their features shot away or already gnawed by dark-time animals.

"I hate this," John Bunyan said. Loudly. It was the first time he had spoken since breakfast, and his remarks back then had been limited to his needs. Thinking about his dead twin brother. And God knew what else. The boy worked steadily, but his spirit was truant.

"None of us likes it," Blake told him.

Back on the ridge, the band played "Rock of Ages." Then they livened things up again with a polka.

Longstreet sat on the fallen tree, eating hot biscuits with farm butter and waiting for Lee's return. General Hood squatted beside him in the Indian fashion, discussing the day's prospects.

"General Lee's a little nervous this morning," Longstreet said, careful of his language but unable to fully resist the need to complain. "He wishes me to attack." Longstreet shook his head with stiff-necked slowness. "I do not wish to do so without Pickett. I never like to go into battle with one boot off."

Hood spit, then said, "Well, get me Law, at least. If we're to go in with only two divisions, I'm going to need those Alabama boys."

Longstreet nodded. "When do you expect Brother Law?"

Hood drew out his watch and found it had stopped. "Damn it."

"Quarter after ten," Longstreet told him.

The Kentuckian shook his watch hard, then set to winding it. "Damn timepiece is mulish as a Mexican. Couple of hours. By one, surely. Maybe before. Law's a hard marcher." Hood thought about it. "His boys'll be tired, but game."

"I believe that General Lee will listen to reason," Longstreet

said. "Regarding Law, at least. But the truth is I don't wish to make this attack." He bit into a last biscuit and talked through the chewing. "If we're to attack . . . if we have to do it . . . I'd prefer to hit them with everything at once. Get it over. Finish it. I don't like piecemeal fights."

Hood refused to share Longstreet's despondency. "Once we get at 'em, I reckon we'll do well enough. Hit them hard on the flank, they'll fold. Always do."

Relieving Longstreet of the need to reply, the foreign observers decided the time had come to ambush the two generals.

"But this is splendid!" Fremantle declared. "What a marvelous thing it is to see both armies in full battle array! One does expect a good show."

"There'll be a show, all right," Longstreet said.

Oblivious as ever, the Englishman plunged onward. "Oh, no doubt, no doubt. Really, General, it's everything one hears, and more besides. Even the weather . . . the sunrise this morning put me in mind of Austerlitz. The 'sun of Austerlitz,' you know. I mean, I thought it rather a good sign, didn't you?" He glanced from general to general, sparkling with delight at himself and the adventure of the day. "I say, what do you think of these rumors about Vicksburg? They say this fellow Grant's been crushed to bits, that he turned tail."

Longstreet snorted. "Sam Grant might be crushed. But he wouldn't turn tail."

"They say he's nothing but a common drunkard."

Longstreet thought of his last glimpse of his friend in that hotel lobby. With Grant's face earnest as a saint's as he insisted Longstreet accept the gold piece he clearly could not afford to give up.

"He's emptied a bottle now and then," Longstreet said. "We all have. But I never knew the man to be a drunk. Nor common."

"But everyone's saying that Vicksburg's been redeemed. That it's a great victory for your cause, that the tide has turned decisively."

"I'd be glad to hear it. But I haven't heard it from anybody with a mite of knowledge on the subject."

He thought again of Grant. Born with a whipped face and a mighty heart, red hair flying as he jumped a horse higher than any

man in the history of West Point. And Grant chafing at his quarter-master's duties in Mexico, finding every excuse to get into the fighting. A man who had never uttered a dishonest word, who could not. Longstreet had sensed an untapped strength in his fellow cadet. Back when "Uncle Sam Grant" had been the quietest man in the barracks.

"Near as I can tell," Hood announced, "the trouble with Grant is that he don't know when he's licked." He laughed, but harshly. "Take Shiloh. Sidney Johnston beat him fair and square. And look what happened. No, sir, if that stubborn sonofabitch ran off from Vicksburg, I expect he was running toward poor Joe Johnston. With a mind to whup him. If I'm wrong, I'll eat my boot and call it a pork chop."

Disappointed by the generals' attitudes, Fremantle changed the subject. "There's a Union signal outpost on the nearer of those hills, you know."

"Saw it," Longstreet said. " 'Long as they don't haul up a battery and a good brigade, it'll be all right."

"Hard to believe they haven't," Hood remarked. "That's one mistake George Meade's going to find costly."

With Fremantle momentarily silenced, Scheibert, the Prussian, thrust in. As the sun browned his face, his dueling scars—livid white—had become more prominent.

"General Longstreet, I must tell you a thing," he announced. "I have spoken with Unionist prisoners, men who are from Germany in their origins. They are disreputable people. Before they fled *wie Ratten* from their homelands, they have rebelled against their sovereigns, against their governments. They are traitors, these men."

Hood looked at Longstreet with a smile that spread his beard around his mouth. They had shared a realization.

Inflamed by his own speech, the Prussian added, "They deserve to be shot."

Longstreet aped deep thought. And tried not to laugh. At last, he said, "Well, now, that isn't quite the way we do things, Colonel Scheibert. Much as a man might like to from time to time. And I'm embarrassed to point out that General Hood and I are in pretty much the same boat as those Dutchmen. General Lee, too. All of us. We're guilty of the sin of rebellion ourselves."

Taken aback, the Prussian stammered on: "But . . . this is different. *Die Lage ist ganz anders.* You . . . are making a fight to keep things as they are, is that not so? The Unionists are those who wish to change all things, to upset society and the proper relations of superior and inferior. For my example, I take the situation of the Negro, who they would raise from the position the *Herrgott* has given him. This cannot be, there must be proper order. Am I not correct?"

Longstreet thought of the pistol-whipped darkey in the chain of prisoners he'd met west of the mountain.

Before he could speak, Hood tore into the Prussian: "It ain't just about niggers. Damn it, man. It's about the freedom of God-fearing men to say, 'This here's mine, and it ain't yours, so keep your dirty hands off it.' It's about states' rights, and damned Yankee bankers worse than Jews. And a Congress that sees more good in a factory than a cotton field. It's about the proper respect due to a man, it's about our freedom." Out of words, he grunted. "You go on over and talk to General Barksdale with McLaws' bunch. He can put it a sight better than me."

"I have not wished to give offense," the Prussian pleaded.

"None taken, Colonel," Longstreet assured him. "General Hood here's just itching for a fight, and he's a fellow takes on all comers. We value your presence . . . and your sovereign's goodwill."

"The Unionists must not be allowed to overturn your society," Scheibert grumbled. "We must defend the proper order of things. That is all I have wished to say."

"And it was well said, sir," Longstreet told him. He just wished the pack of them would disappear. He lacked Lee's faith in the efficacy of foreign opinion. And he didn't care for a one of them, save Ross, the not-exactly-Austrian, who could be merry and had an eye for a dainty ankle. Ross would have fit right in on a fine plantation, raising Hell and taking things as they came. Scheibert would have had a slave uprising on his hands.

Lee returned at eleven. His retinue consisted of more staff officers than had ridden off with him earlier. When the old man dismounted, Longstreet noted that he didn't rush to relieve his afflicted bowels. He looked more vigorous.

Posture perfect and uniform only mildly offended by dust, Lee

approached them. Longstreet and Hood rose. The foreign contingent nodded and stepped back a pace or two. Scheibert cracked to attention and saluted.

"You will pardon us," Lee told the observers and lurking newspapermen. They faded away. No man questioned Lee.

That was a significant piece of the problem, Longstreet believed. The old man wasn't used to having his judgment challenged anymore. He'd been winning too long, making it all look easy. While the butcher's bills swelled.

One of Lee's staff men, Venable, spread the headquarters' map over the ground again. Longstreet spotted Porter Alexander, who would command the artillery for the attack, and waved him over. McLaws had returned to his division, as ordered. Muttering. And justifiably, Longstreet felt bound to admit. He had been as unfair to McLaws as Lee had been to him.

Lee began with Longstreet: "Have your divisions marched for their attack positions, General?"

Longstreet felt hit from the rear. Clearly, he and the old man had misunderstood each other. "No, sir. I thought I was to await your final plan."

Lee's face pinked, but the old man mastered himself.

Might as well get it over with, Longstreet decided. "And I'd prefer to wait on Law's brigade, General. Since I won't have Pickett."

Lee appeared impatient, but asked, "When is General Law expected on the field?"

"Noon hour," Hood answered. "Thereabouts."

The old man nodded. "We can wait no longer than that." He glanced toward the Union lines, but did not really look at them. "We have lost much of the day and will need to move boldly." He knelt to the map.

Instantly, the other officers got to their knees around him. As if it were a prayer meeting, Longstreet thought.

Lee traced his index finger over the heavy paper. It showed roads in some detail, but only the most important landscape features—and those poorly. "General Longstreet, your divisions will attack abreast. Here. As we decided earlier. They will advance up this road and strike those people on the flank. You will have the element of surprise to add to the force of your blow."

"If we're not seen," Longstreet said. "Meade has a signal station on the lower hill now. They might spot us marching up."

Lee dismissed the concern. "Captain Johnston has been over the ground. He assures me you won't be detected. He will guide your corps himself."

Rifle fire erupted to the south, farther down the ridge on which they had gathered.

Longstreet tensed. "That's more than skirmishing."

Lee remained unperturbed. "General Hill is moving General Anderson into position. They doubtless have surprised a forward party."

"Pretty far forward," Hood said.

Lee gave the division commander a sharp look. It quieted him.

"I mentioned General Anderson and his division," Lee said. "You do not have Pickett, General Longstreet, but Anderson will cooperate with you. When you have advanced successfully on the Union's left flank, here and here, he will strike their left-center. It will have the effect of an oblique attack."

"What's Ewell supposed to do?" Longstreet asked. "With his corps?"

Again, Lee was annoyed. "General Ewell will make a simultaneous demonstration. He will bid for General Meade's attention and render him unsure as to where to commit his reserves."

"What triggers Ewell's 'demonstration'?" Longstreet asked.

"He will move at the sound of your guns." Lee scanned the second rank of kneeling officers and stopped at Porter Alexander. "I anticipate, Colonel Alexander, that your gunnery will be loud enough to be heard?"

From Lee, that passed as a joke. His subordinates murmured appreciatively.

"Yes, sir," Alexander replied. "They'll be loud enough."

The old man looked around the assembly of officers, awaiting questions, but not really inviting them.

"We understand each other, gentlemen? As to what is expected?"

No man denied it.

"Then it's time to look to our duties," Lee concluded. "We must strike swiftly now. General Longstreet, you will set your divisions in motion." He surveyed the earnest faces a last time and

swept a hand toward the Union lines. "If God wills it, we will meet again on the other side of those fields."

The meeting broke up. Longstreet sent Hood off after breaking the news that McLaws would lead the march, since his division was better distributed along the farm roads the corps would need to travel. The Kentuckian, who had proven his worth by leading wild Texans early on, didn't like taking second place, but accepted his fate.

Longstreet, though, could not accept his own. He returned to Lee's side a last time.

The old man looked into his eyes, briefly and impatiently, then looked away. As if he found what he had seen distasteful.

"I beg you, sir, don't do this," Longstreet whispered.

He felt Lee tense in anger. When the old man spoke, his voice was as cold as winter at West Point:

"See to your corps, General."

Although it had slowed his political career, Dan Sickles never rued killing his wife's lover. He had shot the craven fellow down in daylight, a block from the White House. Honor had demanded it. Nor was a cuckold apt to advance with New York City voters, unless he acted to guard his reputation.

In the end, he chose not to fault Teresa much—although he had considered killing her, too. She had been young and impressionable, after all. The dastardly Key had abused the privilege of friendship to seduce her, plying her with tales of her husband's amours. Such tattling was, to say the least, ungentlemanly. And if Teresa had not commanded all his affections, Sickles had treated her with consideration. On his wedding day, for example, he had told her mother that their frolic was over. A delectable piece of baggage in her time, the older woman had wept, but kept her senses. Nor had his dalliances with women of the world been indiscreet. The sum of such encounters was no more than common to a man in his prime. In public, he had been the soul of honor. Teresa had not known the extent of her luck.

She knew it now. He might have discarded her as a fallen woman and been petted as a wanton's victim. But the lass had something that spoke to his desires. He wanted her still. She possessed a tumultuous innocence that enticed him beyond reason. Besides, her

family knew details from his past that might have disappointed his constituents. Best to keep Teresa in his bed and the members of her family in their places. So Daniel Sickles had forgiven his wife. Albeit with curtailed liberties.

His star had fallen because of that noble gesture. The public's sympathy had been with him as the wronged party and his acquittal as deranged by passion had been applauded. But when he chose not to discard Teresa, whom the voters wished to see beaten down and condemned, he was judged a blackguard for his display of mercy. But what else could he have done? Cast that white flesh and ready mouth aside? What a waste of horseflesh that would have been! And fortune's wheel had turned around in time: Thank God for the war!

Democrat though a fellow had to be in New York City, Sickles had always been a solid Union man. An undivided country offered far more scope for ambition, political or otherwise. And his Irish constituents, especially, despised the Confederacy, if for no other reason than that England favored the South. The arrogant planters' class too closely resembled the English gentry for Irish sentiment. As for the nigger question, it was of no consequence, except that the Irish resented darkey laborers.

And his credit had held in Washington, God be thanked. In a stroke of what others described as "Sickles' luck," a prime defense attorney at his trial had been Edwin Stanton, now secretary of war. By the time the judge read out the "not guilty" verdict, the two men had become friends. A few years thereafter, Stanton had oiled the hinges at the White House, where Sickles, valued as a top War Democrat, found the president manageable and his wife a vain little fool who could be flattered.

Nor had he done badly on the battlefield, after raising his own men. If he had made errors, all had been bravely done. No man would ever question Dan Sickles' courage.

So on that anxious July day, as he peered into the fuss of Meade's headquarters, he told himself, "Much ado about nothing, ain't it?"

Teresa's family had theater connections, and that rarely left a man short of ready phrases. Oh, his marriage wouldn't have done for Meade's Philadelphia, but played well enough in New York, where vitality reigned.

The headquarters shack was as busy as Delmonico's scullery on a Saturday evening. Poor Butterfield looked worn to a nub, as if he'd been scouring pots and pans for days. Sickles nodded toward his friend, but Butterfield, scribbling on, hardly responded.

Meade had not deigned to notice his arrival. "A grandee dealing with some *arriviste,*" as Teresa's mother might have put it. But Sickles made it his business to know as much about those with whom he had to cope as generous pouring and Tammany Hall could uncover. He knew the old bugger's pockets were shallow, even if his pride went deep. There wasn't much to Meade beyond that uniform, which the "proper Philadelphian" would not even button. Meade looked like an aged clerk gone to seed in his master's absence.

And this clerk with two stars on his shoulders had no time for him. After the insulting messages delivered by Meade's son and a relay of adjutants, *this* was his welcome: to be ignored. By a man whose reputation was built on lighthouses.

Straightening the fine uniform he had put on for battle, Sickles pushed his way through the pack of officers, the lot of whom stank like the privy of a tenement. Meade was playing the sage over a map, with Warren, his vulture-faced engineer, as sycophant. Sickles thrust himself in between the two men.

The commanding general straightened up. For an instant, his features took Sickles aback. He had never seen a man so visibly weary. Meade always had basset hound pouches under his eyes, but now the bags sagged halfway to his chin. He didn't look fit to command a foraging party.

For his part, Sickles had slept nicely, if not at his usual length.

"General Meade, we must discuss my position."

Meade waved him off. "Not now, Dan. In five minutes."

And that was all. Sickles did not believe that Meade would have been so dismissive of the sorriest West Pointer. That was the problem, of course: this brotherhood of "professional soldiers" who didn't know a damn thing about real war. You learned more from an Irish brawl than anyone did at West Point. Look at the bloody mess they'd made, unable to win one clear victory over Lee, despite the wealth and manpower of the North. Sickles did not doubt but that he could do better. *Much* better. After all, *he* wasn't afraid to fight.

But Meade would always favor his fellow West Pointers. To say nothing of his prissy Philadelphians, with their bird-beak noses thrust into the air. One of his two division commanders, Andrew Atkinson Humphreys, was a very pet of Meade's and—Sickles had no doubt—little more than a spy. Birney, who had the other Third Corps division on the field, wasn't much better, but could be steered.

Sickles brushed and bumped his way over to the corner where Butterfield—boon companion of the Hooker days—labored over papers that likely said nothing. The chief of staff looked nearly as worn as Meade. Added to which, he had a volcanic pimple on his nose. Sickles felt pained just looking at it.

"Dan, I'm busy." Butterfield sighed.

"With what? A panegyric to West Point? A hymn to old Philadelphia?"

The chief of staff flexed his writing hand. "A plan of retreat, if you have to know."

"He's planning to run? The old bugger's running away?"

"No," his friend told him. "He's just a by-the-book bastard. He needs a plan for everything. I'm surprised he can shit in a pot without written orders."

"He's given me a god-awful position, you know. Terrible ground. No glory, but the chance of a damned bad thrashing."

Cracking his knuckles, Butterfield said, "Well, maybe you should be back with your corps. Doing what you can."

Sickles ignored the advice. "I think he's setting me up for a scapegoat, that's the gist of it. He certainly wouldn't give that piece of ground to one of his West Point chums."

The chief of staff exhaled. Out of patience with everyone. Even with a friend and drinking companion. "Don't be an ass. Someone has to fill in the line down there. Your corps was on hand. If anything, he's tucked you in fairly safely."

Sickles' hackles rose. "Meaning he don't trust me to put up a fight?"

"Oh, he knows you'll fight. Dan, listen to me. To tell you the truth, Meade isn't doing badly. I can't stand the gilded snot myself, but I'll give him his due for pulling things together. Joe was letting everything run to Hell. We're better off. Although I wouldn't admit it to another living soul besides yourself." Butterfield popped a

last knuckle, then took up his pen again. "The Great Panjandrum's waving you over. Better go." There was unmistakable relief in Butterfield's voice.

Dan Sickles felt absolutely friendless.

Meade didn't give him a chance to speak, but snapped:

"Is your corps in position at last, General Sickles? And why are you here, when you should be with your men?"

"My situation's unclear, sir. The position I'm to occupy . . ."

"What's unclear about it, man? It's been laid out for you, time and again, where you're to extend the line. You're to take up the high ground on the far left, where Hancock placed Geary last night. What could be clearer than that?"

"Geary had no position. He just put out his pickets and let his boys sleep."

Sickles could read men well enough to know that Meade had no patience remaining. But he was not about to be assigned an inferior role in what might be the battle that saved—or destroyed—the Union. Indeed, it could be his last chance to shine as a hero. He needed those laurels for politics after the war.

Meade stepped closer, edging out Warren to make the exchange private. "How plain must I make things, damn it? You are to extend Hancock's line along the lower ridge and place your left firmly on that first round hill."

"It's bad ground."

"It's integral to the defense. Someone has to hold it."

"It's all woods and marshy meadows, all rocks and low ground. My artillery's lines of fire will be restricted. It isn't even any good for infantry."

"It won't be good for Lee's artillery or infantry, either. If any of the Confederates come your way."

"They will. I know it."

"Then you know more than I know," Meade said. "For God's sake, man . . . even if they did come at you, we have interior lines." He turned, almost furiously, to the map on which he'd been working. "Look at this. Our lines form a reversed question mark, with that hill of yours as the dot down at the bottom. I'm positioning reserves to move right or left, as need be. If Lee surprises us all and appears in your front, you'll soon have the Fifth Corps behind you.

And the Sixth, when it arrives. And look at this." He traced a hand over the crude map again. "Those are Lee's lines. Were he to extend them beyond our left—beyond your flank—why, his lines would be over six miles long. And ours less than three. The mathematics aren't difficult."

"I didn't see many reserves as I rode up."

"They're not all in yet."

Sickles looked into the reddened eyes of the tired man before him and saw that he would need to maneuver differently.

"Well," he said, "there are better artillery positions in the vicinity of my lines." Raising his voice just enough to be certain that Warren heard him, Sickles asked, "Do I have the discretion to post my men according to my judgment? Within the limits of your general instructions?"

"Certainly. Any ground you choose to occupy within those limits, I leave to you."

Sickles turned a smile on the chief engineer. "Perhaps General Warren could accompany me on an inspection of my lines? I greatly value his opinion."

He believed that Warren might be persuaded, even if Meade would not.

"Warren's busy."

"General Hunt, then? I'd be grateful for his help posting my artillery. The ground really is difficult."

Meade pondered that for a few seconds, then called out, "General Hunt? I need you."

Hunt broke away from his tribe of gun monkeys.

"Henry, would you ride down to his position with General Sickles? He needs help placing his guns. Do what you can for him, all right?"

Face as drained of healthy vigor as Meade's, Warren's, and Butterfield's, Hunt scowled. "Let me get my damned hat."

The trick was to persuade Hunt that Meade had made a mistake. Sickles hoped the terrain would speak for itself, but he mustered his supporting arguments.

Hunt was a ramrod bastard, though. Proud of his record, of his brevets in Mexico and his authorship of the U.S. Army's latest

artillery manual. The only serious reverse Lee had met had been in front of Hunt's guns at Malvern Hill. But Sickles suspected the man was all façade. Famously the son and grandson of Regular Army officers, he'd been orphaned and raised on the charity of others until West Point took him in and puffed him up. Such a man would have holes in his confidence . . . somewhere. His pride could be manipulated. Hunt always seemed the most levelheaded of the army's senior officers, but, in Sickles' experience of men and their vulnerabilities, a guarded temper could hide the worst self-doubt.

Despite Meade and his West Point ilk, Sickles perceived a splendid day for battle, the heat not too bad and the sky a blue silk petticoat. As the two generals rode down the ridgeline with their aides, skirmishers, the army's gnats, nipped at each other between the waiting lines. Excited batteries fired for obscure reasons, then went silent again. The hour was nearly noon and little was doing. If Lee held off a bit longer and then attacked on the left, Sickles believed he could be the army's savior.

He needed at least one staff general to bless what he intended to do with his corps, though. He had to cover not only his military flank from Robert E. Lee, but his political flank from the likes of George Gordon Meade. He needed one of the pompous West Pointers on record as backing the move he intended to make.

The issue that pressed him hardest, of course, wasn't his corps' position, but whether it would be wiser to stand for the Senate right at the war's end or to take a turn in the governor's chair in Albany. Assuming his Tammany friends had no objection. He could count on the votes of the New Yorkers brigaded in his ranks, on their relatives, on the Irish, and on the machine-owned newspapermen, with their taste for liquor, cigars, and self-importance. And after the Senate, the governorship, or both . . . what might a war hero not achieve, when nostalgic veterans voted?

"You'll see," he called to Hunt as they cantered along, "it's terrible ground, it ain't fit for a dogfight."

"I've seen it," Hunt replied. "It isn't perfect. But someone has to defend it, if the line's to hold."

They diverted their horses around a tangle of guns going into a battery. The sleek barrels of the Parrotts put Sickles in mind of long, black thighs.

"Anyway," Hunt continued, "I've never seen a perfect fighting position. The surface of the earth isn't made that way."

It wasn't the sort of thing Sickles wanted to hear.

When they reached the first regiments of Sickles' Third Corps, Hunt asked, "Why aren't your men throwing up breastworks?"

"It would make no difference," Sickles said dismissively. "Look at this ground. That's marshland out front. And that grove over there. The Rebs could sneak through those trees. Anyway, the line Meade's assigned me is too long for my corps. It's fifteen hundred yards, if it's an inch, and my corps barely musters ten thousand."

Hunt didn't reply, so they rode on, with Sickles pointing out every deficiency he had noted in the ground, while constantly discovering new ones. Just short of the round hill that was such an obsession of Meade's, Sickles turned in the saddle, pulling his horse to face westward.

"Just ride up this lane with me. You're known to have the best eye in the army. Let me show you a *real* position, where we could give Bobby Lee a pleasant time of it."

Spurring his horse across the worthless ground, Sickles led the way past a queer-shaped wheatfield on the left and climbed a low ridge where two groves met, one on each side of the deeply rutted road.

Breaking back into the sunlight on higher ground, Sickles paused for Hunt to come abreast, then pointed forward, toward an orchard that crowned a knoll at canister range. Blue-clad skirmishers dotted the height, but had nothing at which to fire.

"Up there. That peach orchard. That's what I want you to look at. It's Napoleon's own position for massed batteries. A man of your abilities must see it."

He gave his mount the spurs again. The horse shot forward. Hunt trailed slightly, followed by aides and guards, dozens of hooves drumming on the sun-dried lane.

Sickles did not rein up until he had reached the high point, at the far end of the orchard, on the eastern edge of the road from Emmitsburg. The view to the south was commanding, while the lines of fire to the western woodline were markedly better than those Meade had imposed on him.

"Look at this, General Hunt. Ain't this splendid? If I advanced

my corps this far, we could stop the Confederates with artillery fire
alone. The way you did yourself at Malvern Hill."

Hunt didn't rise to the bait, unless he was making a show of
things for form's sake. The artilleryman scrutinized the ground,
first riding southward a hundred yards along the open skirmish
line, then trotting northward toward the nearest farm buildings,
always keeping his course beside the road, but not straying onto it.
Sickles waited, smoothing his mustache and fanning the lazy air:
The flies were up. As Hunt rode along, weightier pests erupted
from the fields surrounding the orchard. A cloud of insects trailed
his horse's haunches.

The instant Hunt returned to his side, Sickles cried, "What the
devil?" He had been so preoccupied with wooing the gunner that
he had missed the obvious. "Where's the damned cavalry? I was
promised a replacement for Buford. Captain!" he shouted to the
nearest dismounted officer. "Have you seen our cavalry pickets? Have
they gone farther out?"

The captain looked dumbfounded. Clearly, the answer was "No."

"Meade ordered Pleasanton to send out a relief," Hunt said. "I
was there, I heard him."

Sickles decided to turn the matter around. "You see how it is,
Henry? Nothing gets done the way it should. Meade's a good enough
fellow, but he ain't up to this. And here I am, with no cavalry watch-
ing the ground beyond my flank. I could be surprised, if I stayed in
that low ground. Up here, at least I could see the enemy coming."

Hunt shook his head. "I don't see it. Oh, the battery positions
are fine, you're right about that. Excellent lines of fire. Although
there's a bit of dead ground down on the left. But look here, Gen-
eral Sickles . . ." Hunt's horse shied at nothing, then settled again.
"This position's impossible, under the circumstances. You told me
yourself your line's already too long. Were you to advance your
corps this far, then stretch back to those hills . . . why, the length
of your line would double. And you'd be out here on a salient, ex-
posed on two sides. You could never defend this ground against a
serious attack."

"I could, with enough artillery. You could send me a few extra
batteries from your reserve. I really was thinking of the example
you set us all at Malvern Hill—what a triumph that was!" He

paused to let his praise sink deep. "Couldn't your men do it, General Hunt? You'd be the hero of the day again."

Hunt was having none of it. "Artillery works best with infantry." The gunner pointed westward. "If the Confederates emplaced batteries along that treeline, this position could not be sustained, sir. Nor could artillery hold it without infantry. Not if the Rebels popped out of those trees in even brigade strength."

"But you admit this is a fine artillery position. In and of itself."

"We have no quarrel there."

"So . . . if Meade could be made to see reason . . ."

"He *has* his reasons. Look, Sickles, I know you haven't been assigned the most desirable position . . . but you drew the short straw this time. That's just how it is. Someone has to grasp the dirty end of the stick. Next time, it could be Hancock."

Sickles resisted the impulse to say that Hancock never seemed to get the short straw. The favoritism in the army was abominable.

"And speaking of Hancock," Hunt continued, "if you advanced your corps this far, you'd leave a gap of nearly a mile between your right and his left. And your own left would have no anchor until it reached that round hill. *If* you had enough men left to get there."

Sickles had hoped that Hunt would be blind to anything beyond the excellence of the battery positions the peach orchard provided. But it was the same damned story as ever: The West Pointers would not break ranks. They'd rather lose a battle than admit that a fellow Academy man might be wrong.

Determined to have his way, Sickles tried again. "All right, then. Look back to the east, toward the position Meade expects me to hold. What if the Confederates gained this ground right here? They'd be firing down on a good portion of my line. Their guns could even reach Hancock on that ridge."

"And Hancock's guns could reach them," Hunt replied. "Really, I'm not sure either side could hold this position long. It's an in-between sort of place, trick ground."

"You like it as an artillery position, though?"

"Merely in a classroom sense. The army's line must be kept as compact as possible."

"General Hunt, let me put this bluntly . . . as one Union man to another . . ."

Artillery fire broke out on the far right flank, at the other extreme of the Union army's position. Hunt alerted. Ready to ride off to see to his duty.

Sickles grasped the reins of Hunt's horse midway back from the bit. His voice grew impassioned. "Hunt, will you or will you not agree that I had best advance my corps to this position?"

The artilleryman looked dumbfounded. "We've just gone through this . . . why, reserves couldn't even reach you promptly out here. You'd be isolated from the rest of the army, it would upset the entire plan."

"You won't back my movement?"

"Not on my authority." But Hunt was no tin tyrant like George Meade. In a more comradely tone, he added, "I'll report your views to the general commanding. That's all I can do for you."

The cannonade on the army's right quelled itself again: The battle just refused to recommence. Still, it was clear that Hunt wanted to be off. To play with his precious guns, his hoarded reserve, his private army. Sickles turned to reviewing Hunt's words for possible justifications for what he intended.

About to ride away, Hunt paused. Both men looked eastward, toward Sickles' waiting corps, most of it hidden by copses or the low ridge.

"I'll put you another argument against moving forward," Hunt told him. "Those groves you complained about . . . and that marshy ground in front of your position . . . if you advanced your corps, you'd have to fall back through all that, if pressed. With the Rebel guns up here firing down on you. As you just pointed out yourself. In my professional judgment, withdrawing from this line could become a debacle."

Disgusted with the West Pointer's timidity, Sickles said, "The Third Corps will not withdraw."

THIRTEEN

July 2, Afternoon

Major General Lafayette McLaws rode at the head of his division, gnawing on a chicken leg. He ate when he was unhappy, and he ate when he was mad. Now he was mad and unhappy. Longstreet had handled him as he might a schoolboy. In front of at least a dozen fellow officers, to say nothing of General Lee. Such behavior was not merely ungentlemanly, it was unforgivable.

As his mount bore his bulk forward, flanked by the horses of Captain Johnston, Lee's scout, and General Kershaw, who commanded his leading brigade, McLaws yearned to get at the Yankees. He felt plain cussed toward his West Point classmate Pete Longstreet, who was a bigger humbug than any Mormon out in the territories. But Longstreet could not be touched, so the Federals would have to do. For now. But Longstreet would get his comeuppance, in good time.

When he finally came down to give the order to march, Longstreet had taken pains to behave civilly. He knew damned well that he had been in the wrong. But making up wasn't that easy: The damage was done. Laff McLaws was not a forgiving man.

At times he wished he'd just stayed home with Emmy.

He'd taken one small revenge on Longstreet, though. He'd defied the order not to conduct his own reconnaissance and had ridden as far as he'd dared toward the Union flank. Now Captain Johnston had led them past that point and McLaws wished he had gone farther on his own. He didn't like the look of the ground, it broke all wrong. He felt the weight of the column stretching behind him, his own division hurrying along—after a string of infuriating delays—and Hood's bunch hard on his rear. Alexander had gotten his guns out early, which kept down the dust, but the

batteries had been swallowed by the earth. McLaws could only hope they'd appear where they were meant to be and when they were meant to be there. The afternoon fled like a thief.

Riding through a shallow valley, he couldn't see much at all. And he didn't like it. Lee's young engineer looked full of confidence, but McLaws didn't share it. Probably another damned Virginian, he told himself. Then he corrected his judgment: If Johnston had been a Virginian, he'd be a damned general.

They passed a shut-up tavern. The engineer paid it no mind.

McLaws would have complained about the meandering to Longstreet, but the humbug was back with Hood, whom he always favored. McLaws felt badly treated and half-abandoned. And this flank march was interminable. The landscape seemed to weave like a battered pugilist.

He tossed the sucked-out bones into the dust and licked his fingers. Captain Johnston led the way up a ridge, but McLaws was determined to head his own division. Just as they reached the crest, he overtook the engineer.

They both stopped. Mortified. Riding up behind them, Kershaw spoke for all:

"Jesus Christ almighty."

Like Barksdale, another politician jumped up to brigade command, Kershaw had the gift of loading the briefest exclamation with a stage actor's emotion.

McLaws raised a hand to halt the staff men crowding up behind him. And he turned to Captain Johnston.

"You low-down sonofabitch, you look at that! You just goddamned look at that, and you tell me what the holy hogshit you see out there, boy."

Abashed by the view before them, the captain shriveled. "I swear, I didn't—"

"Damn it to Hell, boy, they can *see* us. Those goddamned Yankee signal sonsofbitches on that goddamned hill over yonder would goddamned well see every one of us, if we marched over this ridge. And we're still two miles from their lines."

Craving another morsel of chicken, McLaws turned his horse into the field on the ridgeback. He had a mind to draw out his pistol and shoot Lee's worthless toady right out of the saddle. What

the Hell were they going to do now? Might as well have sent George Meade a telegram.

Tracks swirled into the oats from caissons and gun carriages, but they made little sense to McLaws. Alexander had come the same way, then turned around. But where the artilleryman had gone next was a riddle.

Kershaw's orders to his brigade to halt echoed down the line of march. Captain Johnston rode over the artillery tracks on the other side of the field, searching for the long-lost key to paradise. McLaws shook his head and cursed the world again.

Kershaw rejoined him and said, "Best go gentle, sir. That boy's one of Lee's pedigreed hounds."

"I know that, damn it."

Despite his fighting record, Kershaw was a politician still. He added, "Old Pete seems fond of him, too."

"I don't give a wet shit."

The two men heard hoofbeats coming on—and knew what the sound portended.

"That's all I need," McLaws told the brigade commander.

Longstreet galloped up to them. "What the devil's the holdup?"

McLaws cocked his head toward the crest. "Go up and have a look for yourself. This here secret route ain't much of a secret. We march over that ridge, and the Yankees waving their signal flags on that hill will be counting up the buttons on our uniforms."

Longstreet rode on to the crest, followed by two of his minions. As if he didn't trust his subordinate's eyes. Captain Johnston rejoined McLaws as he waited. The engineer had become a meeker man. McLaws ignored him.

Longstreet came back down cursing. When he got his temper reined in, he turned to Johnston: "Why, this won't do. Is there no way to avoid it?"

"Sir . . . I don't know. I swear it wasn't—"

Longstreet held up his hand for silence, shaking his head in disgust.

Even if it meant revealing that he'd disobeyed an order, McLaws was glad of the chance to show up his superior: "I spied out a better route myself. This morning, after we talked. It's back a ways, though. We'd have to countermarch."

"Then countermarch, man."

"It's the better part of a mile to the rear."

Calculations played out on Longstreet's face. "Would you allow General Hood to take over the lead? To save time?"

McLaws straightened in the saddle, marshaling every pound of his thickset dignity. "You granted me the privilege of leading this corps forward, sir. I will not surrender that right of my own free will. I protest any alteration. As a matter of honor."

Longstreet opened his mouth to give a direct order, then apparently thought better of it. He tempered his tone. "You're sure you know a way? Where we won't be seen?"

McLaws enjoyed the tension as his lips formed into a smile. "A little more certain than Captain Johnston, I think."

"Then *march*. It's almost three o'clock." Longstreet grimaced. "I'd like to get this attack under way before the month is out."

The corps commander yanked his horse around and rode back toward Hood.

As Longstreet cantered up, the Kentuckian was pointing hither, thither, and yon. When McLaws' men came to a halt, Hood's boys had gotten tangled with their rear brigade. A passel of generals and colonels sorted it out, while the majors and captains lay low.

Spotting the corps commander, Hood broke from the muddle and trotted over. Grinning darkly, ready to take a few scalps.

"What's the holdup?" he asked. "Laff's horse give out on him?"

When he saw how Longstreet glowered, Hood slew his grin.

"Route's bad," Longstreet said. "Yankee signal station can see the crest up ahead."

"Goddamn."

Longstreet nodded. "Laff's countermarching. Claims he knows another way. You'll need to get your lead brigade off the road, he's headed back here."

Hood's brows pulled in. "Hadn't I better take the lead? He could send me a guide."

"Got a corncob up his ass. 'Point of honor.' I promised him he could lead the march today."

Hood put on a warpath face as he gathered his next words. Longstreet understood that Hood was about to declare that, as their

corps commander, he could damned well order Lafayette McLaws to do anything he wanted him to do.

Longstreet spoke first. "Not worth it, Sam. I don't have time to argue points of honor with Sir Lafayette of Augusta." He made a rare decision to confide in a subordinate. Nudging his horse closer, he said, "You'll be on your own, once the attack goes in. General Lee has ordered me to stick by Laff, once the shooting starts. There's some concern he might need a helping hand."

Hood's ready-to-scalp expression took on a glow. "I can manage, I guess."

Longstreet laughed. "What you mean is 'Good riddance.' I'll be out of your hair."

The Kentuckian permitted himself a rare, wry smile. "I suppose a high general such as yourself might look at things in that peculiar way. . . ."

"I'm depending on you, Sam." Hood's nickname made him think fleetingly of Grant. "I need you to go as far to our right as you can without losing contact with McLaws. Get in behind them, if you can. Just don't lose touch with Kershaw on Laff's right."

"Glad to hear it's Kershaw," Hood remarked. No need to say more.

"How are Law's men?" Longstreet asked. "Footsore, I imagine."

"Not sure they can feel their feet well enough to call 'em sore. But there's not a man in that brigade would stay behind today."

They spotted the head of McLaws' column doubling back toward them. A half-dozen more riders had joined the division commander. The group looked ragged, emanating frustration.

Still well beyond shouting range, McLaws turned off again. In the general direction of the Army of the Potomac.

"I hope the Hell he knows where he's a-going," Hood said.

"I'd better get on up there," Longstreet told him.

He spurred his horse toward the rising dust.

Longstreet and McLaws rode along together, neither saying much. Longstreet sensed the division commander's peevishness and was tempted to tell McLaws to act like a man. With battle ahead.

He let it go. Given that he felt downright peeved himself. Resigned to doing his duty, Longstreet still believed the attack was

foolish. But Lee had made it clear as all ugly that he intended to fight.

A lieutenant spoke as they neared another ridge. "Just over that crest, sir. That's where we'll break cover."

They turned their mounts aside to let Kershaw's men pass.

"How are you going in?" Longstreet asked as the horses quieted. Hoping for an answer that would not require his personal amendment. Sweat drenched his back, but he knew it was many times worse for the men on foot. How many of their canteens were already empty?

"That will be determined," McLaws said coldly, "when I can see what is in my front."

"There's nothing in your front, damn it. You heard General Lee say it himself. You'll be entirely on the flank of the enemy."

Haughty as a Charleston belle, McLaws said, "Then I'll continue my march in columns of companies. After arriving on the flank as far as is necessary, I'll face to the left and march on the enemy."

"That suits me," Longstreet said. For all of his tootling about honor, McLaws was a good, stubborn fighter. Just not the man to cope with too many surprises. "We need to get this attack under way before Christmas."

Longstreet rode back toward Hood, to hurry him forward.

Satisfied that he'd held his own with Longstreet, McLaws watched Kershaw plunge ahead to lead his men through the treeline atop the ridge. Everything had to go crisply now, his brigades would have to quick-march toward the Union flank before deploying into battle order. Surprise was everything.

As soon as the lead troops in gray disappeared from McLaws' line of sight, cannon fire exploded to their front. Seconds later, shot screamed overhead.

McLaws galloped up the slope and dismounted behind the crest. His staff hurried after him. Still on horseback, Kershaw was ablaze with the fire of command, ordering out skirmishers and telling his forward regiments to deploy behind a stone wall that marked a field line.

"Ride back to the other brigades, tell them to rush on up,"

McLaws shouted to an aide. Then he stumped forward, wheezing, toward the battle sounds.

Penetrating the narrow band of trees, he saw a sight that wasn't supposed to be: A line of Union batteries awaited his division, spitting fire at Kershaw's vanguard. Between and behind those smoking muzzles, regiments of Union infantry had taken up positions around an orchard. Their refused flank sat astride his line of attack.

As General Lafayette McLaws tried to figure out what to do, more Federal troops hastened over the fields to extend the Federal line.

Where Lee had promised an undefended flank, Meade's army stood waiting.

"This ain't good," McLaws said.

Accompanied by the key members of his staff, Longstreet rode forward to amend McLaws' battle orders. A courier had instructed the division commander to hold off attacking until Longstreet could survey the changed situation for himself.

The corps commander found McLaws agitated and befuddled.

"I need to attack," he cried out to Longstreet. "I need to attack right now. Their artillery . . ."

"Just hold up," Longstreet barked. "Let me have a look, damn it."

Longstreet didn't dismount, but rode out beyond the trees into the field that faced the enemy. Behind him, Union shells tore away branches. The limbs fell with a thump and a splash of leaves. When Sorrel and Fairfax followed, Longstreet waved them back. The troops who had taken to ground had to see him exposed and full of confidence. But he did not intend to risk the lives of subordinates to no purpose.

Porter Alexander had already rolled his guns out on the right and was giving the Federals about as good as he got. No cannon replied to the Yankees from the front of McLaws' division, though. That wanted fixing.

At first glance, the Union lines appeared formidable through the patches of smoke. The Federals had advanced to a ridge that swept back from an orchard and ran southeast to boulder-studded high ground. The stony crest blocked the way to the two round hills. An attack on so strong a position had never been part of Lee's

plan. Everything seemed upended. Longstreet had learned, though, that few situations were as dire as they appeared at the moment of surprise. Forcing patience upon himself, he began to dissect the Yankee position.

A round of solid shot ripped through the air, shrieking close enough to shy his horse. Behind his back, it smashed through a tree. Falling timber groaned.

Longstreet refused to turn to regard the damage: The men had to believe he was unperturbed. Even if every organ from his brain to his belly jumped.

He coaxed his horse back to stillness.

Peering through his field glasses, he noted that those impressive lines of infantry in blue were, in fact, as thin as a young belle's waist and backed by nothing. The Union batteries covered gaps in the line that were just too wide. Those gaps would be fatal, if struck just right.

Getting up there was going to be costly. Once on that ridge by the orchard, though, his men would sweep those regiments aside. There was an initial advantage, but no solidity, to the Union position. Viewed with a veteran's eye, it seemed an amateur's gambit, all bluff and fakery. Properly attacked, the Federals would have to sacrifice most of their guns.

He rode back toward his gathered staff, letting his mount lope easily. But his heart wanted to escape his chest.

McLaws remained on foot and appeared determined to stay that way. Longstreet dismounted and handed off his horse. He waved to Fairfax and Sorrel, indicating that they should join him. Unwilling to be left out, McLaws hurried over.

"Tom still not back from General Lee?" Longstreet asked.

Moxley Sorrel smiled through sweat and dust. "Even Goree can't ride that fast, sir."

Longstreet turned to Fairfax. "John, I need you to ride down and tell Hood the plan has changed. He's to come up on the right immediately. He'll lead the attack. As soon as he can get his men deployed."

McLaws reddened. "That's *my* privilege."

Longstreet was out of patience. Even as he spoke, he understood he was making an enemy for life.

"The situation's changed," he told the division commander. "Honor can wait. First, we have to deal with those goddamned Yankees."

"I insist on my—"

The pent-up fury of the day threatened to erupt. Longstreet drew McLaws aside. Not gently.

"General, you will do what I tell you to do, and you will do it when I tell you to do it. Or I will take direct command of your division. Do you understand me, sir?"

Longstreet kept his voice low enough to avoid a public shouting match. But it was difficult.

"And on another subject," he continued, "why aren't there any guns in front of your position? Your supporting artillery should be pounding away."

McLaws spouted and sputtered: "If a battery's placed in my front, it'll draw the enemy's fire right down on my lines. And we're all formed up to charge, the guns would be in our way. It'd be demoralizing. . . ."

Longstreet stared right through the man. "You get a goddamned battery up there now, Laff. You expect your men to charge those guns before they've been softened up? Good God, man. Think what you're about."

Underscoring his point, a wave of artillery rounds tore through the trees. To the left and rear, an explosion left men screaming. The carnage went unanswered.

Chastened for the moment, McLaws lumbered off.

"Wait," Longstreet called. "Kershaw's leading on your right. Who leads on your left?"

"Barksdale."

"Good."

"General Longstreet, let me charge. Let me go right now. We'll take those guns. Give me one half hour. If we don't take that gun line, you can hang me from a tree."

"No."

"I can take them, I swear." McLaws looked pathetic, on the edge of tears.

Longstreet cleansed the anger from his voice. "Laff . . . we have to do this in a way that makes a hint of sense. It's not about honor,

yours or anybody else's. It's about winning this goddamned battle. Their position has more holes than a drunkard's conscience, and we're going to give them a lesson in tactics. But we're going to do it right." He softened further, grasping the turmoil within the man he had known since their first, grim year at the Academy. "You'll get your chance. Hood goes in ahead of you, but you're going to finish the job. You'll have all the honor any man could want." That was the most he could offer to McLaws: No more time for coddling. "Now get a battery up there."

Longstreet rejoined Fairfax and Sorrel. Fairfax had brought up his horse, ready to mount.

"All right, John. Tell Hood to attack as soon as he can form up. He's to find their flank and punch through it." Longstreet shook his head, disgusted at the entire situation. "And I don't mean go around them now. We're out of time. He's to punch right through. He'll growl about that high ground in his front, but tell him the Yankees look fairly thin from up here. His right brigade's to go for the low hill dead on, with his left close enough to the road to align with McLaws."

He glanced from one man to the other. "If Hood can bull through, they'll collapse. At a minimum, he'll draw off any reserves they have up. As soon as he's well under way, I'll send in McLaws." For a moment, he looked away. Then he told Fairfax, "Best get going, John. And use your spurs."

"Yes, sir."

Fairfax cooed to his horse and swung into the saddle as smoothly as if riding to his foxhounds. He rode the most beautiful mount in the entire army.

The shelling intensified. Longstreet saw old Barksdale storm up to McLaws. He didn't need to hear a word that passed between them to know that the brigadier was giving Laff hell. Barksdale didn't just want to beat the Yankees. He took a righteous delight in *killing* them. And he wanted to get at them now. The man was one firebrand politician who hadn't stayed safely at home to go on giving speeches.

Laff had his orders. He'd have to deal with Barksdale. As Longstreet had needed to disappoint McLaws.

"Moxley . . . find Alexander. My compliments on getting his bat-

teries up handsomely. Then tell him I damned well want at least a battalion of guns up here to support McLaws. Fifteen minutes ago would've been too late. Get that Georgia pride of his on the boil."

"Yes, sir."

When his aides had ridden off, Longstreet walked back to the crest. In the woodline, a regiment lay belly-down, waiting for the order to advance. Spears of light pierced the treetops, pinning the men to the ground. Longstreet sensed the rambunctiousness soldiers feel as they wait under fire: Visions of what might happen to their flesh in that hour of helplessness provoked a lust to go at the enemy any which way. Sweat-chilled now and chafed by crusted wool, each man had to wonder why the damned fool generals didn't send them forward and get it done. Longstreet understood the private hells in that shell-torn grove. But he preferred to lose a few men to gunnery and falling branches, rather than throw away a thousand lives.

A battery thundered across the field behind them, outriders lashing the horses as they dragged up their bouncing twelve-pounders.

Longstreet felt a legion of eyes upon him.

He maintained his mask.

Entering the exposed field again, he stared across the ground over which he soon would send the men who lay under the trees. Shrouds of smoke hid stretches of the Union line, but the blue sky above touched perfection.

Death came for all men. But it was going to come a sight sooner than necessary for many a man this day. As it had come too soon, years and years too soon, for his children.

Would he and Louise find their way to each other again? What if he himself were killed? How would she grieve? Could she? As once she would have done? Back when they were so happy they both believed that no other love could ever have been so fine, so sweet, so true, as the one they shared?

Looking impatiently to the right, he strained to penetrate the smoke that rose from his own guns. He ached to see Hood's men appear. It was too soon, of course. Fairfax would just be delivering the order. His anxiety was almost that of a child, demanding the impossible. He realized full well that a division of infantry uncoiled slowly from the line of march, no matter how experienced and disciplined.

But knowledge had no power to vanquish emotion. Longstreet yearned to see gray lines break from the cover of the trees and begin their advance. Time was a cruel master now. To have a hope of success, they needed to smash through the overextended Union position before the generals in blue recognized their folly.

As he turned to watch the enemy again, a Confederate shell hit near a Union gun. He raised his glasses, but the smoke from the explosion obscured the view. He waited, forcing himself to be patient. At last, as the fog from the blast thinned to gauze, he spotted bodies sprawled around the field piece, some inert and others writhing. Tiny figures rushed toward them. In the background, horses leapt, fighting their harnesses.

He turned again: Still no sign of Hood down in the low ground.

Longstreet stalked back through the woodline. From the head of the field on the rear slope, McLaws stared at him, a child unfairly chastised. For all the brutality war summoned in men, it could strip away decades, too. The wisdom of adulthood bled to death.

Another battery rumbled up past McLaws' second line of brigades, rushing to fill in the gun line on the left. Alexander, at least, obeyed orders.

The first rider Longstreet spotted was Sorrel on his way back, but Fairfax came on at a gallop just behind him.

Longstreet didn't like the look of it. If all was in order, Fairfax wouldn't whip his horse like that: He was a gentle man with animals.

The Virginia grandee didn't leave the saddle, but rode right up to Longstreet, pausing only to glance upward as a shell on a low trajectory screamed past.

"Sir, General Hood asks that he be allowed to march on the enemy's rear. He's had scouts out and there's nobody on those two hills. Nothing behind them, either. He believes he could sweep right over them."

Longstreet felt a brief rush of enthusiasm. It was what he had wanted to do all along. But that feeling collapsed promptly into anger. At Hood, at Lee, at himself.

It was too late. He couldn't let a lone division peel off by itself. It was just too goddamned late. The battle was on and the afternoon was dying. It was too late for anything but a mutual pounding.

"Goddamn it, John. You ride back and tell Hood I said he's to attack immediately. And to go in the way he's been told. No more delays. I want to see his lead brigades crossing those fields before you can ride back here. *Go!*"

But Fairfax wasn't gone five minutes before Major Sellers of Hood's staff galloped up, interrupting Longstreet and Sorrel.

"General Hood's compliments, sir. He asks your permission to move by the right flank, to envelop that knob hill."

Longstreet liked Sellers. He understood that Hood had selected the man as an emissary because of it.

He fought down the worst of his anger again. "You go back and tell General Hood he is to attack according to my instructions. *Now*. No more delays. He must attack *now*. Tell him Major Fairfax speaks with my own voice."

It was all turning into a farce, a series of witless pranks worthy of a minstrel show. McLaws wanted to attack, but had to wait. Longstreet wanted Hood to attack, but the Kentuckian, who had never shied from a fight, resisted his orders. Sellers had barely disappeared when Longstreet decided he had had enough. He strode over to McLaws, drawing him aside again.

"I'm riding down to see Hood. Do nothing until I return."

He turned his back.

Calling for his horse, Longstreet felt more than half a fool. This pot of confusion was his responsibility. He had never before experienced such a devil's dance of ill luck, misunderstandings, and pigheadedness. Battle was always a welter of confusion, but this took the prize. The attack should have gone in hours before, they should already be inside the Union lines, rounding up the remnants of broken brigades and shattered divisions. Yet, not one regiment in gray had advanced beyond the gun line.

He rode hard, spurring and lashing his horse until it whinnied in terror. Daring it to stumble, to throw him hard and put the load on other shoulders.

It had come to that.

Passing Fairfax on the major's return ride, Longstreet just struck his horse harder. Soldiers bearing armloads of canteens leapt from his path.

When he found Hood, the Kentuckian's forward brigades were finally stepping out to the attack. That was something, at least. Longstreet calmed down to a frozen rage.

Spying him, Hood hurried over. His eyes lacked their usual steel.

"General Longstreet . . . call off this attack, I beg you. Let me go around them."

"You have your orders, General. See to your advance."

"We're throwing men away."

Longstreet refused to hear another word. "We must obey the orders of General Lee. All depends on you now."

But something had broken inside of Hood. Longstreet could feel it. He'd lost the goodwill of McLaws. Would Hood turn from him, too? Command was not the Sunday treat the stay-at-homes imagined.

Hood saluted and rode off to lead his soldiers.

Longstreet sat in the shade on his heaving mount, watching Hood's forward line advance into a cauldron of smoke and sunlight. His own batteries fell silent as the infantry swept past them. The gun-thunder from the Union lines intensified.

"Go now," he told the gray ranks, "and God go with you."

FOURTEEN

July 2, Late Afternoon

Meade would have liked to slash Sickles from his horse. Instead, he mastered his temper yet again and spoke with as much control as he could muster.

"General, I'm afraid you're too far out. You've compromised the army's position." He surveyed the indefensible salient again, the peach orchard before them and the declining fields beyond. Shots from skirmishers prickled the air. "If Lee attacks from both sides, you'll lose your guns. If not your corps."

Fear marred Sickles' eyes now. He knew that he had erred. But the man still possessed sufficient bravado to trivialize his blunder.

"This is higher ground. The lines of fire are better. I needed elevation. This seemed better than the low ground I was in."

The horse Meade rode pranced nervously. Old Baldy had been unsaddled for a rest when word of Sickles' unauthorized movement arrived. Meade had accepted the loan of his cavalry chief's mount, but Pleasanton's horse was odd to the bit and obstreperous.

Meade's temper swelled back toward its breaking point. "*General* Sickles . . . this is, indeed, higher ground than the position you left to your rear. And there's even higher ground in front of you, if you want to keep going. If you'd like to advance right past the Confederate lines, you'll find constantly higher ground all the way to the mountains."

His voice, if not his logic, abashed Sickles.

In a subdued tone, the Third Corps commander said, "I can withdraw."

"You'll have to do it damned quick," Meade told him.

But as he spoke, the Confederate guns opened, condemning them all to defend the ground they occupied. Short or long, rounds

sought the range of the peach orchard, the apex of the position Sickles had chosen. The gun-by-gun battery firing quickly became a steady roar. Pierced by muzzle flashes, smoke fumed and thickened where Lee's infantry lurked.

Sickles' forward cannon replied, booming and recoiling. Stripped of their jackets and even their shirts, artillerymen leapt to swab and feed their guns.

Raising his voice to be heard, Meade said, "I wish to God you *could* withdraw, but it's too damned late for that now." He shook his head in disgust. "The enemy will not permit it. You'll have to fight."

"I just wanted higher ground," Sickles repeated. His face had gone as pale as a man struck by the first pangs of cholera. "I didn't want the Rebels to have this position."

"Damn it, Sickles . . . this is *neutral* ground," Meade shouted. "Don't you understand that?" Artillery shells plowed the fields behind their escorts. Meade's horse rebelled again and had to be reined in tightly. "You can't hold it, and neither can the enemy."

Meade's fury assailed himself above all others. To be beaten by Robert E. Lee would be a terrible thing, but to be defeated by Dan Sickles was abhorrent.

The entire affair was grotesque. Upon receiving word that Sickles had advanced his line without authorization, Meade had summoned the straying commander to headquarters. Twice called, Sickles sent excuses for not appearing, responding only to a third, peremptory order. Then he had galloped up with a swollen entourage—just as heavy skirmishing erupted back on his lines. Meade had been forced to send him back to his compromised troops immediately.

Now the army's scheme of defense was in jeopardy, all the careful planning squandered by one fool politician in uniform who had advanced an entire corps to the most amateurishly chosen position Meade could recall or conjure. All of Meade's faith in an engineer's precise approach to the battlefield seemed laughable now. And bitter.

It galled him to think how much more smoothly things must be going for Lee, who appeared to have granted himself the time for careful preparations, whose subordinates never displayed such bald incompetence. Sickles had advanced into a trap of his own devising, and Lee would not let such an opening pass.

Meade was forced to take Lee's blows where Sickles had tugged the army. The fool had to be supported, or else his corps would be butchered on the cheap. And the roar of the artillery duel suggested that Lee's main attack would come on the left, after all, worsening an awful situation. Even now, though, Meade needed to make certain that this great ruckus was not a mere diversion, that Lee's hardest blow would not hit the Union right and the Baltimore Pike in the end.

It was a devil of a fix.

Struggling with his mount, Meade shouted to Sickles: "You'll need more artillery. Call on the reserve, on Hunt. And God help you."

Sickles began to reply, but the nearby detonation of a shell sent Meade's horse into a panic. The creature careened from the orchard, with its rider fighting to steer it away from the Confederates. The horse bucked and rose, attempting to cast the unfamiliar master from its back. It required Meade's last ounce of horsemanship just to remain in the saddle.

Flanked by artillery bursts, aides and staff men galloped after him, but could not close upon the maddened horse. Meade feared a stumble that would throw him hard, a humiliating way to end his command.

At last, he succeeded in turning the mount toward the Third Corps' rear. He loosened the reins and let the creature run out its vigor and dread.

It was what the animal needed.

As Meade drew up by a barn buttressed with stones, the better horsemen from headquarters swarmed around him.

"George," Meade called to his son, "get Old Baldy, damn it. And tell Pleasanton to send an orderly to fetch this worthless beast before I shoot it. Where's Hunt?"

"He went to call up more batteries, sir."

"Good." Meade stroked the horse, trying to still it completely. Hot horseflesh quivered wet under his hand. He would have preferred to punish the animal, to hurt it. As he would have loved to punish Daniel Sickles. But Meade was learning to do a great many distasteful things out of necessity.

He turned to a courier. "Find General Sykes. Tell him the Fifth

Corps *must* come up on the left, he's to move each brigade the instant it's ready to march."

The captain saluted and spurred his horse, launching clods of barnyard waste behind him. Meade shielded his face and switched his attention to another aide. "Go to the Sixth Corps headquarters. Find out which units are already on the field. Tell General Sedgwick to be prepared to move to the left, on order. Report back here as fast as you can ride."

As the second officer galloped toward the rear, an approaching rider in blue lashed his horse like a desperate jockey. Meade recognized one of Warren's men, a youthful engineer.

The boy pulled up sharply, gasping, and saluted. "General Warren's compliments, sir. The small round hill is unoccupied. Except for the signalers, there isn't a man on it. And the Rebels are on the move, you can see them from up there, they're coming on. It looks like they're aiming right toward those hills. General Warren believes it'll take a division to hold the high ground."

Meade didn't have a division. He didn't even have a spare brigade on hand, not one available regiment. Not yet. Reinforcements soon would be on the way. But "soon" was not "now."

The near fields and groves were bare of Union troops, save the usual stragglers where Birney's division had passed, marching to their fate on Sickles' order. On the right, in the middle distance, Humphreys' men went forward handsomely, faces to the late-afternoon sun, heading toward the Emmitsburg road to spread across the vast gap Sickles had opened.

"Major Ludlow," Meade called to a trusted staff man, "ride over to General Humphreys. He's to wheel his division to the left rear immediately and move double-quick to occupy that first hill."

"The local people call it 'Little Round Top,'" Warren's man put in.

"I don't care what it's called," Meade snapped. "I just don't want to lose it."

Ludlow turned his horse to his task even as he threw Meade a salute.

One risk weighed against the other now. The great gap in the line on Sickles' right was an urgent matter. But the menace to the

hill was even graver. He was robbing Peter to pay Paul, unsure if all of his actions were in vain.

The artillery bombardment had grown more intense. It could only mean that the Rebels had brought up more guns. Probably upon realizing how vulnerable Sickles was. How many pieces did Lee have available? Enough to deliver an equal cannonade on the Union right? Or *was* this the main attack?

Soon the troops in gray and brown would emerge from the far trees. And he would have to place his bet. Indecision was an enemy, too.

Meade's craving for sleep had faded to the feel of a mild hangover. The pulse of battle quickened all his nerves and sharpened his senses. He did a mental count of the units he might draw from other corps to deepen his left, calculating how long it should take each to march up and go in.

Hunt rode up. The chief of artillery was alone. Meade understood. Hunt had already dispatched the last member of his field staff to get the reserve guns moving. For an instant, Meade imagined that he heard batteries racing forward, but knew that bordered on a hallucination. The guns could not come up so quickly. Not even guns that Henry Hunt had positioned.

It was going to be an evening of sweating through each minute.

"Henry . . . ," Meade called, "can you save that damned fool Sickles?"

Hunt shook his head. "I've got plenty of guns on the way. But they can't hold without infantry."

"How much time can you give me?"

Hunt considered the question for a few seconds. "An hour. At most. Probably less. Depending on how Lee comes on."

An errant shell furrowed the dirt in a field between the farmstead and Sickles' threatened orchard.

"Any sense of how many guns they've massed?"

This time, it was Hunt's horse that shied. "At least a full corps' complement. Maybe more."

"Main attack, would you say?"

"It certainly isn't negligible." Hunt's expression grew fierce. "Sickles doesn't have half enough men up to hold that orchard.

He's got Birney covering damned near a mile of front with his division, and on wretched ground that doesn't hang together. I can't employ artillery back in those woods, and we're probably going to lose some guns up here."

Meade understood the shame to an artilleryman of losing a gun, let alone full batteries. But nothing could be done. The cannoneers would have to redeem Sickles' error with bravery, blood, and bronze, with powder and steel.

Time. He needed time.

Leaving the lane that led to the orchard, the first reserve battery to arrive clambered into the high fields, crushing virgin grain. Whips flared and struck, but the cannonade's waves drowned the cries of man and beast.

How much more time would Lee give him? Before the Rebel yell announced the crisis? Mounted on a horse lathered to failing, another courier materialized. Meade didn't recognize this one.

"Sir . . . General Warren has a brigade from the Fifth Corps going into position on Little Round Top."

"Whose brigade?" Meade asked. The Fifth was his old corps and, to him, the best in the army.

"Colonel Vincent's, sir."

Meade nodded. "Vincent will do."

"Any message for General Warren, sir?"

"Tell him to hold that hill. No matter the cost." He waved over the captain of his bodyguard. "Have one of your men switch mounts with this man. Before that horse dies and falls on him."

Displeased, as any cavalry officer would be, the captain saluted and got on with the business. Meade noted, though, that the captain did not turn over the finest horseflesh in the 6th Pennsylvania.

Meade summoned his last available aide. "Ride to General Humphreys. My orders to him are countermanded. He's to reverse direction and extend General Sickles' line along the road, in accordance with his earlier instructions. Now go, man."

Humph's piss would boil at the seesaw orders. Meade imagined his old acquaintance cursing his incompetence. It couldn't be helped. The situation had changed. With Vincent deploying on the round hill and the Fifth Corps coming on, it was now more important to strengthen Sickles' line, to close at least a portion of the

gap that had opened between his corps and Hancock back on the ridge.

The situation was appalling. Brigades and regiments would need to join the line piecemeal, as they arrived, reducing their effectiveness and making a muddle of every command arrangement. It wasn't the way Meade wanted to fight a battle. But Lee and Sickles between them had forced his hand.

Grimly, Meade told himself that the Confederate plan was doubtless running like clockwork. Lee's veterans would never succumb to the confusion plaguing the Army of the Potomac. The thought filled Meade with rage. And determination.

Let Lee come. Meade was determined to fight it out, to give as good as he got. Lee was *not* about to gain another easy victory, Sickles or no Sickles. Meade intended to make him pay for every foot of ground.

The Confederate barrage slackened, then stopped abruptly. Freshly arrived Union batteries sent their shells into the smoke, but the Rebel gunners resisted the urge to reply.

Meade understood. They were coming. Then he heard a distant Rebel yell.

By the time Longstreet got back to McLaws, the division commander was in an argument just short of blows with Billy Barksdale, the Mississippi politician who commanded one of Laff's two lead brigades. Kershaw, the other brigade commander fronting the division, stood off to the side, arms folded, as if deciding whom to wager on.

Barksdale was a strange bird. He could speechify like Calhoun or Clay, or blaspheme like a stevedore. Most men fought because they wanted to win the war and go home. Barksdale didn't seem to mind much how long things continued, as long as he could go on killing Yankees. His hatred had a spice to it that heated his Mississippi soldiers, too. Barksdale's attacks weren't elegant, and he sat a horse as if it were a mule, but he went where you pointed him and got there when you needed him to do so. Once Barksdale was unleashed, the Yankees were going to stop him only by killing him and most of those marching with him. And they might have to do it twice.

Spying Longstreet, Barksdale turned from his division com-
mander and strutted up. Without a by-your-leave, he started in rail-
ing at the man who outranked him by two stars.

"Damn me to Hell, Longstreet, why are my boys sitting here
holding their peckers? With the goddamned nigger-loving Yankee
artillery thumping on 'em?" The Mississippian shook his head in
disgust. "I wish you'd let me go in, General. My boys could take
those batteries in five minutes."

From the middle distance, the clamor of Hood striking the
Union flank underscored the brigade commander's urgency.

"You just wait a little." Longstreet slipped from the saddle, rump
aching. "We're all going in presently."

Barksdale was a beefy man with pale hair thin as a baby's. Once
clipped short, the wispy tufts had grown out to form a halo around
his raw-meat complexion. He always kept his cap on because he was
bald on top.

"My boys ought to go in right now," Barksdale insisted. The
man retained the politician's sense of immunity.

Longstreet was not about to be stampeded. He gave Barksdale a
look that would shrivel an oak tree. "You'll go in when General
McLaws orders you to go in. Meanwhile, General, I expect you to
see to it that the day's orders for officers are obeyed without excep-
tion. Brigade commanders and their staffs may remain mounted,
but all regimental officers go forward on foot. I will not have need-
less casualties among our officers. Is that clear, sir?"

Barksdale snorted. Then he grunted. Then he stamped his foot
and walked away. Heading back toward his nearby brigade. The man
was insubordinate. But Longstreet knew he would fight.

He turned to McLaws. The division commander looked re-
lieved to be free of Barksdale for the present, but the big man was
still unsettled: The waiting was worse than the fighting. But after
the day's long litany of blunders on every side, Longstreet was de-
termined to regain control. Each next increment of the attack would
advance in its proper order. Enough harm had been done this day
through bravado and hasty judgment.

Longstreet glanced at Kershaw, who had not unfolded his arms,
then told McLaws, "Send your right forward."

The division commander passed the command to Kershaw, who had already heard it clearly enough.

"I'm going forward with Kershaw for a bit," Longstreet said to McLaws. "Do nothing until I return."

After ordering his shrunken retinue to remain behind, Longstreet led his horse toward Kershaw's line. He could see the South Carolinians rising in the treelines, eagerness vanquishing fear. Soon they'd step into the sunlight, dress their ranks, and advance.

He would not interfere. Kershaw knew what he was about. But Longstreet wanted the men to see him, to feel they were in his care, that he had confidence in them and the day's plan of battle. Even if he could not feel that confidence himself. Hope, yes. But not confidence. They would carry that first Union position, which was built on air, hanging out on an invisible limb, waiting to be snapped off. But he did not know what George Meade had hidden behind it. They all were paying for Stuart's long and inexcusable absence—the man's appetite for renown had left the army in the position of a blind man in a knife fight.

Still, if Hood grabbed those two hills, the attack would have a chance. Longstreet would have liked to have Pickett's division to exploit any success, but the men ready to attack had plenty of courage. The problem was that Longstreet didn't have plenty of men.

Valor would have to make up for hard numbers.

Billows of smoke, light gray to death dark, obscured the Union lines. Bursts of flame marked the muzzles of Union batteries, but the enemy could be seen only when a quirk of the air made a path through the earthbound clouds.

There was smoke in plenty around Kershaw's forming ranks, too, but shafts of golden afternoon light pierced it, gilding rifle barrels and bayonets.

"For South Carolina!" Kershaw shouted.

The regimental commanders echoed his war cry, but a mighty Rebel yell soon buried their words, its fury defying even the rage of the guns.

The batteries behind which they'd formed up ceased their bombardment and the gray lines passed into the rising smoke. Leading his horse by the reins, Longstreet strode beside them. A battlefield's

sounds played many a trick, but he was certain that Hood was well into the fight on the corps' right. Now it was time to press the attack where the Yankees looked their thinnest.

Make them fear you, Longstreet thought. *Shock them, make them run. Get behind them just once, and it all collapses.*

Panic could do what strength of arms could not.

Noting his presence, some of Kershaw's men gave Longstreet a cheer. He nodded, but did not smile. It was a rough-hewn business now, best left to their own officers.

Union cannon found their range. Men dissolved in bursts of crimson spray. The South Carolinians closed ranks and continued advancing.

As they approached the road between the battle lines, Longstreet mounted and galloped back toward McLaws. Behind him, another grand Rebel yell rasped from thousands of throats.

The division commander had come forward to the edge of the treeline. His face asked, *Barksdale? Now?*

Longstreet shook his head, then drew his field glasses from the case strung behind his saddle and passed his mount to an orderly. The series of assaults had turned into a classic oblique attack, even more so than Lee had intended. Events had dictated what needed to be done. When the situation changed, plans had to be altered.

Before scouting Kershaw's progress, Longstreet swung his glasses to the northeast. Searching for artillery smoke rising from the Confederate left, for any sign that Ewell had begun the diversionary attack the old man had promised.

The sky beyond his own front remained as blue as a baby's blanket.

As blue as the blanket his dead son had favored.

What in the Hell was delaying Ewell? Did Lee understand that his plan was coming apart on *both* flanks now? What, in the name of all the devils in Hell, was wrong with Ewell?

Tom Goree appeared beside him. Longstreet didn't like the dour look on his face.

"Tom?"

Goree raised his voice to be heard above the commotion: "It's General Hood, sir. He's been wounded. He's been carried from the battlefield."

Longstreet lowered his eyes. *Not Hood. Good God. Not now.*

He fought to steady his voice: "That leaves Law the senior brigade commander, am I correct?"

The Texan nodded.

"Ride back down there," Longstreet ordered. "Make damned sure that Law understands he commands the division now, not just his brigade. He'll have to spread his attention, and that's a hard thing to do when a man's in a fight. He's to push the entire division, not just his own boys. And just keep going."

Goree raised a salute and turned away.

Hood was a terrible loss, his wounding a grim turn of fate. Law wasn't ready for division command. The man was a good officer. Just not ready. For a moment, Longstreet was tempted to disobey Lee's order to remain with McLaws. But Hood's attack was well under way and Law would have to manage. He just had to keep up the pressure and not relent, not listen to the inevitable entreaties from subordinates that their casualties were too high or their ammunition too low. On the other hand, three of McLaws' brigades still had to be committed. Putting them in properly would require a steady hand.

He ignored the dismay on McLaws' plump face and turned back to the spectacle in the fields.

He, too, would have liked to send Barksdale in immediately, to commit everything he had. But one of them had to regulate his emotions.

Through rents in the smoke, he watched the long lines of Kershaw's men advance. Their alignment was far from perfect now, but they pressed steadily forward, centered on their flags. It was an odd thing to stand calmly and watch men die from a distance. Longstreet should have been used to it, but sometimes the spectacle bushwhacked him anew.

Kershaw's force had split into two wings, with the left regiments rushing handsomely for the line of Federal guns on the ridge by the orchard. Longstreet watched the proud red banners climb the slope, drawing on soldiers breathtaking in their valor, men bold enough to charge straight into the guns up on the high ground. Where the smoke permitted, he saw Union gunners serving their pieces desperately, ramming canister and case-shot down the barrels.

The artillerymen appeared well-drilled, not wasting a movement as they continued their work amid their mounting dead and wounded. But all their efforts soon would be for nothing: Their batteries were bound to be overrun in minutes.

Then Longstreet witnessed a monstrous, inexplicable turn of events: The gray ranks attacking into the guns wheeled abruptly to the right, exposing their flank to the delighted Yankee gunners. Longstreet watched, riveted, as the Union batteries tore Kershaw's left wing to pieces.

Who could have given such an order? *Why?*

What folly, in God's name, had he just witnessed?

They had come so near, so very near. And now this.

Longstreet turned to McLaws. "Order Billy Barksdale to take those guns."

The boils on Barksdale's rump just made him meaner. There was no way to sit a saddle that felt good, so he stood in the stirrups whenever he halted his horse. Stiff knees aching, he straightened himself and balanced his bulk above the throbbing animal, determined to appear dauntless.

As his regiments formed beyond the pausing batteries, he had ridden along his front to show himself, admiring his men's aura of ferocity. Returning to the middle of the formation, he reined in before his beloved 13th Mississippi.

Rising again, he surveyed the men proudly and shouted, "Hellfire, boys! Y'all going to do your duty by the great and glorious state of Mississippi. I know that. Yankees been fouling our soil for many a month now, disgracing our women and children with their barbarities. *You* know that. Time to water their own damned soil with blood—and I don't mean ours. *What says Mississippi?*"

The ranks growled and warpath voices called, "Damned right!" and, "Turn us loose, Billy . . ."

Then, for one gorgeous moment, by unspoken and common consent, all fell silent along the brigade's dressed ranks. Barksdale savored the splendor of it all, scorning the Yankee guns' lust for Southern flesh to revel in the power and the glory. Aglow with an abundant sense of destiny, lascivious in its richness, he reared up and roared from the depths of his lungs, the volume outstripping

his fiery orations in Congress or out on the stump. The noise he made might have been the roar of a creature half-man, half-lion:

"Y'all see those guns? Those Yankee guns been pecking at us? We're going to *take* those guns, boys. And then we'll keep right on a-going until dead, gut-shot, and quittin' Yankees lie so thick neither man nor beast can climb over top of them." He drew his sword and raised it high. The blade caught the sun as an iron rod catches lightning. "Atten . . . *shun*! For Mississippi! By battalions, *forward*!"

The regimental commanders repeated his order, only to be overwhelmed, swamped, drowned by the grandest Rebel yell Barksdale had ever heard.

This day was rare, enchanted in a way even he, a master of oratory, lacked words to explain. *Destiny?* Perhaps that. A day of destiny. And an hour of delicious rage and satisfaction so encompassing it put him in mind of the day he had watched Brooks cane Sumner to the Capitol floor.

Instead of taking his place behind the regiments, Barksdale dropped into his saddle—wishing the infernal boils would just burst—and rode farther to their front. His white locks bounced and tickled his neck, and he felt himself part of a reborn, noble chivalry. Plagued buttocks or not, he could only grin at the joy of leading *these* men, of being a part of all this, on this day, *here*.

Ragged and proud, his men crossed the shimmering field, careless of enemy cannon, as if their shells were naught but summer flies. Barefoot or shod, each wellborn boy or can't-read-nor-write scratch farmer took pains to keep in step and maintain straight ranks. Now and again, a voice raised a shout of defiance.

They tore down a fence with hardly a moment's pause and brushed aside a Yankee skirmish line. Next, they erased the companies that had rushed to support the skirmishers. As was their custom, the men fired independently, reloading as they marched. A man would break pace for a step or two to fire at the blue smear ahead, then trot up to mend the line again.

Men fell. It made no difference. Mississippi was unstoppable.

At last, Barksdale let the first rank and the second pass him by, careless of the death on every side, but cognizant of his duty to command.

One rapscallion in a ripped calico shirt called, "Done voted for you twice, Billy, and damned if I won't do it a third time!"

Barksdale tipped his sword toward the man.

As he took his place at the rear of the sweeping advance, Barksdale's pride was mixed with the rage that haunted him ever and always. He hoped the rumors about Vicksburg were true, that the drunkard Grant had been put to flight with all his filthy Vandals. But he couldn't trust the camp talk, no more than he trusted that worthless Pennsylvania Quaker Pemberton, Vicksburg's useless defender. Even if the man now wore a gray coat faced with yellow, he was Yankee-born and suspect.

The forward line slowed, then stopped to exchange volleys with the Yankees defending the road, dropping soldiers along the blue line and gunning down cannoneers as they dragged off their pieces. Barksdale let his boys go at it, confident that minutes would tell the tale.

Smoke rose. And screams.

How dare they, though, those infernal Northern busybodies? That was the damnable question at the heart of this. How dare those self-righteous, ignorant, do-gooder Yankees tell Mississippi to raise the nigger high? Yankees didn't want justice: They wanted to destroy the South. As for the darkies, abolitionists didn't know them, not the real ones—only a few tame coons who had their letters. Northerners had no grasp of the nigger's hopeless inferiority. Every white man from the Delta to the red-dirt hills knew the colored man was a shiftless, carefree child, who lived for little treats and wanted discipline. Left to himself he would decline into indolence and crime, even to outrages. To imagine even a scrubbed, hymn-howling darkey as the white man's bed-and-board equal was a joke—and now a deadly one.

His people back in Tennessee had carved a world from the wilderness, while the Yankees carved out profits from other men's sweat. Still young, he had bound his life to Mississippi, with its river-blessed fields and handsome ways of doing. He found an unmatched goodness in his state, where the cool shade of God's mercy welcomed men as a live oak drew a field hand in high summer. His was a fragrant, ordered, peerless world, where virtue thrived.

Now Northern warmongers wanted to wreck it all, in the name

of a perversion of law and religion that would set the black man up on a marble pedestal, higher than a white man's wife and children. Fanatics from the cold vaults of New England, they believed their purpose was worth a sea of blood.

Let the blood be theirs, then.

With a cheer, his men swept through a Yankee line. Barksdale rode on behind them, resolutely overlooking his twisting wounded and the inert dead. A few of the Yankees sent forward still fought on, Zouaves in baggy red pants and filthy turbans. That was fine with Barksdale: If a Yankee wanted to die in coon drawers and a monkey jacket, so be it.

He ignored the disarmed Yankees heading for the treeline his brigade had exited. He felt no empathy, no soldierly brotherhood, with his enemies. Had they all been killed, it would have suited him fine.

From his perch in the saddle, he spotted smoke-wreathed Federal cannoneers hooking lines to a field piece, preparing to drag it off. Spurring forward, he bellowed, "Get those guns! Don't let them take off those guns!"

Whether his men heard him, or took action on their own, was of no matter. They surged forward, heading for the stranded guns and the tumult of Yankee limbers and caissons behind them, where drivers slashed madly at harnesses to cut dead and crippled horses from their teams.

"Shoot the horses!" Barksdale raged. "Shoot the damned horses!"

Defying command protocol, he rode into the midst of the regiment. He was outraged at the thought of the guns escaping. If Northerners wanted a "fiery, swift sword," he damned well had one for them.

On the flanks, other Yankee batteries issued a constant fire, but their attentions were split in two directions now. Barksdale sensed their chain of command collapsing. Flaunting his sword, he urged his soldiers forward, pressing the compact lines to move as one and cursing any officer pausing to think.

The thinking time was done. It was time for killing.

"For Mississippi! Onward, Mississippi!"

A boy in gray, rifle discarded, stumbled toward the rear. With not a spot of blood on him. Nothing but a flytrap, his mouth hung

open as he ambled, arms dangling and twitching. His eyes were those of a blind man, staring eternally.

Barksdale let him feel the flat of a sword across his back. "Damn you for a coward, boy. You get back in the fight!"

But he had no time to waste on shirking wastrels. Not while over a thousand men—*his* men—were killing blue-bellies. Yankees flocked into a farmyard, fighting stubbornly. It wouldn't help them. His boys had the force of God's avenging angels.

Gaining the high ground, Barksdale saw a grand and astounding sight: The Federals were thick enough along the sunken road running north, but to their rear they had nothing for a mile.

Behind this cauldron of fire, smoke, and death, the Yankees had *nothing*.

Up by the orchard, a well-drilled Union regiment stood its ground, protecting the battery that had rolled up to support it. Charging through the fickle smoke, Barksdale leaned down and grasped the shoulder of the first field officer of the 21st Mississippi he could locate.

"Y'all fix those Yankees up proper. Those high-and-mighty sons-ofbitches up there. Open a hole for Wofford to go through, he's coming on. I'm taking the other boys leftwards, tell your colonel. Join up later, if you can. If not, just kill whatever gets in your way."

He kicked his big-boned horse with his spurs, riding tight behind his line, ordering one regiment after another to wheel about and roll up the Yankee defense, to lay into them hard and keep going.

His regiments no longer displayed parade-ground precision, but they held together well enough and turned promptly on his orders, advancing through trampled stalks of grain to get in range of Yankee regiments scrambling to change front.

"Press 'em, don't let them align," he told the heated faces all around him.

An officer dashed up, causing Barksdale to yank back his reins.

"General? Aren't you too close? Those Yankees are doing their damnedest to put a bullet in you."

Barksdale snorted. "Best way to stop Yankee bullets is killing Yankees."

He felt no fear. He was mad as Hell and enjoying it.

In the open fields to his left, between the rattled Yankees and the treeline where other Confederates waited to charge, Southern batteries trotted forward, a spectacle in the gilded dust of evening. Braving desperate volleys to drop their gun trails in the oats and support his attack, they were taking a madcap risk.

How could the South lose, with men as bold as that?

Barksdale watched impatiently as his Mississippians shot it out with yet another regiment of Zouaves—or perhaps a remnant. Mississippi rifles cut the fancy-dress Yankees to pieces, with some of Barksdale's men rushing in for a rifle-butt and bayonet melee.

It was all indescribably beautiful.

Smugly, Barksdale thought of Malvern Hill, where all the valor his men could show had not been enough in the slaughter. No victory since that grisly afternoon had healed the wound that fight left on his soul.

This one might.

"Come on, boys, come on! They're breaking, they can't stand up to you!"

His men did not need encouragement. They burst upon the Yankees like human case-shot.

The thrust of Barksdale's attack had shifted leftward as he rolled up the Union line and Wofford's Georgians came up on his right rear. Wofford could deal with whatever remained past the orchard and back in the woods. Barksdale had his eye on those vacant fields to the rear of the crumbling Yankees.

Turning to take the measure of the Georgian charge, Barksdale saw Longstreet riding amid Wofford's infantry. Even from a distance, the corps commander looked black-miened and determined. But Barksdale could not forgive the man who had held back his troops so long. There would be a reckoning.

He turned his horse back to the fight.

The Union troops resisting his advance crowded around another farmhouse now, gravitating, as men will, toward a hint of shelter, the illusion of safety. The Yankees were fighting staunchly—harder than usual—but their resistance was strained and ready to snap. Wide gaps had opened.

Farther up the road, the next increment of regiments in blue

hastened to refuse their flank and save themselves. But it was too late. Barksdale knew down in the core of his being the Yankees were beaten.

Enraptured and careless, he spurred forward again. "Come on, Mississippi! Give 'em lead and steel, boys, lead and steel!"

The fighting in the farmyard collapsed into ugly brawls. Barksdale pressed his men onward, past the outbuildings, toward those sprawling, undefended fields. That house and barn didn't matter now. Nor did the other farmsteads. Once the remaining Yankees grasped that they'd been left behind, they'd give up quick enough. He would not let them slow down his attack.

You had to keep going, just keep going, no matter what it cost you.

The Yankees were different on their home ground, though. They fought like they meant it, Barksdale allowed them that. Even the last shreds of regiments stood tenaciously, or shook their fists as their officers took them rearward. But the brave would soon be dead or lying wounded. There weren't enough of them left to stop his charge. They'd been caught in the wrong damned place, which was their hard luck.

There really was nothing behind them, *nothing*. Not one intact regiment as far as that distant ridge, where a great gap waited. The way was clear for nearly a mile—maybe all the way to the Union rear, if he hit them right.

Barksdale saw a glorious victory waiting.

In that entrancing moment, he felt the air change. As if a spell from a children's book had been cast. The last Union troops fighting on his right withdrew. As they gave up their grip on the ground, their ranks dissolved.

Wofford pursued them, his Georgians cheering and charging.

Let the Georgians sweep them up. Let Wofford have those groves and their hanging smoke. The purpose of Barksdale's existence now was to hasten across those fields. No enemy on earth was going to stop him.

Wounded men, clad in gray and blue, staggered toward his rear. Some prisoners strolled unguarded, relieved to be out of the fight. Mocked by their captors, others wept in shame. A captain looked

bewildered and bereft. A lad shrieked madly. The dead of both sides lay thick.

Barksdale caught a final glimpse of Longstreet amid the carnage, hurrying Wofford's second line along.

With a grunt, Barksdale trotted forward, horse shying from the dead and the crawling wounded. His boils reminded him sharply of their existence, but couldn't hold his attention anymore. The fight on his left was thickening again, annoying him monstrously, as the Federals up the road rushed to block his advance. The thought of the least delay was unbearable now.

Those Yankees were damnable, insolent fools, and if they needed killing, he'd oblige them.

Then a miracle happened: Those Yankees wouldn't slow him, after all. A gift from the Lord, the first brigade of Anderson's division, Hill's corps, emerged from their hides in the trees on his left flank. Those sweet gray lines could overwhelm the Yankees hugging the road. Barksdale was free to drive into the enemy's heart.

Drenched locks clinging to his face and neck, he rose in his stirrups:

"Onward, Mississippi! Charge 'em. *Charge!*"

FIFTEEN

July 2, Evening

Sickles rode out to stop the retreating soldiers. His headquarters flag had been propped up beside farm buildings tucked in a swale. When the fighting commenced, the site had been safely and soundly behind his lines. Now the shredded remains of those lines rushed toward him.

Amid the trickles and streams of men in blue, Sickles spotted Colonel Madill of the 141st Pennsylvania. The colonel clutched his regiment's tattered colors. Not two dozen soldiers followed him, hardly enough for a color guard.

He never had thought Madill would let him down. The man had been one of his most promising colonels.

Confronted by Sickles, the colonel paused. His soldiers continued rearward.

"Colonel! Can't you hold on?" Sickles begged.

Anger reddened Madill's cheeks, burning through dirt and black powder. He gestured around himself.

"Where are my *men*?"

Sickles let the colonel go. He felt a hollowness in himself that threatened a collapse. Unwilling to leave the environs of the farm, somehow unable to go either forward or to the rear, he had been bombarded by tidings of disaster. The orders he had issued in response verged between meager hopes and sudden whims.

More retreating men came on. Sickles watched as one threw down his rifle.

Over the last two hours, he alternately had been lucid enough to commandeer fresh regiments and dazed by the realization that Meade would invoke a court-martial when all of this was over.

If the insufferable Meade did it publicly enough, his friends

might not be able to quash the proceedings. Even if he avoided a conviction, it would damage his ballot prospects for years to come. If found guilty of disobeying orders and causing a defeat, his life-long aspirations would be dashed: He wouldn't be chosen alder-man from a pocketed Irish ward.

The stumbling wounded were bad enough, but this flood of outright quitters was unbearable.

Even de Trobriand's brigade had failed—after raising hopes it would stop the Rebels. His corps was in collapse on every side. Now, to add to his humiliation, the Fifth Corps was attempting to shore up what remained of his left, with little success.

He would be disgraced.

He knew he should be active, rushing about to exercise control. But, somehow, he could not go. He had contemplated seeking a hero's death on the field. But death had no appeal. Heroism's point was to relish the fame.

Tremain. Where was Tremain? Oh, yes. He'd sent the only aide he fully trusted with a message to David Birney, whose division had made a further hash of things. Could he blame all this on Birney?

Was it too late to order Humphreys back from the Taneytown road? What was the condition of his division? Sickles knew he should ride out and see for himself, showing himself amid the shot and shell.

But he could not go.

What would the newspapers say? Could they be bought off? Before Meade ruined his name? He could claim that Meade had planned to run away, based on Butterfield drawing up that plan. That might stick. He could say that only he had been willing to fight, to stand up to Bobby Lee in defense of the Union.

An orderly approached.

"General, sir? You're exposed here. You should go behind the barn."

Exposed? He hadn't noticed. Yes. The Confederate guns had unlimbered in that orchard now. As he had predicted. *Exposed.* Different meanings to the word. Exposed to danger. Or exposed . . . as what? As a fool? Not a coward, they couldn't make that stick, his record was good.

"General?"

Sickles nodded and turned his horse, flowing with the clots of disheartened soldiers. One called out angrily, "Where's our god-damned bullets, Dan?"

The man was unforgivably insubordinate. But Sickles just looked away, letting his horse lope toward the barn, with its stone foundation as solid as a fortress.

There had to be a way to shift the blame. Not to Hunt, who'd been too visible. Maybe to Birney *and* Humphreys. But the great trick would be putting the blame on Meade. That horse might run. The old sourpuss had precious few real friends.

Sickles thought again that he should rally the remnants of his dying corps. But he simply could not go forward. He had to stay put, that was it. He had to stay here, so couriers could find him. That was a safe explanation. He had to exercise higher command. That was his duty, after all.

Where was Tremain?

He should have seen to it that ammunition was sent forward, that the men were kept supplied. But Tremain was too small a fish to satisfy anyone.

Shells plunged into the trees behind the farm. Sickles did not flinch. He wasn't afraid. Not of that.

Meade, Meade, *Meade*. What had Henry said to Becket's assassins? "Who will rid me of this troublesome priest?" The line played well on stage, even in a wretched performance. Who would rid him of Meade?

He turned his horse rearward and took his stand on a low rise beside the barn. Watching his corps disintegrate. Waiting to see Rebel battle flags aloft.

Some of his men were still fighting. He could tell that much from the noise, although he could not see much through the smoke.

His body jerked. *Nerves,* he told himself. His horse absorbed the motion, remaining calm.

Who was allowing these men to flee to the rear? Where were their officers? He needed to know which regiments had broken first. He might be able to court-martial their colonels before Meade could act against him, to place the blame on a half dozen or so subordinates.

Madill wouldn't do, of course. His record was too solid. And the devil had been clever enough to carry off his regiment's flag himself. But others must have faltered.

The orderly reappeared. The man looked stricken.

"General Sickles! You're bleeding, sir."

Sickles looked down. What he saw astounded him. His right leg was a slop of blood, the knee impossibly mangled.

Viewing the wound made him dizzy.

"I'm wounded," he said dully.

The orderly waved up another man. They helped him from his horse. The animal was unscathed.

"Din't you feel anything? Din't you feel it, sir?"

"Don't let me bleed to death," Sickles begged.

"A cannonball went right straight through your leg. Darnedest thing." The fellow shook his head. The gesture blurred. "Din't you feel it at all?"

"Don't let me bleed to death."

Where was Tremain? Sickles felt faint. He knew that he must not pass out. The world began to craze around the edges.

They propped him against the sheltered wall of the barn, against cool stones. He fought to control his destiny.

"Get a horse strap," he ordered, summoning a voice of command. "Get a goddamned saddle strap for a tourniquet."

Under Sickles' direction, the two men cinched his leg tightly. There was no pain. Where was the pain? There was only a terrible fight to remain conscious.

Revelation struck him: What a piece of luck! Meade couldn't very well court-martial a wounded man, a hero struck down amid a desperate battle. The thought quickened all of his senses.

He considered the mess of his leg. It might have to come off above the knee. The prospect chilled him. Yet, even that might be an acceptable price, he told himself. Assuming he lived, which he intended to do. A leg lost above the knee on the field of battle would play superbly during an election. He would not need to so much as mention his service, his mere appearance would testify on his behalf.

He only had to live. To get through the next hours and days.

Tremain was there. Suddenly, confusingly.

"What's the good news, son?" Sickles asked, attempting to sound jovial.

The aide was dumbstruck.

Sickles fished in his tunic and hooked his brandy flask. Closing his eyes to gather strength, he unscrewed the top and took a healthy swig.

"I want Doc Sim to work on me," he said. "Nobody else. Tell me . . . about Birney . . . his front . . . he'll have to take command now."

And Birney could be blamed for further losses.

Tremain didn't have to speak. General Birney loomed up. Sickles forced a smile. Or thought he did.

"You find me at a disadvantage," Sickles told the division commander. "Hard luck, ain't it? No more than many a brave man has suffered this day. Our beloved soldiers . . ."

"I don't believe we can hold," Birney reported. "The Fifth Corps isn't enough. If Meade doesn't—"

"*Meade won't.* Don't you see it, man? He's left us hanging out, Meade has. *He's* the one responsible. He's to blame for all these fine men perishing. He didn't support us, I begged him to support us. He did nothing . . . nothing . . ."

"I don't know," Birney said. "He's doing all he can."

" 'To and fro, to and fro.' What the hell good does that do us? The man's all show, no substance." He took another drink from his flask, fighting to maintain his ebbing strength. "You have the corps now. But watch out for Meade, I tell you. He'll try to make a scapegoat of you, too. The man has no shame."

He lost awareness, perhaps only for seconds, and was reawakened by the sounds of battle. Artillery grumped.

Birney was gone. Tremain . . . was gone.

"Where's Tremain?" he demanded.

"He went to fetch an ambulance, General."

A horrid thought struck Sickles. "Don't let me be taken prisoner. I mustn't be taken prisoner."

That would look terrible. And it would prevent him from telling his side of the story. Nor would the Rebels be apt to treat him kindly.

"I will not be taken prisoner."

"Rebs ain't here yet, General. Boys are still fighting, just over the rise."

"Where's Tremain? I need Tremain."

"He went for an ambulance. Like I told you, sir."

"Where *is* everybody? Is my ambulance here yet? Where's Tremain?"

The enlisted soldier, his lone companion now, just stared at him.

Clarity returned. As if a cold-water shock had been administered. "Inside my coat, son," he said calmly. "In here. My cigar case. Light me a cigar."

The soldier did as ordered.

His men were still fighting. Someone had told him that. They were still fighting. Perhaps there would be a victory, after all. Battles could be opaque until the end.

He couldn't order his thoughts. He had commands to give. Didn't he? He had been about to do something, but couldn't recall what it was. He thought of his wife. Of her white and perfect breasts, of flesh impassioned.

Tremain appeared at his side again, along with a detail of men. They lifted him onto a litter, then carried him to an ambulance. The canvas had been removed. Smoke smeared the sky.

A damned good target, Sickles thought. They'd have to get him off quickly. Through all of it, he held on to the cigar.

"There's a rumor you've been killed, sir," Tremain told him. The ambulance began jouncing over the field.

He felt the pain now. Oh, did he.

He had to last a little while longer. To put up a good show.

"Prop me up," he told his aide. "I want the men to see me."

Sickles puffed on his cigar as he passed through regiments newly arrived amid the broken remnants of his corps—men who had fled the field but would live to vote.

They saw him, cheery and breathing. He made sure of that. Twice, he even managed to wave to well-wishers.

En route to the field hospital, they crossed paths with a chaplain, who climbed aboard the ambulance and made a wonderful show of prayers for the general. He was Catholic, too, *and* a fellow New Yorker. He'd spread the word back home that Sickles had carried off his wounding with aplomb.

He had to live, that was the thing. The pain was severe now, but pain could be endured. That leg was going to save him.

Barksdale was elated. His beloved Mississippians were unstoppable. No joy in his life had been as thrilling, as exhilarating, as this.

As his regiments wheeled rightward, ignoring the Yankee stand along the road, he rode into their midst again, standing tall in his stirrups.

"Forward, boys, forward! They're broken, you've broken the goddamned Yankee army . . . my brave Mississippians, my brave boys! Give 'em one more charge, just one more charge . . ."

His men swept eastward through ripening fields of grain. Fired upon from the flank and from stray guns to their front, they disdained death. Their ranks had grown ragged and thinner, but they plunged toward the great gap in the Union line, not half a mile distant now. Battle raged on their left and off to the right, but *their* charge had won through.

Two of Barksdale's regimental commanders, Griffin and Holder, strode up and blocked his horse.

"General, we need to re-form. We need to stop and organize our regiments, they're scrambled like Mammy's eggs," Holder said.

"Half my regiment's down," Griffin added.

Barksdale valued these men, but not their opinions. Not now.

"Hell, boys. We're not stopping now. We have those sonsof-bitches on the run. It's time to crowd them." He pointed eastward with his saber, toward the far, still grove. Treetops caught the death-throes of the sun. "We'll re-form over there. Keep your boys moving."

Bodies weary, their ranks dissolved into clans around torn banners, but the Mississippians surged forward again. They ignored stray Yankees seeking to surrender, men who had lost their bearings in the smoke. Nothing short of God's own hand would bring them up short now.

Ahead, the wheat gave way to low ground, a water meadow speckled with brush and briars. Beyond lay the promised land, a glorious emptiness, the end of this battle, perhaps the end of this war.

"Forward, Mississippi, forward!" Barksdale called.

This was the climax of decades of bitter struggle. First, he had

tried to defend his world with words, as a newspaperman. Then he had fought for his way of life as a lawyer. When that failed and the Yankees increased their demands, he had done all he could as a politician to preserve his people's rights. But none of the words on paper, no speeches or bills submitted, had been enough. Northerners made continued union impossible. War had been thrust upon a cornered South.

Here, at last, amid the gore of this battlefield, he finally had achieved something that no Yankee could refute.

His boys were worn, he knew, but their hearts were mighty.

Diminished bands of threadbare men plunged into the marshy ground between them and their goal. Afflicted by the earth, by soil wet even in summer, their progress slowed. As if the earth itself begrudged them victory.

"Go on, boys, go on," Barksdale cried. "Just get on through there."

The light was failing prematurely, bedeviled by clotted smoke. Hellish flames erupted from obscured guns.

Good men fell. Too many were down, too many.

"Keep on moving, press 'em, push 'em. *Go on!*"

Fickle air gathered smoke from other fields, enclosing them in the marsh. They were fighting earth and sky now. His men charged slowly through a twilit world. Time lost its grip, its order. The last pretense of maintaining ranks faded into random figures in a fog.

Abruptly, the smoke cleared. They had gotten through it, if not through the last thorns and mud.

A long blue line stretched before them, rifles leveled.

They weren't supposed to be there. It was as if they had risen from the underworld.

The Yankees fired.

Fewer soldiers pushed forward now as more and more men toppled. A red flag flapped earthward, grasped anew before it reached the mud. It fell again. The Rebel yell was reduced to defiant catcalls.

Barksdale guided his horse through the wretched ground, lofting his sword with a tired arm and calling for one last effort.

A hideous mass of men in blue, the Yankees fired at will.

So close, they had come so close. He could not let those bastards stop him now. Rising in his stirrups, Barksdale roared, furious

beyond words, howling in the voice of a primitive warrior, as if his personal rage could turn the tide. He pointed his sword toward the enemy line, ordering his brigade to keep on going.

And then he saw nothing but the sky, with darkness closing in. Thin as lace, smoke drifted across his gaze. A paleness remained in the heavens, but night held the winning hand.

Why was he looking at the sky? He couldn't understand it. The smoke grew thick as swabs. He had been standing in his stirrups, leading his men. How could he be lying on his back? Wet earth seeped through his garments. Sucking him down.

"I'm all right," he said. Or thought he said. The world spun. As if he had drained a keg of applejack. "Go on, boys, go on," he said. "Victory . . . victory . . ."

Where were his men?

The pain was there, but it had a flirting, roaming quality, a confusing inexactness. A weight within him pushed him down, cooperating with the greedy earth.

He heard the battle he could no longer see. It seemed to be at a great distance.

"Rally the men," he cried. "Holder . . . *rally your men.*"

He could not see his brigade at all. Only purple sky jarred by battle's lightning.

With the greatest effort of his life, he raised himself onto an obedient elbow. A rush of warm wet greased him.

He remembered now. Falling. Faces around him. He had told them to tell his wife and children that he fell doing his duty. Hadn't he? Where were those faces now, where were his boys?

In the gloaming, he saw no upright men. Only bodies, cuddled slugs on the earth.

He was cold. July could not be so cold. Not even here, in hateful Pennsylvania.

Why had his men forsaken him? Surely, only to carry on the attack. He listened for cries of victory, but heard only the guns.

He remembered his boils. They no longer pestered him. He wondered if they had burst in his fall. What a trivial matter that had been. His body felt cold as an ice cellar. There was blood.

A lone figure appeared. Wandering. Unsure of its footing. Barksdale opened his mouth to call out, but could not gather words. He

watched the soldier meander. It was a boy, arm in a hasty-made sling.

He wore a gray uniform. Of sorts. Barksdale's movement caught his eye. He plodded over, stumping through the marsh.

"General Barksdale!" the boy exclaimed. His tone revealed innocent fear. The sling was dark with blood.

"Water."

Obedient, the boy knelt down and opened his canteen. Between them, they shared a total of two good arms. Barksdale struggled to rise far enough to drink.

In velvet light, the boy's eyes flared. Barksdale followed the line of their concern: The water he had swallowed seeped from his chest, along with blood.

"I'm killed, boy. You go on. Tend to that arm."

The young man seemed to fear him, as if blameworthy. Perhaps he feared Death's approach, the unwanted companion.

When would it come? Before his men returned for him? Or the Yankees found him?

"You go on. I'll be cared for. Go on now."

Capping his canteen, the boy wobbled to his feet like a newborn fawn. He began to step away.

"Son?" Barksdale called. "Soldier?"

"Yes, sir?"

"Did we lick 'em?"

"No."

Meade had been fighting two battles throughout the evening. The first was with Lee's army, which had attacked with a fury that shocked even his veterans. The second was a struggle to check his emotions. The only hope he had was to keep his powers of judgment at their sharpest, to view the field with more than mortal clarity. To be decisive, but never rash. He had to maintain control of this unwieldy beast, to give clear orders while others just stared at the slaughter or gave up hope.

It was the hardest thing he had ever done.

Riding from one point of crisis to another, he twice had guided brigades to plug holes in the defense, unable to find the commanders of their divisions. The concentric attacks against his left had

constricted Sickles' lines like a noose on the army's neck. Meade had begun by calling up the Fifth Corps, then, as regiments broke, brigades collapsed, and divisions began to dissolve, he had ordered up units from every corps in the army, save the broken Eleventh, thinning his lines elsewhere to the point of grave vulnerability. Chains of command were a shambles and there had been no time for niceties. Minutes had been purchased with hundreds of lives, entire regiments sacrificed to gain a quarter hour. Amid the mounting troubles, he had called on his generals to give up what men they could from their own lines. To their credit, they complied unstintingly. Every man felt the terrible weight of the moment.

Little Round Top appeared safe, although Sickles' forward line had been broken everywhere. The valley below the Round Tops was a butcher's yard, and the rugged ground to the west had all been lost, while a misshapen wheatfield sprouted corpses from a dozen regiments. The fighting continued in thickets and gloom on the left, but it now appeared that those lines, at least, would hold.

Elsewhere, though, the Rebels kept on coming, pouring in fresh troops in what seemed a brilliantly organized oblique attack of the sort taught at West Point in homage to Frederick the Great. None of the cadets had listened, of course, because their wars were all to be frontier scraps.

Now, from where Meade sat upon Old Baldy—who had suffered a few nicks—he saw a vacuum before him. The center of his line had emptied, except for fleeing men unsure of the shortest route to safety. Humphreys' division had collapsed and there had been nothing behind it.

Any moment now, Meade expected to see gray lines emerge from the smoky twilight. And the force remaining by his side consisted of himself, two junior officers, and two orderlies. Every other member of his staff and even his cavalry bodyguard had been dispatched to hurry on reinforcements or to bully fleeing regiments to make a stand.

His final call for help had gone out to Newton, the general he had picked to command the First Corps on losing Reynolds. The corps had been bloodied badly the day before, but Meade had no one left to whom he could turn. Newton would have to pull his

men off line, and far more quickly than good practice dictated. If he failed to come up swiftly, the path to the army's rear and its trains lay open. The Confederates could walk there unopposed. And the Army of the Potomac would split in two.

This was the struggle's climax. And all he could do was wait.

It seemed an age ago that he and Newton had stood by the cemetery, surveying the fields and the town. But it had not been twelve hours. The confidence Meade had felt in the morning had shrunk to a nugget of hope.

Face impassive, the general burned within. He had done his best to stage an engineer's defense, to teach Lee's army a lesson, only to find himself betrayed by a politician's ambition.

Now Sickles was somewhere in the rear, under a surgeon's knife. Which just might save the villain from a court-martial. The blessing of getting him off the field was worth it, though: Sickles had lost control of his corps early on, then did little to wrest it back. Upon learning that Sickles had been wounded, Meade had sent Hancock to rally the Third Corps' scraps. Win had done everything that was humanly possible. It had not been enough.

Massive and constant, the din of battle sounded left and right, refusing to break off as night enveloped them. Only to Meade's immediate front did there seem to be a corridor of silence. He peered through the smoke and faint light.

He had done all he could. He did not believe any general could have achieved more, under the circumstances. Drained of his last resources now, he could only pray what was done had been enough.

Then he saw them. Their uniforms showed darker in the gloaming, but the advancing lines were unquestionably Confederate. The flags waved by triumphant bearers confirmed it. Not six hundred yards away, across undefended fields, they marched straight for him.

Those Rebel battle lines were uneven now, marked by hard fighting. Not all of Sickles' men had run away. Men had fought for their homes, for the Union, and for the friends beside them. The Confederates had suffered, too.

There was precious little comfort in the thought. The Rebels were *there,* coming on. And Meade had no one left to whom he could turn.

He swung around in the saddle, scanning the world behind the crest of the ridge. Looking for Newton's men. Or for anyone.

To his rear, he saw only night.

The advancing Rebels may or may not have spotted the cluster of horsemen in their path, but they certainly saw the emptiness around them. They sent up a Rebel yell. It was hoarse and much diminished now, but still bloodcurdling.

Was this how it was to end?

Meade glanced rearward a last, urgent time: Ghosts of smoke, no flesh.

The gray ranks loomed, picking up their pace, souls ablaze with the victory in their grasp.

Perhaps this would be the final battle Lee wanted. Perhaps the war would be decided here. And the South would go its way. Because he, George Meade, had failed.

The thought was wormwood and gall.

No! I will not be beaten.

With the Rebel line spreading out to fill the horizon, Meade straightened in the saddle.

He drew his saber.

Without a word, the four horsemen at his side drew their own swords. They aligned their mounts with his, ready to charge and die beside their chieftain.

As Meade began to extend his saber, ready to spur his horse into the foe, an orderly shouted:

"Here they come, General! Here they come!"

Meade was about to snap that, damn it, he had eyes in his own head and could see the Rebels. But the words were stopped by cheering to his rear.

He turned.

General Newton came galloping toward him with his staff, his lead regiments pouring over the ridge, with their country's flag held high in the pale night.

Tears welled in George Meade's eyes, but he restrained them. It would not do for a Philadelphian to weep.

Doubleday's division was coming on, with Robinson's following. Thousands of hurrying footfalls thickened the dying light with dust.

Newton rode up and reined in beside Meade. In splendid spirits.

"With your permission, General, we'll go right at 'em."

Meade nodded. And sheathed his sword.

"I was wondering what you were going to do with that butter-knife," Newton said. Grinning. He waved his men forward, past the relieved horsemen. Newton was a cool fellow, on the whole. But he was enjoying the moment. He drew out a flask and passed it over to Meade.

Meade accepted it. Gratefully. His hand trembled, but he refused to be ashamed. It was enough that the soldiers in blue rushed past him, full of fight.

It was enough, it was enough.

A shell burst close enough to splash the generals with dirt. Meade hardly noticed. Such trivialities didn't matter now.

Arriving in close column by division, Newton's men streamed past at the double-quick. Surprised at the sight, the Rebels had slowed their own progress. The First Corps soldiers deployed into line as crisply as if drilled on that very field.

Meade looked to the rear in wonder and saw more blue columns coming. Those would have to be from Slocum, who must have decided he could spare even more men from his line than he'd already sent. Meade's brothers-in-arms had not let him down. Starved of troops five minutes before, he now had a feast of plenty.

The line was going to hold.

He handed the flask back to Newton and, with brandy burning his throat, he spurred Old Baldy forward. For once in his life, Meade felt unalloyed exuberance.

He guided his horse into the gap between two advancing regiments, urging the men along with a youth's enthusiasm and smiling like a child given boiled sweets. Delighted. Soaring. *Joyous.*

It was all right now. It would be all right.

"Come on, gentlemen," Meade called to his troops, *"come on!"*

For the first time, the Army of the Potomac cheered him.

Longstreet called them back. He knew they would protest, he knew they would blame him. They had come so close, only to be ordered to withdraw. In their recollections, they would have been

on the cusp of an unprecedented victory, when that damnable Dutchman Longstreet ordered them to withdraw, leaving the field of glory to the Yankees.

He would have to live with that.

But Longstreet was not a man to purchase fame with the blood of others. He had never seen men fight better than his soldiers had fought this day. But their courage had not been enough. Numbers mattered, and the Federals had the numbers. Now they even had superior ground, driven onto it by his own men's early successes. There simply was no point in going on.

Through the veiled light he could see what the men on foot below him, down in the fields and gulleys, could not or would not: Their moment had passed. From a low ridge, he bore witness to the deluge of Union troops flooding onto the field. Lines that had been threatened were reinforced, then bolstered again. Fresh guns rolled up, a seemingly endless supply of them. On the far ridge, officers clustered confidently, no longer alarmed by the progress of their enemies. And still more Union regiments came on.

Perhaps, if he had had Pickett, he might have carried the ground to the left of the round hills, splitting Meade's line. Before the Federals had time to recover. But he had lacked the reserves to lend the final, decisive weight to his attack when he had the chance.

Now time had run out.

How his men had fought, though! He had been unspeakably proud of them, had never seen soldiers go forward so handsomely. Now he saw their corpses, and the wounded and maimed struggling to the rear. Up at the sharp edge of the fight, stubborn men still damned every Yankee to Hell: They didn't know when to quit. That was his responsibility.

His men had nearly won. But nearly didn't count. And the odds against them now were insurmountable.

They had taken ground, a great deal of it. But that ground was worthless. They would hold it out of pride, but the Federals had kept both of the round hills. They would not be dislodged, not this day, not the next.

The attack had been misconceived from the very start. And no amount of valor could redeem it. Had he, James Longstreet, done his best this day? He could recall a dozen things he might have

done more wisely. Later, he would remember even more. It was always that way. Battles were fought by men, not omniscient gods. From comfortable vantage points, historians always saw what should have been done. But perfection existed only in their books.

He had played the hand he drew, but lost the round. And that was that.

Tom Goree found him.

"Sir, Law's men don't want to quit. They want to give it one more go, try one more time."

Longstreet shook his head. "Look over there. Wait for the smoke to clear. Tell me what you see."

Perhaps . . . if he *had* had Pickett. Or if Hood had not been wounded and Hill had come in earlier on his left. If Ewell had attacked when the old fool was supposed to. If the afternoon march had not gone astray. If . . . if . . . there was nothing but damned ifs now.

He knew his men had hurt their enemies badly. Meade had not had a merry day, that was certain. But the Union would replace its fallen soldiers, while the South's blood was running out.

The smoke cleared and Goree saw what Longstreet had seen.

"Christ almighty. Where'd they all come from?"

"Ride back down there, Tom. Tell the boys it's over for today."

Goree saluted and yanked his horse about. Angered by all the world. He was a hot-tempered man, who would have gone at the Yankees with a knife. And he, too, would have died.

Whether Longstreet's order to pull back to the nearest ground fit for defense had been received, or if the quitting light had slowed things down, the firing thinned. The men were exhausted. Even if their spirits were willing, their bodies were worn out.

He wished he could tell every one of his soldiers still alive how proud he was of the way they'd fought that day. Pride was all the survivors were going to have, he saw that now. The bitter truth was that they had been defeated, their key objectives untaken. He, and they, had failed. He would not tell them so and would put a good face on it. But this had been their only chance to pry Meade from his position.

And Lee? He already knew what Lee would have to say. This wouldn't be a defeat, but an incomplete victory, with the fight to

be resumed on the morrow. The old man could not bear to leave it at this. They would attack again, with as many men as the bloodied army could muster. They would attack into a Union position that Longstreet now saw was formidable.

Lee would fight again tomorrow, and Longstreet would fight for him. Because that was what soldiers did. Lee would reason that Meade's men had been battered worse than his, that they would break at one more determined blow. Longstreet could hear the old man's voice speak the words: "We must attack them. Those people will not withstand another attack." And the men in gray, from Georgia and the Carolinas, from Virginia and Tennessee, would go forward again, all gallantry and fire and homespun chivalry. And Meade would be waiting. Up there.

Longstreet would go through the motions, try again to talk Lee into maneuvering around Meade. But he knew it would avail nothing. He would do it to ease his conscience, not because he expected results. Lee didn't know how to do anything but fight, once he had been bloodied. His pride would be injured now. He would not quit.

Lieutenant General James Longstreet had lost faith.

done more wisely. Later, he would remember even more. It was always that way. Battles were fought by men, not omniscient gods. From comfortable vantage points, historians always saw what should have been done. But perfection existed only in their books.

He had played the hand he drew, but lost the round. And that was that.

Tom Goree found him.

"Sir, Law's men don't want to quit. They want to give it one more go, try one more time."

Longstreet shook his head. "Look over there. Wait for the smoke to clear. Tell me what you see."

Perhaps . . . if he *had* had Pickett. Or if Hood had not been wounded and Hill had come in earlier on his left. If Ewell had attacked when the old fool was supposed to. If the afternoon march had not gone astray. If . . . if . . . there was nothing but damned ifs now.

He knew his men had hurt their enemies badly. Meade had not had a merry day, that was certain. But the Union would replace its fallen soldiers, while the South's blood was running out.

The smoke cleared and Goree saw what Longstreet had seen.

"Christ almighty. Where'd they all come from?"

"Ride back down there, Tom. Tell the boys it's over for today."

Goree saluted and yanked his horse about. Angered by all the world. He was a hot-tempered man, who would have gone at the Yankees with a knife. And he, too, would have died.

Whether Longstreet's order to pull back to the nearest ground fit for defense had been received, or if the quitting light had slowed things down, the firing thinned. The men were exhausted. Even if their spirits were willing, their bodies were worn out.

He wished he could tell every one of his soldiers still alive how proud he was of the way they'd fought that day. Pride was all the survivors were going to have, he saw that now. The bitter truth was that they had been defeated, their key objectives untaken. He, and they, had failed. He would not tell them so and would put a good face on it. But this had been their only chance to pry Meade from his position.

And Lee? He already knew what Lee would have to say. This wouldn't be a defeat, but an incomplete victory, with the fight to

be resumed on the morrow. The old man could not bear to leave it at this. They would attack again, with as many men as the bloodied army could muster. They would attack into a Union position that Longstreet now saw was formidable.

Lee would fight again tomorrow, and Longstreet would fight for him. Because that was what soldiers did. Lee would reason that Meade's men had been battered worse than his, that they would break at one more determined blow. Longstreet could hear the old man's voice speak the words: "We must attack them. Those people will not withstand another attack." And the men in gray, from Georgia and the Carolinas, from Virginia and Tennessee, would go forward again, all gallantry and fire and homespun chivalry. And Meade would be waiting. Up there.

Longstreet would go through the motions, try again to talk Lee into maneuvering around Meade. But he knew it would avail nothing. He would do it to ease his conscience, not because he expected results. Lee didn't know how to do anything but fight, once he had been bloodied. His pride would be injured now. He would not quit.

Lieutenant General James Longstreet had lost faith.

SIXTEEN

July 2, Night

Sweat and waiting filled Schwertlein's hours, as the battle stormed on elsewhere. The survivors of the 26th Wisconsin had wedged into the line below the cemetery, where Krzyzanowski's stricken brigade held a position that would have suited a robust regiment. The morning had straggled into afternoon, annoyed by sharpshooters hidden in the town. Bands of men seeped out from unscathed brigades to refresh the skirmish line, only to return bearing wounded comrades. A detail from the 26th had been sent forward, but the men, including Schwertlein and broken-toothed Bettelman, no sooner reached a contested fence than they were ordered back into reserve at the edge of the cemetery.

A lone wagon brought up food at last. The commissary sergeant, bellowing, *"Mahlzeit!"* from his bench, had expected to feed twice the number of those who remained alive at their posts, so they had salt beef aplenty: The meal was envied by all those who had scorned them.

Their chewing was serenaded by a barrage on the far left flank, a devil's opera of booms and blasts in the dragging afternoon. The men paid it little mind: The gunnery was sufficiently distant to be the affair of others. Enterprising sharpshooters were of greater concern, but even they had nearer, finer targets. Now and then, a man turned his head at the insistent cannonade, but others would take their turn at dying now.

The mockery making the rounds of the army, the excoriation of the "Flying Dutchmen," filled the men with an impotent fury that left them blistered and listless. Bled out and humiliated, the regiment had never gobbled a meal with so little talk, without a single debate over social reform, abolition, natural rights, true democracy

versus a republic, the relative merits of poets and cooks, or the virtues of Rheingau wines versus those of Baden. The men curled into themselves like salted snails.

On the left, a battle bloomed. Nerves tightened along the lines. As the cacophony edged nearer, smoke aged the evening light. In far fields, lone figures and bunched soldiers retreated.

"*Sieht nicht gut aus,*" a soldier, Theo Fenstermacher, remarked.

"*Na, gut. Lass die Englisch-sprechenden Herrschaften was schönes vom Lee erleben.*"

"*Du Arsch! Meinst Du denn, dass wir nicht hinein müssen, wenn das alles schiefgeht?*"

Schwertlein said nothing. He understood the anger toward their fellow soldiers in Union blue, but speech seemed pointless. What must come, would come. He watched Bettelman instead. The broken tooth plagued his comrade, who struggled to reduce a shred of meat and get it down.

Cannon barked on the right flank now, back among the hills behind the cemetery. But the real fight remained the contest on the left. Down the ridge, a brigade formed in haste and headed toward the gun-lightning. The column disappeared into shrouds of smoke, a premature darkness under the still-blue sky.

Still gnawing his dinner, Bettleman gasped in misery. "Fritz," he moaned to Schwertlein, "you have no idea what pain is, no idea. . . ."

It was true, Schwertlein supposed. Pain was a queer thing, private and unique. Despite all the carnage and horror they had witnessed, none of it lessened the pain from Bettelman's tooth.

During the long day's thirsty, fly-bothered wait, Schwertlein had thought how pain might have done him some good, had it stemmed from a wound a bit greater than the nick that stained his uniform. His limb itched, that was all. A luckier wound might have sent him home, at least for a few months.

He never had allowed himself such cowardly, shirking thoughts in bygone days. But something had changed within him. He had always been able to reason himself into a semblance of bravery, into a numbing belief in a greater cause. Even Chancellorsville had barely shaken that soldierly knack. But this . . . War struck him as no more than a slaughter now. What cause could be so great as to merit *this*?

He was a born believer, but his fine beliefs had failed him. He regretted the loss of his friends, of the dead and missing, of Hannes with his faith in laws and Josef with his poetry . . . but he was *glad* that they had fallen, not him. He knew he should feel nobler emotions, but could not. He was satisfied to remain alive, no matter the cost to others. He felt no guilt, only dread at the thought of perishing himself, and he did not like himself for it. He yearned to live with a lust he had never known.

Peculiar things struck him: the way the heads of artillery horses kept time with their hooves . . . or Bettelman's hand becoming a claw as he tore meat with his fingers. Blades of grass seemed newly distinct, the smoke-rubbed sky immense. Schwertlein had a sense of revelation, but could not say of what. His mastery of words had been his advantage. Now language crumbled. He sensed a new and richer world around him, but could express nothing that mattered.

The guns firing on the right increased in number, dueling in murdered light. Still, the bend in the line, the cemetery knob with its jutting spur, was spared by the cannonade.

Too hard to form for an attack in the streets of the town, Schwertlein told himself. *They won't come this way. We've done our part.*

He had lain down to rest amid graves the night before, dreading the apparition of Otto Schumann, who had risen from the bloody field to embrace him again and again in the endless evening. But instead of fighting ghosts, he had dreamed of Maria. More real than the facts of day, his dream had been rude and delicious, vicious and raw, leaving him with soiled undergarments, with cum-stiffened drawers and a sense of loss past telling. Nor had embarrassment put an end to his wants: He arose so hungry for woman-flesh that he wasn't sure any decency remained in him.

Had other men marked his dreaming? Had he called out? Moved his hips laughably? He chose not to care. He wanted Maria. He wanted a thousand women now. Pure or filthy, he knew what they were and he *wanted* them. Ruthlessly. His desire felt so blinding he feared madness.

Otto Schumann had joined the dead and no longer leapt against him with yesterday's vividness. Lurid dreams had shoved the corpse away. Otto was still there, but on the periphery: Schwertlein could

conjure him readily, still feel the blood and meat slop against his cheek. But Schumann was weaker than the beast who had ravished a pliant Maria in the night.

Schwertlein felt he should use the evening's doldrums to write to bereaved wives, but made no effort. Hypnotized by death and copulation, he sank into fantasies scarlet and impermissible.

What was he becoming? What had he become?

A cynic now, he observed Colonel Krzyzanowski. Kriz limped about, wheezing and wincing, as he inspected, ordered, and rallied his disheartened men. Whenever the Pole's face grew so glum that the men around him mirrored it, he mustered a smile and joked. The men wanted laughter, they craved it. And the colonel understood. But any fool could see the man was suffering.

What was there to joke about? Whose wit could help them now? Was Krzyzanowski insane? Why didn't the damned fool go to the rear and save his life? He had a good excuse. Why didn't the idiot run to his wife and bury himself in her hips? How could men choose a battlefield over a woman's flesh? Once the answers had seemed noble and clear. Now they were mockeries.

Careless of sharpshooters, Kriz paused just beyond his New York regiments, conferring with two generals in the twilight. The officers seemed concerned about the action on the right flank, in the hills to the east of the cemetery.

The battle on the distant left, the great affair of the day, had sputtered out. A last flush of activity, with regiments pulled from the far side of the cemetery, came to nothing. Night draped the fields and hills. The shooting thinned to gestures of defiance.

On the right, the guns dueled on. But the cemetery remained a garden of peace.

For all his new passion for life and its sordid hungers, Schwertlein did not feel a bit afraid. Only sick of all that came with war. He had been reborn as a creature of lust, not fear. If Confederate wraiths emerged from the day's last glow, he would rise and fight. That was his duty. But he could no longer dress the deed in frills.

All the philosophy he had read wasn't worth a dry canteen. Poetry—Goethe, Heine, Hölderlin, Eichendorff—was naught but cakes for children. Only living flesh retained validity. He recalled,

with animal hunger, the prostitute in the alley behind the cathedral. He had taken her standing up, in a stable's archway, his first taste of Eve, in his student days. Drunk when he embraced her, he had spent months dreading the onset of monstrous diseases, but had been spared. He had never again been so rash, but now he viewed his self-restraint as cowardice. He could smell and feel that creature now, exquisite in her squalor, and he wanted her. As he wanted the Maria of his dream, a wanton who took pleasure in his savagery, a squealing, insatiable whore. The battle slew hundreds and thousands, but his mind crowded with orgies, with women named and nameless, real and imagined, all of them naked, hot-fleshed, wet, and shameless.

Bettelman moaned piteously. He had not been dreaming of women.

"Leo?" Schwertlein turned to the watchmaker. "Are you all right?"

"My head's exploding. This tooth, this tooth . . . I want to shoot myself. . . ."

"The doctors will take care of it. As soon as they're done with the wounded."

Darkness prowled around them, unleashing new stenches.

"That'll be months," Bettelman said.

Tears glistened on the little man's face. Schwertlein was seeking helpful words when the sounds of battle shifted. The horrid Confederate shrieking, the screams of damned souls, rose much closer to hand. The wailing swelled just to the right, nearer than the battle had come all day. The Rebel hordes were just beyond the Eleventh Corps' line, where batteries guarded the spur of the hill past the cemetery gatehouse and the Union line curved like a shepherd's crook.

Artillery rounds, shot long, shrilled overhead. All around Schwertlein and Bettelman, soldiers alerted, rustled, grabbed weapons, cursed. The surviving officers herded them into ranks.

The two comrades found their places.

Flashes from cannon and rifle fire tore the darkness. The Rebel howling fell, then rose again.

"Die kommen, die kommen!" a soldier cried. *They're coming.*

"Let them come," Schwertlein snapped, astonished at the feroc-
ity in his voice. "They need to be killed. Every one of them."

He stared up through the hellish light, searching for Krzyza-
nowski, who had left the anxious generals. Schwertlein under-
stood, of course, why the colonel stayed.

Krzyzanowski did not wait for orders to ready his men. As battle
sounds lapped the knob thrusting out from the cemetery, he turned
to the fullest of his depleted regiments, the 58th and 119th New
York, men he viewed as especially his own, and pulled them back
from their places on the line. Forming them up to face toward the
tumult beyond the pike, he shouted to be heard above the chaos,
calling down his Wisconsin Germans and Pennsylvanians to fill in
the gap the New Yorkers had left behind. He knew the latter regi-
ments were too weak to hold, should the Rebs strike here as well.
But they'd do for a bluff, and the risk had to be taken.

Now his New Yorkers stood waiting. But no order came to ad-
vance. The streaks of combat in the night made a hell of the knob
past the gatehouse. He could not be sure, but feared that the Con-
federates had already reached the guns of Wiedrich's battery.

What were the generals doing? When he had left them, their at-
tention had still been fixed on the fighting on the right. Now the
battle had come to them at last. Didn't Howard see it? Didn't Sch-
urz?

"Fix bayonets!" Krzyzanowski barked. Each time he bellowed,
his rib case gripped him painfully. Short of breath and aching, he
tramped down the line of soldiers, struggling to make out the flow
of the fight in the darkness.

The violence, near and confused, intensified.

He decided to wait no longer. Someone had to act. Let them
court-martial him. Someone had to rescue Wiedrich's guns.

Before he could give the command to advance, General Schurz
came up on foot, followed by his aide, Captain Szenowski, a fellow
Pole.

"Howard needs you to restore the line," Schurz called. "*Ver-
dammt noch mal, Kriz*. Can you see what's going on?"

"The guns," Krzyzanowski shouted above the blasts. "They've
reached the guns."

"For God's sake, then, go forward!"

Krzyzanowski turned to his men. This was no longer a matter for generals or strategy. He drew his sword, clutched it tight, and uncased his pistol.

"At the double-quick . . . *forward*!"

Ready for revenge, the soldiers howled.

They had not far to go. Only distance enough for Krzyzanowski to note that Szenowski kept pace with him, leaving his general behind. Krzyzanowski wanted to call out that a Pole just couldn't resist a desperate battle, but needed all his breath to keep pace with his men.

His ribs stabbed him.

"Double-quick!" he shouted again, unnecessarily. "Bayonets! *Gib mal Bajonetten!*"

Mary, Mother of God, be with us now.

They swept across the road past the cemetery, plunging into the melee by the guns. Reality came in cracks and flares of light, revealing Union gunners fighting hand to hand with Confederates in a wild array of uniforms, from a poor-farmer's tatters to the flamboyant garb of Zouaves. Rebels leapt atop cannon, only to be shot or knocked down again. Wiedrich's artillerymen fought with pistols, hand-spikes, rammers, sponge-poles, and discarded rifles taken up as clubs. A cannoneer swung a wooden bucket madly.

The New Yorkers slammed into the brawl, four hundred furious men, determined to avenge themselves for the previous day's debacle. A Confederate officer climbed up on a gun carriage, waving a flag. He was shot, then shot again, and bayoneted as he fell to earth. Men fired rifles a foot from the chests of their enemies, blowing them backward. The quick glare of muzzle flashes lit faces aghast, amazed, bitter, proud, and unrelenting. Men bared their teeth like dogs brought up to bite. Outnumbered now and too pressed to reload, the Rebels swung rifle butts or thrust bayonets into the enveloping blue swarm.

With battle swirling about him, Krzyzanowski knew that he had to maintain what control of his men he could. But he, too, wanted to fight in the rawest physical sense. An hour before, a stray Confederate shell had killed his adjutant, Louis Dietrich, the last of the close-knit staff officers the first day's fighting had left him. He

had felt the loss more grievously than a veteran would have expected.

He fired his pistol into the side of a Rebel struggling, rifle pressed to rifle, with a bearded sergeant from the 58th, then raised his sword as high as his ribs allowed.

"Don't stop, don't stop! Forward, boys! Drive them!"

Amid grimaces glimpsed during blinks of light, and to the accompaniment of mixed cries of spite and triumph, Krzyzanowski strode forward, drawing his men along by strength of will.

Moving again, the soldiers found that they *wanted* to come along, to surge toward the Confederate lines invisible in the dark, to punish a wicked world for all its sins.

The Rebels who had not fallen and could not escape back down the hill raised their hands in surrender. Angry cannoneers clubbed a few to the ground before their officers put a stop to it. But Krzyzanowski's soldiers had no interest in captives now. They charged down the hill, hounds pursuing hares, hurrahing and shouting insults at the men they had defeated.

Soldiers stumbled and tumbled, tripping over each other in their haste.

"Don't shoot, don't shoot . . . my leg's broke," a Southern voice cried out. German curses answered him, but his life was spared. Rifles were as empty as hearts were full.

Captain Szenowski remained near Krzyzanowski, who told him in Polish, "Go back up the hill. Tell Wiedrich to give them canister over our heads."

As they reached the trace of a farm road, he halted his men.

"Everyone down. To the ground! *Now!*"

Unready to be stopped in their rage of triumph, the soldiers had to be cursed down by their officers, who were grudgingly obeyed. Krzyzanowski knelt close to the earth himself, landing between a Confederate sprawled in death and another weeping for his mother and sisters.

On the height above, guns opened. Blind rounds pursued the vanquished through the darkness.

Some of the New Yorkers cheered. Hidden by the darkness, Krzyzanowski clutched his side. It hurt so fiercely it squeezed tears from his eyes. General Schurz had pressed him again to spare him-

self, but Krzyzanowski had refused to go. He would not leave his soldiers in defeat, would not leave his brigade while he could stand upright. Melancholy was in his Polish blood, but quitting wasn't: He was born to long struggles, to wars that lasted centuries, passed down through generations like jewels or silver. But his heritage couldn't ease the hurt in his ribs.

At least he had stopped coughing blood. That was a good sign.

When the cannon on the hill ceased firing for lack of targets, he ordered his soldiers to form up and retrace their steps. There would be no rest even now. Rolls needed to be called and ranks adjusted, pouches topped with ammunition and the wounded carried off to the too-few ambulance wagons and the overwhelmed field surgeries.

Tomorrow would be another day of battle. Krzyzanowski knew it in his bones.

A single candle lit the room where Meade's corps commanders gathered. The shanty stank of sweat and tobacco, of ill-digested meals and burned gunpowder. Every man was exhausted, but the mood was far from despondent. As he stood watching his generals maneuver for position among themselves, Meade believed he knew what each man felt: For all the tribulations of the day, they had stood up to the best that Lee could offer, and if they had not won, they had not lost. If Lee had not been defeated, he had failed in his designs. The Union line had held, if not at Sickles' madcap forward position, then at the line originally intended. It had been a bloody, knife's-edge day, but they had endured it, with fight left in their men as night wrapped the field.

Meade felt starved for sleep, yet mentally sharp, inhabiting a strange mental realm that compressed reality. He ordered himself to stand erectly, letting those who had gotten chairs slump around the table. Latecomer generals leaned on the walls, complaining about inadequate food supplies for hungry soldiers, hinting that Meade had overdone the priority given to ammunition wagons. One-armed Howard bustled in, with the fighting on Cemetery Hill reduced to a flicker. Sprawled on a ragged quilt upon a string bed, Gouverneur Warren had plummeted into sleep. Meade chose not to disturb the engineer. Warren had done good service that afternoon, with a bandaged neck to show for it. Only the corps

commanders mattered now, and all were present. Each man had to be harnessed to one purpose.

George Gordon Meade despised councils of war, but he knew his army. Whatever the morrow might bring, he wanted none of the backbiting that trailed the Army of the Potomac like a stench, arising from accusations by rival generals that their brilliant grasp of the field had gone ignored, resulting in avoidable disasters. Meade was going to give his generals a public audience now, letting each man speak up in front of witnesses. If Robert E. Lee failed to bring him down, Meade would not succumb to army politics.

Further, he wanted to give each man a personal stake in the army's success or failure, to make him feel that his advice was valued. Less than a week ago, Meade had been their peer. He had to allow for the vanity that even the friendliest general wore with his shoulder straps. Meade's preference was to give orders and be done, but he saw that a show of arrogance could be fatal.

He was learning as much about himself as about Robert E. Lee.

Above all, Meade sought clarity of intent. These were weary, burdened men, but if he had to keep them until dawn, he meant to see that every corps commander understood the role he was to play, the position he was to occupy, and the boundaries of his freedom. There would be no more shenanigans in the fashion of Daniel Sickles.

Not that Meade expected any. Each man now in command of a corps had been fitted to the profession and they made up the finest collection of leaders the army had yet fielded. For all their divergence of character and habit, these men were fighters. It was Meade's task to help them fight effectively.

Hancock bellowed out a joke, briefly arousing Meade's envy. Win had the gift of rallying men, of making broken lines whole. His soldiers adored him and even his fellow generals allowed Win a preeminence that strutted beyond his rank. The tallest of them, with fine muscles going to fat, Win outshone other men, as if lit from within. Meade liked him and resented him, wishing he had a touch of that magic himself. Hancock was a prime reason why Meade continued standing, ignoring the chair his chief of staff kept free for him. He needed to tower over Win, who was seated and cursing fantastically to nettle the pure-minded Howard.

Butterfield chased the last of the aides and hangers-on from the

room, and the bantering generals quieted. Looking up at Meade from their chairs, or watching him with hooded eyes as they hunched against the walls, they awaited their orders.

Meade took up the tin cup by the bucket of drinking water and wet his throat. The water was sour. As if death had infected it. Meade would have liked another gulp of brandy. To follow the glorious swig he had taken from Newton's flask that evening.

"All present, General Meade," Butterfield said. Unnecessarily.

The chief of staff wanted to get things going, to get through the meeting so he could return to the many labors laid on him. But this was more important than any routine.

"Returns all in?" Meade asked.

"Yes, sir. I reckon we have fifty-eight thousand men present and fit for duty. Not counting the artillery and cavalry."

Meade almost asked, "So few?"

Butterfield read his mind. Or perhaps his face.

"Casualties have been heavy. Both days. And straggling's a problem."

"I want the straggling stopped. With all necessary force."

As worn as any of them, Butterfield scribbled a note to himself.

"All right, then," Meade said, surveying the room a last time. Men wanted leadership, that was the thing. Even Win Hancock did. Meade hoped he could supply it in adequate quantity. He still had moments when he felt himself an impostor in his position. "Gentlemen, let me begin by thanking each of you for your services this day. We avoided calamity . . . but more than that, much more. General Lee discovered that he could not break this army. Not *this* army. But I believe he will try us again tomorrow. So I have three questions for you. General Butterfield?"

The chief of staff wiped his mustachios, slicking off sweat or spit. He edged a paper closer to the lone candle—shackled by its own wax to the tabletop—and read:

"Question the First: Under existing circumstances, is it advisable for this army to remain in its present position, or to retire to another nearer its base of supplies?"

Speak now, Meade thought. *Every last one of you. This is your chance, and I will not give you another.*

The generals were called upon in order, from most junior to

most senior, beginning with Gibbon and Williams, who had tem-
pory charge of their corps: The regular commanders, Hancock and
Slocum, oversaw the left wing and right flank, respectively. Small
and raw-faced, Gibbon thought the army's position would serve,
but needed corrections. Williams, with his mighty beard and cau-
tious speech, was unwilling to take a clear-cut stand until his seniors
had spoken.

Commanding the Third Corps in Sickles' wake, Birney declared,
"My corps's used up. I don't expect the boys will be much good
tomorrow, they're just fought out. I'm for holding right where we
are, but don't know that I have a right to say so. Given that my men
won't have much to offer."

"General Newton?" Butterfield called on the man who had taken
command of the First Corps only that morning, but still managed
to be fourth from the bottom in terms of seniority as midnight ap-
proached. The battle had already taken its toll of generals.

Muscled like Hancock, but not so domineering, Newton said,
"As an engineer myself, I don't like this position. Lee could turn it,
had he a mind to. The lines themselves are good, we can fight them
all right. But our flanks are hanging out like an old drab's petti-
coats."

"Nothing against petticoats in general," Hancock noted, drawing
laughter.

"Then you believe we should withdraw from this position, Gen-
eral Newton?" Butterfield asked.

"*I didn't say that,*" Newton answered hastily. "I was only pointing
out the risks to staying here. In my view, this is no place to fight a
battle . . . not if we had a choice. But the battle's been joined. . . ."

Newton had disappointed Meade. After the man's superb per-
formance on the field, he was equivocating as badly as George Mc-
Clellan. Meade felt the urge to intervene, to make it clear that they
had to stay and fight. But he heard his wife's voice telling him to let
other men have their say.

Meade glanced at Butterfield: *Move on.*

One after another, the other generals simply said, "Stay."

"Stay and fight it out," Slocum snapped, adding intensity. He
had the build of a sparrow, but the eyes of a hawk. "Come morn-

ing, I'll take care of those goddamned gains those piss-ants made on my flank. They're going to wish they'd stayed home in god-damned Georgia or Alabama or wherever the Hell they came from."

"Sounds like we're of one mind, then," Hancock said, drawing out a cigar. His tone declared that he was as impatient to get through the meeting as the chief of staff. "Rectify the position here and there, but without giving up the field." He bit off the cigar's end and spit it out. "Personally, I think this is a damned good place to fight. If Pleasanton can get his nags out of their nose-bags and watch the flanks for once." He lifted himself far enough from his chair to light his smoke from the candle.

Butterfield called them to order. "Yea or nay to the proposition that the army remains on this field?"

Every officer, including Newton and Gibbon, voted to stay and fight.

"Question the Second," Butterfield said. "It being determined to remain in the present position, should the army attack, or await the attack of the enemy?"

Again, Newton and Gibbon disappointed Meade, both men a stroke too vehement in their insistence that the army was in no condition to attack immediately. Meade knew that. But it didn't have to be declared so loudly.

"Bobby Lee wants to keep battering his head against a wall, why not let him?" Slocum asked. Sedgwick, heavy and calm, nodded his agreement.

Puffing away, Hancock scratched an itch and said, "By all means, let Lee attack again, if he's fool enough. We're in a better position than we were this morning, with everybody up. But I say no attack on our side. Not right away. Unless our communications are threatened."

"Yea or nay, gentlemen?" the chief of staff asked.

Again, the vote was unanimous. Meade was pleased. Thus far, they had given him all that he wanted. And each man had his money on the table.

"Question the Third: If we await attack, how long?"

In the distance, a battery fired, but no guns responded.

The order of answering had broken down and Howard spoke

up first. Enlivened by his repulse of the late assault upon his batter-
ies, he urged, "Attack sooner, rather than later. The army's mettle
is up. Give Lee a surprise."

Skinny and short-tempered, Sykes spit out, "I disagree com-
pletely. Give Lee a fair chance to come at us. We've got good ground
and I don't see a need to hurry things." He snorted. "Took him
long enough to make his arrangements today, and Lee still couldn't
bring it off. He'll be hot now, embarrassed. I say we give him time
to make a mistake." He rocked back in his chair. "And if he doesn't,
there'll be time enough to go at him."

"Unless he moves," Gibbon said, still worried about the flanks.
"If Lee starts shifting his army to our left, we *have* to attack him,
it'll be too late to withdraw."

Again, Meade restrained himself and let his generals talk.

"I'd give Lee a day," Sedgwick told the gathering. He had the
voice of a judge pronouncing sentence. "Give him one day. If he
doesn't attack, then hit him as hard as we can."

"Too long," Hancock said, calculating afresh. "I say wait until
four p.m. That's about when he attacked today. If Lee can't get off
his aristocratic backside by four o'clock, we should go at him while
there's plenty of light." He grinned. "I'll bet you the poor bugger's
missing old Tom Jackson. Every goddamned minute. Our friends
in gray have a bad case of the slows."

The discussion began to wander and repeat itself. Butterfield
held up his hand. This time, he didn't ask for a vote, but just said,
"The consensus is that the army awaits Lee's attack, for a period
left to the army commander's discretion, and with allowance for
local attacks to rectify our lines. Does anyone disagree?"

No nays sounded, no heads shook.

Relieved, Meade sighed. They had given him what he wanted,
what he needed. Even before the council of war commenced, he
had sent a message to General Halleck in Washington, stating that
the army would stay where it was to fight it out. But he was not
about to mention that telegram now. He needed these men to be-
lieve the decision was theirs.

"I'm glad to find you all in agreement, gentlemen," Meade told
them. "You have confirmed me in my conviction that remaining on
this field is the proper course." He looked around at the begrimed

faces lit by the guttering candle. Hancock blew a smoke ring. "General Lee *will* attack again tomorrow. I am convinced of it. And he will be defeated. Thank you. This assembly is dismissed."

As the generals filtered out, Hancock paused beside Meade with a grin. Stinking like a bear with sweat and reeking with tobacco, Win whispered, "You're a sneaky bastard, George, one clever son-ofabitch." He chuckled. "I'd say I admired what you just pulled off, if I didn't feel my pocket has been picked." With that, Win thrust himself through the door, shouting for his horse.

Meade caught Gibbon by the sleeve before he could follow Hancock into the night. With Win still sorting out the army's left wing, Gibbon commanded the heart of the army's position.

"John," Meade said, "if Lee attacks tomorrow, his attack will be in your front. I'm certain of it."

"Does Sharpe know something? From a prisoner?"

"No. But I'm sure I'm right. Lee's made attacks on both our flanks and failed. His next attack will come against our center. He'll convince himself that I've drawn away so many men to the flanks that the center of the line will be our weak spot." Meade tried to smile, but lacked the needed energy. "I mean to check him soundly. With the help of God and a good line of guns, we're going to make your section of the line our strongest point."

"I hope he'll come at me. The Second Corps will give a good account of itself."

Meade felt the tug of midnight, but forced a spark of confidence into his voice: "If Lee comes again, we'll defeat him."

He damned well hoped he was right.

With Gibbon gone and staff men in place of the generals in the cabin, Butterfield asked, "Anything else, General Meade?"

There were a thousand other things. Ten thousand. But it was enough. Let the chief of staff do his work. Meade had lines to inspect and orders to give. Would there be time to snatch a bit of sleep?

He stepped outside, exchanging the rancid air of the little room for the stink of death and blown powder in the darkness. His son approached him.

"General Meade, sir? Father?"

"What is it, George?"

"Are we staying?"

"Yes. We're staying. How's Old Baldy?"

"Hurt. But not hurt bad. He'll be all right. He just needs rest."

We all do, Meade thought. Man and beast. But he moved on: "I was proud of you today, George. You behaved well."

"Thank you, sir."

"But a good officer doesn't take unnecessary chances. Accomplishment, George, not bravado, never bravado. Think of your mother."

With that, Meade sent the boy off again with messages to deliver. Young George had indeed done handsomely, riding about at a gallop to pass on orders and hurry troops along, careless of the death piercing the air. Had Margaret seen the half of what he had demanded of the boy, she would never forgive him. But the day had engulfed them all in its awesome magnitude, and it was a blessing to bob up alive at the end of it.

Whatever beauty men might find in war, it wasn't the sleek, clean beauty of a good lighthouse.

SEVENTEEN

July 2, Night

Betrayed by his bowels, Lee kept to the house his staff had commandeered. He did not want to see his generals now, after they had let him down so badly. It was essential to appear unruffled, to remain at all times a proper Virginia gentleman. But keeping his temper required isolation: It was a struggle to speak civilly, even to his aides. Walter Taylor, of all people, had presumed to suggest a need for firmer control of the army tomorrow. No one seemed to understand these soldiers, his invincible, tireless men. . . .

Appearing at last, Stuart had been chastised and dismissed back to his troopers. Longstreet was another matter, though. A meeting with that man risked a barrage of recriminations: Why had he moved so slowly? Why had he not been able to seize those hills? Why had he halted his men on the verge of success? Lee had to struggle not to impugn his key subordinate's motives, not to think him obstinate unto spite. Nor did he wish to hear more of Longstreet's pleas to maneuver the army around the Union position. The battle was joined, and the battle had to be won. It was unthinkable to let George Meade repulse him after such bloodletting. Leaving this near-won field would be a disgrace.

The army would have to attack again tomorrow, with great force gathered around Pickett's fresh division. Virginia-born and -bred, Pickett would not flag in his sense of duty. For all his frills and fripperies, the man was sound. And his brigade commanders were all Virginians, exemplary men. Courageous. Properly supported, Pickett would need only to be unleashed. Fearing for his battered flanks, Meade would have weakened his center. *That* was where Pickett and his supports would strike him. Meade would not expect a frontal

attack across those fields, and this day's blood would have nour-
ished tomorrow's victory.

Lee *knew* the Army of the Potomac. He had fought these gen-
erals and their soldiers enough times to know that they could always
be beaten. Here, on their own soil, they resisted more stoutly, but
Lee felt in his bones that their breaking point neared. Those people
lacked the wherewithal to withstand the men he commanded. One
great effort would shatter them. He *knew* it.

If only Jackson . . .

Jackson would never have dawdled so inexcusably. Where Long-
street lagged, Jackson would have used every instant to advantage.
The day's attacks had collapsed into piecemeal efforts, allowing
Meade time to shift his men about, permitting him to *think*. To-
morrow would be different: The attack would strike the weakened
heart of the Union line with a blow that would overwhelm George
Meade's defenses.

Longstreet would have to command the attack again, there was
no choice. Mulish though he could be, he was the last of Lee's sub-
ordinates up to the task. A diminished man in more ways than the
physical, Ewell had been sluggish and ill-tempered for two days,
while Hill had spent this day clinging to Lee's headquarters, failing
even to urge his own men forward. Hill's indisposition had dis-
abled not only him, but a third of the army.

Hill's indisposition . . .

Lee found the thought distasteful, a matter that could only be
ignored. Anyway, he had no one ready to take over Hill's corps.
Perhaps Hood would have done in time, but even he lay wounded—
severely, according to his staff. And, Lee told himself, he had to
remember that Hill came of his own kind and must not be shamed
publicly.

He found the mounting losses among his generals lamentable as
to their persons, but tragic when it came to their precious skills. So
many of them were gone now, replaced by men of good heart, but
inadequate talents. It was only the soldiers themselves, his sturdy
soldiers, who could deliver victory to the Confederacy.

But those men needed Jackson's iron hand and will.

Pacing about the chamber, Lee smiled mournfully. Thomas

Jonathan Jackson had been the least likable man he had ever loved. It was hard not to view his death as a desertion.

Perhaps Jackson had been wise to take his leave amidst the war? With his reputation at its apogee? Cross over the river, he'd said. And rest in the shade of the trees.

Jackson, with his lemons, faith, and alacrity.

Lee's bowels throbbed and he stepped toward the next room to use the chamberpot. But the quaking subsided and he composed himself. He knew that Taylor had papers for him to sign. But he was not ready. He needed more time alone.

He had received bad news, but shared it with no one. The rumors that Grant had abandoned his Vicksburg works had been incorrect. The siege continued, with ever less hope of relief. How long could Pemberton resist? Why was Johnston inactive? Could Vicksburg hold until the summer's end?

The news had made it still more vital to win a great victory here, to bring a final relief to the Confederacy. And to Virginia.

It was ever harder to maintain Christian decorum, to prevent a just cause from descending into hatred. Given the barbaric ravages in which those people indulged on his home earth, it took all his strength of will to forbid retribution. Even his Arlington home had been used unkindly.

Truly, they had become separate nations, irreconcilably so. His conduct and that of his men had to be exemplary, and he strove to embody gentlemanly honor. This war was not about slaves, but about civility, about the challenge to a civilization of beauty and refinement posed by a brute, mechanical culture. *They encompassed me about also with words of hatred; and fought against me without a cause.* He longed to sit again in his family pew, in a world well rid of war and rumors of war. But first this terrible issue must be resolved. Yesterday's brethren could no longer live together. Not without destroying the world Lee loved.

So Pickett and the others would go forward. One mighty effort remained to be made on the morrow, a last, decisive victory to be claimed.

Nor could Lee bear the thought, the unthinkable thought, that George Meade might defeat him. It was impossible. He could not

lose to Meade. And his men could not lose to those people. They only needed to be led with vigor.

Lee closed his eyes and saw his legions swarm through the Union lines.

Corny Wright gave up and walked off to sleep, leaving Blake and Cobb by the fire's embers. With midnight behind them, Blake leaned into the feeble smoke, aching to purge the smell of death from his nostrils. They had spent the day handling corpses and covering them over, but the dead just seemed to multiply, an infernal version of the loaves and fishes. The world stank of decay and shit until dried sweat seemed to Blake a sweet perfume. Beyond the fire, the living snored or called out, issuing nightmare warnings of Yankee volleys, or pleading with loved ones conjured in a dream. On a skirmish line, rifles snapped.

Eyes fire-brightened, Cobb cackled: "Behold, how good and how pleasant it *is* for brethren to dwell together in unity!"

Blake considered him through the twists of smoke. "Psalm 133."

Cobb's black maw widened into a grin. "That's right good, Quaker. Them Virginny folk brought you up right."

Blake had spent much of the day amid unaccustomed thoughts, wondering not about the phenomenon that was Cobb, but about its creation. After so many months of living and fighting together, it was the first time he had pondered the possible misfortunes of the other man, the tangled path that had led him to this place. And he had realized that, beyond the common mistrust of Cobb's kin back in the hills, he really knew nothing about the man beside him.

Blake felt for his tobacco and realized he had none. He let it go.

"Billie?"

Cobb looked up, eyes narrowed at Blake's use of his first name. As if he knew it was prelude to a challenge.

"Hear that boy sawing wood?" Cobb asked, shaking his head. "That Bunyan boy puts a battery to shame."

"I'm glad he's sleeping," Blake said. "I suppose losing a twin brother's even harder than losing a regular one."

"Lot harder," Cobb told him, "than losing some little gal you set your eye on for a time, but who never bound herself to you."

Blake understood the reference. It wasn't deep.

"Billie, tell me one thing. Without giving it a hard mouth." Blake breathed in the bitter smoke. "Why have you hated me so much? What have I ever done to you?"

A horse whinnied back in a grove. Other horses took up the noise, as dogs will, then quieted again. Cobb pondered the questions.

At last, the little man said, "Now, what makes you think I ever hated you, Sergeant Blake?"

Blake snorted. "I'm not joking, Billie. Nor mocking. I'd just like to know. Why you never miss a chance to dog me. To get downright mean, if you want me to put it plain. Why me? What did I ever do to you?"

With a sigh almost parental, Cobb met Blake's eyes dead on. The gaze was so fierce Blake found it hard to keep steady.

"Why do I hate you, Tom Blake? That assumes you're big enough for a man to hate. And I don't mean the tallness of you and the broad shoulders, that's not what I'm talking about."

"If I'm not big enough to hate, then *why*? Why all the devilment?"

Cobb poked the embers with a blackened stick. A flare of light sharpened his features. "Ain't what you done to me. You never did a thing to me. Not the way you mean. It's what you do to yourself. It just makes me angry."

"Would you two shut up?" a man called from his blanket.

Cobb shifted closer to Blake. His voice hissed. "Look at me," he commanded. "You look at me, Thomas Blake. You don't have to tell me what you see. I know it well enough, oh yes I do. But take a good look, boy. Then you go on and look at yourself. Come first light, you borrow yourself a mirror, and you look." Cobb shook his head. "And what'll be looking back at you? A face as comely as the beloved of the Rose of Sharon. *And* the lily of the valleys."

"And you hate me for that?"

"Damn me to Hell, you don't *listen*. Can't you listen just once, boy? You ask me a question like that, then you don't listen none?" Cobb's voice remained a whisper, but he seethed. Mad enough at Blake to come on with his fists.

"I'm listening."

"Then you listen good, for I won't tell you but once. You look

at yourself now. You know the look of yourself. Big, strong. Handsome. Even if some jumped-up little dolly in a poor-built brick house run off on you. That's you right there, right now, strong and handsome. Born so, a gift from God. Smart, too. Maybe not wise, but smart. The way it takes to get on in life, when there ain't no war to skew things. And are you grateful? No, sir. Some worthless no-good on a horse his daddy bought him hollers that your daddy was a drunk. And you sulk and sorrow like Job himself, as if the whole world ended. And all the while, you're a buck-handsome fellow with a half-interest in a store back home, and, from what I hear, some land bought up, and you ain't but twenty-six nor -seven, give or take. Then you look down at me and want to know why I hate you." Cobb spit. "You're not man enough to hate, 'least not yet. You're just a grown-tall boy who won't stop picking at scabs a true man would forget. Look at you, Thomas Blake. You got everything. And you cry unto the hills that you got nothing."

The little man's grimace spoke of anger, but not hate. "Sure enough, I'm jealous. But I've been jealous worse. That ain't the point. It's the resentment that the Lord done give you all these gifts, and you refuse to be grateful. You're a blessed man in search of a curse he can hide behind." Cobb sat back. "All I ever wanted from you was one sign that you knew how lucky you were. Just one sign. You're the fortunate son, beloved of the daughters of Zion, blessed with groves and vineyards unto a surfeit. And what do I see? The luckiest man I know pitying himself like a girl no one asked for a dance." Cobb looked into the glowing ashes, ruined face carved with despair. "They should've named you 'Cain,' you know that? Heaped with gifts, and killing's all you take to."

"I've never seen a man who likes to kill as much as you do."

Cobb snorted again. "If I do, I've got reasons. *If* I do."

"So why are *you* the way you are? You know so much about me. Or you believe so. What about you, Billie? All anybody knows is that you grew up on the Cobb side of the McCaslins, made no great impression, then disappeared. Folks figured you either went west, or got knifed up some hollow. Then you turn up ten years later, mean as the cholera."

"Ugly," Cobb said, "and mean." He snickered emptily. "A leper, without the Savior's healing hand. I suppose I ought to wear bells."

"That's putting it hard."

"Look at me, Thomas Blake. How would *you* put it?"

Blake reached for words of comfort, but he found none. Instead, he asked, "What happened, Billie? Where were you all those years? Yesterday . . . graveside . . . you were different. And tonight. Bible verses all over you. What happened?"

"Maybe I done beheld a pale horse?" Cobb looked away. "Or maybe I finally come far enough away from the Whore of Babylon."

"I'm no good at riddles."

"You know your Good Book, though. But you wouldn't say a word over James Bunyan yesterday. Left me to do it. Which wasn't right."

"Why wasn't it right?"

"Because those words don't belong in my mouth no more. They come out sour."

"If you don't want to tell me, fine. But I'm asking you. What happened to you? What made you so damned hard?"

Cobb smiled. "You know something, Quaker? This is the first time anybody in the company . . . in the whole damned regiment . . . asked me anything about myself. Beyond my name and age, when I enlisted."

"Well, I'm asking now."

The little man scraped the earth so fiercely with his stick that it snapped in two. But he spoke with ghostly calm. "I wasn't much of a McCaslin, tell you the truth. Nor a Cobb. Just never took to the ways of my own folk." He tilted his head, considering the broken twig. "Some say there's a tinker strain in us. Others say just bad blood, just plain, old wickedness. And I saw some wickedness, yes I did. Couldn't miss it. Doings up in them hills that even a beardless boy knew had to be wrong. Pleasurable, in the ways of Sodom and Babylon. Or Cherkey Hollow, anyway. But wrong. And I just didn't fit the muster. Oh, I got along, I wasn't trouble. My brothers and folks just thought I was queer in the head. But I worked a good day, and that was all they needed. Then, thunder and lightning above, I felt the Call. Didn't want it, didn't ask for it. But damn, if it didn't come over me."

His eyes saw other landscapes. "I had my letters. Taught them to myself, with some talk-help from my gram, the one came over herself.

She'd gone blind, but knew the verses, and I spelled them out. Can't say it did me no good, neither the letters, nor the Good Book." He cackled, almost the old Cobb. "Barely man-ready to deal with the world, and I fall to my knees by a corncrib, blinded by the light. Caught on the road to Damascus. On my way to feed the hogs, anyway. And I knew I had been chosen by the Lord, that he had favored me."

Cobb tossed the broken stick into the embers. Weak sparks rose. "I come preaching to the dinner table that night and my brothers laughed like men troubling a hoor. Beat me bloody, to bring me to my senses. The way brothers do." He frumped his chin, remembering. "Come morning, I was gone. With nothing but cold biscuits and that old Bible."

Staring into nothingness, Cobb took up his tale again. "You wouldn't of knowed me. I was a good preacher, a downright wonder, a natural hollering man. Not for the quality folks, nor in a church of my own, but down in the corners and hollows, in the shade groves and barns. I laid my hand upon many a good man's head and blessed many a woman. They believed me, Quaker, because I believed myself. I was called, and never had a doubt." He grinned. "Folks took to calling me 'Little Elijah,' though I never got around to smiting heathen priests in significant numbers. But folks give each other names for their own reasons. Anyway, I traveled west of the mountains, far as the Mississippi, even across that great Nile into Arkansas, and rarely wanted for a meal. Folks were hungry for salvation and starved for the Word, and I had a beautiful shout and a veil of rapture. Of course, I fell into the sin of Pride." He cackled again, at himself now. "I got to thinking my powers truly could redeem the Sinner, male or female, child or elder."

Cobb laughed a soft, surprising laugh and scratched beneath his shirt. "Don't go thinking I was one of these hellfire-and-brimstone fellers. No, sir. I put more stock in Jesus than Jeremiah. And I never tried to tell a man Jesus really turned that wine into water, not the other way around. Just tried to persuade him that getting hog-drunk and killing his own brother wasn't Christian. Same with fornication. Oh, my Lord. I'd seen enough before I was twelve years old to know men nor women weren't going to give *that* up. Just wanted them to stop doing it with their own sisters." He wiped a

dirty hand across his mouth. "Tell you the truth, there were times when I think I just loved the roll of the words in the Bible verses, loved to hear my voice ring out across the beauteous vale of this old world. I truly felt the Call, from head to toe, though some days it lay stronger on me than others." He nodded over a congregation of memories.

"Trouble started when I took all that talk about Mary Magdalene too serious. I'd come on to Natchez. Ever heard of Under-the-Hill? Down by the river? Silver Street? Well, you're none the poorer for it. More sin packed into one little row than any place since Sodom and Gomorrah. That's where I met her. Susan. My Susan. Susan Wyatt. Susan Cobb. Or whatever she calls herself these days. I went down among the heathen to save souls, and lost the best part of my own. But a man lies to himself, and never more so than he does about a woman. I saw her 'as the lily among thorns.' And she was beauteous. And I took her unto me." He laughed, grimly now. "I believed, I truly did, that I could lift her up and save her soul. But *you* know what I was interested in, Quaker. Even if I couldn't say so to myself. And she was willing. Oh, that she was. Always laughing. I told myself my Susan was an innocent led wrong. And I took her unto me as a wife. 'And I said unto her, Thou shalt abide for me many days; thou shalt not play the harlot, and thou shalt not be for *another* man. . . .' Hosea 3:3."

Cobb closed his palms over his eyes, whether from weariness or sorrow come to a surfeit. "My heart was filled with joy, and my loins with lust. Even her own people tried to warn me off, but at a time like that a man's a mule. And I was halfway to Heaven, telling myself, 'Live joyfully with the wife whom thou lovest all the days of the life of thy vanity, which he hath given thee under the sun. . . .'" He unveiled his eyes. "Know that verse, Quaker?"

"Ecclesiastes 9:9."

"What's 9:18 say?"

"'Wisdom *is* better than weapons of war: but one sinner destroyeth much good.'"

"Quaker folk beat that into you? Anyway, it's true enough. About the sinner destroying much good. If there was any good left in me, after I tarried with her. With the woman I loved more than eternal salvation. Know what I meant to her? After giving her my name

and pledging my immortal soul? I was a riverboat ticket from Nat-chez up to Memphis. No more than that. Wasn't a month thereafter, and she'd gone off in the night. With my last two dollars." His grin spread his ravaged nose. "Even took my Bible. I suppose she figured it might bring enough for a breakfast. And what she *did* leave me with made me into a thing that makes decent folk turn away." He spit into the ashes. "Like I said. 'A leper.' Even if it ain't the leprosy in the Bible. And there ain't no healing Savior here among us."

Blake considered Cobb a while longer, then looked away. There was nothing to say that wouldn't have been a lie.

Cobb slapped his thighs, as if he meant to rise and slip off to sleep. But the little man remained seated until the last coals faded and left them in the dark. As for Blake, sleep had no charms to draw him. Not that night.

At last, Cobb said, "Figure it's true? About us going in again tomorrow?"

Blake nodded at a darkness rimmed by darkness. "What's left of us. Unless the Yankees march off."

"They won't."

"No. I expect not."

"Something's changed. Can't say exactly what. But something's changed."

"They're fighting for their homes now."

Cobb's disembodied voice said, "It's more than that. It's like they took a while to figure out they had that much fight in 'em. And now they know."

"Now they know."

"Well," Cobb said with a dead-of-night yawn, "I expect we'll have a chance to cover ourselves in glory again in the morning. You ought to try to get yourself some sleep, Quaker."

"You can stop that now. Calling me 'Quaker.'"

"All right. Sergeant Blake."

"I like 'Tom' better."

Cobb cackled. "Why, I wouldn't feel sufficiently respectful, you a sergeant and all. I might get court-martialed."

A shot, close by, startled both men. Blake rose to his knees, grabbing for his rifle. A voice cried, *"Jesus, oh Jesus, I'm shot . . . I'm shot and killed . . ."*

"That Corny?" Blake said.

"Sounds like."

"Somebody help me! Jesus Christ. I'm shot."

The two of them hurried toward the voice, blundering over men whose sleep had been broken. Others, too, headed for the wounded man. A lantern emerged from an officer's tent.

"Corny? Where are you? We can't see you."

"Git off me, you big sumbitch."

"Corny?"

"He's here, Sergeant Blake." It was Charley Campbell's voice. He had leapt to the side of his friend.

Blake felt along the ground and found a blood-slopped leg. His hand pursued the blood upward into a hot, wet pulse.

"Who shot you, Corny?" Charley asked. "What happened? Where'd they hit you?"

"My belly, my nuts. I don't *know*. Oh, Jesus, don't it hurt? I never hurt like this. . . ."

The lieutenant scared up to command the company found them with his lantern.

"What happened here, men?" the boy demanded.

"Bring the light here, Lieutenant."

The lad did as Blake bade him.

Prodded, Corny screamed.

"Shut that damned feller up," a voice called. "Shoot him, if you have to."

"Corny, I can't tell where you're hit," Blake said. "You have to help me."

"Down there. Oh, my God. Down *there*. It hurts me so."

Every spot Blake touched had been slimed with blood or still pulsed with it. There was gore all down Corny's legs, where it made no sense.

A hand closed over his forearm, gripping it tightly. It was Cobb.

"Over here," the fallen preacher said. He tugged the lantern from the lieutenant's hand and held it beyond Corny's feet, leading Blake's eyes.

Young John Bunyan had blown out his own brains, rifle under his chin. The big corpse lay shapeless, with a wrecked jaw shocked open and a hole where an eye had been. The bullet had passed on

to strike Corny's groin, and much of the slop along Corny's leg was brains and blood from the twin.

"What a damned fool thing," Charley Campbell said, "what a damned fool thing."

Corny sobbed in agony, but the whole men stared down at the twin.

"I figure he just got a head start on the rest of us," Cobb said.

PART
IV

THE LIMITS OF VALOR

THE PICKETT-PETTIGREW CHARGE, JULY 3RD

1. Meade's headquarters
2. McGilvery's batteries
3. 69th Pennsylvania & Cushing's battery
4. Union trains
5. 26th North Carolina with Marshall's Brigade
6. Garnett's Brigade
7. Kemper's Brigade
8. Armistead's Brigade
9. Late attack by brigades of Wilcox & Lang

KEY

Infantry
Cavalry
Line of attack
Attack continues
Path of retreat

All locations approximate
Artillery not shown

EIGHTEEN

July 3, Morning

Hints of light revealed the waste of battle. Horses loitered among the dead, masterless and shimmering with gore. Just below the rise where Lee and Longstreet stood contending, a stallion nuzzled the grass in search of breakfast. Its mutilated hindquarters quaked, part of a separate creature. The morning twilight revealed a dangling leg. Breaking from the cluster of staff men shadowing their generals, John Fairfax strode out and shot the beast.

As the Army woke, a yawning artilleryman quickstepped from the soldier-infested treeline to undo his britches and squat, soiling the ground ten yards in front of his gun so he and his fellows would not step in the turds when serving their piece. Only as he plucked stalks to clean his fingers did the fellow note that he had distinguished company. Undismayed, he touched a paw to an eyebrow and sauntered back into the woodline.

"*Ecce homo,*" a high-toned voice called from a cluster of staff officers.

No man for sacrilege, Lee turned sharply toward the few who laughed. Without resort to words, his bearing chastised them. The officers eased back, allowing the disputing generals another layer of privacy as they watched the landscape emerge from the dark's retreat.

Many of the wounded had been collected, but moans still rose from the fields between the lines, distinct in the morning calm. There were no screams, though. Not this side of the field surgeries. Yesterday's worst sufferers were dead.

In the distance, a bugle sounded: one of the newly written Union calls. Summoned, a crimson sun fought through the clouds,

exciting the landscape. The night had been almost chill, but hard heat lurked.

"It can be done," Lee said. "The men can do it."

A breeze licked them with the stink of death.

Longstreet met Lee's eyes. Caught by a spear of light, they glowed with a belief almost fanatical: His soldiers were expected to make miracles.

Struggling to keep his voice tolerably subordinate, Longstreet said, "General, I've been a soldier all my life. I've been with soldiers engaged in fights by couples, by squads, companies, regiments, divisions, and armies, and should know as well as anyone what soldiers can do." He broke the stare and faced toward Meade's lines, willing Lee to follow his gaze. "It's my opinion that no fifteen thousand men ever arrayed for battle can take that position. This wouldn't be an attack, but a useless sacrifice."

Lee turned away. The old man stood erectly, as rigid as a cadet on post at West Point. But Longstreet sensed the turbulence within. They waged a contest not only of wills and visions, but over who could best restrain his temper: two gentlemen, deciding the fate of thousands of trusting men held at their mercy.

Turning toward the Union lines, the old man raised a fist.

"The enemy is there," Lee said, "and I am going to strike him."

Longstreet's gut refused to welcome his breakfast. Lee bewildered him. He could not understand how any man—let alone one of Lee's experience—could fail to see the folly in attacking across that mile of open fields. Longstreet had pushed out his scouts in the night, then ridden out on the enemy's flank himself. There were multiple opportunities to outflank Meade. Even now.

Lee refused to hear him. Upon his arrival at Longstreet's position, he had flared at the lack of preparations for a dawn attack, at the realization that Pickett's men had not yet come up on the line. But Longstreet had had no inkling that an early attack was intended. He had been with Pickett the evening before when a message arrived from Lee telling Pickett to hold in place, that he would be called upon when he was needed. But Lee had not called upon Pickett, or on anyone else thereafter. Then the unsettled old man had wanted McLaws and Law—now commanding Hood's division—to attack alongside Pickett the instant he marched up. That had

sparked another bitter argument, with Longstreet pointing out how battered the two divisions were in the wake of yesterday's fight, along with the danger of the Federals striking his flank, if Law and McLaws were to move out of position. Only when he drew Lee out into the open to see the terrain for himself had Lee relented regarding McLaws and Law. But the grand attack, with Pickett at its heart, would still go in.

Longstreet had then pleaded for Hill to attack as well, with the bulk of his corps. He believed that Meade's current position would not yield to fewer than thirty thousand men. Lee insisted that half the number would do.

Finally, at sunrise, Fairfax shot the crippled horse and Longstreet made his final, desperate plea. It failed. He felt half a wish that Fairfax had shot him, instead of the stallion.

Longstreet had never been less confident of success, never so burdened by the thought that thousands of men would be wasted— the flesh-and-blood lives of soldiers who put more trust in Lee than they did in God.

How could Lee fail to see it?

Behind them, the Army of Northern Virginia rose from its uneven rest. Most of the birds had fled the groves, yet a few trilled their daily greetings to the world. The aroma of campfires pierced an array of stenches. Regiments groaned and rustled, awaiting a boiled treat of captured coffee. Orders snapped.

Lee softened his posture. But not his resolve. Taking Longstreet's arm, he told him, "We must pull together, you and I. The men must not believe we are divided. They must have confidence."

Longstreet nodded.

Light gripped the fields and colors fought clinging shadows. Off to the left, on the high ground where the blasted orchard stood, Porter Alexander shifted a battery. The artilleryman had more energy than anyone else in the army. Longstreet had already decided that the young man would command all the corps' guns that day. No one else was as capable. Certainly not fussy old Pendleton. And the artillery would have the devil's own work to do.

"Let us go forward a little," Lee said, almost gently. "Toward the road, the better to see. You will have many labors this morning, General."

They mounted and rode out, trailed by their retinues. Nearer now, Alexander busied himself with another section, laying each gun himself.

Riding beside Longstreet, Lee said, "The artillery will have to prepare the way, of course. To silence the batteries in the center. If the artillery does its work, I do not think it will be so very difficult. Meade has been weakened to the breaking point."

Longstreet did not reply.

They dismounted on another of the low crests that rippled the fields and examined the Union lines through their field glasses. They had entered the realm of the dead now, ground upon which both sides had bled, only to abandon it. The cluster of horses and officers presented a splendid target, but the Union cannoneers declined to open.

Lee took his time, shielding his lenses from the rising sun with a hand that was not quite steady. The old man had not yet been this far forward, but Longstreet knew the ground from the thick of battle. He sensed that Lee was only now discovering the topography's disadvantages. The old man said nothing.

A Yankee corpse in blood-crusted Zouave dress stared into the sky. His shoes had been taken, along with his stockings. His naked feet seemed ridiculous and obscene. Close on his toes, a bearded corpse in homespun had spilled its brains. Beyond lay more, far more, whose lives had stopped suddenly.

Toward the town, skirmishers pecked at the morning.

A cavalcade broke from the wood that concealed the army. Gaunt Powell Hill took the lead, instantly recognizable, followed by Harry Heth, the latter's head white with bandages. Staff officers and escorts completed the little troop. Hooves thumped the earth as the riders made for Lee.

There was plenty of bad blood between the corps commanders Longstreet and Hill. As well as the bad blood in Hill's veins, Longstreet told himself. He did not believe that Hill was the man to command a corps. But the Virginian had been Lee's choice.

Longstreet was sorry now that he had ordered Hill's arrest the year before. The action had been petulant, but could not be undone. The dislike and resentment had been there on both sides, though, with Hill hounding after glory undeserved and Long-

street behaving poorly, as he realized now. He did not believe that Hill was an honest man, or a good one. Possessed of bravery, Hill was also capable of malice, his style of command a brew of impulse and indolence. But they were thrown together now, and would have to make the best of it.

The riders pulled up. Hill looked somewhat recovered from his latest indisposition, but Heth was hard to read. For that matter, Lee also seemed healthier, sounder, than he had been for days.

Longstreet turned away to scribble orders for Tom Goree to carry to Pickett, who was to bring up his men and find a sheltered spot in the army's center. Sleek as a Comanche, Goree galloped off with the message.

Bemused that no Union gunners had opened on the henhouse gathering of generals, Longstreet stepped back into the command circle in time to hear Lee tell Hill and Heth, "General Longstreet will, of course, command the attack. General Hill, you will provide a division to cooperate with Pickett, as well as any brigades wanted as supports."

Longstreet caught the look from Hill: half jealousy and half relief that the responsibility for the day would not be his.

"I believe," Lee said, "that General Heth's division is well positioned to join Pickett."

Hill and Heth exchanged a queer look, but Lee appeared not to notice. Longstreet wondered what that was all about. Something had gone unsaid.

Longstreet caught Heth watching him. Discovered, Heth looked away, showing Longstreet the stain on the bandage wrapping his head.

"I believe it best," Lee said to Heth and Hill, "to allow General Pettigrew to continue to lead the division for today's attack." Attempting a smile—a facial contortion Lee had never mastered—he turned to Longstreet. "Our friend General Heth must be allowed time to recover."

"I'm all right," Heth said, by way of excusing himself. "Just not all right enough. Things don't look right, not half the time. Wouldn't do, I suppose."

"Pettigrew will serve all right," Hill put in.

Longstreet knew Pettigrew just well enough to worry. His

brigade's attack on the battle's first day apparently had not been quite as refined as the gentleman himself. Now the embroidered cavalier was to lead a division he had commanded for barely one day in a near hopeless charge.

But who else was left? That was the damnable thing: Glorious attacks were killing and maiming generals and colonels faster than a new crop could be grown. Yet, they went on squandering their best, as if good leaders were cotton or tobacco and could be replaced by another bale from the warehouse.

Pettigrew was universally acknowledged to be a brilliant man, but Longstreet wondered if his lauded genius mightn't get in the way of sensible soldiering. He'd heard that, at New Bern, Pettigrew had made a knightly show of attempting to limit the bloodshed, with the result that he and his men received a whipping. Soldiers had to think, but they also had to know when to stop thinking and just plain *do*. Pettigrew struck Longstreet as a wellborn gentleman whose valor belonged to his role as a cavalier, public bravery of the sort that cost other men their lives. If that judgment was unfair, Longstreet told himself, it was no more unfair than giving inexperienced men the charge of attacking divisions.

For all that, there wasn't a damned thing to be done about it.

Barricades of clouds resisted the sun's assault, but the breakthrough was coming, Longstreet could feel it with the certainty of a man who had lived much out of doors. The day would be Texas hot by noon, and the temperature would side with Meade as Pickett's men and Pettigrew's crossed those fields.

A scrap developed around a cluster of farm buildings short of the town, the sort of fight that was ugly enough if you were caught up in it, but that hardly counted to anyone who wasn't.

After dismissing Hill and Heth, Lee turned to Longstreet and interrupted his thoughts. "General? Shall we show ourselves to the men? And greet General Pickett?"

As soon as Lee left them, Longstreet took Pickett forward to see the fields he had to cross and the deadly slope his men had to climb. Ordering their staffs to hold at the tree line, Longstreet led the way into the open. He wanted—needed—to hear Pickett speak

frankly: In the company of others, George would feel obliged to pose as fearless.

He had known Pickett since they were lieutenants in Mexico, in the 8th Infantry. At Chapultepec, Longstreet had carried the regiment's flag until shot in the thigh. George had taken it from his hands and planted it on the ramparts of the citadel. They had been hardly more than boys then, exuberant in victory, still unaware that life held more than laurels.

Longstreet had gone on to a happy marriage and four children, until scarlet fever robbed him of three and cast a pall over a love he'd thought indestructible. Still, he had been granted happy years, unlike George Pickett. Standing on that parapet in Mexico had been a high point for George. Not long thereafter, his much-loved wife had died. The Army sent him off to Indian country, where he took up with a squaw and fathered her child. He had served in dull eclipse until his defiance of the British up in the Washington Territory revived his name at last.

In this war, his performance had been dashing, if not always wise. His valor at Gaines' Mill had earned him a bad wound and promotion to divisional command. But the army murmured that his convalescence—under the care of a willful girl who was hardly more than a child—had made him wary of danger for the first time in his life. And Pickett made no secret of his attachment to his Sallie: He was downright tetched with moon-calf love, wearing ribbons begged from her hand without the least embarrassment. If others cast themselves as cavaliers, Pickett was a knight in gray-wool armor.

Longstreet found himself hoping that the worst of the slanderous gossip would prove true. If the prospect of those fields daunted George Pickett, they could go together to Lee and petition the old man to stop the attack. Longstreet knew he was out of credit with Lee, but Pickett was like a darling, indulged son whose voice might catch the old man's ear in time.

Well forward of the batteries being readied, Longstreet reined in his horse and suggested dismounting. He noted how Pickett took his time, eyeing the Union lines from up in the saddle. George never quite broke his stare at the ground he must cross and the lines he had to capture.

Longstreet let him look.

At last, Pickett said, "My, oh my . . . ain't that a sight?"

"What do you think, George?"

Pickett shook his head, oiled ringlets tossing below the cap he wore at an angle. "Looks like those boys are expecting our company, don't it? Can't say old Meade's done himself any harm settling in." His face was downright grave by Pickett standards.

"The position's formidable," Longstreet said carefully. "Can it be taken, George? I need your honest view. Between us."

Pickett hesitated, staring across the broad expanse that led to the Federal lines. Lifting a hand to extend his cap's visor, he slowly shook his head.

Longstreet began to hope. Perhaps, even now, Lee could be made to see reason.

Pickett changed in an instant. Dropping his hand from his cap, he turned out of the sun, smiling as grandly as if about to dance with his beloved Sallie.

"My boys can do it, Pete. It'll be hard, ain't saying it won't be. But damn, if we won't do it." He cocked his head, almost forty years of age and still as much a boy as he'd been in Mexico. His grin widened. "Only good manners to take a stroll up there, in my opinion. With Granny Meade expecting us to call, we'd be downright rude to decline the invitation."

Longstreet felt betrayed. They'd known each other for so long, why did George have to put up so much front? Pickett thought his prospects were grim, that much had been evident from his long look at the lines. Couldn't any of them be honest, with so much at stake?

The infernal problem was that there wasn't a man in the army who would risk dishonor by saying a thing could not be done or didn't make sense to do. If the Confederacy died, it would perish of pride.

"Take a good look, George," Longstreet said, locking up his emotions. "Take a good, long look. Then get your men ready."

James Johnston Pettigrew watched Longstreet approach with a surge of anger he knew he dared not reveal and with trepidation that must remain equally hidden. The division placed in his hands

was in no condition to match Pickett's fresh men in a grand attack and his reputation might suffer in comparison. The carnage of the battle's first day had gutted the best of his regiments, their valor confirmed by their grimly shrunken rolls, and he could rely upon only two reduced brigades of the four he now commanded. All would go forward, but what each brigade would achieve was rather in doubt: His own, under Marshall now, had been severely bloodied, but would fight, and Fry would do well enough leading Archer's men, who were hardy veterans. Brockenbrough's troops were worthless, though—no matter who led them—and Davis had a brigade only because he was the president's nephew. It was folly to send these men in, when General Hill had others fresh and ready.

It was an honor, of course, to lead the division in an attack that must decide the battle. But he'd already found that controlling four brigades was rather a different thing from commanding one. Errors today could savage his reputation. Nor did he think the prospects especially good for the planned attack. He even suspected General Heth of using his wound to avoid responsibility.

He continued to smart from the general's earlier insults, after he had followed Heth's orders to the letter and declined to engage the Union regulars encountered in front of Gettysburg—only to have it suggested that he had lied about their presence, while revealing cowardice through his behavior. Heth had not used the monstrous word, but the implication had been clear to everyone present. It had driven Pettigrew to press home his attack on the first day of battle, to show the stuff of which he had been made, but even that gallantry had not cleared the blemish. He could not show the least weakness this day.

Longstreet dismounted, passed off his horse, and stumped up the slope toward him. Pettigrew always found the man uncouth. Except for Lee, few former regulars were men of social distinction.

He had much preferred the company of the French officers in Italy—wellborn men who behaved with *savoir faire*—and the charming villages of Piedmont or the Veneto ran more to his taste than this odorous Dutch town. But he had not received the desired commission in time to fight at Magenta or Solferino, after which there had been no point in pursuing one: Only the glory of war ennobled soldiering, which was, in peacetime, rather a dreary affair.

Now, of course, he was fighting for his own land, which gave matters a colorful patriotic dash, allowing a gentleman to make the best of things. Yet, the soldier of fortune's romantic cast retained a certain Byronesque appeal.

It struck James Johnston Pettigrew that the man would have looked an ass in a fine French uniform.

"How are you getting on, General Pettigrew?"

"Well enough, I think, sir. Although one regrets General Heth's indisposition."

"Indeed," Longstreet said, considering him with eyes that belonged to a grizzly bear. "Indeed."

"I trust General Heth's convalescing satisfactorily, sir?"

Longstreet raised an eyebrow. "He hasn't been down here?"

"Not this morning, sir."

"Well, don't worry about Harry Heth. Wound isn't serious. Just gave him a hangover won't quit. How's your division?"

Pettigrew feigned surprise at the query. "The men are splendid, sir. As always. And honored that you've selected us to participate in your attack."

Longstreet didn't seem a man of nuance, but his face was hard to read.

"I didn't select you," the corps commander said. "General Lee did. With General Hill's acquiescence." He snorted. "More's the honor, I suppose."

"Yes, sir. Supremely so."

"You had a hard day of it Wednesday."

"The men won through, sir. Their performance was simply inspiring. They covered themselves in glory."

"I've heard that said."

"Hard fighting, sir. But we've had our day of rest. The men look forward to avenging their fallen comrades."

"Do they now?" An unmistakable smirk disfigured Longstreet's mouth above his beard. "General Pettigrew, have you had a look at the fields your men are to cross? Have you seen what's waiting on the other side?"

He had. The prospect was mortifying. In his brigade's attack two days before, the distance had been short and the landscape partly wooded. This attack would cross a mile of open fields, every

step of it under the Union guns. It seemed nothing short of murderous.

"Of course, sir. I examined the corps' front yesterday. Upon receiving today's orders, I took in the prospect again."

"And?"

"I trust in your leadership, sir. And in General Lee's."

Longstreet laughed one crude syllable. "Well, God bless you. It's always nice to meet a man of faith." His features turned to stone. "You believe your men can make it across those fields? And penetrate the Union lines? And stay there? Do you *believe* that, General?"

Pettigrew was bewildered. Why was Longstreet questioning him like this? Did he doubt his courage, his competence? What did he want him to say? That it couldn't be done? Such words would never issue from his lips.

Longstreet's demeanor was almost as insulting as Heth's had been.

Correcting his posture to a rigid perfection, Pettigrew said, "Sir, my men can do anything General Pickett's men can do."

Longstreet grimaced. "No one suggested otherwise, General Pettigrew. That wasn't my point." He tugged his beard and snorted. "I regard this attack as . . . more challenging than most. I only wanted your opinion about your division's prospects."

"And now you have it, sir."

Longstreet veered between fury and despair. Pettigrew, he decided, was a lying, prissy bastard who'd kill every soldier entrusted to him to preserve his precious honor, then probably get himself killed and be hailed a spotless hero of the South. Pickett at least had weighed the matter, before electing suicidal chivalry. And George had a division that wanted to fight. Riding through the muddle of Pettigrew's men, Longstreet had seen faces resigned to duty, but hardly impatient to start across those fields.

Word would have gotten out, of course. About the day's line of attack and its obvious difficulty. And rumors would make things worse.

The clouds had burned off and green foam lined the mouth of Longstreet's horse. In the meadows between the groves, the sun

pressed down. Soldiers bedecked with a dozen canteens each sought the streams that had washed the first day's dead. Water would be as important as ammunition. It always was.

Men sprawled listlessly in the shade, waiting in bored torment. A band played "Wait for the Wagon." No one paid attention to the skirmishing beyond the ridge. The men knew, as they always did, that bigger things were coming.

Longstreet rode for his own corps' lines, hunting Alexander to discuss the artillery's role in the attack again. Instead, he crossed Lee's path.

The two men halted in a shady lane. Lee looked stronger, dignified, imperturbable. If the old man had any doubts, they were not evident.

"Well met," he told Longstreet. "I've just come from General Hill. Lang and Wilcox will support Pickett on the right, their brigades are already in the desired position. And Trimble will follow Pettigrew with two brigades."

Longstreet nodded. He was torn between adding forces to the attack and sparing as many soldiers' lives as possible. "Pettigrew may need the help. His men look blown to me."

"They'll fight," Lee said. Closing the topic.

"Harry Heth hasn't been down to his division. And Pettigrew's not as confident as he lets on. Big leap, from brigade to division command. Harry should've looked in on him."

"I suspect General Heth doesn't want to appear to be meddling."

"Pettigrew might do with some meddling. He's game enough, but I'm not sure he's ready."

"Pettigrew will do his duty."

"No doubt. The question is whether he can control that division."

"He need only maintain his alignment with General Pickett."

A battery rushed up the lane. The generals gave way, guiding their horses onto an island of sunlight between the trees. Soldiers rose up amid the weeds and brush. Out of respect for Lee, not fear of hooves.

On impulse, Lee turned to the nearest men. "Do you know what you must do today?"

The men nodded. Some edged closer. Into Lee's aura.

"Will you drive those people?" Lee asked.

A reassuring hubbub erupted: "*Sure enough, we'll whip 'em, Gen'rl.*" "*We'll do it for you, sir, you know we can.*" "*No Yankee born's going to stop us, Gen'rl Lee.*" "*You just turn us loose. . . .*"

The old man turned a glowing face to Longstreet. His expression said, *You see?*

What Longstreet saw was an eternity of soldiering. He had heard men complain bitterly countless times, wracked with fear or furious at some idiocy, only to parrot the words expected of them when a superior—even a hated one—asked if they were ready to give battle. And Lee was loved.

No one would ever tell the truth to Lee. How could these soldiers in their rags be expected to reveal their doubts when their generals wouldn't?

The soldiers wished to touch Lee, a boot, his saddle, his horse. But none of them dared. It was as if he were a living saint.

And this looked to be an afternoon of martyrdom.

A few minutes after eleven, Colonel Alexander reported to Longstreet. He had seventy-five guns deployed along the corps' front. Most of Hill's batteries were positioned to support the attack as well. Flanking fire against the enemy batteries in the cemetery could be expected from Ewell's corps. His own guns would concentrate on the Union center to open a gap for Pickett. There had been nothing like this in the war, the bombardment would be massive.

"I don't want you just making a noise," Longstreet cautioned his favored artilleryman. Irritation sharpened his voice, but Alexander wasn't the cause of it. Longstreet had issued more orders that morning than he'd ever given prior to a battle—only to find too many of them taken lightly. "Don't just make a damned noise. I need you to cripple those bastards. Tear their limbs off. You understand me?"

"Yes, sir. What artillery can do, we'll do."

"How many guns do you figure in all? That can fire to good effect?"

Alexander chewed his lip. His trim beard stirred. "Walker can bring at least fifty of Hill's guns to bear . . . so that's a hundred

and twenty-five. I've had no contact with General Ewell's people, but they should go after the batteries up in that cemetery. Problem's not the number of guns, but ammunition, sir. We fired for five hours yesterday."

"How much damage can you do?"

The younger man gleamed with sweat. Longstreet had never known a fellow more tireless. But he needed effectiveness, not just activity. There was going to be activity aplenty.

"Oh, we can hurt them," Alexander said. "Bad, I think. But we can't keep it up for more than half an hour, not without emptying the limber chests. Frankly, sir, I'd prefer to limit the bombardment to twenty minutes. In case the Yankees get up to some tricks later on. We need to hold something back. There's no more shot or shell this side of Staunton. . . ."

"Make it thirty minutes." Longstreet wondered just how much to say, then decided on honesty. "If you can't put the guns in Meade's center out of action, this attack isn't going to succeed. That's the plain and simple of it. Marching into rifle volleys is bad enough. I don't want all those boys walking into canister. You understand me?"

Alexander waved off a pestering fly and stared into the face of a troubled man.

"Yes, sir. My guns are ready."

Colonel Edward Porter Alexander waited for Longstreet's signal guns. Positioned in front of Wright's brigade, where the line of sight was best and couriers could go quickly, he drained the last water from his canteen, wishing he'd taken the time to fill it that morning. The quiet gripping the field as noon approached was thick with dread. He was about to unleash a storm of death unlike any other witnessed in the war. In his twenty-eight years of life, he had never been so tense, alive, and impatient.

A front-porch political stalwart from Georgia, Rans Wright had the thickest beard in the army and a taste for visiting. He strolled out from the treeline for a chat.

"Going to be some hot work today, Alexander," the brigadier general said.

"Yes, sir. You're not going in?"

Wright shook his head. "Got to leave somebody back to mind the store. Had my time yesterday. Bad enough."

"I hear you nearly broke through, sir."

Wright spit. No wetness came out. " 'Nearly' don't do."

The two men stared across the sun-pressed fields. Just looking drenched your armpits.

"Take a gander," the brigade commander resumed. "More guns up there than yesterday, maybe twice as many, and yesterday wasn't no pie-eating contest. You're going to have to even up tall odds, son."

A rider galloped toward them. Alexander recognized one of Longstreet's couriers. The sergeant leapt from the saddle, saluted, handed over a folded paper, and was off again, showing them horseshoes.

Alexander opened the note. Dots of sweat darkened the paper. The words struck him like a fist:

> *Colonel. If the artillery fire does not have the effect to drive off the enemy or greatly demoralize him, so as to make our efforts pretty certain, I would prefer that you should not advise Gen. Pickett to make the charge. I shall rely a great deal on your good judgment to determine the matter & shall expect you to let Gen. Pickett know when the moment offers.*

He handed the note to Wright, who read it and whistled. "Sounds like Old Pete might be having second thoughts."

"I *can't* do what he asks," Alexander said, still stunned. "*I* can't decide whether Pickett goes in or not. I won't be able to see enough to judge, the smoke from the guns hides everything." His hand shook as he took back the note from Wright. "We'll be shooting blind after the first few minutes, praying we've got the range and elevation right. The only way I could read the effect of our fire would be their return fire, if it slackens off."

"Write him back. Tell him just what you told me. But you have to put it in writing, son." Wright whistled again. "Never figured Longstreet for a man who couldn't make up his own mind."

Alexander didn't understand it, either. It was as if a hand other than Longstreet's had written the message.

He scribbled down his reservations and sent the note off by courier.

"Want some eats?" Wright asked him. "I can offer that much. In return for the splendid gunnery we're expecting."

"Thank you, sir. I couldn't eat, not now."

"I suppose not." Wright peered across the fields. The air was heavy and dead. "Shame you couldn't open up this minute."

Alexander gave him a quizzical look.

"Look yonder," Wright said. "Those Yankees trotting back and forth, flags and pennants and all kinds of carrying on? Generals preparing a reception committee, that's what that is." He chuckled, as if contemplating a practical joke to be played on friends. "Put a couple shells on 'em, and they'd remove themselves most expeditiously."

He nodded along with the Georgian, but it was what he didn't see that interested Alexander. Except for those knots of busybody riders, the Union line looked graveyard still from a distance. The Federals weren't bringing up guns or shifting regiments anymore. That meant they felt they were ready for whatever might come their way.

Were they?

Alexander's mind darted about. Bringing his thoughts back under control was like trying to catch a fish with his bare hands. Longstreet's note had raised new possibilities, none of them pleasant. He had assumed this attack was Lee's inspiration, that all had been decided for the best, that there was a plan and its features were inevitable.

He stepped away to piss and fumbled anxiously with his buttons. The stream was brief and dark. He could smell his urine.

Too damned hot. A man could burn his hand on a cannon's barrel before it fired a shot. The gunners nearest him had stripped off their shirts and they'd brought up every bucket in their battery, setting the water out of the path of their drills. He considered walking over and scooping up a handful or two of water, but didn't. The water was theirs, not his.

He walked back toward Wright.

"Waiting's no pleasure," the Georgian commiserated. "Just a-watching through the bars as they build the gallows. Or waiting

on a ballot count. Which is pretty much the same thing, in my experience."

The courier returned from Longstreet. The second note was not much of an improvement:

> *Colonel. The intention is to advance the infantry, if the artillery has the desired effect of driving the enemy's off, or having other effect such as to warrant us in making the attack. When the moment arrives advise Gen. Pickett. . . .*

He could not believe that such an equivocal message came from the hand of General James Longstreet. ". . . *if* the artillery has the desired effect . . . *if*. . ." Thousands of lives depended on a guess. *His* guess.

Alexander passed the second note to Wright, who seemed unjustly amused at the situation.

"He's put the responsibility back on you again," Wright said, grinning. "Hell of a situation to be in, son. But, damn it, you know we're going to attack, no matter what happens. All you have to do is call the time, that's all this is."

"I won't even be able to *see*."

The Georgian shrugged. "Just judge things the way you told me. Their fire dies away, you've done your part. Then it's up to Pickett and his boys. And all the rest of them."

"And if their guns keep up with ours?"

"Look here, son, this isn't about you. Longstreet's just in one of his black Dutch moods. Probably feuding with Lee again. They've been at it like man and wife for on to a week now, so I hear. Longstreet's just passing down the unpleasantness—that's why officers come in different ranks. And you're handy."

"He's put a terrible burden on me."

Wright spit dry-mouthed again, a man with a chewing habit who lacked tobacco. "Truth is, your guns won't decide this. Oh, they'll help. Wouldn't want to go in without 'em, if I was part of this grand and glorious circus. But today's going to be about numbers, about who's willing to throw in the most and take the hardest hammering." He shook his head, entertained by the ways of the world. "Anyway, there won't be any holding back Georgie Pickett. We're

past that point. Ain't a man in this army could do it, short of Marse Robert himself. You'll be lucky if Pickett waits until you call for him."

Alexander didn't answer. He was listening and not listening. Thinking about how best to advance his guns during the charge, about the commitment of the small reserve he'd withheld, about his ammunition stocks, ranges, and trajectories.

"Tell you the same damned thing I just told Pickett," Wright went on. "It's mostly a question of supports. It's not as hard to get up there as it looks. I was there yesterday, with my brigade. The real difficulty is to stay there after you get there. Whole Yankee army's up there in a bunch. If Lee himself hasn't seen to proper supports, we'll be crying in our whiskers come this evening."

A cannon boomed on the right. Alexander quickened. The signal? When Longstreet was ready, the Washington Artillery would fire off two rounds.

There was no second shot.

Their meal was hard biscuit and bacon grease, mean fare in the heat. Blake had wanted to send his men's canteens back to the creek again, but the new lieutenant with whom they had been graced worried that they'd be called to form in the meantime. That wasn't the boy's only worry. He'd gone over the ridge with the other officers to have a look at the ground where they'd make their attack. The boy had come back speechless.

Blake understood. Since moving up near the line the evening before, he and plenty of other men had wandered over to survey the battlefield, so they knew the immensity of the fields they were now expected to cross. A few men were all for it, but most were just resigned, scratching out last letters home or cleaning their rifles.

There were so blessed few of them now, only a few hundred still on their feet from a regiment that had begun the battle with more than eight hundred men. All of them would fight, out of the blind obligation that passed for a sense of duty, out of suicidal pride and orneriness. But few looked forward to it.

Cobb had pared him like an apple, skinning him down to the raw, the night before. Everything that Cobb had said about him had been as true as it was difficult to shoulder. He had been the

on a ballot count. Which is pretty much the same thing, in my ex-
perience."

The courier returned from Longstreet. The second note was
not much of an improvement:

> Colonel. *The intention is to advance the infantry, if the*
> *artillery has the desired effect of driving the enemy's off, or*
> *having other effect such as to warrant us in making the*
> *attack. When the moment arrives advise Gen. Pickett. . . .*

He could not believe that such an equivocal message came from
the hand of General James Longstreet. ". . . *if* the artillery has the
desired effect . . . *if* . . ." Thousands of lives depended on a guess.
His guess.

Alexander passed the second note to Wright, who seemed un-
justly amused at the situation.

"He's put the responsibility back on you again," Wright said,
grinning. "Hell of a situation to be in, son. But, damn it, you know
we're going to attack, no matter what happens. All you have to do
is call the time, that's all this is."

"I won't even be able to *see*."

The Georgian shrugged. "Just judge things the way you told
me. Their fire dies away, you've done your part. Then it's up to
Pickett and his boys. And all the rest of them."

"And if their guns keep up with ours?"

"Look here, son, this isn't about you. Longstreet's just in one of
his black Dutch moods. Probably feuding with Lee again. They've
been at it like man and wife for on to a week now, so I hear. Long-
street's just passing down the unpleasantness—that's why officers
come in different ranks. And you're handy."

"He's put a terrible burden on me."

Wright spit dry-mouthed again, a man with a chewing habit who
lacked tobacco. "Truth is, your guns won't decide this. Oh, they'll
help. Wouldn't want to go in without 'em, if I was part of this grand
and glorious circus. But today's going to be about numbers, about
who's willing to throw in the most and take the hardest hammer-
ing." He shook his head, entertained by the ways of the world.
"Anyway, there won't be any holding back Georgie Pickett. We're

past that point. Ain't a man in this army could do it, short of Marse Robert himself. You'll be lucky if Pickett waits until you call for him."

Alexander didn't answer. He was listening and not listening. Thinking about how best to advance his guns during the charge, about the commitment of the small reserve he'd withheld, about his ammunition stocks, ranges, and trajectories.

"Tell you the same damned thing I just told Pickett," Wright went on. "It's mostly a question of supports. It's not as hard to get up there as it looks. I was there yesterday, with my brigade. The real difficulty is to stay there after you get there. Whole Yankee army's up there in a bunch. If Lee himself hasn't seen to proper supports, we'll be crying in our whiskers come this evening."

A cannon boomed on the right. Alexander quickened. The signal? When Longstreet was ready, the Washington Artillery would fire off two rounds.

There was no second shot.

Their meal was hard biscuit and bacon grease, mean fare in the heat. Blake had wanted to send his men's canteens back to the creek again, but the new lieutenant with whom they had been graced worried that they'd be called to form in the meantime. That wasn't the boy's only worry. He'd gone over the ridge with the other officers to have a look at the ground where they'd make their attack. The boy had come back speechless.

Blake understood. Since moving up near the line the evening before, he and plenty of other men had wandered over to survey the battlefield, so they knew the immensity of the fields they were now expected to cross. A few men were all for it, but most were just resigned, scratching out last letters home or cleaning their rifles.

There were so blessed few of them now, only a few hundred still on their feet from a regiment that had begun the battle with more than eight hundred men. All of them would fight, out of the blind obligation that passed for a sense of duty, out of suicidal pride and orneriness. But few looked forward to it.

Cobb had pared him like an apple, skinning him down to the raw, the night before. Everything that Cobb had said about him had been as true as it was difficult to shoulder. He had been the

most ungrateful of men, making the least of the gifts he had been given. As strong as he was in body, so weak had he been in spirit. Surrendering his soul to a fickle girl and a drunken father's memory. When all the world had been given him, he had closed his eyes and wickedly clenched his fists.

He thought of John Bunyan with his brains blown out. And Corny with his private parts shot through, waking from sleep to screaming pain. Then bleeding to death. Pike Gray and Jack Ireton, Art Peachum and Ollic Wright. James Bunyan and Tam McMinn. Hugh Gordon waiting to live or die at a field surgery. All of them, all of them . . .

Death. Where is thy sting?

Everywhere.

And he had thrown away the gift of life.

Tapping his empty canteen, Charley Campbell said, "I hear a feller just died of the heat. In Company C."

"Probably fainted," Cobb said, "when he heard we were going to charge over that prairie."

"No," Charley said, "he died. God's truth."

Cobb managed to grin, black-mouthed, and snarl at the same time. "'God's truth'? I'd call that another matter entirely. But sticking to the business here at hand, I'd say a feller goes down with the heatstroke, he might be the lucky one. Better'n having your balls shot off while you're sleeping. Or lying out in them fields, bleeding in the sun."

"Why you always got to be pestimistic?" Charley asked.

Blake opened his mouth to correct the word, then thought better of it. "Pestimistic" suited Cobb. Like a hand-sewn set of drawers.

"Look on the dark side, you get a nice surprise every so often," Cobb explained. "Look on the bright side, you're apt to be disappointed."

"That ain't no way to live," Charley muttered.

Cobb grinned again, delighted. "Won't be too long and many a wondrous hero of the Twenty-sixth North Carolina—which covered itself in glory, if you ain't heard—well, he won't have to worry about how to live no more. Deliverance courtesy of His Majesty, Jefferson Davis, and the Confederate States of America. Just toss

that heroic sack of meat in the pit and throw on the dirt. *Hallelu-jah! Amen!*"

"Billie, you sonofabitch," Charley said, "you'll probably be the one who walks away without a scratch. I swear there ain't no justice in the world."

"No, there ain't. Been saying that all the while, but nobody listens. Blowing my horn like the Angel Gabriel, and all you're worried about is your share of the drippings."

The lieutenant strutted up, a determined child. Blake stood. The others didn't. No one saluted.

Standing stiff as a board, the boy looked them over. "I thought you men should know that an order's been given to shoot any man who malingers or tries to run."

"That's nice," Cobb said. "Officers included? You were back in the rear the day before yesterday, ain't that right?"

The lieutenant reddened. "I was detailed to guard the trains."

"These men won't run," Blake told him. "I can vouch for them."

"They're insubordinate, Sergeant. Especially that one." He pointed at Cobb, who showed him his black teeth. Repulsed, the boy turned on Blake. "If you want to keep those stripes, I'll expect appropriate discipline in the future."

Little Cobb rose off his haunches and tugged up his filthy trousers. "You shit yourself already, son? Or you holding it in to dump one on the Yankees? Up real close, like?"

"*I'll bring you up on charges!*" the lieutenant cried. He sounded as if he were about to weep.

Cobb laughed.

NINETEEN

July 3, Noon

Brigadier General Henry Jackson Hunt loved the army. He believed in the Union's practical advantages, but despised his government's nagging corruption. The army, not the pork barrel, was his passion, an obsession nurtured quietly behind a disciplined front. When he had been orphaned at the age of ten, army associates of his father and grandfather ensured he was never homeless. It was thanks to those loyal men, as well, that he and his younger brother got to West Point. Thereafter, the army had been his home and the artillery his calling, with room in his life for precious little else.

The practice of artillery was a beautiful thing to Hunt, with its combination of science and honed instinct, of art and mechanical skill. It set the purity of mathematics and the laws of ballistics against barometric pressure and the wind, against the countless tricks of the earth's relief—and, not least, human foibles. In Mexico, he had received brevet promotions, first to captain, then to major, for his valor from Contreras to Chapultepec, but he was prouder still of his work on the army manual *Instructions for Field Artillery*. Hunt believed that any soldier could stand in the line of fire, but more of them needed to think.

If there was any resentment in Henry Hunt, it was that the men who served his guns never got due credit for their work. When glory was apportioned, the artillery would receive, at most, a nod. Promotions stagnated, while infantry officers and cavalrymen leapt upward. But Hunt knew what his men did. Yesterday, they had held a line the infantry could not hold, long enough to save the entire flank. If there had been a hero of that shambles, it had been McGilvery of the artillery reserve. But Hunt had lived long enough

to know that the lieutenant colonel's name would not be crowned
with laurels.

Now Henry Hunt reined in his horse on the blasted forward
slope of Little Round Top, beside the battery Rittenhouse had inher-
ited from the fallen, valiant Hazlett. The position was spectacular for
gunnery. Hunt regretted that the ground would not admit more
cannon. Rittenhouse's rifled ten-pounders could range nearly every
target on the field.

Hunt gazed past the shot-up groves to the quieted fields be-
yond, envisioning what must come: long ranks of Confederate in-
fantry, determined to cross that expanse and steal a victory. Hunt
agreed with Meade that the attack would strike the center, hitting
the long ridge that declined from the cemetery. He found it hard to
believe that some of his fellow generals—not least, Hancock—
remained unsure of what the Rebels would do. Hunt knew: An old
artillery hand saw the terrain and its hidden laws more sharply than
others did. And the logic of this battlefield was inexorable: Lee
would come at the center.

He had spent the morning watching the proof develop. The
Confederates had been shifting guns all morning, amassing an im-
pressive concentration directed unmistakably at the ridge. The odd
shots that had pocked the calm were obvious ranging efforts. Yet,
Hancock had argued with him that, while an attack *might* be in the
offing, an artillery barrage could also provide cover for Lee's with-
drawal. That was nonsense. Lee wouldn't have enough ammuni-
tion left to waste on a deception. And the Army of Northern
Virginia still had fight in it. Lee had come close to a win the eve-
ning before. He wouldn't quit now. The artillery bombardment,
when it came, would play for all or nothing.

Without resort to his field glasses, Hunt could see the distant
ranks of cannon in front of the treeline, from the high ground by
Sickles' damned orchard to the southern edge of the town. Lee was
massing everything he could.

Hunt was ready. Meade had left him a free hand to direct the
army's guns, and he'd made the most of it. Rittenhouse's lone bat-
tery on the heights was only a tiny part of his scheme of fires. Hunt
was determined to devastate the advancing Confederate infantry so
severely that few, if any, would reach the Union lines. Let other

men claim the glory if they craved it, the third day of this battle would hinge on gunnery.

Before riding back down the hill to begin his third inspection of the day, Hunt turned to Lieutenant Rittenhouse.

"No nonsense," Hunt said. "Every shot to be aimed, and delayed if the target's obscured. One round per minute, no more. No squandering ammunition. Ignore the rate of fire of the enemy. Excitement is no substitute for effectiveness."

A gleaming boy, the inheritor of Battery D, Fifth U.S. Artillery, nodded earnestly. He saluted sharply as Hunt turned his horse to lead off his detachment of staff men and couriers.

Discipline was everything. Or damned near it. If he could prevent the gun crews from firing madly into the smoke, they'd have rounds in plenty to meet the Confederate infantry—while leaving enough reserve stocks to carry on. For all of gunnery's geometry and formulae, the ultimate calculation wasn't hard: You needed more ammunition than your enemy when the crisis came, and you didn't achieve that superiority by creating thunderous shows that accomplished nothing. Fools measured success by rates of fire—which only mattered for canister and close combat. Accuracy and discipline were the keys.

Convinced by long experience that anything neglected would go wrong, Hunt headed down to the low ground and the great surprise he had got up for Lee. He let his horse go easy and a few members of his retinue edged ahead of him. Their horseshoes sparked off the rocks of the forlorn hillside. Only when they reached a farm lane did Hunt spur his mount to a trot.

McGilvery occupied the bottomland that Sickles had so detested. His concealed gun line stretched from the sunken meadows where the evening's attacks had withered, to the flank of the corps defending the Union center. As Hunt led the way past cannon after cannon, he was pleased to see their crews had filled again. Infantry volunteers replaced yesterday's casualties, some of them men who imagined they'd have an easier time with the guns than in their old ranks. They had no idea of what was waiting for them.

Absorbing bad habits as well as good from the veterans, many a man had stripped to the waist to stoke the guns in the furnace of the day. A believer in a soldierly appearance, Hunt let the violations

pass this time: The heat was heavy and worsening, and all that mattered now was the work ahead.

He found McGilvery at the foot of the ridge inspecting a field piece.

"Well, Freeman?"

Face smeared with yesterday's powder, the lieutenant colonel smiled. "It's the most beautiful site for guns I've ever seen."

Hunt thought so, too, but declined to be effusive. It was no time for overconfidence. The position was superb, though, although it took a seasoned gunner to see it. Few of McGilvery's thirty-nine pieces were visible to the Confederates. Neither could his men see the Rebel gun line, but that didn't matter. The purpose of these batteries wasn't to duel tit for tat with Lee's artillery, but to sweep the attacking infantry from the flank, and neither the Lord nor the devil could have better shaped the ground to such a purpose. The batteries sat on a rising lip in the trough Sickles had abandoned. As soon as the Rebel infantry passed the middle of those fields—focused straight ahead and unsuspecting—they'd be exposed to McGilvery's raking fires. The effect would be shattering.

Hunt spared McGilvery one of his lectures. The fellow knew his trade. Nodding his approval, Hunt trotted on up the long ridge to the batteries in the center, the guns that would bear the brunt of the Rebel barrage and had to hold on to send canister into any attackers who made it through his crossfire. Not all of these exposed guns or their crews would survive, and he had positioned reserve batteries to their rear, their number another cold-blooded calculation.

He paused at Cushing's battery, its guns positioned between a small grove and a sharp jut of the fence that marked the line. The guns here belonged to Hancock, who could be difficult. A master of leading men, Hancock was less skilled at employing artillery, the sort of officer who judged the effect of his batteries by the amount of noise they made.

"Ready, Cushing?"

"Yes, sir."

"General Hancock been round?"

Cushing smiled. "Of course, sir."

"Offering advice?"

"Mostly encouragement. 'Give 'em the devil, boys.' That sort of thing. I appreciate the replacement limbers, sir."

"Lucky we're not both dead. Your boys gave as good as they got, though."

Just hours before, a Rebel shell had hit one of Cushing's limbers, with the knock-on chain of explosions destroying three of them. He and Cushing had been talking with a sergeant just yards away. Their escape had been miraculous.

"Who's got Brown's battery now?" Hunt asked.

"Walt Perrin, sir."

"Know his business?"

"Walt's steady."

"Good."

As the morning tightened into noon, Hunt stared across the fields again, imagining it all one more time. Cushing and his fellow Second Corps officers just had to survive the coming bombardment, which would concentrate on their portion of the line. Everything about the ground, its little tricks, the drops and folds a hasty glance overlooked, told Hunt the attackers would funnel down to a point near this nick in the line, that stone wall and clump of trees. Charging men invented goals to aim at. In the absence of better landmarks, the copse would draw them.

He considered sharing his ruminations with Cushing, then decided against it. There was a line that must not be crossed between alerting subordinates and alarming them. Cushing was a sound officer, he'd sort things out for himself.

By way of good-bye, Hunt looked down from the saddle and said, "General Hancock will roar like a bear, but you keep back enough rounds to repel an assault at close quarters. He'll be thinking of his infantry, he'll want you to fire just to keep up their morale." Hunt swept a hand toward the waiting soldiers. "It's up to you to keep those poor bastards alive, Cushing. Your guns are the best friends they've got." He gee-upped his horse and rode northward.

Another ranging shot struck behind the men of Hays' division, beyond the right-angle turn in the boundary fence. They were coming. Soon. A great damned lot of them. Only a slumbering fool could fail to see it.

Hunt wondered why the Confederates were waiting.

That ranging shot encouraged him, though. The Confederate gunners were still firing high and long, their usual practice. If they failed to correct their elevation now, they'd put most of their shells behind the ridge, once the smoke made everything a guessing game.

He spotted Hancock atop the ridge, haranguing an officer whose men were hurrying forward. Hunt decided not to pay his respects. Hancock would only demand more guns for his front, where there wasn't space to deploy any more effectively. Hancock was the kind of man who wanted more of everything, field pieces, food, or glory: a magnificent fighting soldier, but ever a bit of a trial.

As he rode up along the next stretch of the line, Hunt saw regiments ranked behind regiments, as if the fields had sprouted thick blue crops. Whatever his artillery failed to finish, these men would conclude. He believed he sensed something different today, an alacrity—a vengefulness, perhaps—as if not a few of the men foresaw everything as he did. After so many heartbreaking reverses, the time had finally come to turn the tables.

Hunt knew soldiers. For virtually all of his life, he had lived among them, often in intimate circumstances that let no man hide weaknesses. From syphilitic drunkards to shining knights from the pages of Walter Scott, he had known them by the thousands, even in childhood. He had not been quite eight when his father took him along on the expedition he led across the Missouri, founding Ft. Leavenworth on the western bluffs. Hunt remembered days of boundless prairies, food that you just got down any way you could, lilting songs raised by dusty throats—music hoarse and wonderful— and the disappointment he felt upon meeting Indians at last: Instead of whooping, attacking, and making a spectacle, they had carried themselves submissively, men broken and ashamed. He recalled the immense, immeasurable strength of his father, a captain in Army blue, who died two years later and was thereafter hopelessly, terribly gone. A man in his prime years himself now, Henry Hunt could not imagine another life with such an eminent purpose. He pitied the man who never had served in uniform.

At last, Hunt came to the cemetery atop the commanding hill, where Osborn had staged the Eleventh Corps' strongest batteries. The prospect was even grander than the view from Little Round

Top, a flawless panorama of the Confederate gun line glinting a mile away. Behind them, hidden in those distant trees, how many Rebel soldiers waited to charge? Twenty thousand? Thirty? Hunt would not have liked to cross those fields, no matter the numbers allotted him, but it struck him that even thirty thousand men would be hard-pressed to carry his army's lines.

Say what you wanted about the Eleventh Corps, Osborn had the stomach for a fight. Already protected by the terrain, McGilvery had been able to dig in his guns and throw up a parapet, too. But Osborn's best lines of fire were from the cemetery itself, which hardly lent itself to eager digging: No gunner wished to disturb a grave, fearing bad luck to come. Major Tom Osborn could put shot and shell on nearly every point likely to be crucial, but the Rebels could answer in kind. If Lee's artillerymen were smart, they'd concentrate on Osborn, giving his batteries precedence even over those in the center. But Hunt doubted they'd be smart that way—the pressure would be on them to knock out the guns positioned directly in front of their infantry. Unless Lee had artillerymen with sense as well as backbone, enough of Osborn's cannon would survive to play Hell with the charge. Lee's gunners were brave, even daring, but Hunt regarded their skills as second-rate. Having trained a number of them himself in the pre-war army, he regarded their failings as a personal embarrassment.

An infantryman could afford to think in terms of a few hundred yards, but artillerymen had to grasp the entire battlefield.

And Hunt had arranged the entire line to his purposes: McGilvery would rake Lee's infantry from the Union left, making a grim surprise of it, while Osborn poured in shells from the other flank, achieving a crossfire as close to perfect as Hunt had ever seen outside of a textbook.

Lee would have to be mad to send his divisions across that field. And Hunt was sure he would do it.

The artillery commander dismounted, stretching his forty-three-year-old bones and marveling at the prospect laid out before him.

"Rebs were damned fools not to take this hill two days ago," Osborn said. "Could've done it, too."

"But they didn't."

"Well, they're going to pay for it."

Hunt nodded, then said, "I expect you'll take some fires from your own flank, from your rear there. It may get hot."

Osborn chuckled. "I hear it got a little hot for you this morning, sir. First report was that you'd been killed by a lucky shot."

"Ranging shot. Not lucky enough."

"Cheroot, sir?"

Hunt declined. He didn't believe it was proper to take a subordinate's cigars or his credit. He would have liked a smoke, though.

Lighting up, Osborn asked, "Who's got that battery out in front of Hays? Devil of a place to be, thrust out like that."

"Woodruff."

"Brave man."

"Following orders. Not my orders, by the way. Speaking of limbers, you might want to move yours back behind the ridge."

"I'll need the rounds handy," Osborn said. He, too, had his plan.

"You know my instructions. Preserve ammuniton. Wait before returning fires. Only fire at identified, worthwhile targets."

Osborn smiled. "'No more than one round per minute.' Yes, sir. I understand." He gestured toward the fields beyond the town and below them, at the baking expanse awaiting triumph or tragedy. "They come marching out of those woods, we could fire blindfolded and knock 'em down like pins." Lowering his eyes, the major shook his head. "Almost hate to see the poor devils try it. Sheer murder. Nothing but."

"Murder's what we do," Hunt said. "Make sure your men have water."

Black murdering buggers they were, the English, and 'twas down to their account that Daniel Francis Gallagher never married. For he had no wish to wear himself the black shame he had seen on his father's face, the shame of a man who knew not how to feed his wife and brats. They were Mayo people, his Gallaghers, and the wind from the sea carved the faces of the women, just as the poteen muddled those of the men. But a life it was, if never grand, until black '47, with the praties gone mush in their beds and the black English shipping off cargoes of grain while starvation whittled Irish bodies boneward. Black bastards they were, the landlords, absent or not,

come over to the one true church or not, black buggers and bastards all to ride past the shame of a man who cannot feed his kind, riding horses whose price would buy up a village. Then the black typhus came in that black, black year, and his mother, father, and sister did not starve to death, for the spots on their slack, white skin did the trick for the hunger, the three of them dead, all three, and him left to wonder what doing should come next, for the rest of his people were dead or tramping about the lanes worse than tinkers, or gone to America. All but the house-proud Castlebar Gallaghers, shopkeepers so mean the cholera always spared them, his blood kind to whom he walked in that black year, only to be shut out of doors and kept there for fear of the typhus. He'd learned to steal, but better to hate, for little there was to steal in those black days and hatred filled the belly better than love, oh, didn't it, though?

Born to hate the English he was, to spit in the tracks of the county families who traipsed off to London to avoid famine and plague, their great houses shuttered and looked to by keepers with shotguns at the ready, not even a bed in a barn allowed to a boy of ten, but a great lesson he gave them, for all that, for killing was in him. And the family fool enough not to go when the going was still fair, the Cuthberts of Sligo, had a son, and the son had a pony. And when the boy rode down that narrow lane, between the fields gone bad, he was not known to Daniel Francis Gallagher by name, not yet, but white were his golden curls and his riding suit bright as a flash girl's borrowed petticoats, and Daniel Francis Gallagher, aged ten and proud, brought him down with a rock well hurled, and as the boy lay bleeding on the ground, all the lovely sight of him, the same rock retrieved came smashing down between the stunned blue eyes, again and again it came down, until there were no blue eyes left, only a pulp, and no coins in the young master's pockets, but thick slabs of bread with butter and jam in the saddlebags, and him, Gallagher, no murderer but his blood's avenging angel, rolled the corpse over and sat on its rump to eat, caring not, for life had no more value than that and hunger the master of all. He ate the bread with a trembling hand, shaking not from fear but from the joy of feeling the soft, sweet bread give in to his teeth. They could have hanged him on the spot, for all he cared

in the moment, so lovely it was to have a full mouth, if not yet a full belly.

Two tramps were hanged for the murder, and guilty they may have been themselves for doing something shameful to the body, but not for the killing, and when he heard about their taking he was halfway across Sligo going the other way, outraged that another man—men—should have the credit of his bold deed. He always had a good eye for the land and the ways of it, even then, and made his conqueror's way back to the cottage that was little more than a shed for human animals, but no one had taken the bodies away and they were gone black as the year itself, as black as English hearts.

There was nothing left but America, his passage paid by doings of which he tried never to think, shaming even now, and if the hunger left him smaller than he might have been, oh, he was a mean one, a hard boy, steeled by the shame on his father's face before he had luck and died, and the chimney-by tales on cold nights of his ancestors rising, all hanged by the lobsterback beasts in the '98, and more than a few, his father included, suspected of being Whiteboys long thereafter, hobbling Englishmen's cattle for practice while waiting to hobble men. For if all the tales of Oliver Cromwell were true, they were as nothing to the slow-murdering policies of London come to pass, and the hunger, the shriveling hunger, his mother naught but cheekbones and a nose above the skeleton clutched by her rags, his sister thin to vanishing, and his father weeping for shame and helplessness, with not even a glass to stop his thoughts. And then the typhus, which spared him, he was certain, for this day.

This day on a sun-punished field, with a sergeant's stripes upon his sleeve and the boyos of the 69th Pennsylvania sweating around him, taking up the good time by rattling in brogues so thick that even Colonel O'Kane, sweet man that he was, when he wasn't a right bastard, could not catch but stray words of it, for O'Kane was a Derry man, who knew not the secret languages of the West.

"Get out there again, boys, go on," Gallagher said, in a voice that could empty a shebeen by the docks, "and farther this time, get on with ye, for there's beautiful rifles and such to be had, just laying there for the taking, with the Johnnies who left 'em awaiting for their comeuppance."

"Cripes, we were halfway to their batteries last time."

"Then go the other half, dearies, and give 'em all a kiss from Sergeant Danny. Now go bring in every rifle ye can find. Ye'll be thanking me, come the circus. Now go on."

"Will we be having our dinner, then, d'ye think? It's been two famishing days." Walsh was a fellow Mayo man, but a cocky one.

"Ye won't need to eat when you're dead, me boy. Now get ye over the wall and do as you're told."

The point might come when Walsh wanted a thrashing.

Gallagher turned back to the other task, the holy work of filling barrels with death, then laying the rifles nicely side by side behind the low wall, ready to greet the high Southern gentlemen bound to come calling round. For Daniel Gallagher could smell a fight from the Delaware to the Schuylkill, and old Pennsylvania was bound for some killing this day. Let the generals prance and the gun-navvies do their duty, the hour would come and soon enough when the high English Rebels, those narrow-nosed gents in gray, would get worse than he'd given that young master. *Oh, let them come, do*, Daniel Gallagher thought, *and I'll have the manners to greet them as befitting.*

The 69th Pennsylvania were fighting lads, as their strength for the day, hardly 250 of the thousand Irishmen who'd marched out two years before, would tell anyone who wasn't a fool or an Englishman. They were men let loose to do all the damage they could to an aristocracy that couldn't put chains on Irishmen over here, so clapped them on niggers. And damage they did do. Gallagher himself took special pride in keeping his wits about him, cool as a jug laid by in a mountain stream, and taking careful aim at the Rebel officers, the finer the uniform, the sweeter the satisfaction when the man tumbled bloody in agony, and may his last thoughts be of Mother. Given a choice between shooting down a colonel in an old coat and a lieutenant in a uniform fresh from the tailor, he'd shoot the boy first, returning to the colonel, time permitting. Such killing was a joy, a *joy*, as it had been for the warriors of legend. And the landlord's son, on the old sod or here, was always Erin's enemy.

Before the war was kind enough to come, he'd worked his way, not twenty-four then, to a mastery of the docks along the Delaware, ensuring that what was meant to be paid on the sly was paid

on time, and no man challenged him twice. And if the high and mighty of Philadelphia looked down on Paddy and Mick, any man could see they'd be broken, too, that this was the promised land for the suffering Irish, that a man could get up, stay up, and then climb higher, if man enough he was to bust his knuckles. Even the stones thrown at the regiment's flag as they marched down Broad Street had not soured Daniel Gallagher. For he took things in their turn, thinking, *First the Rebels, dearies, then you're next.*

He had no watch, for the last one he'd picked from a beautiful corpse in gray had gone smash the day before, in repelling the last attack, and a donnybrook that was. But watches there would be in plenty, not too long from now. Meanwhile, he judged that the sun had inched past noon.

Oh, let them come, dear Jesus, let them come. Let them march over those fields to say hello.

The detail he had sent forward returned with two dozen more rifles. Gallagher took those in the best condition for himself. He'd not stand behind the boys this day, encouraging them to hold their ground and keep their blue lines tidy. Today was a day for sport and plenty of it. The old Philadelphia Irish Militia was in the ring and ready.

Detail done, a few of his boys worked up shade using their blankets. Bayoneted rifles stabbed in the earth lofted the wool. Others undid their canteens and drank too deeply. A few men mumbled, eyes closed. Gallagher knew they were praying, but too embarrassed to get on their knees in the daylight. He granted them all peace in the sultry hour, other than barking at Flannery not to drink up his last drop, with plenty of thirst to come. Himself, he went back to inspecting the line of spare rifles.

Killing made it clear that a man existed.

Gallagher still had plenty to prove to the blackhearted, bestial English. And to their landlord kind in coats of gray. Oh, he had no love for the nigger, who was an animal. But there was a greater principle involved.

He could not understand how any famine-born Irishman could take up arms to serve the Southern cause. Unless it was for the sheer pleasure of the fighting, a reason Daniel Gallagher could respect.

Ever wary, Gallagher was a difficult man to surprise, but Colonel O'Kane came up on him in his reverie.

"Sergeant Gallagher? How are the men?"

Gallagher rose, panting a bit. "Hot, sir. But ready for mischief."

The colonel gestured at the hundreds of extra rifles lying ready. The men had wanted to prop them against the stones, barrels high, but the artillery that was bound to come would have played havoc with them. A nice grassy bed would do for the rifles. For now.

"Not sure I'd want to be on the other side of that wall today. If they come at us."

O'Kane was a born saloon-keep with his banter, keeping the feel for his lads on the line as any good publican minded his paying customers. Better he was, a thousand times, than the Welsh drunkard gone before him.

"Colonel, sir, 'tain't a matter of 'if.' The blackhearted buggers are obligated."

O'Kane raised an eyebrow, amused. " 'Obligated'?"

Gallagher smiled. He knew his smile was not pleasant, but that was the good of it. It kept men, even colonels, at the right distance.

"To me, sir. After all the work my lads have done."

The regiment's commanding officer appeared about to extend the conversation, then changed his mind. Pivoting, he said in a fare-thee-well voice, "Remind the men to aim low, Sergeant Gallagher."

"That I will, sir, that I will," Gallagher assured him. As far as his own aim went, he shot for the groin.

Meade felt like a cadaver in the saddle. He had slept for three hours in the night, but it had not been enough for mind or body. Moving about, inspecting the lines, seemed the only course to avoid collapse—the way you had to march soldiers through their exhaustion, or see them fall apart when allowed to rest. He envied the men lounging under the shade of blankets or tentage rigged as flies and felt that he could sleep all the day and night, had he the freedom.

After Meade had a brief exchange with Hays, in which his speech sounded slow in his own ears, Hunt rode up on him.

Meade reminded himself to show good posture, to look every inch the commander. It took an effort.

"Well, Henry? How are your guns?" The question did not have to be asked. Hunt was one man who never let others down.

A substitute for the injured Old Baldy, Meade's horse pawed the ground, a creature of more energy than its master.

"If Lee comes on, he'll be sorry," Hunt told him.

"What do you make of the big display?" He meant the Confederate gun line. Hunt understood.

"They'll hear the noise in China. Sir, I've ordered our guns to refrain from returning fire for fifteen minutes after Lee's batteries open." The artilleryman made a lemon-eater's face. "Given how junior officers tell time when the guns go off, they might wait ten. If I'm damned lucky. I just don't want them squandering ammunition."

"We're not short?" Meade heard the alarm in his own voice. Hunt had assured him, a few hours before, that their remaining stocks would be more than enough. With the question blurted out, Meade steadied himself again.

"No," Hunt said. "Not in terms of reserves. But there won't be time to replenish the guns on the line between the bombardment and the charge. The forward batteries need to have rounds in their chests to repel the infantry." Hunt slapped at a fly. "An artillery duel's a fool's errand for us, anyway. Our guns are Lee's problem, but Lee's guns aren't ours. Our problem's their infantry."

Meade's horse swished its tail, attempting to lash its rider, as if the beast were determined to wake him fully. Meade forced his thoughts back into a functional order: Hunt was right. His artillery and Lee's did not have a symmetry of purpose on this field. His guns were meant to kill soldiers on foot, while Lee's were obliged to stop them. He and Hunt understood each other, sharing the veteran's taste for parsimony: The time to spend without restraint was when the crisis arrived, not a moment earlier. The day before, Meade had lost his temper with an artillery lieutenant who had opened up on an obscure, worthless target.

Waste not, want not. The old verities.

Breathing deeply to fuel his fading senses, Meade said, "Hancock won't much like it."

"No, he won't," Hunt agreed. "He thinks ammunition chests are bottomless and the artillery exists to put on a minstrel show. He'll

be sorry enough, if he doesn't have canister loaded when they're on top of him."

But was Lee going to charge them, after all? Meade had been thinking more about that and confusing himself. Fighting down new doubts. The night before, he had been clearheaded and certain that Lee would come against his center, that it was inevitable. Now he found himself fearing a move past his left again. Who had raised that last night? Newton? Gibbon? The candlelit argument of twelve hours before had blurred. His thoughts were a smear.

"I've been thinking, Henry . . . Lee *could* come around our left flank, after all. Those guns might be a ruse. Or a barrage could even cover a retreat, give Lee time to get his trains moving, start his men. That's what Hancock suspects he might be up to."

Hunt looked at him sharply. As if he only now sensed the depth of Meade's weariness. "No. Lee's coming straight across those fields. And he's going to hit Hancock dead on."

"You sound damned sure."

"General Meade . . . they'll come. And we're going to squeeze them with fires from both flanks and stampede them into a mass in the middle of that field. They'll bunch toward their own center, as soon as they take raking fire. It's the way infantry react. They do it every time, our men or theirs, and I don't care how disciplined or experienced they are. They'll come at Gibbon and Hays in a shot-up, angry mob. And if Hancock doesn't waste his ammunition, his guns will finish them."

Meade followed Hunt's description as best he could, envisioning the flanking fires and the crowding of the attacker's bloodied ranks. Hunt understood battlefields and men, not just his guns. But the images filled in more slowly than they should have done.

I must get through this day, Meade told himself. Surely, this day will end it.

"Malvern Hill again?" he said.

"Better. Or worse. Depending on which side of the guns you're on."

"You're awfully sure of yourself, Henry. Lee's always been one for surprises."

"Not today," Hunt said fiercely.

Meade closed his eyes, then snapped them open again. He hoped

that Hunt was right. That, for once, Lee would do what they expected, wanted, needed him to do. "I wonder why they haven't opened fire. Artillery issues?"

Hunt shook his head. "They spent all morning fiddling with that gun line. Then they stopped, about an hour ago. Either their infantry isn't ready, somebody's having doubts . . . or their chain of command's gone to Hell." Hunt smiled. His smiles, notoriously, were almost as rare as Meade's. "Maybe all three. I'd give twenty gold dollars to listen in on the talk over there right now."

Meade found himself drifting away from Hunt's words again. When he realized the artilleryman had finished speaking, he said, "Very good . . . good . . ." A bright red impulse gripped him. "I really must see Hancock . . . haven't defined his responsibilities, not precisely . . . make sure he's ready . . ."

"For God's sake, sir. Give yourself time to breathe, you need to rest yourself. Hancock's ready to fight. The man's *always* ready to fight." He pulled a face. "I just hope that bull elephant's ready to think."

The image of Hancock as an elephant charmed Meade. His mouth widened. A war-elephant, to be sure. Still, an elephant. Win had trouble buttoning his coat over his belly nowadays. It was a rare man who gained weight on a campaign.

"And you?" Meade asked. "You've been riding up and down all morning, Henry. If you won't spare yourself, at least spare that horse of yours. . . ."

"I need to have one more look from Little Round Top."

Meade's thoughts caught up with the muscles around his lips, which were oddly pleased with the world, despite countless worries. "You're going to be a disappointed man, Henry. If Lee doesn't follow your plan."

Hunt looked at Meade ferociously.

"He will," the artilleryman said.

Heading for the back side of the ridge in search of Hancock, Meade let his horse find its own way between the regiments. The ghosts and hobgoblins of error plagued him, insistent fears that, despite Hunt's bolstering confidence, he had been mistaken all along and had deployed his army poorly for what was to come. His

tactical flanks were well defended—but what if Lee swung deep and turned his left? Or surprised his right and cut the Baltimore road, as he'd feared from the outset? He had bet on a late-night hunch, trusting his instincts, and had strayed from the rigor of an engineer.

General Gibbon intercepted him, hurrying up on foot despite the heat.

"General Meade! So glad you could take me up on my invitation!"

Meade stared down at the man who had stopped by his stirrup: What invitation?

Oh, yes, yes. Breakfast. But it was already past noon. Was there something else he'd forgotten?

Gibbon chattered on: "The cook rustled up what he claims was an old hen—more likely a rooster, but no point arguing. Made us a stew fit for our delicate palates." The division commander raised and dropped a good-natured shrug. "Won't rival the finest dinners in old Philadelphia . . ."

"I have to find Hancock," Meade said.

"He's here, sitting right over there." Gibbon grinned. "Surely, you don't think Win would miss a free meal?"

"I can't eat," Meade said. "The men haven't eaten. Those Philadelphia Irish . . . haven't had a cracker in two days. My fault . . ."

Gibbon's face went taut. "George . . . listen to me. You look like a dead man. When's the last time you've had a meal yourself?"

Meade couldn't remember.

"You *must* keep up your strength," Gibbon insisted. "What good are you to the army, if you drop?"

Suddenly, Meade realized he was famished.

His horse followed Gibbon's footsteps. As if the animal had taken Gibbon's side.

A brilliant aroma taunted Meade's empty stomach. Up ahead, Hancock's big haunches spilled over a keg. Win's face hovered protectively close to his plate. Pleasanton, who should have been at Meade's headquarters, wiped up the remains of his stew with a crust. The favored diners sat in the shade of an apple orchard. Nearby, soldiers waited in the sun.

Meade watched General Newton approach from the other side of the trees. His black horse gleamed with sweat.

To make it go round, the stew was served in portions too stingy for Hancock's mighty appetite—Win eyed other men's plates with doglike interest—but there was cheese, hardtack, and a pile of boiled potatoes on a mess chest to serve as belly-fillers. And coffee for all. An orderly brought up a cracker box so Meade could have a seat.

"Well, gentlemen, this is fine," Meade said.

Gibbon took a plate from an attentive cook and delivered it to his guest. Meade had to restrain himself from downing it like an animal. He could not remember ever being so hungry.

He remembered something, something important, something he had forgotten. He looked around at the assembled generals. "Order the regiments and companies on provost guard to come up. We may need every man."

Hancock gave him a sideward glance. "You gave us that order this morning, sir."

Embarrassed, Meade blustered, "I . . . just wanted to be certain. If Lee comes on, we may need every man."

"I don't know," Hancock said. "I think he might not. Lot of dawdling over there. As if they just want to hold on to our attention. Old Marse Robert might be halfway back to Chambersburg, we wouldn't know the difference. Either that, or he's up to some damned trick. He's taking too much time, it isn't like him."

"He attacked late yesterday, too," Newton put in.

Hancock ignored his fellow corps commander. "That gun line out there could mean any number of things. Not necessarily some kind of madcap attack."

Win had spoken Meade's own doubts, yet, hearing them from another changed his mind again.

"No. He'll come at the center. At you. Hunt's convinced."

"I think so, too," Newton said. Subordinate to Hancock, Gibbon stayed out of it.

Meade returned to his stew, each spoonful a joy in the mouth.

"Hunt's always convinced of something," Hancock said. "If not of this, then of that. I've never met a man who's so cocksure."

"Hunt knows what he's about," Newton said. "The man was splendid yesterday. From everything I've heard."

"Nonsense," Hancock snapped. He was not a man who liked to

be contradicted. Infinitely brave, "Hancock the Superb" was also Hancock the bullheaded. "Nonsense," he repeated. "Hunt would've lost at least a half-dozen batteries if it hadn't been for us rescuing his guns. I had to send men out to take them back. His cannon jockeys just left them, walked away."

That was untrue. Hunt and his men had done wonders. And they'd paid a high price in blood. Meade wished to defend Hunt, but was too weary. Chewing a shred of antediluvian rooster, he turned to his cavalry chief to change the subject:

"Sharpe tells me Stuart's back with Lee."

Pleasanton growled his response: "Fool should've been with Lee's army from the start. Off on a romp. Jolly old Jeb Stuart, the sashaying cavalier. What did he accomplish, tell me that? Captured some wagons. Horse's ass, if you want my opinion."

His cavalry's performance at Brandy Station notwithstanding, Pleasanton still felt a sting at the mention of Stuart's name.

Meade set his empty plate on the trampled grass.

"Cheese ain't bad," Hancock told him. "Have some. It's on John's mess bill."

But Meade could eat no more. He put himself all too vividly in the place of the hundreds of nearby men waiting with empty bellies for the battle. He nearly spoke of the matter again, but decided it helped no one to spoil the mood. Which was testy enough.

Gibbon handed round cigars. Meade accepted one. That was all right. He would not have minded a brandy, either. He had reached the point at which strong drink would not have put him out, but would have jolted him back to life.

I just have to get through this day, he told himself again.

"Lively morning over on the right," Newton said.

Meade nodded. There had been some bad moments early on, out past the heights the locals called Culp's Hill. But the Confederate gains had been redeemed and now that flank was quiet.

"Win," Meade said abruptly, "I don't believe you'll be needed on the left today. Forget commanding the wing. Just see to your corps, the center needs all your attention. If Lee does come on—don't argue wth me now—John will have his hands full with his division."

Hancock stiffened, but swiftly came around. He was a model

soldier, for all his swagger, and knew what made sense and what didn't on a battlefield. He puffed his cigar and nodded his acceptance.

The conversation swooned. They were all exhausted men. If they had eaten better, they'd slept far less than their soldiers.

Flies swirled around the remnants of the meal.

The recognition of how well he understood these men—men so like himself, for all their differences—penetrated the haze afflicting Meade. Everyone was fighting to stay awake until the fight began. But they'd come back to life with the first shots, their minds saber sharp and bodies pulsing with energy. It was just the way it worked.

Expressing what each of them felt, Hancock declared, "Bobby Lee needs to shit, or get off the pot."

With a champion effort, Meade got to his feet. It was time to ride the lines again, to stop by his headquarters, to see that everything remained in order, that there'd been no acts of folly in his absence.

What was Lee doing?

"General Gibbon," Meade announced in his most majestic voice, "the finest cooks of Society Hill could not compete with your mess. My compliments, sir."

Gibbon rose and bowed. For a moment, they stood at a Philadelphia ball. "The honor's entirely ours, General Meade! I'll tell Cook we shan't hang him."

Win got over his grump and snorted a laugh. "My goddamned compliments, too, John. Next time, though, chill the champagne. . . ."

Meade's orderly brought up his horse. The animal lurched toward the scraps of crackers on the mess chest. Meade grabbed the bridle and yanked the animal back. Bad enough for the men to see their generals eating like hogs while they went hungry, but let them see a horse get at the vittles and there'd be a mutiny . . . as well as a defining story of the battle in every newspaper.

"Well, now that General Meade's demoted me again," Win announced, "I think I'll have another look at my guns, make sure Hunt hasn't got them aiming at each other." He touched his fingers to the brim of his hat.

"I'll ride the line, then I'll be at my headquarters," Meade said. As if suspected of truancy, he felt a childish need to declare his whereabouts. He still was not fully comfortable lording it over these men who had been his peers mere days before.

He saw now that he could do it, though. He *could* command this army. He had not failed the test.

The plate of stew had helped him more than a fresh corps would have done.

He saw Gibbon watching him, judging him.

Meade spurred his horse into the gap between two waiting regiments.

The day had grown eerily quiet while they were eating. The stillness of noon, much multiplied. How could thousands of soldiers be so quiet? Even the flies on his horse were deathly still. The sun itself seemed to have stopped. As it had for Joshua.

On whose side would the Lord God be this day?

The men had not been given their daily bread. But he had eaten his. He hoped it would not bring bad luck. Soldiers had to eat. And their hunger was, at least in part, his fault. He had brought up every reserve, every gun, all his ammunition, at the cost of crowding all else from the roads, certain the battle would end and the men could be fed. But what if it didn't end? Or ended badly?

His horse neared a redheaded boy with a supplicant face. Was he going to beg for food? The lad saluted, expression confused, perhaps crazed by the heat.

What was Lee up to?

As Meade reached the crest of the ridge, with the spectacle of his army stretched out before him, a cannon boomed over on the Confederate lines.

His heart and mind quickened: *This is it. It's starting.*

The army tensed around him.

But the ponderous silence returned. To a world smothered by the heat. One shot, then no more. One shell, on an obscure trajectory. Then nothing.

The wait was horrid.

The sun had not stood still, of course. The first afternoon shadows were creeping east, slight but certain.

Another gun sounded from the opposing lines, followed quickly by a second round. The shells flew over Meade's lines and burst in the rear.

And then came pandemonium.

TWENTY

July 3, Early Afternoon

Hancock's fury swelled more swiftly than his horse could gallop. He had already torn into Hazard, his corps artillery chief, but decided he had to see to things himself.

Corps flag following closely behind his stirrup, he led a staff contingent forward, racing between explosions that splashed gore, careless of the dismembering solid shot. Most of the shells screamed overhead to play Hell in the rear, but enough struck home to make it hot for his regiments: The howls and shrieks of men, horses, and ordnance quickened the air. Soldiers clawed the earth in search of safety.

The men of the 69th Pennsylvania lay sardined behind their wall, driven to pack together by animal instinct. Poorly disciplined off the line, the Irish 69th was fierce in battle, a regiment that gave its officers headaches, then redeemed itself with maddened valor. Hancock knew the men would show their pluck, once they caught the stink of Rebel assholes. Other units were hardly blooded, though, or had new brigade commanders yet unproven.

Beyond the pack of Philadelphia micks and an idle gun section, a shell tossed bodies and bits into the air.

"Goddamned sonsofbitches," Hancock barked.

A few feet short of riding down young Cushing, Hancock yanked back on his reins. Oblivious, the lieutenant stood beside his guns, watching the enemy batteries through his spyglass.

Alerted by his first sergeant, the boy looked up at the general in the saddle. Cushing was beardless and pink-faced. West Point was turning out infants, officers who'd barely learned to wipe their own asses. Hancock doubted that the lieutenant had ever had a woman, or knew which part of himself went between her legs.

"Cushing, why the Hell aren't your guns firing?" he shouted to be heard about the din. "D'you think they're decorations for Mother's garden?"

The lieutenant wore a guileless look of a sort Hancock disliked. Boys. Damned boys.

"General Hunt said to hold our fire, sir. To conserve ammunition."

"To Hell with that horse's ass. You take commands from *me*, not some fucking gun monkey."

His language startled Cushing. Evidently more than the bombardment.

Good. The boy needed startling. Hancock had polished his skills at speaking to solders of every rank over many a year.

"Yes, sir. . . ."

"Well, jump to it! Get your guns into action. The men need to know we won't let those buggers shit on us. *Move!*"

The baby-cheeked lieutenant stood his ground a moment longer: "Sir, I have to conserve ammunition for their charge."

"Shut your goddamned mouth and see to your guns, boy. Or you'll face a court-martial the minute this turd-fight's over."

Expression fiercer and stronger than Hancock expected, the lieutenant collapsed his telescope, saluted, and turned to his battery, shouting by-the-book gunnery commands.

Tugging his horse about, Hancock called to an aide: "Tell Hays to get his batteries into action. I'll see to the left myself."

Behind him, he heard Cushing's number one gun fire, followed quickly by the number two.

Hunt was a puffed-up mechanic, a creature of the staff, with no proper sense of soldiers and their needs. You couldn't expect men to lie there and take such a pounding without their own guns speaking on their behalf. Hunt needed a cannon rammed up his ass.

A shell struck beside a caisson, detonating the contents and hurling fragments of metal, wood, and horseflesh in every direction. The team horses that had not been killed outright leapt and kicked, showering blood about them and neighing in agony, struggling against their harness.

He did not have to stop at every battery. Most had commenced

firing at the report of Cushing's guns. But Hunt had his loyalists among the artillery officers.

Shells struck in quick succession, stitching through the waiting ranks of soldiers. The battering threatened to crush morale among the weaker regiments. Hancock felt he had no time to lose.

Calling up another courier, he waved a hand toward the nearest troops—who watched him in both admiration and terror. "Find their colonel. Tell him to move his men just over the ridgeline, but keep them ready. The same goes for the other second-line regiments. Just behind the crest, not another inch."

The courier snapped a salute and spurred his horse.

Smoke thickened over his gun line now, as action by section and battery stiffened the mood. If his guns hit nothing, so be it. The men had to have confidence, that was the thing. Soldiers liked the noise of their own cannon.

Beyond his flank, Newton's guns began firing, too.

Good.

But as Hancock rode through a break in the rising smoke, he saw that not a single gun on the far left flank had opened. Hunt had at least forty guns lined up down there. It was intolerable.

Digging in his spurs so fiercely his horse whinnied and leapt, Hancock was ready to burst like a shell himself. George Meade had made solid work of bringing up the army, Hancock gave him that. But Meade put too much trust in that bugger Hunt, who saw the world through the aperture of a gun-sight. Now it was time for Meade to keep out of the way, and high time for Hunt to get his damned comeuppance.

The shrinking retinue pounded into the low ground. The army's reserve artillery stood at the ready, doing nothing. Down where they couldn't see one Confederate gun and would serve no purpose until the Rebs were on top of them.

Hancock charged toward the first battery commander he could identify.

"Your battery taking a holiday, Captain? What the Hell's going on here?"

"We're delaying our reply," the captain said with provoking calm. "General Hunt's orders, sir."

"Hunt's not in command of this goddamned line. *I* am. And I

order you to open fire. Immediately. Or I'll have you charged with cowardice, you piss-ant."

That caught the captain's interest. He glared at Hancock, who remembered that, in fact, he no longer commanded the left wing. But that was a minor detail. George Meade would back him up.

"Give me a written order, General," the captain said. "And I'll open fire under protest."

Lieutenant Colonel McGilvery, another insolent sonofabitch and one of Hunt's pet creatures, trotted up.

As if intent on worsening the general insubordination, McGilvery spoke first to the battery commander, rather than to Hancock.

"What's the difficulty, Captain Hart?"

Before the artilleryman could reply, Hancock barked, "Why the Hell aren't these batteries firing, McGilvery? You taking a goddamned Mexican siesta? My men are going through Hell, and you're scratching your balls. . . ."

"General Hunt has a scheme of fires, sir. The time hasn't arrived for these guns to open. Your own guns are wasting rounds they're going to need."

"Don't you tell me how to run my guns, McGilvery. Just open fire, damn you. That's an order."

McGilvery refused to become flustered: "I take my orders from General Hunt, sir."

Hancock exploded, voice roaring over the racket back on his line. "I outrank Henry Hunt, goddamn it. And every whoreson cocksucker in the artillery. I *order* you to open fire."

"I must decline to obey the order, sir."

Hancock fought down an impulse to knock McGilvery out of his saddle.

"Put your guns into action, you sonofabitch."

An errant shell screamed overhead and disappeared behind them.

"They haven't got the range," McGilvery said matter-of-factly. "They don't even know these guns are here, sir, don't know what's waiting for them. General Hunt's orders were given to meet this very case, he's doing his best to support you."

Hancock snorted. "With silent guns. While you let the Reb artillery shit on my men." He saw that he was not about to change

McGilvery's mind, though. The man was a dry-docked sea captain from Maine, stubborn and useless.

There was going to be Hell to pay later, Hancock decided, but now he had to get back to his corps and his men. The Confederate bombardment had intensified, but it wouldn't last forever. Then they'd come on, a great goddamned gray mob. Old Meade had been right about that much. Meanwhile, his men had to see him, mounted and fearless.

"Your guns aren't worth a prayer book in a whorehouse," Hancock said. He pulled his horse around and rode back to the fight.

As Meade watched from the porch of his headquarters shanty, a dud shell struck a line of horses tied to a nearby rail. The impact gutted the beasts in a burst of gore.

Long bones cracked like rifle shots. Flesh flew.

In an instant, the line of staff mounts became a tangle of writhing meat. With shells screaming overhead, a new man on the staff plunged forward to put the beasts out of their misery. He shot the only unwounded horse in the head.

Explosions furrowed the earth of a nearby field, propelling grit over orderlies pulling down tents. Another shot pulped a line of corpses waiting for a burial detail. The Confederates had mistaken the range and most of their rounds spared the troops up on the line and the Union guns. But the barrage pounded the supply wagons staged in the low ground behind the headquarters, and panicked teamsters fought for a place on the crowded road that offered the only escape. Wagons careened and crashed. Some men just ran. Ammunition wagons stood abandoned, waiting for the shell that would ignite them. Amid spectacular wreckage, an ambulance burned.

A round of solid shot fanned Meade, inches away from killing him, and crashed into the house with a burst of splinters. Poorly fused, another shell pierced the attic. Two staff officers rushed out of the shanty, covered in dust but whole. Others, still inside, coughed and cursed as they gathered up their papers.

Meade had hoped to maintain his headquarters here, just behind the line, but the notion was suicidal. And he still had a day's work to do before he died. After stepping down from the porch

with studied calm, he walked past the slaughtered horses toward the road. One beast clung impossibly to life, eye bulging as it spewed blood.

A round shot tore off the front steps where he'd stood.

As the personnel of his headquarters scattered around him, Meade slowed his pace to set them an example. The truth was that he found it all exhilarating: Fear of bodily harm was not one of his weaknesses.

He smiled at what he saw next: A covey of staff men had taken shelter behind the rear wall of the shack. The old planks offered not the least protection and already had been splintered in two places, yet the soldiers and their officers crowded against them. Meade tried to rally their spirits with a tale from the Mexican War, but the effort at humor failed. He rued, again, that he lacked Hancock's way with soldiers.

An explosive shell—no dud this time—struck amid the horses of his bodyguard. The blood and meat splashed all the way to the shanty, slopping over the men who had huddled behind it.

Meade's chief of staff came up beside him, the last man to leave the cabin. Clutching a roll of maps, Butterfield opened his mouth, but Meade spoke first:

"This won't do. We'll try that barn down the way."

Their horses stood among those that had been spared. Mounting, Butterfield held on to the maps. Those officers and couriers who still had untouched mounts leapt to follow the generals, with the remainder of the staff coming after on foot.

We're hardly an example for the men up on the line, Meade told himself.

Down along the Taneytown road, two wagons warred for precedence, locking wheels, then breaking apart abruptly. One turned over on its side, narrowing the escape corridor.

A caisson waiting with Hunt's reserve exploded, triggering serial detonations. Meade cringed at the loss of ammunition.

Still, the men on the line were being spared, relative to what they might have suffered, had Lee's artillerymen been better shots. That was the thing that mattered in all this, that regiments in blue would be ready to stand and kill the best men Lee could muster.

He paused to order a company left on provost guard to go forward and rejoin their regiment. Delighted to get away from the worst of the shelling, the men went toward the crest at the doublequick.

At the barn, Butterfield spread the best map on the ground. Orderlies rushed to help, but the chief of staff told them to stay out of the way. Hooker man or not, Butterfield was giving all he had to his duties. Despite their personal friction, he wanted to win.

Meade waved up a captain, barking to be heard above the confusion: "Ride to General Slocum. Tell him the attack's coming at the center. He's to send another brigade to back General Hancock. And he's to hurry."

He could risk thinning the right now. He had already positioned reserves behind Hancock's line, ordering up brigades from various corps, but he wanted real depth. Lee had to meet blue wall after blue wall.

As the staff hurried to reorganize itself, a shell burst in the road. At first, Meade thought the only casualties were horses again. Then he saw Butterfield quivering on the ground, clutching his neck with fingers bright with blood. Another man lay still beside the map.

No place along the road would serve for headquarters work.

His son appeared. "Sir . . . General Slocum's headquarters is back on that hill there. He's just out of range, and he's got a signal station."

The boy was clearheaded, the mark of a true soldier. Meade felt a flash of pride.

He knelt to see how serious Butterfield's wound was. The man was conscious and would live, but his role in this battle was over. Meade wished him well, and went back to the war.

Bellowing to his staff to follow, he mounted again and led the way rearward through the rain of shells. He was determined not to lose control of the army as Hooker had at Chancellorsville, or as Burnside had done at Fredericksburg—where Meade's men had been forgotten under fire. Hancock, Newton, and the others would handle the coming charge. His purpose now was to care for everything else, to keep the great beast of the Army of the Potomac properly in harness and pulling obediently.

Spurring his mount, Meade outdistanced the men who served him. He rode past the wreckage of wagons and smashed gun carriages, past the corpses of men who'd imagined they were safely tucked away, past others bloodied and weeping, dazed or waving blankets to put out fires. The plight of the horses was nothing short of a massacre.

When he reached Slocum's hill, he didn't even dismount. He saw at once that the signal station could not reach his flag men back on the ridge, who had gone to ground. Exasperated, infuriated, and sweating like a slave, he cursed and kicked his horse back into a gallop, retracing his path through the torrent of death, mortified at the time he had just squandered.

He cared nothing for the stragglers in his path now, willing to ride down any man to return to a place where he could command his army. Unwilling, after all, to accept that his part was done, that the battle had passed to subordinates, he lashed his horse as if he meant to skin it.

Few wounded men staggered rearward. Initially, the observation pleased Meade, promising that Lee's guns had done little damage up on the line. Only after another minute of pounding toward the ridge amid bursting shells did it strike him that no wounded man would willingly leave the line and risk greater chances of death walking to the rear. The battle had gone topsy-turvy, its dangers upended.

He spotted a blue column on a course parallel to his own, quick-marching from Slocum's flank right through the bombardment. Turning his horse, he rushed toward the officer heading the column. It was General Shaler, bringing up his brigade.

Skipping the courtesies, Meade called, "Take your men over there, to Hancock's left. Head for that orchard."

As he turned to ride off again, a plump man in civilian clothes materialized, astonishingly careless of the shelling. He grasped Meade's bridle.

"Cheneral, dem solchers . . . dem solchers uff yours has took *mein* house for the woundit mens und made in *mein Garten* a graveyard. I make a claim on the government!"

Meade barely restrained himself from whipping the man with his reins. "You fool! You don't even know if you'll *have* a government after today. Get out of here, or I'll send you up to fight!"

Followed by his son, his flag, and the motley group of riders who had caught up with him, Meade rode straight for the crest of the ridge that trailed down from the cemetery.

He found himself facing a valley filled with smoke, with his own guns firing into dirty clouds. It surprised him that Hunt would waste so much ammunition.

He watched, appalled, as a section of guns limbered up and rolled to the rear.

"George! Ride over there and find out why those guns are leaving the line."

Guiding on Meade's flag, a courier found him.

"From General Warren, sir. He says it's urgent."

"Where's Warren now?"

"The first round hill, sir. He's been trying to signal, but there's too much smoke."

Meade took the note and unfolded it. Warren's impression merely confirmed his own: The Union gunnery only obscured whatever Lee was doing. Lee could launch an attack behind the smoke.

George returned. He blurted out, "The lieutenant said he's out of ammunition, that's why he pulled back his guns."

"God*damn* it," Meade said. "George, I need you to find General Hunt. Send riders to both ends of the line. And to the rear. *Find Hunt.* I want our guns to cease firing, this is pointless."

"Yes, sir." His son rode off into the acrid fog.

Meade felt his eyes sting as he watched the boy go, with the smoke only partly to blame.

Distant points of light blinked and disappeared again. Now and then, a shell struck among his waiting regiments, but most still howled overhead. It was all a waste, every bit of it.

He wondered what was happening across those fields.

Wasn't a battle a beautiful thing, as lovely as May in a meadow? Gallagher mocked any nearby man who fidgeted, twitched, or cowered. As for those who fainted in the heat or fell to raving, 'twas weak they were and worthless, undeserving.

"Just lie steady, dearies, and take in the pretty show they've all got up for yiz." He laughed like the devil over a priest gone bad. "Ye may never see another such day, if ye live to see any at all."

"Jaysus, Sergeant Gallagher," Walsh complained, "an't it noisy enough without your catterwawling?"

"Walsh, me dearie, ye're needin' to put them ladylike nerves back under their darling skin." He laughed, then called, "Can't anyone give us a song? For I'm weary o' the tune the Rebs are playing."

"He's crazy as English George," Lonergan declared. "Nothing to eat for two damn days, the world's coming to an end on every side of us, and the man wants a minstrel show. He's crazy, he's mad . . ."

"That's why the great, high powers made me a sergeant," Gallagher said. "Because only the devil himself could master the likes o' ye. Reilly, give us a song, then, for the day's gone drab and dreary, for all the racket."

A simple lad with a succulent voice, Reilly dutifully tried to lift a tune. Naught but a croak emerged. Canteens were as empty as their bellies, and every man's throat was scorched with the taste of powder.

Gallagher gave them a bit of the quiet then, if quiet there could be amid the goings-on. He marveled over the foolishness of the colonel and the major, prancing about on their hind legs to show they weren't fearful, behaving like idiot Englishmen. Gallagher saw no point in risking death without a fair chance of killing the other man first. But officers had their own queer notions about what inspired the lads, all high thoughts and nobility, when Gallagher knew damned well and enough that nothing roused the boys like drawing blood. Give them some lovely killing to do, and a fair enough chance to do it, and every lad among them would stand proper.

Raising himself to see what he could see, he found precious little on view to the regiment's front, naught but smoke fit for smuggling contraband and flashes bright and gone again, quick as a sleeve-slithered ace in shebeen poker. He turned then to see what was on beyond his own lot, and spied the boy-lieutenant still by his guns, blood-smeared and clasping a rag against his shoulder. The lad's face was foul as a navvy's with burnt-up powder, but pretty enough even now to come to grief, if ever he took himself for a dockside stroll. The lad called out adjustments to elevation in a voice that struggled to sound like a grown man.

Gallagher knew the type, he did, for he had slain such a lad all

those years ago, a sweet young man who was not meant for this world. So unsuspecting they were, all doomed by virtue.

Gallagher only hoped the lieutenant would last until his guns were truly needed, for he did like to watch the application of canister.

Hunt wished Meade were present in the cemetery. Hancock had made a mess of things, bullying his batteries to open early and blast away. The Rebels were firing at a breathless rate, excited Union gunners responded in kind, and the duel had already lasted a good half hour. Lee's ammunition stocks would be running down, but so were his own. And Hunt knew his guns were vital to the defense. It was all so . . . so damned amateurish.

"This is idiocy," Hunt declared. "I'd fail any gunnery student who made such a shambles."

Just below the vantage point where he stood beside Ollie Howard, guns fired by section, spitting flame and recoiling between the headstones. The noise was numbing, even to an artilleryman.

Empty sleeve dangling, General Howard shook his head and asked, "What do *you* make of it, Osborn?"

The Eleventh Corps artillery chief peered through the man-made fog, reading the twinkle of Confederate muzzle blasts. "I agree with General Hunt, sir. Either they think their fires are doing a lot more damage than they are . . . or they're keeping it up just to drain off our ammunition."

"Of course, they want to exhaust our ammunition," Hunt said. "It's common practice before a charge. I taught the fools that much, at least."

"Not proud of your former students today, Henry?" General Howard asked.

Hunt didn't respond, but stared into the smoke.

"I wonder," Major Osborn said, "if we mightn't put one over on them?"

Hunt turned.

"Suppose we just stopped firing?" Osborn continued. "By the time word passed down our lines to cease fire, they'd assume we were running out of ammunition. Or that they'd silenced our guns."

Hunt lifted an eyebrow as he looked at Howard. He often

wondered what old Ollie would do if he lost the other arm. Grim thought.

"Could work, you know," Howard offered.

Yes, it could. Trailing off your fires was an age-old trick. Hunt was miffed that it hadn't occurred to him first. He'd just been so damned furious at Hancock.

"How much ammunition do you have left, Tom?" Hunt asked. "Right here. In those battery caissons."

Osborn took Hunt's point and said, "Plenty left to tear a charge to bits. If we stop firing soon."

"And your men won't quit their posts?" Hunt asked cautiously. "If Lee's fire keeps up after ours has stopped?"

Howard's expression showed that he felt the slight on his corps' reputation. The tee-totaling abolitionist let it pass.

Osborn shook his head. Decisively. "I'll let them rest by their guns. They won't run. I guarantee it."

"Then stop," Hunt said. "Immediately. Have your batteries cease firing." He looked at the Eleventh Corps commander. "If General Howard approves, of course."

"We could all do with less noise," Howard said.

Osborn took off at a run, nearly knocking over Howard's Polish colonel, who limped along like a cripple and looked ghastly.

Howard confided, "I've told Kriz he looks like a beggar sent out from the Court of Miracles. He didn't understand the reference, I fear."

Hunt made no sense of it, either. But it made sense to stop firing, then see what Lee's boys made of it. He'd have to ride down along the line and give the order himself to make it stick, though.

He believed Meade would approve. If he didn't, Hunt was willing to take full responsibility and bear the consequences. Winning the battle was all that mattered now.

First Lieutenant Alonzo Cushing, commanding Battery A, Fourth U.S. Artillery, felt blood slime under his uniform. The fragment had torn through his shoulder. The pain made him want to cry out, but bearing it was the manly thing to do. Many a man around him endured a worse wound.

And then there were the dead sprawled by his guns.

He raised his telescope again, one-handed, peering into a thick gray sea in the hope of following the trail of his next shot.

"Number two gun! Fire!" he shouted from a parched throat.

As its muzzle flared, the cannon bucked, then settled. Devoured by the smoke, the round's impact escaped him.

"Lieutenant . . . you have to go to the rear," First Sergeant Fueger told him.

"I'm fine. Just see that the volunteers are swabbing properly."

Ever obedient, Fueger turned back to his gun crews, their depleted ranks filled out with men culled from nearby regiments—many of them Irish, moon-faced, short, and brawny. Most had served around cannon long enough to grasp the drills. And they were brave, willing to stand in the fury while others cowered.

Cushing had done as Hancock ordered, opening counter-battery fire on the Rebels. But he did not fire madly. Instead, he tried to see that each round had a target, at least an approximate one. But as things worsened, with one gun out of action and ever more gunners maimed or lying dead, it was a struggle to keep men from yanking the lanyards before their guns were ready.

Blood coursed down his chest. Earlier, he had envied the enlisted men their freedom to strip off tunics and undergarments. Now he was glad he could not see his wound.

A Rebel shell fell short, exploding in the field beyond the wall. Fine specks of dirt reached Cushing, despite the distance.

Don't think about the wound, he told himself. *Concentrate on what you have to do.*

He feared the surviving corporals and gunners were cutting their fuses too long. But he couldn't tell for certain. And he had to limit his movements just to stay upright.

Suddenly, unaccountably, the smoke put him in mind of a fog at West Point, a very specific fog, when he had marched off some forgotten infraction and missed the New York City ball at which he had hoped to kiss a girl whose name he had now lost. He had never wanted anything more in his life than to kiss her lips, just once. It had seemed the summit of all human ambitions. But the opportunity slipped away as he paced back and forth in the fog, and now she was just a ghost amid the slaughter.

He snapped back to his duties, sharply aware of the soldiers

cowering behind the wall and stretch of fence—scant protection against explosive shells. His guns had to be ready, when the test came. For their sake.

How much longer could the duel go on? The roar seemed to have lasted hours. He had husbanded all the ammunition he could and called up extra canister, but his long-range rounds were swiftly running out. How could the Rebels keep up such a fire?

He tried to raise his glass to his eye, but found himself too weak.

Turning to call a command to First Sergeant Fueger, he flew, spun, twisted, encompassed by fiery heat and colossal noise.

His thoughts collapsed. He flailed.

The pain . . . was huge . . . unimaginable . . .

He wasn't dead, wasn't dead. He curled upon himself, clutching his belly and private parts with a frantic hand. A wet mess had escaped the cloth of his uniform.

His sight came back, his hearing. Screams. All around him, screams.

The pain was vast and thick. He didn't want to cry, wouldn't cry, didn't know if he was crying.

He twisted on the ground, which only worsened the pain. He stilled himself, but that was awful, too. He pawed his exploded belly.

Fueger knelt over him, looking down. The first sergeant's face was dark against the smoke, but his shadowed features still betrayed his horror.

"I'm . . . all right," Cushing muttered.

The first sergeant only stared.

". . . to my feet . . . get me on my feet . . ."

"You can't, sir, you daren't. Don't get up. You can't."

"Help me." He struggled to lift himself, but his body moved oddly. Things went in improper directions. Meat slithered.

"Your . . . your innards . . . ," Fueger said.

Cushing tried to nod, didn't know if he succeeded, didn't even know what he meant. He felt his guts spilling out. It was an impossible, unimaginable thing.

"Get me up."

A big man, Fueger heaved him to his feet. Cushing held his abdomen together as best he could. He did not dare look down.

"Hold me up!"

"Sir . . . you're . . ."

"Hold me up. That's an order." He told himself the pain was easier to bear now that he was standing. It was a lie.

Was the fire slackening?

Surely, on his own gun line . . . were the other batteries out of ammunition? Had they been so wasteful? What would they do when the Rebels came? What was happening?

". . . stopped . . . firing . . ."

"Yes, sir. We've been ordered to stop." He renewed his grip on Cushing. The first sergeant was weeping. "We've got to get you to the rear, sir."

"No." He almost added, "There's no point."

A horse. General Gibbon. Staring down.

"Cushing! Go to the rear. Good God, man. Sergeant, take him to the rear!"

"No," the boy cried. "I won't leave my guns. Not now."

Gibbon appeared surprised that the man before him could summon such vehemence. Cushing felt his stare. Inspecting. What did the general see? A dead man? A fool? A boy? All Cushing knew was that he could not leave his guns.

Gibbon turned his head and rode away.

The fire began to slacken on the other side of the fields.

"They'll be coming now," Cushing said.

"Yes, sir. That they will."

Cushing remembered what he had to do: "Advance the guns!" he shouted. "Guns to the wall!"

Nothing happened. No man responded. They stared at him. At his belly, his crotch. Cushing still refused to look at himself.

He had learned to measure many things. But who could measure pain? It could only be expressed in astronomical degrees.

On the battery's flanks, soldiers scrambled to their feet, crowding up to wall and fence, preparing to take their revenge for what they'd endured.

"Advance the guns!" Cushing called out again.

"They can't hear you, sir," Fueger explained. "Your voice . . ."

"Then repeat my orders," Cushing said. "Stay with me, don't let me fall. Repeat my orders."

"Forward the guns!" Fueger bellowed, his big-man's voice a roar. "Guns to the wall, let's go! The lieutenant's still in charge here."

In the vastness of his pain, Cushing found a clear space. He learned that his legs still worked. It amazed him, pleased him, a wonderful gift. Pressing his hand against his leaking guts, he started forward, supported by the first sergeant, almost framed by the larger man. They went slowly. Cushing stood as erectly as he could manage.

He'd lost his hat. He regretted that.

"Just keep me on my feet," he told his first sergeant. "Whatever happens."

After the crews had manhandled his guns right up to the wall, settling them where they had splendid fields of fire, Cushing said:

"Load spherical case."

Blood and bowels overwhelmed his hand, oozing through his fingers, as desperate to escape as captive animals. His purpose in life had contracted now, from dreamed-of kisses and plans for a long, fine life to a fierce determination to do his duty.

TWENTY-ONE

July 3, Afternoon

O*n your feet!"*
The command echoed down through the regiment's sur-
viving officers. Blake and his men rose up amid the trees. Here and
there a soldier, weakened by wounds or the heat, collapsed after
struggling to stand. Thrust into command of the 26th North
Carolina, Major Jones had scoured the nearby hospitals, bringing
back every one of the regiment's soldiers who could walk. Most
came willingly enough, eager to rejoin their comrades, or ashamed
to appear reluctant. Blake figured the 26th's numbers had been
lifted to three hundred men.

They weren't all going to impress the Yankees. One man in two
wore a bandage tanned by the dust, with some a downright patch-
work of bloody rags. Forming their lines, a soldier dressed to the
right with his one good eye, while the next man clutched his rifle
with one good arm.

Blake had kept a look out, hoping to find Hugh Gordon still
alive. But Hugh did not appear.

Major Jones walked down the lines, inspecting his army of inva-
lids and survivors. Knock Jones wasn't a talkative man and said
even less than usual. When he realized that one boy with a swad-
dled head couldn't see well enough to recognize him from three
feet away, Knock sent the lad rearward. But the boy was the only
one who was dismissed.

"Old Knock don't like this at all. No, sir, he don't," Cobb mut-
tered. "*He* knows what's a-coming."

"What the dickens they waiting on?" Charley Campbell asked in
a dried-out voice. "Why don't they just git it over?"

The thunder of the guns had dropped off sharply. Hundreds of

men checked their weapons, rustling about in dappled light and shade, tapping empty canteens, or calling defiance at Yankees who could not hear them. Blake knew each man was gorging himself on his thoughts, whether of the impending ordeal or of loved ones, regrets or dreams. Lying under the artillery fire had been Hell itself, but standing and waiting in the close air was worse.

Lives crammed into moments.

Blake recalled things he'd wanted, but nothing he'd truly loved. Not since his mother's death. He had wanted Lenore, prized her, but love had not figured into it, he saw that now. It had been all pride and some body-wanting. Not love as the word was meant. Another girl would have done as well, or better.

Better.

He wondered, for the ten-thousandth time, what had driven his father to a drunkard's fate. Why was the love of his mother insufficient to turn a man's heart from a bottle? And how had his father been able to care so little for him that he preferred freezing to death to raising a son? What devils had got at him? For all the disgrace his father had brought upon them, for all his wildness, he had still been known as a Bible-reading man, if not a Bible-living one. Had he struggled with sulfurous demons, only to fail? Or had he just been heartless and self-given? Those questions would never be answered, whether Blake survived to ask them again or not. But those were the matters that had shaped his life, that had deformed it.

Cobb had been right, too right: He, Thomas Fox Blake, had relished the wrongs done to him, real or imagined, instead of embracing all that was right in his life, all he had been granted. Was he his father's son, merely turned to other vices? It was a hard thing to ponder on such a day.

The air stank of blown powder, of death-rot and shit, of sweat. Yet, as the smoke rose and faded, a magnificent sky reappeared, burned pure by the sun. It was inhumanly beautiful.

Glory be to God, Blake thought unwillingly. The words burst upon him. Insistent. Unreasonable. Invincible. *Glory be unto Him.* Even if all of religion were a fable, he saw now that it was a needed thing. The truth ground into him: Whether God was real or a lie, God gave. Had his father been just like him, unable to bear the gift? Were both of them born to see darkness amid the light?

Blake thought he understood where he had strayed: He'd thought too much on what men did to God, and that had poisoned him.

Shells had torn pathways through the branches, leaving pale wounds on the trees. Spared leaves shivered, moved by the breath of angels. Dark and pale, dark and pale, their flesh glistened in the sun as they rode the air. Beyond that green infinity of leaves, the sky remained rendingly blue. No stain of black smoke defiled it now.

It struck Blake that only an intimate knowledge of horror let a man grasp the power of redemption. Nor was it a matter of eternity, but of the here and now, of overcoming the trials of this life, not some candy-apple immortality of wings, white robes, and somnolence. Redemption belonged to the earth, it was proffered to the hand that held the sword, not the quivering sheep. Terror afflicted Abraham, not Isaac: The dread of the deed had been with the old and knowing, not the innocent. And when the angel of the Lord reached down to stay Abraham's hand, the sky to which he raised his awful eyes must have been one such as this, pure above the abyss of mortality. The angel had saved Abraham: The spared life of his son was incidental. The killers quickened God's interest, not the innocent, since the innocent could never know His power. His clemency was not for the pure of heart. Why give, where there was no need?

Had his father been Abraham? Blake could not see it, not exactly. But the notion hovered, a persistent summer fly.

Glory be to God! He gave all men this sky. If they had the eyes to see it. The world seemed a place Blake had never truly known.

"Bayonets!"

The men of the 26th North Carolina joined metal to metal, clanging, rattling, grunting as they locked their blades in place. More men dropped, some victims of the heat and murderous thirst, others surely feigning. A few of the wounded men had had enough. The miracle was in how many stood to go forward.

"If they don't get a move on, I'm like to piss my pants," Charley Campbell said.

"You're like to piss 'em soon enough, either way," Cobb told him.

Charley reared up. "Damn you, Cobb. You and me are like to have us a meeting, this is over."

Grinning, Cobb sang the word of Charles Wesley, in a tenor

startlingly pure: *"Soldiers of Christ arise . . . and put your armor on . . ."*

No other voice took it up. Cobb dropped the melody, cackling. But even his gutting-knife humor had a hollowness.

Except for random shots, the artillery on both sides had plain given up. What *were* they waiting for? If there was a right time to go, it was now. Before the Yankees could gather themselves again.

Colonel Marshall rode up and leaned from the saddle to confer with Knock Jones. Marshall was another fine-faced boy whose birth had placed him over other men.

"Got some nerve," a voice said to Blake's rear, "sending a no-good Virginian to command a brigade's all North Carolina men."

"He ain't a no-good, Jimmy Marshall ain't," another man responded. "But he *is* a damned Virginian. Give you that."

"He don't get down off that horse, once'n we get out there, he's going to be a *dead* Virginian. They all think they're going to impress themselves some ladies by getting killed brave and dandy." The speaker snorted a hate-this-whole-world laugh. "Boys, *I* know a lady or two I'd like to impress with something else entirely. . . ."

"Jesus Christ," Charley Campbell said, "everybody sounds like Cobb now."

Blake sensed a change in the atmosphere and alerted. Well to the right, there was movement, something big and animal, amid the greenery.

General Pettigrew trotted up to Colonel Marshall and Major Jones. The general wore an immaculate uniform and appeared excited, high-strung. Blake thought he caught the name "Pickett," spoken in a tone of urgency.

Knock Jones shook his head at something. The major's expression was dutiful. And black.

Cobb leaned close to Blake.

"Listen here, Quaker," the little man whispered. He stopped himself, then started afresh: "Tom . . . you listen to me now. Ain't no use in playing the fool today, it ain't going to make no difference. . . ."

Caught in radiant sunlight, General Pettigrew rose up from his saddle, lifting his sword. "For the honor of the good old North

State," he called. His voice was high and elegant, forced into strength. "Forward!"

Colonel Marshall turned in the saddle, scanning his new command a final time. "For the North State! For*ward*!"

Jones and the company officers repeated the command.

In the distance, a band played "Dixie."

Why didn't Pickett come on? Why was he dawdling?

Alexander stood along his gun line, alternately seeking paths through the smoke with his field glasses and turning to see if Pickett's men had appeared.

The last note he had scrawled to Pickett had read, "For God's sake come quick . . . or I can't support you." He had noted the time of the dispatch: one thirty-five.

Ten minutes had passed. He had fired long past his own deadline. Ammunition chests were draining rapidly. Either encouraged by the fading Union fires, or out of shot and shell, many of his own batteries had stopped firing. Without orders.

Where was Pickett?

Instead of the Virginian and his men, Longstreet appeared, a black-miened man on a black horse. At the height of the artillery duel, Alexander had watched him ride calmly through the fields behind the gun line, showing himself to the men waiting in the trees, exposing himself with no regard for his safety, an inspiring figure, daring the Yankees to kill him, almost as if he would have welcomed death.

Longstreet got down from the saddle. His expression was as fixed as that of a corpse.

Alexander reported: "Sir, the enemy have withdrawn their guns from the center. Most of them, I think. We gave them Hell."

Longstreet said nothing, but only stared. His eyes were dreadful, those of a preacher abandoned to Satan's mercy.

"We can get off to a right fine start," Alexander continued. "But General Pickett must come up, or I won't be able to support him the way I'd like." Wincing in anger at his next thought, the artilleryman continued, "I had nine guns held back as a reserve, to go out with him. But they disappeared. During the firing."

Longstreet spoke at last: "I didn't know you'd kept a reserve."

"I wanted to surprise you, sir. To give you a nice surprise. I meant for those guns to roll out ahead of Pickett. Flying artillery."

"Well," Longstreet said, "sounds like they flew, all right."

Neither man smiled.

The corps commander sniffed the air like a coon dog and faced the Yankees. The smoke was easing. The distance to the Union lines looked vast.

Longstreet squinted and leaned forward with his shoulders, as if a few gained inches might let him see all. "Are those fresh batteries coming up?"

Alexander hastily raised his field glasses. But Longstreet spoke again before he could find the spectral guns.

"Go and halt Pickett. Stop him right where he is. And replenish your ammunition."

Alexander's innards froze. Despite the oven heat behind the guns. "Sir . . . we don't *have* more ammunition. Not enough. We near emptied the trains last night. There is no more. And even if we had it, it would take hours to bring it up. Meade could bring up more, faster. Now's our only chance, we have to strike while the iron's hot."

Longstreet's features furrowed above his beard.

"I don't want to make this attack. I believe it will fail." The general shook his head with funereal slowness. "I don't see any way it can succeed." He turned hurt eyes to Alexander again. "I would not make it even now. But General Lee has ordered it and expects it."

Again, Alexander felt an unfair responsibility shoved toward him. Did Longstreet want him to agree? Was that it? He believed he had done great harm to the Union guns, that opportunity beckoned. And when he had sounded out Pickett in midbombardment, the noise of the gunnery had excited the Virginian, who had been ablaze with enthusiasm and like to break his leash.

Now Longstreet had shocked him. And Pickett would not come up.

Alexander feared to say a word. For the attack, or against it. Playing for time, he took out his watch and clicked open the cover.

It was two o'clock.

Red banners waving, Pickett's first rank of soldiers emerged from the trees.

* * *

As he led his brigade forward, Dick Garnett whistled one of his favorite tunes, "Willie Brewed a Peck of Malt." His lips didn't shape a carrying sound—he hadn't the breath for that—but it helped him stay in the saddle. He'd been sick as an Injun in a smallpox year, but had got down from his ambulance wagon to mount his horse and go forward. He was not about to let his brigade make this attack without him, not with Jackson's charges after Kernstown still in the wind, but he knew he was too weak to go afoot.

The heat threatened him with the dizzies, but he kept his horse in hand. He rode between his first rank and the second, filling a lane between regiments with his staff. Wherever he looked he saw his splendid men, dressing their lines as they marched into the open, their ranks as straight as their uniforms were ragged. Freed of the shade in the groves, their bayonets shone like a fence of polished silver.

Garnett felt himself to be father and brother to all of them. He had always been that way around his soldiers, in the old days when his boys had worn blue coats, and now, in their dirt-proud, tatterdemalion glory. Pondering their fates could wet his eyes.

As the brigade divided to sweep around the guns, Porter Alexander rode up beside him.

"How do, Porter?" Garnett asked. "Ain't this fine?"

"Yes, sir."

"Hot, though."

"Not as hot as the Great Plains, sir. Remember?"

"Oh, I do. That I do." Garnett peered across the fields toward the Union lines. Distance and the sun turned regiments into caterpillars, bristling black, not blue. "These here fields are plains enough right now, though. I'll settle."

The young artilleryman at his side clearly had something weightier to say. But the words didn't come and Garnett didn't press him.

The Yankee guns held their fire. Were they low on ammunition? Sweet Jesus, let it be so. His entire brigade was in the open now, its soldiers helpless for the next three-quarters of a mile.

Behind him, his men unleashed a Rebel yell.

"Scare a Comanche and terrify a Sioux," Garnett said. "Ain't they something?"

"Yes, sir."

"Something chewing your tail, son? You look half-scalped."

"Just thinking about supporting fires, sir. I'd best get along. I need to move up some guns."

Garnett managed a not-quite smile. "Be glad of them."

They saw the first red-orange-gold muzzle flashes. The Union guns on the round hill to the right had a fine position, perfect for enfilading fire.

Nothing to be done about it.

The shells fell short, killing dirt. But the explosions quickened the pulse.

"See how long it takes 'em to get the range," Garnett said calmly. He steadied his horse. "Or if they mean to just let us walk into it." Leaning as far toward his younger companion as illness let him, his tone grew earnest. "You find the time, you might pass some words with Lo Armistead, he'll be coming up. Just say how-do. Lo's got fond memories of you, stories he tells. Kindly ones. About the three of us. Out there, those endless days." He smiled. "Never did care for the rattlesnakes, but the rest wasn't a bother. You go on back and find Lo. Give him my regards."

It struck Dick Garnett that his long days were at an end. All that had come before had pointed him here, toward this field, on this bright afternoon.

"Go on now," he told Alexander. "You have work to do."

The artilleryman snapped a salute and turned his horse. Unwilling or unable to say more.

The Union guns on the round hill fired again and batteries near the center went into action. The Yankee right—Garnett's left—remained silent, though. The cemetery bristled with guns, but not a one of them opened. The range was long, but they should have been firing on the attack's left flank by now.

He rode back to have a look at things.

And Dick Garnett was shocked by what he *didn't* see: One of Hill's divisions was supposed to advance beside Pickett, on the left. But all Garnett saw were idled guns and the torn trees to their rear.

He and Kemper were hanging out like an old Apache's teats. And Lo's men were already coming on to their rear.

* * *

As he led his brigade forward, Dick Garnett whistled one of his favorite tunes, "Willie Brewed a Peck of Malt." His lips didn't shape a carrying sound—he hadn't the breath for that—but it helped him stay in the saddle. He'd been sick as an Injun in a smallpox year, but had got down from his ambulance wagon to mount his horse and go forward. He was not about to let his brigade make this attack without him, not with Jackson's charges after Kernstown still in the wind, but he knew he was too weak to go afoot.

The heat threatened him with the dizzies, but he kept his horse in hand. He rode between his first rank and the second, filling a lane between regiments with his staff. Wherever he looked he saw his splendid men, dressing their lines as they marched into the open, their ranks as straight as their uniforms were ragged. Freed of the shade in the groves, their bayonets shone like a fence of polished silver.

Garnett felt himself to be father and brother to all of them. He had always been that way around his soldiers, in the old days when his boys had worn blue coats, and now, in their dirt-proud, tatter-demalion glory. Pondering their fates could wet his eyes.

As the brigade divided to sweep around the guns, Porter Alexander rode up beside him.

"How do, Porter?" Garnett asked. "Ain't this fine?"

"Yes, sir."

"Hot, though."

"Not as hot as the Great Plains, sir. Remember?"

"Oh, I do. That I do." Garnett peered across the fields toward the Union lines. Distance and the sun turned regiments into caterpillars, bristling black, not blue. "These here fields are plains enough right now, though. I'll settle."

The young artilleryman at his side clearly had something weightier to say. But the words didn't come and Garnett didn't press him.

The Yankee guns held their fire. Were they low on ammunition? Sweet Jesus, let it be so. His entire brigade was in the open now, its soldiers helpless for the next three-quarters of a mile.

Behind him, his men unleashed a Rebel yell.

"Scare a Comanche and terrify a Sioux," Garnett said. "Ain't they something?"

"Yes, sir."

"Something chewing your tail, son? You look half-scalped."

"Just thinking about supporting fires, sir. I'd best get along. I need to move up some guns."

Garnett managed a not-quite smile. "Be glad of them."

They saw the first red-orange-gold muzzle flashes. The Union guns on the round hill to the right had a fine position, perfect for enfilading fire.

Nothing to be done about it.

The shells fell short, killing dirt. But the explosions quickened the pulse.

"See how long it takes 'em to get the range," Garnett said calmly. He steadied his horse. "Or if they mean to just let us walk into it." Leaning as far toward his younger companion as illness let him, his tone grew earnest. "You find the time, you might pass some words with Lo Armistead, he'll be coming up. Just say how-do. Lo's got fond memories of you, stories he tells. Kindly ones. About the three of us. Out there, those endless days." He smiled. "Never did care for the rattlesnakes, but the rest wasn't a bother. You go on back and find Lo. Give him my regards."

It struck Dick Garnett that his long days were at an end. All that had come before had pointed him here, toward this field, on this bright afternoon.

"Go on now," he told Alexander. "You have work to do."

The artilleryman snapped a salute and turned his horse. Unwilling or unable to say more.

The Union guns on the round hill fired again and batteries near the center went into action. The Yankee right—Garnett's left—remained silent, though. The cemetery bristled with guns, but not a one of them opened. The range was long, but they should have been firing on the attack's left flank by now.

He rode back to have a look at things.

And Dick Garnett was shocked by what he *didn't* see: One of Hill's divisions was supposed to advance beside Pickett, on the left. But all Garnett saw were idled guns and the torn trees to their rear.

He and Kemper were hanging out like an old Apache's teats. And Lo's men were already coming on to their rear.

Nothing to be done about that, either.

As Garnett turned his horse to the front again, a shell struck close enough to sting him with dirt. A solid shot found the range and tore the first hole in his line.

Brigadier General Dick Garnett soothed his horse, breathed deeply to tame the dizzies, and went back to whistling.

They broke from the trees into light that was almost blinding. Blake gave no orders. None were needed. The few men remaining straightened the line on their own, proud despite all, mountain-born. For all his sly rebelliousness, Cobb marched as straight-backed as any man, rifle at right shoulder shift, lean face pointed forward like a weapon. Worried and determined, Charley Campbell's look was that of a farmer threatened with losing his land. But it was life, not land, that was at issue. Unless you counted the mile to be covered and the troop-lined ridge that rose across the fields.

Blake marched at their shoulders now. There were sergeants enough ready to hold back as line-closers. And it was more than that: He felt compelled to soldier right up front. There was no reason to it. Reason stood against it. Spite and kinship drove him, the blood brotherhood with even Cobb, with Charley Campbell, with the litter of their dead, with all the men who had marched, still marched, or would march with the regiment. Men who downright hated each other went forward side by side, this strange, iron-hard bond making kin of all.

The frail-hearted had already slipped away. The few who dropped out now were felled by the sun, by a heat so thick a man could almost grasp it and fold it over. No guns fired on them, not yet, but insects rose before their tramping feet, erupting in all directions. General Pettigrew urged them on, flirting about the lines on his dapple gray.

Their ranks parted as they engulfed the gun line—silent now, silent as death—and one cannoneer doffed his worn black hat and placed it over his chest as they passed by, the way hill folk did at buryings.

They straightened their lines again, ragged men with polished weapons, nothing between them and their enemies now but an awful stretch of emptiness and time.

"Steady, boys, steady!" The officer's admonition was unnecessary. But Blake understood the fellow's urge to speak. The sound of a man's own voice affirmed his life.

Barefoot or badly shod, they surged across the hot earth, breaking stocks of barley underfoot. And still the Union guns refused to open on them. The shelling that could be heard on the right did not reach their lines and belonged to the fates of others.

The land—which looked flat, but wasn't—reshaped itself. The front rank climbed out of a swale and Blake spotted double lines of soldiers—brown, gray, dirty white—well ahead and far off to the right. Pettigrew's unease back in the woods made more sense now. They'd gotten a late start, for whatever neglectful reason, whatever sheer damned Southernness, and had to come up on line with the other attackers.

Couldn't order double-quick and exhaust the men before they got to the fight, either. All the officers could do was to keep the men moving steadily, hoping they could negotiate the fences and ditches ahead without too much delay.

It was hard to see past Fry's front rank, but there looked to be a senseless gap as well, extending from Pettigrew's right flank hundreds of yards to the troops who had gone on ahead.

Cobb saw it, too.

"Goddamned nigger barn dance, that's what this is," he said.

The gap was officers' business, Blake decided.

A rail fence loomed. Skirmishing fire pecked. A man toppled, hurling his rifle.

"Push down that damned fence," Knock Jones hollered. "Just go right at it."

They did. Becoming one great, many-legged beast, the soldiers quickened their pace nearly to a run, slamming into the fence rails with bodies and the stocks and butts of rifles. The successful act of destruction raised spirits to an even higher pitch. They realigned their ranks without losing momentum and surged toward the retreating Yankee skirmishers.

Ahead and just to the left, farm buildings smoldered. Stubborn flames played peekaboo, taunting the men with the distance still to cover before they could reach the marker of those ruins, still not halfway to the Union lines.

The rhythmic swish of thousands of men advancing through the grain put Blake in mind of a scythe wielded by a giant.

A terrible harvest was coming, that was sure.

Yet, the sky remained a magnificent blue, not yet marred by fresh smoke. The only unkind color on the earth was that of the Yankees lined up on the ridge.

Nudged rightward by their officers, the men began to crowd and their lines to ripple. Maintaining parade-ground ranks was a hopeless chore while striding to overtake men with a good head start. Knock Jones and his handful of officers kept their regiment mostly in hand, but its strength was little more than a brace of companies. The Tar Heels to right and left bulged forward or lagged.

They knew what was coming, all of them did, and they wanted to get it done with. Despite the heat, they would have liked to run, knowing full well it would play them out before their time had come. Knowing a thing in the head was no longer enough. Body and soul had their own special ways of figuring.

And still the Union guns didn't open on them. Shelling lashed the brigades up ahead on the right, beyond that infernal gap, but Pettigrew's command felt nothing worse than the sting of withdrawing skirmishers.

Spontaneously, the men raised a Rebel yell. Earlier than was their habit. The purpose now was not to terrify the distant Yankees, but to bolster themselves. Every man, barefoot or shod, walked on needles now, on coals, on blades. Not one of them had ever made such a long attack, across fields that refused to end and against an enemy who never seemed to get any closer.

"Why ain't the damned Yankees shooting?" Charley Campbell asked the world. "All them goddamned guns they got up there."

In answer, the Union artillery opened fire.

TWENTY-TWO

July 3, After 2:00 P.M.

Lieutenant Colonel Freeman McGilvery waited. Rittenhouse opened first, firing from Little Round Top, exploiting his view of the battlefield and the long range of his rifled cannon. General Hunt rode off to guide arriving reserve batteries to the center and McGilvery cantered to higher ground to have a look at the Rebel advance for himself. His line of guns could have opened long before the attackers could see them. But he waited.

Batteries began firing from the First Corps and Second Corps sections of the line, hurling shot and shell westward.

McGilvery waited.

Through the unsullied corridor fronting his own batteries, he witnessed a thrilling spectacle: Advancing by brigades, at least a full Confederate division of ten thousand men or more marched relentlessly over the sun-swept fields, ranks dressed smartly and red flags catching the breeze. The attackers ignored the shells tormenting them, as if their lives were things of little consequence. Bayonets shimmered like scales on just-caught fish.

And McGilvery waited.

The Union fires bit, erasing bodies from existence and hurling others upward like spurned dolls. Immediately, soldiers from a following rank rushed forward to fill the gaps. Flags fell, only to rise again.

He glimpsed the flags of still more Confederate brigades off to the north, trailing the initial wave. At least ten thousand men were in that field, perhaps far more.

And he waited.

McGilvery had learned patience. The sea had taught him. Cap-

taining vessels out of Maine, destined for splendor and squalor in southern climes, he had grown accustomed to doing every thing in its proper order and at its proper time. As an elder seaman had warned him years before, "No matter how badly you want the land to come out to meet you sooner, it just plain won't."

His guns were about to become the reef on which the Rebels splintered. He had only to wait a little longer now.

With a whopping roar, Osborn's guns opened from the apex of the line, up in the cemetery. Osborn knew his trade, he did. Every one of his cannon would have been carefully aimed and ranged to devastate the brigades on the Rebel left.

McGilvery watched the Confederate right advance.

The Union line barked and billowed smoke. Except in front of McGilvery's hidden guns. He watched the Rebels dying bit by bit, unaware of how much death awaited them. Even their forward skirmishers appeared oblivious, their attention fixed on their counterparts in blue. He welcomed their ignorance, their confidence, and almost pitied them. Fine, brave soldiers they were, he gave them that: fine men led by fools.

After galloping back down to his gun line, he positioned himself at its center to see exactly what his batteries saw, waiting for the Confederates to crest the swell of ground that would expose them.

Their banners reported first to his waiting eye, followed quickly by a line of bayonets.

And they still didn't see him. Riveted by the blue lines to their front, the Johnnies just kept marching.

McGilvery held back for a last few seconds, until it became impossible to miss.

"*By battery! Fire!*" he shouted.

His subordinates repeated the order and the ground shook mightily. Even on horseback, McGilvery felt the tremors.

A combination of solid shot and spherical case gashed the Rebel lines at an angle, ripping through the front rank to the second, leaving oblique gaps as wide as roadbeds. Johnnies from the rear rushed forward to fill the holes again. The nearest brigade's line of advance was about to bring it within canister range.

The Rebs dipped into the trough of the creek at the bottom of

the swale, presenting his guns with densely clustered targets. His batteries massed their fires into the funnel, scouring the low ground. The result was a slaughter.

"Left batteries! Load case! Right batteries! Canister! Fire at will!"

Firing swiftly was no waste of ammunition now. The combination of targets, terrain, and range was a gunner's dream.

Anxious to judge his effect through the building smoke, Mc-Gilvery rode a few yards forward, advancing through the seam between two batteries.

His own rounds tore past him, savaging the air.

He saw his tormented enemies through a bright mist. Crowding together, they began to turn, herding away from his guns, unwilling to take the punishment. Their movement made no tactical sense at all: They were wheeling northward toward the Union center, executing the movement so close to the First Corps lines that regiments hastened into the fields to unleash volleys into their exposed flank. The Confederate maneuver appeared suicidal.

McGilvery was convinced that his guns had deflected the Rebels from their intended target, upsetting whatever plan they might have had.

Nor was he finished.

From his vantage point amid the headstones, Major Thomas Ward Osborn watched the Confederates advance. Calculating finely, he delayed calling his gun crews back to work for as long as he could: The men were blown from their labors in the heat and lay on the ground like corpses. And he had time, a little more of it. On his flank, the Rebels were either poorly coordinated or up to something odd, since they had emerged into the fields hundreds of yards behind the foremost brigades. Then there was that bizarre gap between the attack's two wings.

Osborn watched as the guns on Little Round Top opened at long range, followed by some of the batteries down in Hancock's stretch of the line. The effects were slight, a waste of powder that only encouraged the Rebels. The brown-dappled gray ranks advanced as smartly as grenadiers. Punched by the Union artillery, they closed ranks again without breaking their pace. He noted, too, that most of their officers were on foot, a sign that they understood the

odds they faced: Those who remained on horseback were no more than targets.

McGilvery held back, too, down in the far bottom. The old salt was prickly, but had become a professional. The Rebels were going to get a series of shocks, shellings so brutal Osborn winced to think of it, as if he were down there in those fields himself. He brooked no charity for the cause of the men he was going to kill, but had to admire their valor.

Yet, there was madness, too. He did not see how the attack could succeed, even if Lee piled on his divisions and corps. Ordering such a charge was lunatic, a wanton sacrifice. In the end, it was no more than mathematics.

He restrained his guns until the lagging Rebels—totaling at least another division—had crossed a third of the ground between the lines. The brigades he meant to target began to hurry their march, lines quivering on the uneven terrain. It told him that their delay had been unintentional, that this was not a planned oblique attack, but one gone awry from the outset. And that gap remained between the advancing wings.

That gap wouldn't last, Osborn told himself. Artillery fire from both flanks would drive the separate wings toward the center, as Hunt had forecast. It was going to be a mess, plenty of guts and precious little generalship.

"Batteries! Attention!" he shouted. Wondering if, in his fascination, he had waited too long.

He glanced at his blackened gunners as they sprang to life. Their officers and sergeants had needed to ration the water from the battery buckets in order to keep back enough to soothe the guns. Nonetheless, the thirsty crews leapt up, with each man standing to his position, ready. He noted their expressions, the excitement, as they got their first proper look at the targets before them.

Osborn had pre-sighted the guns and loaded them, certain of where his fires should first strike. Growing up on a farm gave a man a feel for the ways of the land, for the tricks of a landscape others thought flat and simple. You learned where errant animals hid from view. That taught you where men couldn't hide.

"Ready!"

The command echoed down the gun line, as the voices of his officers strained against the thunder down the ridge.

"Fire!"

During the lull, he had schooled his battery commanders on his priorities, aware that the noise would allow little active direction once their gunnery commenced. Now he watched black dots arc toward the Rebel formations, caught in the strange moment between their escape from the muzzle and their impact.

Perhaps half of his shells had an effect. For an opening salvo, that was splendid.

The captains and lieutenants, the sergeants and sweat-gilded gun crews, took over now, correcting range and elevation to meet the Confederate advance, moving swiftly and steadily to apply as many shells to the quick gray lines as they could before clouds of smoke left them shooting blind.

What Osborn saw through the thickening haze was butchery. He had gone from farm boy chores to college in New York, and had read the law on the eve of Southern secession. But Blackstone never addressed this form of murder.

On the flank closest to the town, a wavering Rebel formation broke for the rear, even before his fires had much effect. The prime brigades continued coming on, though, utterly undeterred and scornful of death. Along the distant treeline, barely visible now, more gray ranks appeared. A battery limbered up and trotted forward beside the infantry. Scattered fugitives plunged toward them, tiny creatures runnng for their lives. The Rebel attack had already gone off-kilter.

The fleeing men did not break the ranks of the second echelon, but Osborn wondered what grim thoughts arose in the soldiers marching through the runaways.

His guns pounded the leading brigades. As the salvos took their toll, the efforts of those in gray to restore their ranks with fresh meat began to break down. Lines bent and buckled. But they would not stop.

As the Rebels neared the road leading south toward Emmitsburg, with their flank almost perpendicular to his guns, they began to bunch and intermingle, inclining toward the Union center, driven hence by his fires. Through his glasses, Osborn watched men bend forward, almost doubling over, as if making their way

against high winds and driving rain. But this storm was of iron, steel, and lead.

Running the trace of his gun line, Osborn shouted, "The road! Concentrate all fires on that road! Hit them when they're coming over those fences. *Hit the road!*"

Some of the officers and crew members heard him. Enough of them. Hands waved an acknowledgment. Exhausted faces flashed their comprehension.

Struck by a surge of faintness, Osborn paused. Placing his hands on his knees and breathing gunpowder. The heat behind the guns was at least ten degrees higher than the sun had made it. It amazed him that his gunners could keep it up. Some had been firing for over an hour in total. Pieces had to be splashed with precious water, with no more to spare for the men. Stripped to their trousers, many of the gunners were as black as Negroes. Some crews maintained the crispness of their drill, while others just worked the guns as best they could, needing no commands. But all kept firing into the gypsy smoke, seeking targets through its rips and tears.

Returning to his lookout, Osborn raised his glasses again. Waiting. Scanning. Aching for the smoke to part.

When it did, he saw a mass of men struggling in the roadbed, caught between two fences, beasts for slaughter.

Lieutenant Cushing clutched his guts and ordered his men to load again. Propping him up, First Sergeant Fueger passed on the command. Fantastic pain competed with excitement for Cushing's attention, but he remained unwilling to indulge himself.

He had watched the Confederates approach, guiding his remaining shells into their handsome ranks, admiring them, hating them, hoping to hang on until they were vanquished. His exposed intestines squirmed over his fingers, but he still refused to examine his body's wreckage. His men, too, averted their eyes.

He was down to a single gun now. But one gun could do great damage. And Cushing—aware he was dying—intended to do his duty to the end.

At first, the gray lines had been a blurred mass centered on lofted flags. His gun and others along the line tore passages through their ranks. The Rebels howled. Then, as they approached the

road, their lines became a collection of individuals: Bearded men could be distinguished from those who were clean-shaven.

One shot from his gun struck at the feet of an advancing line, tossing men about as if they were weightless. Cushing took no satisfaction in the cruelty of it, but reveled in his effectiveness. He did not seek vengeance. He wanted victory, and knew it must be his last desire on earth.

If he had to die, he intended to die well.

The Rebels on his left made a great, befuddling turn, their ranks dissolving into a mob as they aimed straight at the wall his gun defended. Crossing the road, they rushed at gaps torn in the fences, truly charging now and wailing like demons, ignoring death, heat, thirst, wounds.

Cushing felt an equal resolve to stop them.

He ordered his men to load canister.

The little balls made red clouds out of men.

"Canister! Load!" he called again. Desperate to get off at least one more volley before the running men could reach his wall. Faithful to the end, his first sergeant repeated his command.

"Ready!"

The charging forms acquired faces, mouths, eyes, their expressions sharpened to a peak of intensity more than human and less. They rushed straight for his gun, directly at the muzzle, racing against his last remaining crew's effort to ram home the charge.

The Rebels howled their death-rage, and Cushing sang out his:

"Fire!"

He had never seen the effects of canister unleashed so close to living men: It was a crimson massacre. Yet, more of them came on. Running toward him. Screaming. Falling. Limping. Crawling. Hellbent on getting over the wall, no matter the cost.

"Load canister!" he cried a last time, hearing the death in his voice and hanging on to his first sergeant to stay upright. His guts lurched against his paw.

Some of the Rebels paused to aim their rifles. One of their bullets found Cushing's mouth and blew out the back of his head.

Glorious it was, as lovely a sight as ever a man did see. With the Rebels running forward from the road, the lot of them all but trip-

ping over themselves, the officers called the sweet 69th to rise from behind its wall and pour it into them.

The volley dropped a line of Johnnies, as if they'd been commanded to lie down and sleep, and the quivering of their bloody wounded made a fine beginning to the day's proper work. Gallagher tossed one rifle rearward for reloading and picked up the next from the number he'd amassed. He hadn't the time to choose only officers now, with the Rebs coming on full flush, so he just gave it to the biggest men he could spot, to take them out of the donnybrook that was coming. By the time he took up rifle number four, he could see the wide, crazed eyes of them, the terror and the madness, and it pleased him so. Some were in a right rage, they were, with others running toward him only because they could no longer think of anything else to do. If heroes they were, they were all of them fools as well.

To his delight, Gallagher spotted a fancy officer, after all, waving his men onward. He put a stop to the waving soon enough.

Glancing to the right for a reloaded rifle, he saw the boy artillery lieutenant give up his brains. But his last, lonely gun got off a gorgeous round of canister, chewing a great hole in the Rebel mob.

The collision came quickly thereafter, with one last shot fired off and the Johnnies over the wall just to the right, knocked back by a volley, only to surge over the stones and guns again.

Gallagher's officers screamed to refuse the flank, and two companies on his right drew back in good order. But the arses in Company F blundered about, only to disappear in a swarm of gray.

They were over the wall, the buggers were, a hundred men or more, wailing like banshees. A dirty pack of them turned to take on Gallagher and his boys, but his lads were all for it. Driven from Galway and Fermanagh, from Cork and Kerry and Wicklow, his men crashed into the gray-clad, slave-fucking bastards for the sport of it, welcoming them with rifle butts and knuckles.

A soldier in a sorry straw hat came at Gallagher with a bayonet, but he wasn't a pig for the sticking this fine day. He parried, then smashed his rifle's stock against the Johnny's fingers, crushing them on the guard of the man's musket: When you couldn't reach a man's private parts, there was no better way to cost him his purpose than to take him in the head or on the fingers. In the instant

of shock and pain that crippled the Reb, Gallagher brought the heel of his rifle up into his jaw, cracking bone with a sound as sharp as a pistol's shot. When the Reb went down, Gallagher rammed his empty rifle into his face. The second stab pierced an eye.

Another Reb, perhaps a friend of the first, came for Gallagher, but Carnahan caught him with a bullet fired so close to the man's chest that his rags took fire. Serve the shite-arse right, it did.

Straight on behind the brawling clutter of men, Gallagher spotted a high Rebel officer trying to climb up on the dead boy's cannon. How he longed for a loaded rifle in his paws, but 'twas not meant to be. The colonel or general or whatever he was got one foot up in the spokes of the carriage wheel, raising a sword with his hat impaled upon it and the noggin cover slipped down to rest on the hilt. Immediately, the sorry bugger buckled and twisted and clutched himself, hit twice and true and merry.

Well, prizes enough there were. More men of his own pack came swarming in, while some other devils—perhaps the 72nd, those great Ulster-tainted malingerers—let go volley after volley, knocking down the Rebs who had penned themselves on the wrong side of the wall.

'Twas a gay day for the Union. Then:

"Jaysus, they're shootin' *us*!" McGuire shouted hard on Gallagher's ear.

"Well, what do you bleedin' expect?" the sergeant asked.

"No, no! Our own boys it is, coming through the grove."

"To Hell and Derry, then, the best way's forward."

Sure enough, some fools were firing into the melee, as if they were as color-blind as stupid. But at the same time he felt the animal presence of his own side crowding into the fight, men from a muddle of regiments, coming in for the kill.

Gallagher watched a boy in gray—no more than a lad he was—as he loaded his rifle amid the happy to-do. He bloodied his hand on his own bayonet, but didn't stop ramming home his powder and ball.

The instant the boy withdrew the ramrod with his scarlet mitt, Gallagher struck him a blow with his fist and took the weapon from him. Turning from the boy for richer meat, he spied a gray-

clad officer, fancy as a Dublin pimp and fine as the squire on Sunday. The man was struggling to fill his revolver's cylinder.

Gallagher shot him point-blank in the belly, spoiling the lovely uniform and the bugger's afternoon. A slow death, that one was going to have, and let him lie in agony.

He took a wicked blow from behind, hard to the back of the head. But Gallagher had been struck far worse on the docks—if not by his own da—and he turned to find a bayonet lunging at him.

If any man on the field could dance a jig, 'twas Danny Gallagher. He took him a shallow slicing, the hot biting shock of it skittering along a rib, but it didn't sum up to the weight of a proper punch, let alone a killing thrust. With his rifle gone missing from his mitts, he punched the Reb on the side of his snout, then hit him again and a third time, before tripping him and elbowing him down.

He dropped atop the creature in gray, a full-grown man this bucko, with a ginger beard and teeth already out. The devil was a fighter, though, and got in a kick as Gallagher dropped toward him, reeling him back for a plowman's dance before Gallagher did some kicking of his own, right in the devil's woman-tickling glories. Then he landed a knee on the bugger's chest, took up a rock, and beat his skull to a pulp.

'Twas growing to be a hard day's work, if a sweet one.

The worthless buggers from the 72nd, good soldiers all, came on now, ranks in fair order, countercharging down toward the wall.

In a moment, the air went out of the Rebels in the killing field. They'd had enough. Weapons dropped, hands went up, and here and there a handkerchief waved at Nellie. Those who fought on were soon put paid and sent to visit their forefathers.

From up the line, where the volleys continued thick from the boys in blue, cheers went up and then a triumphant chant:

"Fredericksburg! Fredericksburg! Fredericksburg!"

So quick it all was, in the end. An eternity of instants. A joy too fine for words—and then it was done.

"Fredericksburg! Fredericksburg!"

Men cheered on every side.

A whore's miracle, several of the lads from Company F reap-

peared, as pleased as punch with themselves, leaping back from the other side of the wall.

When Gallagher got himself up, he registered all the confusions of a retreat, of failure, of humiliation, as the Johnnies with proper legs took themselves off, leaving back the sorriest. Between the wall and the line of the road, dozens and more of the Rebs raised their hands in surrender, or lay on the ground waving rags. Others, mean as landlords, kept firing back through the comrades who had forsaken them, determined to kill a last Union soldier or two.

"Get on with you, Johnny, get along now. Go on, the lot of you, that's the way." It was Walsh's voice, lording it over a wonderful shame of captured Rebs.

Some of his own kind advanced beyond the wall, racing toward the road, with the doings-and-done a fire in them now, the scent of the hunt in their nostrils and blood in their hearts. Some fired into the backs of Rebs running away, while others contented themselves with claiming prisoners. The wise lads and the officers gathered flags.

"Sergeant Danny," Walsh addressed him, standing there proud as a whore with a ring on her finger, "it's bleeding ye are, like the blind butcher's pig in the kitchen."

But Gallagher knew he had no serious injuries. Nor pains that couldn't be mastered.

Off to the right, bits of skirmishing continued, and the sound of a squabble rose from the guns on the left. But here it was done.

The Rebel batteries tossed out some rounds to cover their retreating soldiers, and a bit more damage was tallied. But the thing was over. Naught but a memory now, as unforgettable as a man's first woman.

The officers, ever busy when all the work was done, cried out for the men to sort themselves out and rejoin their regiments.

"All in good time," Gallagher told them all and none of them. For he had a last task to do to finish the victory.

He traced his way back through the maze of bodies, strewn and piled and twitching, with the wounded clawing the air and calling their mothers, until he found the officer he had shot. Gallagher didn't want him dying uninstructed.

Hardly more than a lad he was, with sweat-darkened tawny hair and wisps of beard. A captain, Gallagher decided, and never to be a major. The fellow wore a silk scarf around his neck, of the sort that must have been given him by a ladyfriend.

Gallagher knelt by the fellow's side and unknotted the scarf, drawing it away from the pulsing flesh.

"I suppose ye'd like some water, me lad," he said.

The man's eyes blinked, but his body didn't move.

"Well," Gallagher went on, "there's none to be had, not a drop. It's your ill luck."

He wiped the blood from his face with the scarf, then thrust it under his blouse to sop up the gore where the blade had scraped his rib. Reassured that the slicing was nothing to interfere with business, he pawed through the wounded man's pockets and soon came up with the finest watch he had ever held in hand. And ticking it was, like an English heart at the sight of an Irishman's misery.

The gut-shot captain, who had suffered additional injuries in the tumult, struggled to raise a hand to stop Gallagher's theft. But he was too weak.

The captain was dying. But not yet. His eyes were alive and intelligent, his expression aware of his last bit of God-given life.

Gallagher scouted the captain's hands for rings, but found not one.

With a grin he summoned when beating men on the docks, Gallagher brought his mug close to the boy's fine features. Close enough to feel the lad's breath tickle his own whiskers, to smell its dry-mouthed staleness. The man's eyes flashed no more defiance, only a delicious dread.

Kissing close to the captain's ear, Daniel Gallagher whispered, "It's not just your watch I'm after taking, boyo. After this fine war's over, I plan to take meself south, if ye didn't know. And I'm going to fuck your sweetheart and your sisters. And when I've had me fill and grown tired of their weeping and begging for mercy, I'm going to pass the lot of them on to your niggers. You think about that now."

Gallagher rose, a victor.

TWENTY-THREE

July 3, Afternoon

Brigadier General Dick Garnett had never wanted any of this to happen. As he waved his soldiers—his brave boys—onward toward the stone wall, hoping against collapsing odds that, somehow, the attack might be driven home, he felt their excitement multiplied within him, the peculiar human inability to stop when the stopping was good.

And now it was too late. Kemper was down, and he had last seen Armistead disappearing into the melee around the guns. The grand charge had become an affair of curses and screams, of rifled muskets swung as clubs, of heaved rocks and cracked skulls, of rage and numbers.

"Come on, boys! Come on! You're there, by God, you're there!"

He waved his hat at the sweat-streaked, battle-carved faces rushing past him. Their hides spit blood as they fell. Bullets wasped around him, too, biting into the horseflesh bearing his weight, and he knew it was only a matter of minutes until he joined the fallen. But he could not stop any more than those men could. His dizzies surged again, trying to unhorse him, but his sense of duty—what was life's purpose but duty?—glued him to the saddle amid the slaughter.

Garnett jerked his stallion about and rode back through the thinned-out mob in gray. The men had lost all military order, their brigades intermingled after that fateful left wheel and the shock of the flanking fire. Now they just plunged forward, leaderless, because going on was the one thing left to do.

"Over that wall, too!" he cried. "Git on, boys, git among 'em!" He waved his hat toward the scrambled blue line south of the copse. "Turn 'em, boys! Git around 'em! Cut 'em off!"

He had learned war—or thought he had—fighting the Seminoles and cornering Mormons, and in the minor Indian spats that briefly broke the boredom of Ft. Laramie. He had missed active service in Mexico, to his shame, but had done his best to comprehend its lessons. He had never imagined this, though: the magnitude, the bravery, the waste . . .

It was a bewildering thing, how a man could hope to win when he knew he couldn't. He rode amid his men and hoped. For their sake, if not his own. Striving with all the will remaining to him to crack that dark blue line, to force a miracle.

Yet, even now . . . here . . . in this final place, he sensed that all of it was a great wrong, that firebrands South and North had wrought this day from vainglory and spleen. It was not the end he had wanted for his service. But duty lay where the soldier found himself.

Garnett had been a Union man at heart, against secession. But when the parting of the people came, he felt compelled to go with his state, Virginia. So many years after leaving Rose Hill for West Point, his heart could not break its tether. He had murdered his ideals for blood and soil.

Now this: Smoke and madness. Raw screams far more blasphemous than curses. Southern voices, Irish voices, flat-voweled Yankees, shrieks past all allegiance. Rifles fired point-blank. His own revolver empty.

"Go on, go on!" he called to a wavering soldier. But the man only stood stock-still, planted in the middle of the battlefield, suddenly used up.

They were so few now, so few.

He strained to see through the haze. More Yankees coming up, entire tribes of them. Sweeping in, disorderly but enthused. Shouting unintelligible war cries.

So many, so many.

And so few with him now. He had expected to see supporting brigades appear through the earthbound clouds, to hear Rebel yells of reassurance nearing. But all he had was a bleeding horse, an empty revolver, and the remnants of three stricken brigades cast into this devil's cauldron, cheap as beans.

He could not bear to think it was all for nothing. Even now.

Aware of the odds growing each moment more impossible, he could not give up. It could not be for nothing. . . .

Could it?

His horse was struck again, but would no more quit than Garnett would quit himself.

At his stirrup, the beard and jaw tore off a startled face. Blood splashed Garnett's boots. Aware and unaware, the shot man staggered on toward the Yankees.

Armistead had taken his boys over the stretch of wall left of the copse. Then Lo had disappeared into the tangle.

They had to punch through on the right of those trees as well. To have any hope of making the lodgment stick. They had to widen the break, to complete it, to outflank the battle-crazed men in blue—Irish as porridge and poteen, by the looks of them.

"Come *on*, lads!"

So close.

But as his men approached the wall, fresh-laid rifles knocked them down by the dozen. Union cannon began to bark again.

Where in the devil was Pickett? Where were the supports? They were so close. . . .

Broken-hearted and raging, dizzy and shamed, Garnett steered his horse directly for the wall. He waved his hat at his soldiers one last time.

The long line staggered. More shells struck. Reduced to bags of blood, men splashed their comrades. The flag of the 26th went down, but fresh hands took it up. Exploded dirt hit Blake in the face like buckshot.

"Dress your ranks!" Knock Jones called from their rear, while other voices cried, "Guide right, guide to the right!"

The men recovered from the first shock of the perfectly ranged Yankee guns, correcting their buckled line as they surged ahead, passing the hot ruins of the farmstead on their left and quick-marching down an incline toward a ditch that jagged across the fields.

A round of solid shot tore a bloody trail through the ranks to Blake's left.

"Get across that damn thing, get across any old way."

The ditch contained no more than a hint of wetness, but lay just deep and wide enough to trouble them. The line bristled in both directions as some men leapt the obstacle or clambered down into it, while others hesitated, hunting urgently for a better spot to jump or stepping back to get a running start.

Blake leapt. A small man, Cobb had to fuss his way down into the trough and back up again. Charley Campbell paused, then mimicked Cobb. Blake reached down to give him a hand up.

A shell-burst tumbled him into the ditch. He just missed Charley's bayonet. After the shock, they sorted out arms and limbs, their rifles and fallen caps. Blake wore blood now, but nothing much seemed awry. Charley got up cursing.

Beyond the ditch, the line paused to re-form, punished all the while by the Yankee batteries. The hill that held the deadliest guns grew cotton bolls of smoke. As the soldiers of the 26th marched forward again, the distant goal of their charge grew indistinct. Hiding from them. Or hiding a surprise.

"Guide to the right, guide right!" a young voice called again. That damned gap yonder. Between them and whoever was on their flank.

Angry now, they knocked down another fence, leaving a trail of their dead and dying behind them.

A wheatfield stretched ahead—infinitely, terrifyingly wide—and ended at stout fencing that marked a road. Beyond, obscured by smoke, their enemies waited.

Crowding away from the deadly flank and the batteries on the hill, soldiers bunched together, offering denser targets to Yankee gunners. As officers struggled to keep control, the ranks drifted rightward toward the Yankee center. As if there were in fact a guiding hand—perhaps that of a God overcome with pity—the brigades advancing to their right made an abrupt leftward wheel. The movement was huge and clumsy, but angled their thousands toward a meeting point with Pettigrew's men, just where the Union line stuck out its jaw.

They would hit the Yankees together, after all.

Stride by stride, the line of the 26th formed a shallow wedge. A shell exploded at the toes of soldiers who had strutted beyond the flag, tossing them into the air. One man did a perfect skyward

somersault, dying a clown's death. A second explosion followed, fired by the second gun of a section, and butchered the men who had rushed to close the gap.

Still others came forward, lest the Yankees think them weak. Pride trumped life. Dry-throated men howled a painful cheer. But its force was less than it would have been minutes before.

The fence. Just get to that damned fence, Blake told himself. Eat the bear one little bite at a time. Cobb and Charley Campbell were still with him, and the new lieutenant more or less kept up. The boy looked determined and terrified.

The Yankee fire grew still more intense, more accurate, despite the wreath of smoke around their batteries.

Hard to miss, Blake figured. What the hell had all that noise been about in the hour before, if the cannonade had not even dented the might of the Yankee guns?

Cries of agony trailed them through the wheat.

Crossing that field took hours, days, weeks, months. Blake felt the urge to run forward, to get somewhere, anywhere. But he stayed in the rank to which he had committed himself.

"Close up!"

Blake did not know the brittle-as-flint voice. Looking around to put a name to it, he saw the flash of a shell-burst and Colonel Marshall tumbling from his horse.

The young man sprang back up, though. Fending off helping hands, he shook himself and straightened his fine, new uniform, then remounted. An aide turned the colonel's horse in the proper direction.

Get down, you fool, and walk, Blake thought. You won't be worth a shit to us if you're dead. He had to fight an urge to pull the boy down again.

He marched on. They all did. But the damned fence would not come closer. Blake could see it clearly, though: They weren't going to knock this one down, it was thick-made. A few more steps, crushing wheat underfoot, and he realized there were two fences, not just one.

A penned-in road to get across, and close enough to the Yankees for their infantry to fire down into them.

Goddamn it to Hell.

Torn by ever more gaps, the line broke from its quick-march rhythm as men rushed for the first fence. Lung-biting smoke had drifted across their path and they plunged into a midafternoon twilight. As if God had darkened the sun. As if the Lord did not want to see any more. Or Hell was fuming.

God or Satan, it was hard to say who was busier.

Before a single man laid hand on the fence to hurl himself over it, the Yankee batteries switched their loads to canister. It tore the attack apart.

Stunned men left on their feet meandered or stood. Gaping. A few shot their rifles into the smoke in fury, needing to do something, anything, to try to hurt their tormentors in return.

"Over the fence! Get over the damned fence!" That was Knock, hoarse and unmistakable. The major still had his head about him.

Others took up the cry. Up the line, men rallied to fire a volley, perhaps at an order that never reached Blake's ears.

"Come on!" Blake yelled. He launched himself at the first fence. Along with dozens, hundreds, of other soldiers. "Come on! Run! Get past the fence!"

Cobb was with him. Cobb was always with him.

Blake vaulted the slats, surprising himself with the ease of it, and turned to help any others who needed aid. At his fingertips, a barefoot man just topping the fence fell backward, chest punched bloody. Behind the mass of men clambering over the obstacle, Colonel Marshall waved his sword, encouraging them with words Blake could not hear.

A bullet struck the colonel in the forehead.

Blake pulled Charley Campbell into the lane. A few men leapt over the second fence and went on, but most knelt or flattened themselves along the road. Dead, wounded, whole . . . it was hard to sort the bodies at a glance.

Voices cried that the Yankees had outflanked them. One man knelt in midroad and prayed wildly, shouting to God, as if at a revival meeting.

The Yankee gunners up on the hill kept blasting them with canister. Some of their muzzles aimed right down the road.

It was nothing but a slaughter pen for pigs. And Blake did not intend to die like a pig.

Knock Jones ran along the road, bellowing, "Get up, damn it, y'all get up and get over that goddamned fence. We're almost there, the Yanks can't stop us now."

Blake heard his own voice repeating the commands. He dragged Charley Campbell to his feet. Cobb didn't need any tugging. Evil-eyed, he was ready. Other men rose up, too.

The lieutenant had gone missing.

It was all a matter of seconds, then, after the eternity in the fields. A last mass of men began to climb the far fence, determined to get at the Yankees and do some killing, to have their revenge at last.

"Come on, come *on*!"

As they topped the fence, a Yankee regiment poured a volley into them.

Charley Campbell plunged into the field. His head struck the earth and twisted away from his shoulders.

But the flag went forward. *Their* flag.

Of one will, the men in Blake's stretch of the line—a ghost of a line—paused to fire into the blur of men up in the haze. The Yankees were lined up behind a fence of their own, pouring out an impossible volume of fire.

Men began edging forward again, reloading as they advanced. A few went back over the fence, leaving the hard souls alone to finish the work.

The regiment's flag fell.

It rose again.

And fell again.

A boy grabbed it and ran headlong for the Yankees, a friend keeping pace beside him.

Brave souls tried to follow, bending their torsos forward, fighting a headwind only they could feel, planting one foot in front of the other, undaunted.

To the right, where a strip of the line had appeared undefended, a fresh Yankee regiment rose up from the earth, leveled their muskets, and fired.

It was the end.

"Buck and ball!" an outraged voice cried. "The bastards . . ."

The Yankees began to cheer and chant. At first, Blake's ears could not find the word they repeated.

Then it rang clear: *"Fredericksburg, Fredericksburg!"*

Through a mist that would have suited a mountain hollow, Blake saw a herd of Yankees surround the boy with the flag and his companion. Their rifles were leveled. Blake waited for them to fire, dreading the moment.

Instead, the Yankees grabbed the two boys—and the flag—and dragged them back over the fence, as if they were truants.

Blake wouldn't have it. Not that flag, not now.

He ran toward them, thirty yards away.

"No!" Cobb screamed.

Blake could not comprehend what his antagonist sought to deny him. He raced for the spot where he had last seen that flag. Nothing else mattered anymore, not on this earth.

Stumbling over a body, he quickly righted himself and looked up. Straight into the Yankee line.

A bareheaded boy in a gunner's trim held a lanyard in his hand. The muzzle of the cannon aimed at Blake.

The boy hesitated.

A sergeant descended on him. Shouting.

The boy yanked the lanyard.

The last thing Blake saw and heard on this earth was Cobb, kneeling over him and grasping his rags, crying, "Don't die, damn you, Tom Blake, you *can't* die . . ."

Lieutenant Colonel McGilvery was astonished. He had been certain that the attack was over. His guns had been firing at distant clots of men retreating over the fields they had recently crossed with flags and heads held high. The great din from the center of the line had grown less insistent. He heard cheers.

Then they came on again. Two last brigades of them. Or, perhaps, a brigade and a stray regiment, judging by the size of the formations. Whoever had ordered them forward had to be mad. Their numbers were far too few to make a difference, and even their line of advance made no damned sense. As if they had set out only to offer themselves as targets for his guns.

"What the Hell?" a sergeant asked the sun, the moon, and the stars. The man doffed his cap, wiped his sweat, and shook his head.

"Load spherical case," McGilvery called. His throat was raw,

but they heard him well enough. "Crews without spherical case, load solid shot. Prepare to switch to canister."

The advancing Confederates might as well have been stranded on rafts at sea, so isolated and hopeless did they appear. Yet, they came waving banners, that cross of washed-out blue on faded red, marching proudly through the thinning haze, their spirits as indomitable as their bodies were doomed.

The senselessness of their effort repulsed McGilvery. He understood desperation. But not stupidity.

His gun crews bustled about in the smoke-queered light. Some men still had their bloodlust up, but others moved with the dreaminess of exhaustion. They, too, had assumed that their work was done, or nearly so, and those not maddened by the additional labor now required were dully resigned.

The Rebs just came parading on, dressed so neatly into ranks they might have been marching through Richmond behind a brass band. But the only music sounded from distant guns—Osborn's, he figured.

Horses began to neigh behind the gun line, unsettled by the change they sensed in the air.

McGilvery raised his glasses for another look. The Confederates were so perfectly in range he could tell when a man changed his stride to avoid a body.

Soon there would be more bodies in that field. He had a strong stomach and plenty of leftover anger, yet, somehow, the thought of knocking down these men fouled up his guts. This wasn't a battle anymore. It was set to be a massacre.

Officers and men looked toward him. Waiting for his command.

He let the Confederates cross the ridge upon which he'd slain their predecessors. Then he let them come on a little more. Secretly hoping some officer would recognize their folly and turn them around. Knots of retreating men passed them, the refuse of the grand attack, headed for the rear and a chance to live. The forlorn-hope brigades did not break step.

Disgusted, McGilvery lifted his right hand. Raising it high for every man to see. And he paused. Giving his enemies one last chance, a few last seconds to come back to their senses.

Rage filled him. Rage at anyone, in any army, who would commit such a criminal blunder.

"Commence firing!" he shouted. "Fire at will!" He dropped his hand for the benefit of the more distant gun crews.

Nearly forty cannon spit flame and recoiled in quick succession. The sound briefly deafened every man, but the resumption of battle made sense to the horses, who calmed.

He didn't need his field glasses to see the gashes torn in the Rebel ranks. The range and trajectory made it hard to miss.

The gray lines quivered, but came on. These men didn't turn as the others had, but senselessly plunged ahead, aiming at a worthless stretch of ground that led to nothing but another trap.

His batteries fired with malice and fresh energy.

The Rebel discipline held for a clutch of minutes, but once they got down in the swale where the creek meandered, where his guns could sweep them with loads of doubled canister, they began to run: A few dashed back toward the Confederate lines, but most charged straight ahead like blinkered horses, racing deeper into killing range, heading for the false protection of the rocks and scrub trees just beyond the low ground.

McGilvery raised his glasses again. In time to see men ripped apart amid their terrified comrades, set upon by devils disguised as artillery. Their last order disintegrated, becoming the strangest rout he had ever seen, in which men ran toward their enemies and threw themselves on the earth.

His gun crews hardly bothered to aim. Their discipline was breaking, too, but in an ugly, bloody, vengeful way.

McGilvery watched men claw the earth and cower behind trees too thin to protect them. Men clutched each other like lovers or crawled behind corpses to hide.

His batteries had never done such slaughter.

The Rebels were broken. Few of them tried to fire and none were sure of targets. They had come to a place as hopeless as it was worthless.

White rags waved, only to be shredded by double canister.

One blast swept up a line of cowering men, hurling their quartered bodies over their comrades. Fresh meat caught on branches.

The well-salted sea captain feared he was going to vomit.

"Cease firing," McGilvery shouted. *"Cease firing!"*

The near guns obeyed, but the far sections roared on.

"Cease firing!" He turned to an aide and his last remaining orderly. *"Stop* them, damn it. It's enough. *Enough!"*

His subordinates dashed for the far stretches of his gun line. In the distance, he saw advancing men in blue, sweeping toward the grove to gather prisoners.

The firing stopped and McGilvery turned away.

What have I done?

Lee sat on his horse, deep in the fields, as his soldiers streamed back around him. Even now, they took off their hats at the sight of him, releasing their grips on wounds to uncover their heads. Many wept.

Others called out in pain and shame and anger, "We can go again! Let us go again! We can whip them!"

But they could not go again, not on this day. It took all of Lee's reserves of personal discipline to restrain his welling tears.

"It's all my fault," he told the passing soldiers. "It's all my fault this time. . . ."

Stepping nearer, the blackened, bloodied men shouted, "No! *No!"*

But it was true: This debacle was his fault.

What have I done?

Men helped each other rearward, their private friendships all that remained of organization now. Hideously wounded, some defied belief as they kept their feet.

Most still had their weapons, that was something. Not all was lost.

But so much had been wasted, so much, so terribly much. He did not know if he could bear the shame.

The attack had been folly. He saw it now. But the future had been veiled. He had been too proud, too sure, and the Lord had humbled him.

But at what cost had his chastisement come? How was this just? His faith in the Lord was unshakable, but much passed Man's understanding.

He had believed that these men could do anything, that those people could not resist their ferocious courage. But even valor had limits, he saw that now.

Lee rode farther into the field, away from the advanced battery where Alexander, bless him, kept the Englishman locked in conversation. Lee did not have the stomach for the man now, but did not want to be ungracious.

"God bless you, General Lee!" a man cried out. He had no hat to doff, but covered an eye with a hand that streamed bright blood.

A lieutenant passed in silence, glancing timidly at Lee. The downcast remnant of a company trailed him.

"Form your ranks when you get back to cover," Lee told the defeated men. "Obey your officers. We want all good men to hold together now. . . ."

What have I done?

He could not, would not, think of General Longstreet. The injustice of resentment was too tempting.

I have been proud, Lee thought. It is a terrible sin in the eyes of God.

Another pack of men came up. Four of the ragged soldiers bore a litter, its burden clearly an officer of rank.

Lee nudged his horse closer.

"Whom have you there, boys?"

"General Kemper, sir."

Something in Lee's features made the men set down the litter. Kemper had tugged the blanket over his face against the sun. With an effort, he showed himself. His features were taut with pain.

"I hope you are not badly hurt?" Lee asked him.

Their eyes had met, but Kemper looked away. "I think they've got me this time," he said.

"I trust not," Lee said. "Oh, I trust not."

What have I done?

The soldiers took up the litter again and moved on. Who else had fallen? Of these fine men the army could not spare?

Enough fight remained in Lee for him to hope that Meade would come charging in his turn across those fields, into *his* guns and the rest of General Hill's corps, to take an equal punishment,

if not a greater one. But as his soldiers struggled by, and he listened to the cheering across the fields, Lee sensed that General Meade would not oblige him.

Still . . . if Meade could be lured to attack . . . perhaps all could be redeemed?

Meade would not attack. Lee knew it bone-deep and plain. But he could not stop hoping. Even now.

Wandering back across the fields with a handful of his men, General Wilcox spotted him and approached. At the same time, the Englishman intruded, pursued by Alexander.

Earlier, Lee had needed to console Pickett, who was hurt and angry. He did not know if he possessed the self-mastery to face another chiding from a subordinate. He knew what he had done to these men, he knew it all too well. But a man could bear so much, and then no more.

On foot amid his staff, Wilcox wept openly. Halting at Lee's stirrup, he declared, "General Lee, I came into Pennsylvania with one of the finest brigades in the Army of Northern Virginia . . . and now . . . now all my people are gone . . . they're gone, all killed . . ."

Lee reached down for the general's hand and took it as he would have the hand of a child.

"Never mind, General Wilcox, never mind. All this has been *my* fault, I'm the one who lost this fight." He did not know if he could go on without breaking down himself. And someone had to remain strong for the army.

For the first time, Lee felt dangerously old.

"I'm the one who lost this fight," he repeated. "But you must help me out of it. In the very best way you can. We need all our good men now."

Wilcox nodded, cheeks shining with tears, and went on to rally what survivors he could.

Still they came on, so many of them. And not all their wounds were visible, Lee knew.

"It's all my fault," he told them, again and again.

Among the last men to retreat, a gore-covered soldier limped along, helped by a filthy comrade. When he realized that Lee himself hovered before him, the wounded man jigged over, clearly suffering at each desperate movement.

Propped up by his equally bloodied camp-mate, the old soldier found the voice to say, "General Lee, sir . . . I'm a dying man. Let me shake your hand." He raised a crimsoned paw.

When Lee reached down to grant the doomed man's wish, soldiers crowded around, expecting a miracle.

Meade rode through havoc and confused shouts, reassured only when he grasped that the men coursing toward him were his prisoners. A great mass of them.

The roar and racket of battle had diminished to the front, but a new wave of cannon fire growled on the left, in the direction of Hunt's concealed gun line. Beside the herd of prisoners, a few men in blue were taking themselves off as well, with one of them screaming, "The Rebs are in the line, the Rebs done got us . . ."

One of the captive Confederates, a blood-smeared little man, cackled derisively.

Approaching the crest of the ridge from the rear, Meade spotted Lieutenant Haskell, Gibbon's aide-de-camp. The fellow was bloodied himself, but energetically called out orders to this man and that.

Haskell saw him and turned. They met on the ridgetop. Down the slope, where rifles still cracked, smoke teased over a mad scene.

"How's it going here?" Meade asked. Half fearing the answer.

The lieutenant smiled through the grime and gore disfiguring his face. "I believe, General, the enemy's attack . . . is repulsed."

"Already?"

"I believe so. It is, sir."

Meade's eyes ached, skinned by weariness, singed by smoke. He strained to see. And got a start: Rebel banners waved over his lines.

His mind caught up with his eyes. The flags had been captured. His own men were flaunting them. Through passages in the smoke, he saw his soldiers gathering in more prisoners, hundreds of them. Deeper into the fields, in a luminous haze, thousands of Confederates retreated in disorder.

"Thank God," Meade said. Then he added, "This is General Hancock's victory."

The wounded lieutenant's expression took fire. Meade understood: Haskell had forgone promotion to continue to serve Gibbon and would not have his general slighted.

"And General Gibbon's, of course. With credit to General Hays, as well." He breathed deeply, yearning for fresh, clear air. Instead, he got the stink of powder and mankind. "I'm told that General Hancock has been wounded."

"He remained on the field, sir. Commanding. Until the Rebels broke. General Gibbon's been hit, too. Although I don't believe his life is endangered. And Colonel Webb, sir. He may be rather bad. But we won, sir. We *won.* . . ."

Meade tasked his brain to think, but the sluggish beast behind his eyes resisted. He gave up and asked, "Who's the senior general, then? In your corps?"

"General Caldwell, sir."

Of course. Caldwell. He knew that.

Below him, he saw an army in disorder. But it was a *victorious army.* Unless . . . Lee came again. The firing on the left was a burr to the relief he almost felt.

He heard his wife's frequent caution: "Oh, George, you'd see rain clouds in Heaven itself!"

Yes. Margaret. Oh, but she would be proud. *If* this were so.

As if summoned, his son rode up behind him, trailed by a few gathered officers from his staff.

Meade watched for a moment as his soldiers—*his* soldiers— brought gray-clad prisoners over fences and walls, their spirits broken.

"Thank God," he muttered again.

The lieutenant before him wobbled. Wounded. Hot. Meade felt embarrassed by his lack of consideration, his selfishness. At this moment, of all moments.

"Haskell, you're wounded yourself."

The lieutenant declined the sympathy. "Not so badly, I don't think, sir."

"You must be tended to."

"Yes, sir. A few more things . . ."

Meade realized still more: The aide had been left to take charge of the division. And the lieutenant had been doing so when Meade interrupted him.

"All right," Meade said, embarrassed. "And my compliments to

General Gibbon. When you see him. Well fought, Haskell. Well fought, indeed."

Still, those guns were roaring on the left.

Nonetheless, the rising, thinning smoke revealed a true disaster for Robert E. Lee.

Meade turned his horse toward the hill and the cemetery, seeking a clearer view from higher ground. Exuberance rose within him, quickening his nerves, waking him fully. As if from a troubled dream.

Followed by his son and a swelling crowd of horsemen, Meade rode a zigzag course through the confusion left in the fighting's wake: shouting officers, limping wounded, still more prisoners, intermingled regiments and brigades. Men sprawled everywhere, some of them wounded, others drained of all but life by the heat.

He realized that what they had accomplished still had not sunk in for those soldiers any more deeply than it had for him. They were all too accustomed to losing, their minds resisted the evidence of victory. Not a few officers stared in a daze as the army's commander rode past.

They had beaten Lee. He warned himself not to be lulled into folly, to wait, to be certain to the last degree. But everything he saw around him said that Robert E. Lee had been defeated. In what looked to have been the greatest attack of the war.

He also saw that his own plans would have to change. There would be no prompt and sweeping counterattack by his own men, that had been a fantasy. His soldiers could barely keep their feet—indeed, many men could not—and the confusion appeared immense. The army had survived, but it was stunned.

The men needed ammunition, water, and food. He had eaten, but these men who defeated Robert E. Lee had not.

For all that, it struck George Gordon Meade again that he commanded a *victorious* army. An army he had led for less than a week. That no other general had managed to lead to victory. He had faced the worst that Lee could do. And he had won.

He turned to tell his son that his mother would be terribly proud of them both, but young George had trailed off somewhere.

Meade kept riding.

He found Howard and a bevy of his officers standing on the hillside in clear air, just below the gun line.

Before Meade could dismount, the corps commander and a dozen others crowded around his horse, calling out congratulations and reaching to shake his hand.

More officers rushed up. Enlisted soldiers gathered to see him, stepping as close as they dared.

It was . . . overwhelming.

Beaming, the normally somber Howard touched Meade's hand with the fingers that remained to him, but immediately broke the contact to point southward.

"Look there!" Howard cried. "Look there, on Round Top."

Meade turned. A semaphore message flashed up the line.

"What does it say, Wheeler?" Howard demanded of one of his officers.

The captain took up his field glasses.

They all waited. Less than patiently. Meade realized, only now, that the guns on Hunt's line had ceased firing.

"Is it all right?" Meade asked.

The captain replied with a grin, directed first at Meade, then at Howard, and back to Meade again.

"It says, sir, that the enemy has been repulsed on every part of the line."

The officers erupted in a cheer.

Meade saluted them. Howard stepped closer to his stirrup. The bearded, severe face shone above the grave beard.

"General Meade," the corps commander said, "you must ride the line. The men will want to see you."

Would they?

Meade had never dreamed of such a day. He had not dared. Even his rarest hopes of victory had not reached to this.

Forgetting that he had just saluted the gathered officers, he saluted them again, reined his horse about to clear a path, and applied the spurs.

Followed by his retinue, Meade thundered down the hill, leapt a battered portion of fence, and led the way into the clearing fields. He would have liked to gallop, despite the danger of blowing his mount completely, to tear along the line for the sheer joy of it . . .

but his progress was limited to a trot as his horse picked its way between the dead and wounded.

At first, nothing happened. Then shouts went up: "Meade! Meade!" The few shouts became many. Soldiers rushed forward, climbing wall and fence, standing atop gun carriages to see, forming a thick blue wall along the front. They crowded and jostled as if his ride were the spectacle of their lives.

Meade touched the brim of his hat in a salute.

And they *cheered*.

He saw his son come up, differently mounted now, but young George and all of the staff men kept a respectful distance to his rear.

Meade rode before his army, amazed and proud.

The men cheered and cheered.

For him.

TWENTY-FOUR

Epilogue

Lieutenant Colonel Arthur James Lyon Fremantle lay back and thought of England. Might as well have been there, what with the rain and dreariness. Hardly the picture one had of America. "Sunny Southland" and all that. Of course, this was the North. Still. A cooling drizzle might have been welcome enough, but this deluge was rather much.

Fourth of July. The date only deepened the gloom among Lee's people. Who were not the grand Cavaliers Englishmen imagined. Hospitable enough, in their countrified ways. But Lee was no more than a rustic squire, while Longstreet was, at best, the yeoman-farmer sort. And the rest were as conniving as Welsh colliers. Only Fairfax seemed a thorough gentleman. Blood always told.

Bloody mess, overall. Now this bout of camp tummy. Nothing severe. But unpleasant. Dreadful conditions. Not the least proper discipline. Fought like tigers, but without adequate direction. Proper bollocks the generals had made of it.

Daren't breathe a word of that in the regimental mess. His brother officers were convinced that the Southrons were splendid chaps, and they weren't the sort who welcomed contradiction.

Didn't do to lie, of course. Just leave things out. Bit like dealing with women. Great deal you couldn't tell them. Dreadful creatures, really.

Old drain wouldn't stay sealed. Damned embarrassing. Even in defeat, Lee's staff was given to tasteless humor.

Packing up, the lot of them. Going home to Virginia. That Union fellow hadn't obliged them, no attack had come. No gambler, that one. Unlike these gadabouts. Born for the card table, fine horseflesh, and debts.

Would have rather liked a bath. And a glass of Napoleon brandy.

Trick now was to get across the lines and hurry home. He had his story. Devil of a fight, if a disappointing outcome. A decisive Southron victory would have made him. Eyewitness. Greatest battle since Waterloo.

But this shambles? Not what his people wanted to hear at all. The right sort back home imagined Lee as an Arthur, his paladins as knights of the Round Table. Left a fellow in a bit of a pickle.

Fellow from *The Times* had explained it to him. Never change the facts—you'll get caught out—but shade 'em so you won't spoil his lordship's breakfast.

He needed the nod from the generals who had already crowned old Lee with victory's laurels. They were the ones who had to say, "Well done, Fremantle!" Had to put a tasty sauce on a nasty cut of beef.

Hadn't had a stand-out career thus far. Promotions, thanks to the memory of the pater. But he'd missed out on the Crimea, great bollocks that it had been. No service in the Mutiny, either, although that was hardly a thing to be regretted. The right sort didn't go out to India. Squabbles over bum-boys on the Frontier, cholera and niggers everywhere. Nasty as Manchester. But service as a military secretary in Gibraltar wasn't the way a fellow made a name.

Now he had his chance. "Daring fellow, that Fremantle! Has the spark, that one! Shall we ask him round? Hear it all from the horse's mouth?"

But what could he say about the dreadful losses? Fifteen generals dead, wounded, or missing. Lee's paladins certainly didn't keep to their tents, say that much for them. Mad as drunken Scotchmen, though. And the rank-and-file losses were appalling.

Dreary, dying afternoon. Trains already off. Infantry waiting to go. Line of guns putting up a show to keep the Yankees guessing. Hundreds of wounded to be left behind.

At least the Federals weren't savages. Englishmen fighting Englishmen. Basic decencies and all that. Even if their Englishness was rather a tumbledown business.

Really did want a bath. Probably have to drag the old bones to New York City for a decent soak. Then a proper ship. Dinner at the captain's table.

His belly quivered nastily.

He might stress that the Union could not win the war. No matter how many battles its generals won. Land too vast, the Southrons too determined. Have to let them go their way, in the end. That approach might be the ticket. No need to stress the scale of the defeat.

Arrows in the bowels, one after another. Up you get, old man. Didn't do to disgrace oneself. Up, and out into the rain. Muck and mess, all of it.

Had to outshine the old pater, that was the thing. And it looked to be damnably hard, when the only available Napoleon was a nasty sort all tangled up in Mexico. Nor had his beginnings been as auspicious as he had let on to the Southrons. Out of Sandhurst, he'd been thrust into the 70th Foot, a regiment of no standing. And the best he could do was to get himself transferred promptly to the 52nd, which was precious little better. Memories of their mess still made him shudder. And not one proper hunter in the stables. It had taken a beastly long time for his father's friends to get him properly placed in the Coldstream Guards. Now he had to make a name for himself. Although it wouldn't do to seem too thrusting. Bit of adventure, firsthand account of war. Service done for the common good. Present oneself with a light touch. That sort of thing.

The outbuilding to which he rushed was occupied and Lieutenant Colonel Arthur James Lyon Fremantle, future general in service to Her Majesty, was forced to squat in a cluster of trees, where others had preceded him and from which his embarrassment might be viewed by the multitude.

As his bowels eased on the Pennsylvania earth, he was certain of one thing: As an officer, he had nothing to learn from these American amateurs. No English general would ever order his infantry to attack *en masse* across open fields in the face of entrenched modern weapons. It just wasn't done.

On the Fourth of July 1863, as rain drenched the wounded left on the fields of Gettysburg, Vicksburg surrendered to Grant, Longstreet's old friend.

The 26th North Carolina suffered 85 percent casualties at Gettysburg, the worst loss of any regiment on either side. Morale dropped

in the battle's wake, but by autumn, the survivors recovered from the blow. Reinforced with new recruits, the regiment marched with Lee until he surrendered. When the last roll was called, 131 men answered.

Rushed west after the Union disaster at Chickamauga, the 26th Wisconsin fought in twenty-five additional battles and engagements, including Missionary Ridge, Kennesaw Mountain, the sieges of Atlanta and Savannah, and Bentonville. The survivors were present in North Carolina when General Joseph E. Johnston, who had struggled on after Lee laid down his arms, surrendered the remnants of the last great Confederate army to General William Tecumseh Sherman.

On the afternoon of July 3, the 69th Pennsylvania lost 143 of the 258 men who had filled its ranks that morning. The regiment's colonel, its lieutenant colonel, and two captains fell. No regiment of native-born Americans played as great a role in Lee's defeat as these sons of Erin.

Major John "Knock" Jones of the 26th Carolina ended July 3 in command of the brigade General Pettigrew had led on the first day of battle. Promoted to lieutenant colonel, he was mortally wounded the following year at the Wilderness.

Lieutenant Colonel John Randolph Lane, the second in command of the 26th North Carolina on July 1, had much of his jaw and tongue shot away in the regiment's attack on the Iron Brigade. His men gave Lane up for dead, but he was tough as a hickory stump. When Union cavalry threatened his train of ambulance wagons, Lane refused to surrender, took off on his own, made his way south, and, defying his wounds, returned to command the 26th as its colonel later that year. He was wounded again at the Wilderness, then a third time at Yellow Tavern, and a fourth time at Ream's Station. John Lane survived, married, built a fortune in a web of businesses, and died a hero of the South at age seventy-three.

Edward Porter Alexander, Longstreet's devoted artilleryman, rose to the rank of brigadier general. Gravely wounded as the Federal noose tightened on Petersburg, he rose from his bed through strength of will to rejoin Lee's army in the war's closing days. After

the surrender, he returned to Georgia and became a railroad president. Porter Alexander wrote wisely and honestly about the war. He died in his seventy-fifth year.

Committed to personal gallantry above all, Brigadier General James Johnston Pettigrew was mortally wounded in a trivial skirmish during the final hours of Lee's retreat. His men took the dying officer back to Virginia.

Lieutenant General James Longstreet and Robert E. Lee reconciled, each recognizing the importance of the other. Longstreet's tactical skill saved the Army of Northern Virginia at the Wilderness, where it had been stunned by Grant's ferocity. Within hours, Longstreet suffered a severe wound, but returned to active service in the fall. He was present with the Army of Northern Virginia when Lee surrendered at Appomattox Court House.

The day after the surrender, Longstreet encountered Grant near the home of Wilbur McLean. Overcome with emotion, Grant grasped Longstreet's hands, then, unable to contain himself, threw his arms around his cherished friend.

As worship of Robert E. Lee intensified through the years, the Gettysburg disaster required a scapegoat. Given that he advocated reconciliation and served his old friend Grant during his presidency, Longstreet became the obvious choice. He then made the mistake of replying angrily and sometimes disingenuously to his critics, fueling decades of acrimony as the South's surviving generals and colonels refought lost battles in print.

At last, justice was done. In Longstreet's twilight years, his veterans rallied around "Old Pete" again, acknowledging him as a titan of the Confederacy. He died in 1904, the last of the great Southern generals.

At his best, Robert E. Lee fought brilliant battles and admirable campaigns. His weakness was as a strategist: His beloved Virginia was the center of his universe and the need to defend it at all costs blinded him first to the importance of the Mississippi Valley, then to the fatal blows struck by Sherman in the Southern heartlands. When Grant came east in 1864 and gripped Lee's army, it proved all too easy to fix him in Virginia, while Grant's brilliant, ruthless subordinate swept around the South's strategic flank.

Lee's pride did not permit him either to give up Virginia or to

surrender his army until it was impossible to fight on. He prolonged the war uselessly, with magnificent skill.

After the war, Lee declined all offers of gifts, position, or fortune, becoming, instead, the president of threadbare Washington College in Lexington, Virginia. To the end of his life, he declined to belittle his former foes or to cast blame on his subordinates. He died in 1870, but lives on in Southern hearts.

Lieutenant Alonzo P. Cushing received a posthumous Medal of Honor. In 2010.

Former sea captain Freeman McGilvery, unsung hero of the fighting on July 2 and July 3, suffered a minor wound to a finger the following year. The wound failed to heal. In the course of an amputation, McGilvery died from an overdose of chloroform.

As a result of the damage done to his body on that first afternoon at Gettysburg, Wlodzimierz Bonawentura Krzyzanowski's health remained impaired for the rest of his life. Nonetheless, he continued to serve in the field, rising to the rank of brigadier general. After the war, in an age of spectacular government corruption, he had the misfortune to be an honest man. He was, of course, accused of corruption by those whose schemes he challenged. Deemed innocent, he served in a succession of Federal posts, interrupted by spells of private enterprise. His fortunes rose and fell, but he never ceased to love either the land of his birth or the country in which he found freedom. He died in genteel poverty in 1887 in New York City, beloved to the end by those who had served under him. General Krzyzanowski is buried in Arlington National Cemetery.

Brevetted as a major general for his service at Gettysburg, Henry Jackson Hunt continued to feud with Winfield Hancock over the proper lines of authority on a battlefield. After the war, Hunt remained in the Army, although it meant reversion to the rank of lieutenant colonel. He could not imagine another, better life. Promoted again to full colonel, he remained the U.S. Army's undisputed expert on artillery matters.

Despite suffering a wound on July 3 that never healed completely, Winfield Scott Hancock returned to his corps in time to lead it in the Virginia campaign of 1864. That autumn, his wound flared again, removing him from the battlefield for the final time,

but he always retained the devotion of his soldiers. In 1880, he ran
for president of the United States, losing to James Garfield, a fellow
war veteran, by a handful of votes.

The day after the amputation of his leg, Daniel Edgar Sickles
overruled his surgeon and had himself carried to the nearest rail-
head in a litter borne by infantrymen. By July 5, he was in Wash-
ington, reclining on a feather bed in smart quarters near the White
House. He knew the president would call on him for a firsthand
account of the battle, and Lincoln fell into the trap. Sickles filled
the president's ears with tales of his personal bravery, declaring that
Meade had thought only of retreat, while he, Dan Sickles, forced
the army to stay and save the Union. Lincoln believed only half of
what he heard, but that was enough to poison his mind against
Meade.

Sickles never stopped banging the drum in support of his claim
that *he* was the hero of Gettysburg. He repeated his lies about
Meade so often and so forcefully that they became common cur-
rency. A rogue to the end, he died in 1914. He had outlived every
other senior general.

The right man at the right place and time, George Gordon Meade
won a crucial victory at Gettysburg. But his triumph left him with
a battered army, stunned by its success. Rolls had to be taken, units
reorganized, ammunition and other basic supplies brought up and
distributed. Thousands of wounded soldiers needed care, and
thousands of prisoners had to be removed. The Army of the Po-
tomac was in no shape to launch an immediate counterattack to
annihilate the Army of Northern Virginia. Lee remained danger-
ous, and Meade had accomplished the mission assigned to him:
preventing the capture of Washington, Baltimore, or Philadelphia.

He organized a pursuit as rapidly as circumstances allowed, de-
termined to harry Lee's army as it retreated. Had the right oppor-
tunity presented itself, Meade would have attacked in Maryland.
But his sole chance would have meant frontal attacks against far
better fortifications than his own men had occupied on Cemetery
Ridge.

Impatient to end the war and accustomed to poor excuses from
tardy generals, Lincoln believed enough of Dan Sickles' lies to

erupt in anger at Meade for not destroying Lee's army. Meade offered to resign, and the president came to his senses. But great damage had been done. In the autumn, Meade's Mine Run Campaign foundered on absurd interference from Washington and the inadequate troop strength allowed him. Nor was he willing to waste soldiers' lives to further his reputation.

Nonetheless, Meade's qualities were such that he remained in command of the Army of the Potomac until the war's end. Overshadowed in reputation by Grant, who soon came east as general-in-chief, the victor of Gettysburg served efficiently and loyally for two more years. Despite politically driven calls for his dismissal, he was the only commander of the Army of the Potomac who was not relieved. As Lincoln could not spare Grant, Grant could not spare Meade.

But performance was not as potent as publicity in the long run. Dan Butterfield rallied back to his old friend Sickles, and the two men began spreading calumnies about Meade. Jealous, "Fighting Joe" Hooker chimed in, too. After Meade's early death in 1872—his war-ravaged health could not resist pneumonia—his reputation suffered further at the hands of detractors, north and south. His no-nonsense command manner had alienated key comrades, while Southern chroniclers could not forgive him for defeating Robert E. Lee in a fair fight. Fatally, he was not a political general and had little patience with newspapermen—with the result that he was damned by partisan scribblers or, when not attacked, ignored in favor of self-promoters and liars. The man who grasped the reins of an army literally overnight and saved the Union in the course of three desperate days of battle was demoted in the public mind to a drab second-rater, his victory credited to his subordinates. It was the worst injustice ever done to an American general.

Author's Note

The Killer Angels will remain the most beloved Gettysburg novel. Michael Shaara's skillful writing, mythic portraits, and romantic view of the battle make it incomparable. Yet, the events of those three days were so dramatic and rich in personalities that a dozen novels might describe them, each with its own focus, and still leave gaps in the line for other authors. And each generation will have its particular needs: *The Killer Angels*—which I read with awe on its first publication—was perfectly pitched for the mid-1970s, when our military suffered low regard and citizens had to be reminded that towering heroes wore our country's uniform.

Today, we have multiple generations of Americans who have not served in the ranks; who have not been taught history; and who learn about war from politically biased films. A novel about Gettysburg for our time must demonstrate war's horror and appeal, while depicting the complex humanity of those who shoulder rifles or lead armies. Immigrants crowded the battlefield, with enemies to their front and to their rear. Generals did not always speak in the innocent cadences of the Victorian stage (Hancock, for one, could be staggeringly profane). Fateful decisions had to be made without decent maps or reliable intelligence. Inglorious but vital, good staff work saved one side, while inadequate coordination doomed the other. At least 150,000 men had to eat, find water (much of it polluted by the dead), and empty their bowels. Amid ineffable valor, depraved soldiers looted corpses and the wounded. Men died by the hundreds because a command went unheard or ignored, or a flawed command was given. Personal rivalries and negligence worsened the slaughter, and pride too often triumphed over sense. There was more to the battle than picturesque charges and gallant stands.

It demeans the heroes of Gettysburg to depict them as flawless saints. Not one was cut from marble in the womb. Imperfect men fought an imperfect battle and so preserved "a more perfect union" for all.

Heroes are men who overcome themselves.

My own relationship with those fields and groves dates to my 1950's childhood. Propelled by cloudy lore of a Civil War ancestor, my mother and father took my brother and me on annual pilgrimages to Gettysburg (Bruce picked out a gray cap; I chose a blue one). The impending centennial of the war produced a deluge of magazines and pamphlets, as well as a flood of books and even trading cards packaged with bubble gum. The illustrations leapt to life in my imagination as no postmodern digital effects ever have. In seventh grade, I even wrote a history of the Civil War—to the chagrin of a very busy teacher—and it was almost published by Scribner's. In the end, the work's inadequacies trumped its novelty.

Later, I studied the fields surrounding Gettysburg with a soldier's eye and, in 1985, found myself tasked to produce a leadership class, built around the battle, for the U.S. Army Intelligence Center and School. *The Killer Angels* was much in vogue on military reading lists, so I designed a case study from the other side, from the perspective of the exhausted, ferociously brave men of the 15th Alabama, who marched over twenty miles in killing heat only to shatter before the 20th Maine.

As a captain in an era of meager paychecks, I scrimped to buy the complete *Official Records of the War of the Rebellion* (130 volumes) on an installment plan. With that bill paid in full, I bought the collected papers of Ulysses S. Grant. Even as career twists took me from the detritus of war in the Caucasus to panoramic bombardments along the Israel-Lebanon border, I knew, deep down, that the Civil War was my subject.

I wrote a series of Civil War mysteries under the pen name "Owen Parry." Told from a cranky Welsh immigrant's viewpoint, the novels sought to get at the grit, as well as the glory, and developed a cult following. A volume of Civil War Christmas stories, *Our Simple Gifts,* remains a source of unembarrassed pride to me. But with the approach of the 150th anniversary of the Battle of

Gettysburg, I saw it was time to grow serious and take on the challenge of reincarnating the battle that has haunted me since childhood.

The result is the book in your hands.

I have read about Gettysburg for over fifty years, only to find there is always more to read. Beyond the original records, veterans' memoirs (some more trustworthy than others), letters, files, and regimental histories, I've profited greatly from the work of dedicated historians. Some of these men and their books influenced me so deeply that they must be acknowledged. The authors may disagree with any number of my interpretations of why or how specific decisions were made or events developed. I can only respond, respectfully, that some things make sense to a soldier that can only baffle those unafflicted by staff time, or who never had to rouse weary soldiers from their cocoons of mud. For all that, I could not have written this book without relying on the exhaustive research of men who've devoted their lives to the study of history.

No matter how long a list of books I offered, some deserving works would be forgotten, so I'll limit my commendations to books that directly influenced *Cain at Gettysburg*, as well as a few fine studies of the battle for general readers.

As I inspected regiment after regiment in search of inspired choices to "carry" the battle, I encountered no finer book than *Covered with Glory: The 26th North Carolina Infantry at the Battle of Gettysburg*, by Rod Gragg. This is splendid historical writing, dazzling research revealed with narrative verve. Gragg's account of the regiment's charge on July 1 is the best narrative depiction of Civil War combat I have found. My own portrayal of the action has been erected on Gragg's solid foundation.

Of equal importance and inspiration were two revelatory works by James S. Pula, who has dedicated himself to teaching us about the role of immigrants in our nation's history. His admirable book *The Sigel Regiment: A History of the 26th Wisconsin Volunteer Infantry, 1862–1865* helps redress the injustice done to idealistic German immigrants maligned by nativists unwilling to blame their own kind for disasters. This is great work by any standard, and it led me to a second book of Dr. Pula's, the indispensable *For Liberty*

and Justice: A Biography of Brigadier General Wlodzimierz B. Krzy-
zanowski, 1824–1887. For far too long, Krzyzanowski has been only
a name on a monument on the drive to Barlow's Knoll. Dr. Pula
memorialized a great soldier whose commitment to freedom eclipsed
that of many a native-born officer. The book inspired me, and I am
deeply in Dr. Pula's debt.

As a side note: I did not feature the 26th North Carolina and
26th Wisconsin in this book for the sake of twinning their num-
bers to make a symbolic point. It was purely coincidental that these
two regiments best fit the tale I hoped to tell.

There are legions of Gettysburg books in stores, libraries, ar-
chives, and attics and for sale online. For readers who wish to learn
more about the battle, I recommend *Gettysburg* by Stephen W.
Sears for an excellent introductory account. On the first day of
battle, David G. Martin's *Gettysburg July 1* is comprehensive, while
Harry W. Pfanz's *Gettysburg: The First Day* reveals a profound fa-
miliarity with the battlefield. Pfanz also authored *Gettysburg: The
Second Day*, which stands as the definitive account of the encoun-
ters on the Union left, but which should be read together with his
Gettysburg: Culp's Hill & Cemetery Hill to complete the picture on
the Union right. For Pickett's Charge, which has captured the in-
terest of writers from Faulkner to Foote, *Pickett's Charge: The Last
Attack at Gettysburg,* by Earl J. Hess, offers the best contemporary
scholarship.

For biographies and memoirs, try *Fighting for the Confederacy:
The Personal Recollections of General Edward Porter Alexander,*
edited by Gary W. Gallagher. If that excites your interest, pick your
general—nearly every senior officer who failed to die on the battle-
field seems to have fought on with pen and ink.

Among modern accounts, *General James Longstreet: The Con-
federacy's Most Controversial Soldier,* by Jeffry D. Wert, is a highly
readable introduction to Old Pete, while James A. Hessler's *Sickles
at Gettysburg* puts the best possible face on an odious man (who
was, for all his faults, a Union patriot). Glenn Tucker's *Hancock the
Superb* remains a vigorous pleasure, while *Toward Gettysburg,* by
Edward J. Nichols, humanizes the valiant, tragic Reynolds. But
when it comes to Meade, it's disheartening how little has been
written about this great, if difficult, man. After fifty years, the best

biography is still *Meade of Gettysburg,* by Freeman Cleaves, although it's also worth reading the stiff-necked Isaac R. Pennypacker's *General Meade* from 1901. Meade deserves better. (I can attest that gifted generals are not always affable.)

Finally, I must pay tribute to Philip Laino, whose *Gettysburg Campaign Atlas* is a wonderful tool for those of us who are entranced by the battle. Mr. Laino has created 421 maps that clarify events remarkably. Infuriatingly, this superb work has not yet been published in the high-quality edition it deserves. Life's as unfair as war.

The Civil War remains with us in countless ways, from the oddity of Confederate flags flown in West Virginia—a state created because its residents sided with the Union—to the long, infernal hangover of slavery. The greatest battlefields are national parks, flooded with tourists, and a novel about one battle fought a century and a half ago can still charge into bookstores. It is the war that made us who we are.

It was also our bloodiest war, with over six hundred thousand Americans dead, and our most evocative. The enduring power of its music attests to it. We can listen to "Yankee Doodle," "Over There," "Don't Sit Under the Apple Tree," or "Feel Like I'm Fixin' to Die" with recognition and amusement, but they do not stir us.

Play "Dixie." It summons images of unrivaled courage. Then play "The Battle Hymn of the Republic." The heart swells with a sense of justice triumphant.

Courage and justice. They belong together.

biography is still *Meade of Gettysburg,* by Freeman Cleaves, al-though it's also worth reading the stiff-necked Isaac R. Penny-packer's *General Meade* from 1901. Meade deserves better. (I can attest that gifted generals are not always affable.)

Finally, I must pay tribute to Philip Laino, whose *Gettysburg Campaign Atlas* is a wonderful tool for those of us who are en-tranced by the battle. Mr. Laino has created 421 maps that clarify events remarkably. Infuriatingly, this superb work has not yet been published in the high-quality edition it deserves. Life's as unfair as war.

The Civil War remains with us in countless ways, from the oddity of Confederate flags flown in West Virginia—a state created be-cause its residents sided with the Union—to the long, infernal hangover of slavery. The greatest battlefields are national parks, flooded with tourists, and a novel about one battle fought a century and a half ago can still charge into bookstores. It is the war that made us who we are.

It was also our bloodiest war, with over six hundred thousand Americans dead, and our most evocative. The enduring power of its music attests to it. We can listen to "Yankee Doodle," "Over There," "Don't Sit Under the Apple Tree," or "Feel Like I'm Fixin' to Die" with recognition and amusement, but they do not stir us.

Play "Dixie." It summons images of unrivaled courage. Then play "The Battle Hymn of the Republic." The heart swells with a sense of justice triumphant.

Courage and justice. They belong together.